NO SAFE PLACE

A Joe Hunter Thriller

MATT HILTON

Sempre Vigile Press

NO SAFE PLACE
MATT HILTON

Published In Great Britain by Sempre Vigile Press 2016

1

ISBN Hardback: **978-0-9935788-2-3**
ISBN Paperback: **978-0-9935788-0-9**
ISBN E-book: **978-0-9935788-1-6**

NO SAFE PLACE

Praise for the Joe Hunter thriller series:

"Matt Hilton delivers a thrill a minute. Awesome!" (Chris Ryan)

"Hard-hitting and fast-paced, I was hooked from start to finish."
(Simon Kernick)

"Roars along at a ferocious pace..." (Observer)

"Electrifying." (Daily Mail)

"Vicious, witty and noir. Hilton is a sparkling new talent." (Peter James)

"Another brutally fast and brutally addictive novel from Matt Hilton. Ne'er-do-wells beware, Joe Hunter is coming for you!" (Crimeandpublishing.com)

"Explosive and deadly . . . the prolific penman strikes gold again."
(Crimesquad.com)

PROLOGUE

The splintering of a door jolted Ella Clayton from her thoughts. She jumped up, pushing back her chair in her haste and the legs squealed across the tiled kitchen floor. The glass of wine she'd been nursing at the breakfast counter fell from her fingers and shattered in a welter of red gobbets that stained her shoes and jeans. The two startling crashes happened almost simultaneously, both snapping Ella's attention one direction and then instantly the other. The broken wine glass was unimportant; the smashed door something else entirely. Her first instinct was to call out for help, but her voice was pinched in her throat.

Who could she shout for anyway?

Her husband had left an hour earlier, taking their son, Cole, up to his dad's fishing lodge on Lake Tarpon on the hunt for largemouth bass. She'd watched Andrew load their nine-year-old in his SUV, handing the boy a bottle of juice to keep him hydrated on the short trip. Ella had waved Cole off, and he'd waved back, but it was while barely shutting up as he fired instructions at his dad to get going. Cole had been eagerly looking forward to the trip, keen to catch his first freshwater fish, be that bass, tilapia, bluegill or sunfish. Andrew had already said his goodbyes, out of Cole's earshot, and he'd only hung a hand out of the window, flicking his fingers in farewell as he'd driven away. If their fishing expedition had been aborted for unforeseen reasons, and her husband and son had returned early, then Andrew would have used his key, come in by the front door, not made this noisy entrance through the utility room door via the garage.

Ella stood rooted to the spot. She was as confused as she was frightened, and indecision held her rigid: should she investigate or run? Only when the door into the kitchen was kicked open, slamming the wall with a sound as violent as gunshot did she lurch away. Shrieking, she reached for the phone on the wall, got her fingers on it, but in her urgency knocked the receiver out of its holder. The phone clattered across the floor, and she chased it, aware of how close the invader was on her heels. She gave up on the phone, running instead for the vestibule. If she could get to the front door she could scream for help. But again, who would hear? Their house was on a private lot, a good four hundred yards from the nearest house, and even then it belonged to an old couple, both so deaf neither would hear a grenade detonate in their own living room. But she had to try.

She could barely breathe. Her legs were rubbery beneath her. It was as if she was running through a quagmire.

Her pursuer wasn't as hindered. He came after her, striding purposefully. She could sense him reaching for her, to snag her hair in a gloved hand and she twisted away, fleeing instead for the family room. A boot kicked at her ankle. It was enough to trip her and she fell against the open door, and then to the floor. She scrambled on all fours, seeking to place the settee between them.

There was a sharp crack.

She recognised it as gunfire. Waited for the shocking impact of a bullet through her flesh. But it didn't come. The bullet had drilled a hole in the settee. Ella swerved on hands and knees to one side, croaking in terror. The shot into her settee was a warning, but the next might be placed more accurately. She collapsed to one side, rolling onto an elbow, shuffling away sideways as she placed her feet ineffectually between her and the man looming over her. He was dressed in a nylon coverall, the cuffs taped to his boots and gloves with duct tape. He wore a ski mask and goggles, and had a rucksack on his back. Disguised from head to foot she couldn't be certain: did she know her attacker though? His shape said yes, she knew him, but she couldn't believe *he* would do this?

She stared at him, from his huge boots up to the soulless goggles, and the gun he held in each gloved hand.

Absurdly the wine stains on her jeans drew her gaze, and it was as if her blood had already been spilled. She knew the image was a portent, and screamed in defiance at the inevitable. The man fired again. This time it was at a wall, and it punched a small hole through the drywall and into the kitchen beyond. He'd fired only one of the two guns he held, the other was aimed at her gut.

'Please!' Ella cried. 'Why are you doing this?'

The man didn't speak. He didn't have to, not when her plea fell on deaf ears. He only shrugged, then took another pot shot at the same wall, this time lower than where the first bullet hit. The other gun didn't waver off target. Ella lifted her left hand, as if intending to swat aside the promised bullet like an annoying bug, and the gold of her wedding ring twinkled dully. The man grunted at her, amused, and he pulled the trigger. This gun wasn't as loud as the first, but the sound was cataclysmic to Ella: it was the sound of her doom. The bullet cut through the palm of her outstretched hand, didn't slow and punched her gut harder than any fist in creation could. The impact folded Ella around the bullet as it drilled into her. She unfurled in the next instant, her legs spasming, her hands flung over her head behind her. Her damaged hand fluttered against the plush leather of her settee.

'Does it hurt?' pondered her attacker as he bent over her. He snorted in pleasure. 'I just bet it does.'

His voice was muffled by the ski mask. But Ella recognised it. She was right: she did know this man. And suddenly she understood what this was all about.

'Why?' she croaked. 'I…thought you…loved me.'

'Don't flatter yourself, bitch.'

'You won't…get away…with this…'

The man crouched alongside her, moving his second gun closer.

'Oh, I think I will,' he crowed. 'All my bases are covered.'

Ella could see her shocked expression reflected in his goggles. Her face was so pale it was limpid, her mouth a stark wet oval beneath equally wet eye sockets. She watched as the reflection of the gun probed the space beneath her chin. Could feel the subtle tremor of his finger on the trigger passing through the hot metal and into her flesh.

There was a scarlet explosion.
It was the last thing she ever experienced.

1

The sand gave beneath every footstep, making jogging difficult. If I'd followed the strip of asphalt separating the beach from the road it would've been easier. But I didn't mind the extra effort. I welcomed it. Going the easy route was never my intention, and I'd made things harder again by loading building bricks wrapped in newspaper in my rucksack. I needed the work out, and was determined to get back to full health. Over the past month I'd set similar challenges so I could evaluate my progress. I wasn't back to full fitness yet, but I was getting there.

Not long ago I'd been shot in the chest. As luck would have it, I'd been wearing a bulletproof vest. Unluckily, the vest wasn't impervious at close range and a bullet had found its way through and buried its tip in my left pectoral muscle. I'd survived, but the wound had proved a bitch to heal. Perhaps it hadn't helped that my recovery was hampered by having to rescue an abducted woman from a compound full of armed mercenaries, but there you go. I was forced to take things easy while I recuperated, and was better for it, but the time I'd taken to heal had played havoc on my cardio and strength. I don't recall taking as long to regain my fitness when I was a young soldier, but had to face the truth. Now in my early forties, I wasn't exactly a young soldier any more. In fact, I wasn't even a soldier.

It's over three hundred and seventy miles from my house on Mexico Beach to the office of Rington Investigations in Tampa, Florida, where I work. Meaning I've a five and a half hour commute if I obey the posted speed limits. On bad days the journey can take longer. My friend, and business partner, Rink, has often encouraged me to move closer to the office. I've considered doing so, and checked out a house between Clearwater and Palm Harbor a few months ago, but didn't go through with the move, thinking at that time I'd miss my home from home.

Mexico Beach was about as far removed from my old house in Manchester in the north of England that I could imagine, without stepping off the fine white sand into the turquoise water of Saint Joseph Bay. I enjoyed eating at Toucan's or taking a cold Corona at any of the beachside bars, or sitting on the pier, watching the boats and the frolicking holidaymakers. As I was doing now, I regularly ran the beach from Port St Joe, through Mexico Beach, or up towards Tyndall AFB following the contours of Saint Andrew Sound. My beach house was just far enough away to feel removed from my day-job, allowing some peace of mind during downtime, but I could get back to Tampa if necessary.

But I couldn't call it a safe retreat anymore: trouble had come to my door, most recently in the shape of one of those mercenaries seeking to avenge a brother whose death he blamed on me. I hadn't killed his brother, the situation had been more complicated than that, but it didn't matter to him, and things had grown violent before we were finished. Allowing that the home invasion had been a trap I'd helped set up, it shouldn't bother me now. But the violence had left an indelible stain in the house that I couldn't ignore, or maybe the stain was on my psyche. More often than not I stayed away, sleeping over at Rink's place at Temple Terrace, or bedding down in the back room at the office, rather than return home. It wasn't fear that made me avoid my own home, more a feeling of unease that my private sanctum had been violated. I couldn't find peace there now and a move was looking more attractive. But I'd promised that when I did move, it'd be a new start, and I wanted to be back on form before then.

So I ran. Feeling the sand give beneath my boots, and the loaded rucksack bounce against my back with each step. Sweat lashed off me, my T-shirt was sodden, and my shorts adhered to my thighs. I looked directly ahead, my sights set on the hazy distance. I might have run all the way past the air force base and on to Panama City, except I heard my cell ringing. I wanted to ignore its summons, but I slowed, moved down by the surf and unhooked my rucksack. Breathing heavily I delved in the pocket on the rucksack's flap and pulled out the phone. It had stopped ringing, but I could see whose call I'd missed. I hit buttons.

'Rink,' I said, by way of greeting.

'Where are you, Hunter?' he asked.

I looked out to sea, watched a pelican flap lazily above the turquoise surface. There were some kayakers out, and I could faintly hear them talking. The sun boiled off the sweat from my forehead.

'I'm running,' I said. 'Or I was til you stopped me.'

'It sounds like you needed to stop; catch your breath, brother.'

'I'm fine,' I said.

'Sounds like it,' he replied, meaning the exact opposite. 'Seriously, though, are you good to go?'

'Depends what you've got in mind.'

'Easy job.'

'If it were that easy you wouldn't be calling me, Rink. You'd put Velasquez or McTeer on it.'

'Val isn't ready yet,' he said, 'and McTeer is on that close protection gig down in Miami.' He snorted out a laugh. 'You're it, brother, whether you like it or not. Besides, the client asked for you in person.'

I thought about what he said. Since taking a severe beating during a job down Mexico, Raul Velasquez had been pulled off the front line. Like me, he was eager to show he was fit for service again, but Rink was uncertain and had put him to work on office duties. Jim McTeer was another of Rink's employees, an ex-cop. He was currently working private security for some visiting soccer player down in Miami. McTeer had hinted it was David Beckham, but I didn't believe him.

'So what's the job?'

'Like I said, it's an easy one.'

'"Easy" isn't in my vocabulary,' I reminded him.

'So what they say is true. You do learn something new every day. "Easy" should suit you just fine, Hunter, until you're back to full strength.' Rink must have put a hand over his phone, because his next words were muffled. Didn't matter, I heard an equally muffled response but didn't recognise the voice. It was probably Velasquez, I decided. When he came back on Rink's voice was much clearer. 'How soon can you get here?'

I looked at the sun. It was dipping towards the horizon. 'I'll have to get back home, shower, throw a few things in a bag, but I can be there this evening.'

'Soon as, brother,' Rink said. 'The job's an easy one, meaning not too strenuous, but I didn't say it wasn't urgent.'

'A clue what to look forward to wouldn't go amiss.'

'That'd spoil the surprise.'

I wondered what was going on. Mentally I checked the calendar, but there were no significant dates I could think of. Apart from one, but that couldn't be it. 'If this is a ploy to spring a surprise birthday party on me, I'll kick your arse,' I warned him in good humour.

'Hunter, I'm with you on that one. Once I hit the big four-oh I stopped counting. Look, sooner I get off, sooner you can get your sweaty butt home and shower. I'll be done here when you arrive, so just come to my place, OK?'

'Will do.' We hung up. I again searched the horizon to the north. I wasn't done running. Still, I'd to run back the way I'd already come. I hefted the rucksack onto my shoulders, cinched the straps so the weight of the bricks was equally balanced, and set off. This time I did use the asphalt path, and made better speed. Rink had been purposefully guarded about what he had in store for me, and it made me think. I felt a buzz of nervous anticipation as I pounded the path home. There'd been something in Rink's tone he'd tried to veil. But it weren't a bad thing. He'd been pleased to summon me, and he was never one to get excited about a big payday. There was something else. Something I'd actually be happy about; I just had no idea what. Suddenly I wanted to dump the bricks and sprint all the way back.

2

Rink lives in a condo within spitting distance of Busch Gardens, the theme park next door to Temple Terrace. Some days, when standing on his balcony, you could hear the faint whoops and screams of delight of those riding the rollercoasters, the whooshing, rushing sounds of the coasters themselves, but that was dependent on the prevailing wind direction and how heavy the traffic was on the nearby I-75. When I drove up East Busch Boulevard there was little traffic around, and the theme park had closed for the night. I'd made good time getting from Mexico Beach, but it was still late, and even the parking lots of Red Lobster and Taco Bell had emptied by then. I kept going, past the public library, then peeled off, using surface streets as short cuts through to Rink's place. Tampa is a low-lying bayside city, and there isn't much in the way of high-elevation in the topography of its suburbs either, but Rink's condo sat on what would be termed a hill by locals, though it was barely more than a bump in the landscape.

I pulled my Audi onto his drive, behind his Porsche Boxster, checking out another vehicle I was unfamiliar with. It was a bog-standard Ford with Florida plates. The car gave me no clue to Rink's visitor. Lights were on throughout his apartment, but I could see nobody inside. Rink's place was at the end of a row of similar apartments staggered along the crest of the hill; all with their own dedicated parking bays. Most bays were occupied, so perhaps the car belonged to a neighbour's visitor, and they'd parked in the first available space. Speculation wasn't helping. I got out my Audi, grabbed my bag and shut the door. The clunk alerted someone inside, and a figure moved through the living room to the window. I recognised Rink's muscular shape, though the light behind him set him in silhouette. He raised a hand, then headed for the door. I went to meet him.

'You musta hauled ass,' Rink said by way of greeting.

'I might've been a little heavy-footed on the gas,' I admitted. I craned to see past him. 'Why the secrecy, Rink? What's going on.'

He surprised me by cupping a hand at the back of my neck, and leaning in. It was a surprisingly intimate gesture. For a second I thought he was going to kiss my cheek, until he whispered. 'You're gonna like who's here, brother.'

'Who?'

'Best you see for yourself.'

He urged me inside, and I'd be lying if I said I didn't pause. I suddenly felt nervous, squinting an eye as I checked him for any deceit. If I went in and a group of well-meaning friends jumped out singing "Happy Birthday" I'd struggle to make out I was happy to see them.

'Go on through,' Rink said. 'You know the way.'

I was tempted to head for the spare bedroom, to drop my bag, but Rink closed the door and followed on my heels, ushering me towards the living room like a trusty old sheepdog. I was propelled, to avoid being trampled by him. I could feel the buzz of expectancy rising off him like an electrical charge. Who had got my usually calm and collected buddy all excitable?

Rink's an ex-soldier, and like many disciplined veterans he keeps a neat and ordered living space. He's also part Japanese so has that Zen thing going on. So immediately on entering his lounge, I spotted the signs of his visitor, but these gave no immediate hint of who it was. I saw the empty plates and cups on his coffee table, and a rumpled cloth bag set alongside his settee. The settee cushions bore indentations from a body. But there was nobody there, and I glimpsed at Rink for direction. He nodded at the door that opened onto his balcony, and through the reflective glass I caught movement as somebody shifted, getting up from one of the recliner chairs outside. The person who entered stopped me in my tracks.

I don't know whom I was expecting but it wasn't Bryony VanMeter, a homicide detective with Tampa PD's Criminal Investigations Division.

'Hey,' I said.

'Hey, Joe,' Bryony said, and lifted a half-quaffed bottle of beer in greeting. 'Long time no see, lover boy.'

I smiled at her pet name for me, though it was somewhat through embarrassment. Rink chuckled at my discomfort, and gave me a prod in the kidneys. I'd have squirmed like a schoolboy, but Bryony was watching me too keenly. So I stood stoically.

'It's been too long,' I said. She'd changed her image since last I'd seen her, but she was every bit as lovely. She now wore her auburn hair short and feathered around her freckled face, and small diamond studs in her ears. Her lips were moist from the beer she'd enjoyed, and I noted a small nick on her bottom lip that wasn't there when we'd last kissed. I wondered if I kissed her now the small imperfection would make any difference to how her mouth moved against mine. We'd enjoyed a fling a couple of years ago, after I'd assisted her in bringing a rich scumbag called Mick O'Neill to justice. O'Neill had a penchant for throwing people off skyscrapers and I'd ensured he got a taste of his own methods. By doing so Bryony and her partner Detective Holker had cleared a few latent murder cases off Tampa CID's books. Bryony had shown her appreciation as much as Holker didn't. But then, I hadn't dated him afterwards. Our relationship hadn't lasted, because it wasn't doing her career prospects any good being associated with a suspected vigilante. We'd gone our separate ways, though it was under friendly terms, and with no lessening of the feelings we had for each other. I turned up the corner of my mouth. 'Then again, I hope this is a social call, Bryony?'

'Depends on what you'd like to confess to,' she said.

'His undying infatuation?' Rink asked, and expelled a wet laugh that smelled of beer. Bryony shook her head at him, but there was a gleam in her hazel eyes, and a quirk on her lips. I tutted at him, and would have prodded my elbow in his gut but that would only have made me look as immature as his humour.

'I think Rink already told you about the job I'm offering,' Bryony said.

'*You* want to hire me? A Major Crimes Bureau detective?' I said.

'Not me personally,' Bryony corrected. 'I'm here on behalf of someone else, a private client. But,' she strung out that word, 'you would be working alongside me, Joe. Whether or not your client needs to know about our arrangement is another matter.'

I gave Rink a look. 'You said this was an easy job. Sounds as if there could be some complications you didn't mention.'

Rink showed his gleaming white teeth. 'Easy doesn't mean things have to be boring,' he said. He recalled his duty as our host. 'C'mon...now the greetings are done with, lets go outside. I've more beer on ice.'

We went out onto the balcony, where recliners were arranged around a low glass table that was ringed with moisture. As promised there was an ice bucket with bottles sweating inside. Rink handed me a Corona before I could even sit down. There was a chair placed for me, and the others took the ones they'd already used. Rink was opposite me, Bryony to my left. It was warm despite the late hour, and the cicadas were in full volume. I aimed my untouched Corona at Bryony. 'Want to tell me about this job, seeing as I rushed to get here.'

'And I thought you broke the speed limit just to see me,' Bryony teased. She held up a finger. 'Except Rink didn't tell you it was me who was hiring, did he?'

'*Rink* likes to keep *Hunter* on his toes,' said Rink, purposefully emphasising the third person POV.

I wondered how many beers he'd already drank, and by his shit-eating grin decided it was more than his usual intake. He was tipsy, and enjoying playing matchmaker. He'd told me numerous times I was nuts to let Bryony go, and to be fair, looking at how beautiful she was I couldn't agree more. But this wasn't about rekindling a love affair, it was about employment, so I made sure one of us from Rington Investigations remained professional.

'Want to tell me about it?'

'Have you been following the news lately?' Bryony asked.

'I tend not to: it's too depressing,' I said.

'You haven't heard about the spate of home invasions that have happened these past few weeks?'

I had. We'd talked around the office about the violent robberies that had recently plagued the city, but that was as far as we'd gone. Tackling the gang responsible for the home invasions was in the remit of the Major Crimes and Strategic Investigations Bureaus of Tampa PD, and they wouldn't welcome the interference of a lowly PI outfit. But that shows you what I knew.

'You want me to help bring this crew to justice?' I wondered.

Bryony laughed, then excused her disbelief with a wave of her hand. 'No, Joe, I'd prefer you kept out of the way of this one. We want arrests, not a blood bath.'

I held up my palms, made an "I have no idea what you mean" face, but didn't really take any offence. Bryony wasn't easily fooled though. She knew about some of the things I'd done in the past, and even if in private she silently applauded me, she couldn't go on the record to do so. It'd ring the death toll of her career.

'I'll give you the short version,' Bryony said. 'There have been six home invasions to date. Thankfully, though the crew used firearms and other weapons, the fatalities have been few. An elderly widower died, but that was due to cardiac arrest, when he tried to fight for his wife's jewellery back. The other fatality was Ella Clayton. Shot to death while trying to escape when her house was broken into. In the other invasions the properties were empty at the time, or there were only kids home. On those occasions the crew didn't need to use their weapons, but that doesn't mean they won't next time.'

'They're punks,' Rink said. 'Cowardly punks.'

Bryony briefly raised her eyebrows, but she was in agreement. 'We have some leads on the crew responsible; hopefully we can stop them before anymore victims die.'

'Amen to that,' Rink chimed in, and raised his bottle to his lips.

I was busy thinking. 'So if you don't want my assistance with this crew, what exactly do you want, Detective VanMeter?'

Bryony squeezed me a smile. 'I was just getting to that, Joe. I mentioned Ella Clayton. Because of the violent nature of her murder, there's a lot of pressure on CID to catch her killers. She has become a figurehead for critics of Tampa PD who claim we aren't doing enough for their tax dollars to find resolution in her case. So it stands to reason that the brass has rolled the crap downhill to Criminal Investigations, and on to the investigating detectives in particular. One of which is *Moi.*' She touched a hand to her chest. 'Now, ordinarily I wouldn't ask, but I need someone to alleviate some of the pressure I'm under, and I think you're the man for the job, Joe.'

'I can't see what I can do to help that Tampa PD would sanction.'

'I'm not asking that you catch the killers,' Bryony explained, 'I want you to babysit Ella's family.'

'Babysit?' I frowned.

'OK, that perhaps wasn't the best choice of words, but you know what I mean. I want you to keep an eye over them, keep them safe until we have Ella's murderers in custody.'

'They're in danger from the home invaders? That doesn't make much sense, unless they personally witnessed Ella's murder?'

'They didn't. Ella's husband and son were fishing up at Lake Tarpon when she was attacked.' Bryony paused to take a pull at her beer, and I knew then there was more to this case than initially believed. She rolled her bottle between her palms, while she ordered her thoughts, then it was as if she decided to hell with it. She might as well say what was on her mind. 'You know how when a murder happens, we look first at family and close friends as suspects? Andrew's alibi stands; he was with his nine-year-old son when Ella was murdered. There's no disputing the fact. But in my opinion that doesn't make him innocent.'

'You think he might've organised the attack and had his wife killed by proxy?' I asked.

'It's always something we have to consider, and investigate.'

'But to do that effectively you need someone on the inside,' I finished for her. I studied my own beer, then tilted it and drank most of the bottle in one long swallow. I glanced across at Rink and caught his slight grimace. He knew what was going through my mind. I'd not long ago agreed to protect Billie Womack, and got shot for my trouble, when really others required protection from her. I'd been used, made to look a mug by a supposed old friend named Brandon Cooper. He was with the Bureau of Alcohol, Tobacco, Firearms and Explosives — commonly referred to as an ATF agent – but it hadn't made him trustworthy. Was I really prepared to jump into the middle of a case where it was apparent a law enforcement officer would manipulate me again? I wondered how much of the debacle at Hill End Bryony knew about from Rink.

'We've nothing on Andrew Clayton,' Bryony went on. 'So we also have to consider that he's innocent of any involvement in Ella's murder. If he is innocent he deserves our sympathy, and our support. There's also the boy to think about.'

'Yeah,' I agreed, a nine-year-old child should be protected. 'Do you think he's in danger?'

'Not directly from his dad. But there are others to be worried about.' Bryony tugged gently at an earlobe as she spoke, rotating the diamond stud. 'It's not only Tampa PD who has been criticised over Ella's murder; it appears some people have their suspicions concerning Andrew, and they've made their opinions heard. He's attracted a bit of a hate campaign, and more than once patrols have been dispatched to his home to chase off the rebel rousers. Two nights ago someone threw a brick through his front door. Andrew has also reported a prowler he caught staring through his kitchen window, but we were unable to locate the person responsible. Andrew wasn't being hysterical, we did find signs that someone had been standing on the flowerbed below the window.'

'Why hasn't a patrol car been allocated to sit outside the house?' I pondered, though I suspected the answer.

'Budget constraints, manpower issues, conflict of interest where a possible suspect is concerned…take your pick.'

'And that's where I come in?' I said.

'Exactly. Andrew claims he isn't worried for himself, but he doesn't want any harm to come to Cole, and nobody can blame him for that. When I informed him that Tampa PD couldn't supply round the clock protection he asked me if I knew anybody who could.' She pointed at me. '*That's* where you come in, Joe.'

I exhaled slowly.

'You don't want the job?' Bryony pressed.

'It doesn't matter what anyone thinks of Andrew Clayton; there's an innocent child involved. Was there ever any doubt I'd take it?'

3

When he used to be a cop, nobody would have got the drop on Jed Boaz like this. Back when he'd carried a shield and a gun, he'd been switched on. Neither a badge nor a firearm was armour against assault from those who had little respect for the accouterments of a detective. So he'd always ensured that he was alert, on-guard, prepared for when the shit came down. He'd never been caught napping. But that was eight years ago now, and in the intervening years the fall out from an acrimonious divorce, and a dependency on prescription painkillers and bottles of scotch, had dulled him. He'd shattered both legs in a pile-up on the I-4. Ironically it hadn't been during a high-speed chase – many of which he'd been involved in during his law enforcement career – but on a slow Sunday afternoon after visiting family up at Lake Buena Vista. He didn't recall much about the collision afterwards, but he'd the State Troopers' report to go on: a car full of French tourists had blown a tyre, and over-reacting the driver had yanked the steering, throwing their car under the wheels of a truck. The truck had jack-knifed, swatting Jed's vehicle across the central median and into the path of an oncoming bus. His wife's injuries had been blessedly superficial – minor cuts and bruises - but Jed had to be cut out of the mashed wreckage, and it had been touch and go as to whether he'd keep his right leg due to the crush injuries. The surgeons had saved his leg, if not his full mobility. Recuperating from his injuries had been a bastard, but so had his behaviour. He was unfit for work, and was pensioned off on medical grounds, but he hadn't welcomed early retirement. Less than a year after the accident his wife, Barbara, said goodbye to the boorish man he'd become, taking half of everything with her including a cut of his pension. In hindsight he couldn't blame her, because he had been a spiteful asshole. He could try to blame the meds or the bottle, but really it was down to him. He'd lost pretty much everything: His job, his wife, his home, and his self-respect. But he'd tried to climb back out of the hole, though the private work he'd undertaken didn't give him the same credibility he once had, but it paid his bills and put scotch in his belly most evenings, so he wasn't complaining. Not much. What it hadn't done was remind him that there were dangerous, evil bastards out there just waiting for the moment you dropped your guard so they could inflict pain on you.

Most days, when he was sober, he conducted business from the seat of his Honda Civic, the tools and paperwork associated with his business scattered on the seats both front and back, all of it smelling of take-out fried chicken or burgers, and sour whisky breath. When he wasn't sober enough to be behind the wheel, he used a room he rented above a tool hire shop in a strip mall off West Waters Avenue. The room was small, cluttered, but cheap enough, and was in staggering distance of a Panda Express and McDonald's for when he got hungry, and a Walmart for when he grew thirsty. He required a business address, and somewhere his mail could be delivered. Also, he needed somewhere he could crash out when he was too drunk to haul his ass home to his miserable condo a few blocks away in River Oaks. Tonight was such a night.

He wasn't as drunk as he wished to be, but he was soused enough not to trust himself to drive and arrive home in one piece. His legs were aching like crazy, and twice his reconstructed left knee had almost given out on him since he'd left the bar. His right leg, atrophied an inch shorter since his accident, was the weaker leg of the two. He walked like a constipated duck, even when he wasn't loaded. His gait made him a target of jokes, and sometimes of predators, and for that reason he kept an equalizer on hand to teach those who'd target him a lesson. He reached in his jacket pocket and racked out his extendable truncheon, even as he turned to confront the guy who'd followed him down the alley behind the strip mall.

The tool hire shop closed at six p.m. and it was now fast approaching the witching hour. That meant Jed had to use the back door to gain entrance to his office. Ordinarily it wasn't a problem – not if you discounted the steep narrow stairs he'd to mount – and going down the poorly lit alley didn't ordinarily concern him. If he came across anyone in the alley, it would be a homeless dude scratching through the Dumpsters for discarded food behind Subway or Krispy Kreme. He knew the local street people and they him. Occasionally he'd slip them a few dollars and stay on side with them. But this guy was no hobo.

'You want to fuck with me,' Jed challenged, as he lifted the steel baton towards the man, 'you made a big mistake, boy.'

He'd made more mistakes than lowering his guard. The first was showing his weapon so openly; the second was misjudging the guy who continued towards him unperturbed. This was no kid who thought he'd roll a drunk for the contents of his wallet. The guy had come prepared for a fight, and had dressed for the occasion in an all-in-one coverall, boots, gloves, ski mask and opaque goggles. He also held a weapon, and Jed's only sense of relief was that it wasn't a gun. But it was a knife, and every bit as deadly if it stuck him in the right spot.

Before he lost an inch in height, Jed had been a big man. He was still big, and if he were still fit and healthy, he'd be confident of matching this guy in a fight. But now, unsteady on his feet from both booze and injury, he felt a ripple of terror pass through him. From the confidence in his approach his opponent held no such fear.

In a choice between fight and flight Jed had only one option. He swung the truncheon in a wide arc that fell a full yard short of the man. 'Keep the fuck away from me!' he yelled. 'Just take one step closer, buddy, and I'm gonna smash you in the head.'

The masked man halted. But he didn't back away. He simply stared at Jed, his gaze impenetrable beyond the smoked glass of his goggles. The only visible hint of the man's identity was in the white of his skin around his mouth, and the whiteness of his teeth as he grinned maliciously at Jed's bravado.

'I'm telling you, man. You don't know who you're messing with.' Jed swept the baton back again in a second vicious swipe.

'I know exactly who you are,' said the man.

'Well you know more than I do, man!' Jed glanced for an escape route. The door to his office was still a dozen paces away, and locked. No way could he make it in time before the weirdo could pounce on his back. He aimed the tip of the steel rod at the man's face. 'Who the fuck are you, anyway? What do you want from me?'

'Everything, Boaz,' said the man, 'I want everything.'

Jed slapped at his pocket. 'Buddy, I've about ten bucks to my name. You want it, fucking take it. It's more than my trouble's worth.'

The man shook his head, but didn't yet approach. He folded away his knife and slipped it into a deep pocket on the coveralls. His confidence was growing exponentially to a point the baton didn't require a counter weapon. Jed also shook his head in warning: the fucker would learn his mistake at his peril. Jed's legs were crippled, but he could still swing a metal bar with the best of them.

'I'm giving you one last chance to walk away, buddy. If you don't, well, I'm putting a dent or two in that skull of yours.' Despite his words, Jed began backing away. His left heel went into a puddle of filth spilling from the base of a rusting trashcan. The stench of decomposition wafted up around him, smelling much the same as the rank stink pouring out of his pores.

The man opened his arms, holding out his hands thumbs up, as if begging a question. Or inviting Jed to take another swing. Jed didn't. He still held the baton between them. It suddenly felt flimsy and insubstantial in his fist.

'I don't know what you want from me,' he said, and hated that he almost whined.

'I told you. I want everything.' The man inched forward. '*Everything* you took from me.'

Realisation struck Jed as hard as a punch to the gut.

'It's *you*?' he asked.

'Don't act shocked,' said the man. 'You must have known I was coming for you next.'

'Son of a bitch,' Jed wheezed, and he knew it was now or never. He pushed off his bad knee, jerking forward even as he whipped the baton over his shoulder, building momentum for a slash at the man's skull. But the man was moving too. Not away, but directly at Jed. His right arm chambered as well, but it was to block Jed's blow as he snapped down the truncheon. The extendable metal rod whacked the man's forearm, but with little effect. The baton was designed to concentrate kinetic force into its tip, not up near where it was gripped by its wielder. The blow would leave a welt, but it wasn't strong enough to break bone, or even deaden nerves, as Jed intended. He yanked back his arm, aiming for another more satisfying cut to the man's ribs. But the opportunity didn't arise to land the blow. The man's clenched left fist struck him under his ribs, and Jed folded over it. He almost vomited, even as he staggered back, his vision threatening to abandon him in a flash of scarlet agony as his guts contracted.

He sensed more than saw the man move towards him, and he swept the baton sideways out of instinct. A gloved hand snapping down on Jed's wrist checked it. He attempted to roll his arm free, but as he did so, the man's other hand grasped the baton and wrenched it away. Jed reared up, shielding his head with his free arm, expecting a blow from his own liberated weapon. Except his head wasn't the intended target. The tip of the truncheon whipped across his reconstructed knee, putting paid to hours of surgery and years of physiotherapy in an instant. Jed hurt too much to scream. He collapsed over his shattered leg, falling in a huddle at the man's booted feet, grimacing in torment as he tried to pull his injured knee into an embrace. He was shown no pity. The baton came down on his other leg. This time it was his ankle that exploded in agony. Jed pulled up his freshly hurt limb, huddled over both legs to protect them, but that only left open his head and shoulders to the prolonged and brutal attack that followed.

4

'It looks as if Andrew will be good for my fee,' I noted as Bryony VanMeter drove us up the driveway towards a waterfront house off Hillsborough Avenue, near to Double Branch Bay.

It was the morning after we'd met at Rink's place, and she'd returned early to pick me up, in order to personally introduce me to Andrew Clayton. Despite having downed a few bottles from Rink's stash of beer she appeared bright and breezy, and was freshly showered and perfumed. By comparison I felt and possibly looked as if I'd enjoyed a heavy drinking session, though it had nothing to do with imbibing too much alcohol. I'd had a restless night, my thoughts churning while considering if I'd done the right thing by accepting the job. Instinct had warned me to turn it down flat. But I was there, now, at Andrew's home, and it was too late to change my mind.

'He's good for the cash,' Bryony assured me. She sniffed, and I took it there was a good reason Andrew was still on the suspect list. 'He's even better placed considering Ella's life insurance payout he has coming.'

'I doubt he was short of money before that.' As soon as the words left my lips, I shut up. The fact that the family's wealth had made them targets of violent thieves shouldn't be forgotten.

The Clayton house was impressive, both large and spacious, on its own landscaped plot that edged up to a wide natural pond. On either side were groves of Southern Live Oak and Bald Cypress, strung with garlands of Spanish moss that dripped from their branches. The house emulated the architecture of Saratoga Springs – a style more popular over near Orlando than in Tampa - and was comprised primarily of wood cladding over a timber frame. It was robin egg blue, cream on the window and doorframes, and with grey stone columns highlighting the first floor bay windows. There was a raised porch, picturesque arched windows, and a two-door garage, and if a brief count of the windows was any estimate then a gazillion rooms inside. In my opinion the house was far too large for a small family of three – correction: only two now that Ella Clayton was no longer in residence – but I guess that was down to personal taste, or the whim of a huge wallet. Affluent residents of Tampa tended to live on Harbour Island, or on the Golf View or Parkland estates, and this house could easily have belonged to any of them.

As we approached it didn't look like a house of death, until I spotted the singular mar on its bright façade. The front door window had been so recently smashed it hadn't yet been repaired, and as a stopgap measure a sheet of plyboard had been fixed to cover the hole. The plyboard was an ugly reminder of what had recently occurred to blight this family, and what continued to. I was angry on behalf of the Clayton's, more so that small-minded idiots should torment a grieving child.

Bryony parked her Ford, one of the pool cars used by Tampa PD CID, on the drive comprised of crushed seashells. When I stepped out, the shells were loose underfoot, crunching as I shifted to haul out my bags. Nearby an American flag snapped lazily in the breeze, the flagpole centred on a manicured lawn. Bryony got out and led the way to the raised porch. There were railings up the steps and on the porch, and thicker beams supported a peaked roof. All that was missing were rocking chairs. I could have easily imagined I was setting foot on the veranda of a ranch or plantation house. The planks barely creaked under our combined weight, and they were freshly scrubbed and oiled and gleamed wetly in the morning sunlight. I checked that I wasn't leaving tracks on the surface, but there was no hint of my passing. Bryony paused a moment, straightening her clothing, and it was more to conceal the gun in her shoulder rig than it was to make herself presentable. There was possibly a small boy inside whose mother had been recently gunned down: seeing a gun might have an adverse effect on the boy's recovery. She aimed a finger at the doorbell. I didn't hear a corresponding chime, but the bell must have worked because from within the soft thud of footsteps approached the door.

Because of the plyboard over the broken pane, I had no view inside, so had no idea what to expect. I'd pictured Andrew Clayton based upon his affluent home and expected one of those guys who wears golfing attire even when he was off the courses, a pullover tied around his shoulders, and quite often a trophy wife hanging off one elbow. But when he opened the door, Andrew Clayton burst my bubble of expectation. I tried not to show my surprise. He was a bull of a man, with wide shoulders, thick legs, and a round shaved head. He wore wireframe spectacles perched on the flattened bridge of his nose, dressed in a plaid shirt and jeans, and loafers on his feet. There were old scars on his forehead, and as he held out a hand to usher us inside I saw more scars on his knuckles. He was older than I imagined the father of a young child would be, maybe in his forties like me. I thought of him as a heavyweight boxer who hadn't been active in the ring for a decade or more. We stepped inside.

'So this is the tough guy, huh?' Clayton said to Bryony, but appraising me. He was three inches taller, and about five stone heavier, than me, and his arms bulged with muscle. Judging by his lop-sided smile he didn't appear too impressed at his first impression of his bodyguard.

'This is the guy,' Bryony confirmed. Then with a teasing smile at me, she added, 'Looks can be deceiving, Andrew. You're in good hands.'

Clayton held out a paw to shake, and I accepted. He squeezed, the way some big guys with an attitude did, and I felt the bones of my hand begin to grate. I met him eye to eye, and returned the Neanderthal grip. Clayton grunted in mirth, then withdrew his hand and rubbed distractedly at his forearm as if I'd pained him. 'So what do I call you, buddy?'

'I'm Joe Hunter,' I said. 'Suit yourself. My friends tend to call me Hunter.'

'Then Hunter it is.' Clayton glanced briefly at Bryony. 'My friends have been in short supply lately.'

He led us into a spacious sitting room towards the rear of the house. There was a large picture window, and through it I could see the lawn where it dipped down towards the pond. Sun-bleached reeds formed a tall barrier between the mowed grass and the still water. My gaze went to a pale splotch on one wall. Spackling paste had been applied to fill an indentation in the wall, but to my trained eye I recognised a bullet hole. I made a brief scan of the other walls and saw more cover-up work. Bryony had already explained how the invasion crew had broken in via the garage, entering through a utility room to the kitchen where they'd given chase to Ella. She'd fled into this room, where more than one shooter had tried to bring her down. From the placement of the bullet holes she must have given them quite a run around, or they'd been simply shooting for shooting's sake. There had also been bullets found embedded in a settee, as I recalled, but Clayton must have replaced the furniture because the current settee looked unmarked.

Clayton watched me as I made my perusal. 'Yeah, this is where it all happened,' he said. He nodded to a spot on the floor. 'That's where Ella finally died. The bastards chased her in here and shot her like a dog.'

'I'm sorry for your loss,' I intoned.

The only indication he accepted my words was a jump of one eyebrow, before he turned aside. He moved across the large room, adjusting his spectacles, and I thought perhaps containing his emotions. Even big tough guys grieved, I had to remind myself, even if they didn't like to show it. I myself had gone through the process too many times not to feel sympathy for him.

Bryony knocked my elbow. 'Want me to hang around?'

'No. I'll get settled in. I think Clayton will be more relaxed without a cop around.' What I meant was that he'd probably speak more openly if he thought his every word wasn't being judged. Bryony understood.

Raising her voice, she said, 'Mr Clayton. Can I leave it to you to show Hunter around? I've a lot to do, I…'

Clayton turned so abruptly it caused Bryony to falter.

'Yes, Detective.' The sunlight coming through the picture window glared off Clayton's spectacles: I couldn't see his eyes behind the whiteout of their lenses. 'You've a lot to do. You should be out there finding the sons of bitches responsible for murdering my wife. If you can't manage that, then find whoever the asshole is that keeps coming round here and throwing bricks through my goddamn windows.'

Bryony's mouth formed a tight slit. But she nodded in acceptance of the berating. 'Speak with you later,' she said to me, and turned on her heel. Bryony had already told me that Clayton had proven awkward, but little wonder when he knew he was still a suspect in her eyes, and those of others with Tampa PD and beyond. She left, and I heard the front door snick closed. I looked at Clayton, and saw he had a hand over his mouth. He wiped, as if disgusted by his words.

'I'm sorry,' he offered. 'I shouldn't have spoken to her like that. Detective VanMeter's one of the few cops I have any faith in. She's the only one who seems to give a damn, when all the others have just treated me like a suspect.'

I shrugged away his apology. It shouldn't have been given to me, but Bryony. If only he knew that Bryony also suspected him of involvement in Ella's murder, he might not apologise at all. Then again, I could also understand his frustration: if he was innocent, and I'd no reason to think otherwise, then he had a right to criticise the police.

'Bryony is a good cop,' I told him. 'Your faith in her is well placed. She'll catch Ella's killer.'

Clayton waved a hand, inviting me to sit. I put down my bag, but I remained standing. He didn't seem to notice and slumped into an easy chair. He glimpsed up at me, and now I could see his eyes clearly. They danced over me, appraising again. 'She speaks highly of you too. Tells me you used to be a soldier. Special Operations guy.' He sniffed, but it wasn't in disdain. I'd noticed the stars and stripes banner waving on his lawn. Clayton was patriotic, and probably one of those that stood up and saluted veterans and firefighters at ball games. Perhaps he extended the same gratitude to veterans of US allies. 'You're a Brit, right? You sound like those northerners from Game of Thrones on TV.'

'I grew up in Manchester, England. I've been around the world a lot since then.'

'So are you a United or City man?'

'Not much of a soccer fan, I'm afraid,' I admitted.

Clayton held up a scarred fist, inspecting it. 'Can't say as I am either. I'm not much into team sports. Prefer it when a guy has to rely on himself to win.'

I wondered if that was his way of saying he didn't believe he needed me.

'I used to fight,' he said.

'Boxing?' I asked.

He snorted, as if the suggestion was beneath him. 'Iron Man. King of the Cage.'

'Mixed Martial Arts,' I said. Rink was active in the game, after a long time fighting in Kyokushinkai knockdown karate tournaments.

Clayton waved that description aside. 'Nah, I did it before the introduction of all the rules and regulations, before it grew soft. Back then we just had two guys, bare knuckles and the last man standing won.'

He wasn't simply making conversation, but I didn't believe he was being a braggart. Again I think he was pointing out he didn't need my protection, but really he was trying to convince himself. He could be the hardest fighter on earth and it hadn't done a thing to protect his wife.

He hung his head, and I watched him rub at the scarred knuckles of one hand. 'That was years ago,' he sighed, and transferred a hand to his right knee. 'I blew out my ACL fighting a pro-wrestler and that was my career over with.'

'You seem to have done all right out of it,' I said with a general nod at his accommodation.

'Huh! This didn't come from my purses. All I've got to show from all those fights are the scars I carry and a limp on damp mornings. No, all of this came from investing in boat rental. Me and a buddy started off with two fishing boats we had out of Sarasota, built our business up to a small fleet, and from there went into importing and supplying boats to other

31

start-up outfits. Things slowed down for a while after the financial crash, but business is picking up again.'

'So boats are still your passion?'

'Angling,' he corrected. 'The boats are a means to an end.'

'You were on a fishing trip with your boy when Ella was killed,' I said, and even I felt I sounded accusatory. But he didn't take offence.

'I'm away on fishing trips most weekends. It's no secret. I think now that was why my home was targeted when it was. Whether the assholes expected my wife to be home or not is another thing.'

'They came with guns,' I pointed out. 'They prepared for the worst. The thing I don't get is why they murdered your wife. A bunch of guys with guns, they could easily have controlled her while they took what they wanted.'

'They obviously didn't want any witnesses,' Clayton said.

But I thought of other incidents where the invasion crew had allowed witnesses to live. Bryony mentioned there were kids who had simply been locked in rooms while they went about their business. One old guy had died, but only when he resisted and his exertions brought on a heart attack.

'What did they take?' I asked.

'You mean as opposed to a wife and mother?' Clayton shook his head. 'Sorry, man. I know that's not what you meant. Just stuff. Electronics mainly: two TV's, a Blu-ray player, our tablets, other bits and pieces. All of it was replaceable stuff. But they also took personal items, my wife's jewellery from our room, my collection of watches, couple of Breitlings and a Rolex among them, some pocket cash we had lying around. Worst thing they did was take Ella's wedding ring off her finger after she was dead.'

The haul wasn't unusual. In the other home invasions the gang had targeted high value, easily transported goods. But there was an anomaly. The taking of Ella's ring from her finger didn't fit their *modus operandi*. But then she had been their only female victim to date, so maybe temptation was just too much for the thieves. Having chased her through the house, perhaps they felt she owed them extra payment for their effort. They were monsters, but Clayton didn't really need reminding.

'How is your boy doing?' I asked instead.

'It's been tough on him, but you know kids, right? They're tougher than adults at times like this. You're probably wondering where he is.'

'I am.'

'School. He's better off there with his friends than hanging around his old man.' Clayton must have thought about the boy's vulnerability, because he added, 'He gets picked up and dropped back again at the gate by the school bus. The school has security guards on patrol, and particularly at this time the principal has assured me she'll keep a close eye on Cole.'

'When he's home, I'll be here for him,' I said, and meant it. 'He's my priority, you can bet on it.'

Clayton stood up, and extended his hand a second time. When I accepted his grip this time there was no associated pissing competition.

5

Andrew Clayton was watching a movie on his recently acquired replacement TV. It was a huge flat-screened affair that took up almost an entire wall in his den. It had a surround sound system that'd accommodate an auditorium crowd. The movie was a Stallone actioner, and I could hear the muffled sounds of explosions and gunfire even down by the pond where I stood. I looked back at the house and saw lights behind a number of windows. Blue flickers came from beyond the blind over Cole's bedroom window, and I took it he was sneaking some late TV while his dad was engrossed in the celluloid mayhem a few rooms over. I'd come out for some peace, but also to do a circuit of the grounds. Best that I was familiar with the outside as I was growing with the interior of the house. Earlier I'd scouted nearer the building, checking out the flowerbeds where a prowler had recently stood, while peering inside. The soil had been forked over, so there was nothing left of the footprints discovered by the responding police patrol. There were indentations in the lawn, but Andrew, Cole, or even the gardeners employed to keep the grounds in tip-top shape could have made them. Now, standing by the pond, I checked lines of sight, and saw that the grounds were largely clear for a good forty or fifty paces on three sides, protected on only one by the expanse of water. The moss-hung trees looked eerie in the half-light of the moon, and any number of prowlers could approach through the woods before they were spotted. They'd have to be determined to travel through the tangled thickets though, and unalarmed by the proliferation of insects. Easiest way in was via the drive, but a sturdy wall and a wrought iron gate with an electronic lock protected access from the main road.

I could hear the soft hush of traffic on Hillsborough Avenue, and from more distantly on the causeway that took commuters from northwest Tampa across the bay towards Clearwater. A dog barked over in Bayport West, barely decipherable over the sound of cicadas. But I could hear yapping closer, too. I immediately walked up the lawn, rounded the house and on to the drive. I stood there and listened. The yapping came again, and this time I recognised the high-pitched vocals as those of a girl and boy in an excited flap. I moved adjacent to the drive so they didn't hear the crunch of my feet on the seashells. When I got to within twenty feet of the gate I stood still, but was hidden from them by the shadows from the trees flanking the drive. A young guy leaned against a parked car, gesticulating with a beer can at a teenage girl who was peering intently between the bars. She was answering without looking at him. She sounded tipsy, and I thought she'd had something stronger than the beer he was quaffing.

'I dare you to climb the gate,' the guy challenged the girl.

'I'll do it if you do it,' she countered. She held onto the bars with both clenched fists, leaning back so that her hair hung loose over her shoulders as she eyed him. 'C'mon, Bobby, you said you would.'

'You have to be nuts. Crazy Clayton will get us.' The youth pushed a hand through his floppy blond hair, grinning absurdly at her, as she used the gate as a pivot to swing sideways.

Just a couple of kids doing what kids do, I decided. Daring each other to approach the murder house. I wondered if already rumours of hauntings at the Clayton House were going around the nearby high schools. On top of the harassment Andrew was getting from those with an axe to grind, he didn't need drunken would-be ghost hunters creeping onto his property. I stepped into view. The youth spotted me immediately, and made a visible jerk of surprise. He hissed a warning at the girl and she spun around, her mouth falling open, eyes widening as I approached from the gloom. She immediately released the bars and took a couple of backwards steps. She glanced at her boyfriend, at me, and then at him again in an exaggerated double take. I wondered if she was about to run and jump in the car, and that would have suited me, but she didn't. Her immediate shock had been replaced by inquisitiveness.

'Hey, mister! Is it true a woman got murdered right here?'

'Hush, Mel,' Bobby cautioned, because he'd no way of knowing who I was. I could have been the notorious Crazy Clayton for all they knew.

I didn't answer directly. I said, 'It's not a good idea hanging around here.'

'Why not?' said the girl, as excitable as before. 'Will the crazy man get us?'

'No,' I said. 'But the cops might. You know you're trespassing on private property, right?'

'It isn't private out here, this side of the gate,' argued the girl.

I pointed back the way they'd arrived from. 'All the way back to Hillsborough,' I said, with no idea if I was right or not. 'It's all private property. Maybe it's best you go back up to the main road and park there, eh?'

The youth, Bobby, reached for his girl, but she pulled gently out of his grasp. 'Who are you?' she asked me directly.

'An employee,' I said.

'Some sort of security guard?' She sneered at me. 'Maybe if you'd done your job right, nobody would've gotten killed.'

'I wasn't here then.' I didn't need to explain myself, and doing so might have encouraged more questions from the girl. I could see Bobby was already keen to leave, but didn't have the *cojones* to command his girl to get back in the car. 'You know the police are still patrolling around here, right?' I made sure both of them got the point.

'It's not like they're going to arrest us or anything,' Mel said, and laughed at the absurdity of my warning.

'They won't for trespassing, but they might be more interested in how much you kids have been drinking.' I pointed at Bobby. 'Especially you. I take it you want to hang on to your driver's licence a bit longer than you've already had it?'

Bobby looked at his can of Budweiser and the thought of throwing it clear must have gone through his mind. Visions of being forced to take a sobriety test were enough to send him packing. He grasped Mel a second time, and this time when she tried to prize free, he held tight. 'C'mon, Mel. Let's get out of here. If I get run in on a DUI charge, my dad will kill me.'

The car was his father's, I'd have bet. I took out my cell phone. I'd no intention of calling the cops, but the suggestion was enough for Bobby. 'C'mon, Mel, for crying out loud!' He tugged her towards the car. She pouted, scowled daggers at me, while I dabbed buttons on the phone, actually calling up my empty voicemail account. She flipped me the bird. But Bobby pressed her inside the car, then ran round to clamber into the driver's seat before she decided to get out again. He gave me a pleading look before ducking inside, and I raised a thumb and put away the phone. Bobby drove off.

I waited until the brake lights first flared then died as the car turned right on Hillsborough Avenue a few hundred yards away. Rink had promised an easy job: well if seeing off a few ghoulish kids was the extent of my duties then I could live with it. Of course, that wasn't all I was here for. I was Bryony's eyes and ears on the ground, but up until now I'd nothing to report. Andrew Clayton had given me no reason to believe he was anything but a grieving husband, with a small child to contend with. Earlier, when the school bus had dropped him at the end of the drive, Andrew had brought Cole in after explaining who I was. Cole had been polite, but distracted, had hung his head and then followed his dad to the kitchen for chocolate milk and cookies. Afterwards he'd gone to his room, giving his X-Box his full attention. I thought the boy would come around in a day or two, and wasn't about to push him into accepting me. It wasn't easy filling a hole in your heart, and I wasn't the one to bridge the gulf that had opened in Cole's when losing his mom.

I sauntered back towards the house. Andrew had left his room. He was backlit as he moved slowly through the sitting room. He might have wondered where I was, but I'd mentioned to him earlier I'd probably patrol the grounds, so maybe not. He stopped, stood staring out, but he couldn't possibly see anything but his own reflection in the picture window. His mouth worked silently, and his spectacles were again blank mirrors. I moved away. Went around the side of the house and stopped to check the double garage doors. They were unmarked from where entry was made, but I recalled that Andrew and Cole had not long left on their fishing trip when the home invasion crew entered. Perhaps one of the garage doors had been left open when Andrew took out his SUV and they hadn't needed to force inside. I'd taken a look earlier. The locks had been replaced on both the utility room and kitchen doors. Both doors still retained the dusting powder used to lift the latent prints the police had discovered: they had been partial imprints from footwear. One was identified as a brand of work boot; the other of a sneaker with a distinctive tread pattern. Similar tracks had been found indoors, as well as other shoe prints, but these had long since been removed by a professional cleaning firm who'd also scrubbed all trace of blood.

Moving away I went around the back of the house again, took a quick glance up at Cole's room and saw he'd either personally elected to turn off his TV, or his dad had busted him and made him go to sleep. The room I'd been allocated was two over from Cole's and in darkness. Something plopped in the pond, and I turned to check it out, but couldn't see a thing. I walked across the lawn, not so much to check what had caused the splash but just to be moving. I could feel the ache in my muscles from yesterday's run, and had missed the one I should've done today. Distractedly I rubbed at the healed wound on my chest. It was only one of many scars I wore, but the most recent, and it still occasionally tingled with residual discomfort.

There was a crackle of underbrush.

I came to a halt.

Waited for the sound to repeat.

It didn't, but it wasn't the only thing to have fallen silent. The cicadas had momentarily seized their incessant chirruping. I began a nonchalant saunter towards the pond, but drew up short before I reached its boggy edge. The reeds barely stirred in the faint breeze blowing inland from the Gulf of Mexico. I stood as if unconcerned, my head slightly tilted as if I peered up at the moon, but I was listening, and allowing my gaze to zone out, using my peripheral vision to check for even the tiniest hint of movement. I didn't catch anything moving, but my senses were on full alert. Back in the days when I'd soldiered in some of the most dangerous places on earth, I'd honed my senses to a point I'd almost come to believe in the fabled sixth sense. The military had designated the talent of detecting a hidden watcher, or sniper, or lion crouching in the long grass, the title "Rapid Intuitive Ability". The military liked their designations. But really, the RIA gift isn't anything wondrous or preternatural, but simply instincts we all possess from back when we were still prey to more savage beasts. Most people have suppressed what they no longer need, but a soldier can't afford to drop his guard. As I stood, pretending to be unaware of my watcher, I felt a prickle on my neck and the hairs on my forearms rose almost as if there was a buzz of electricity in the air. I could almost feel eyes boring into me from the trees to my left.

My SIG Sauer P226 was a comforting weight in its carry position in the small of my back. But I didn't reach for my gun. I simply turned and returned the stare, though I could see nothing in the deep gloom beneath the moss-strewn boughs of the trees. Without averting my gaze I began marching purposefully forward. Whoever was hiding there held their position. But not for long.

As I got to within five paces of the trees there was a scuffle that turned into full-on crackles and snaps as someone – or something – large forced a route away from me. My gun stayed in my belt. I didn't believe for a second it was an animal; it was human. I could hear the thuds of feet, and the muffled curses of a male getting snagged on the undergrowth. I didn't think it was one of the home invasion crew – what purpose would any of them have for lurking in the woods? – and it might not even be the prowler who'd been spotted previously. Perhaps Bobby and Mel hadn't arrived at the gates alone, and this was some other stupid kid, half-pickled on beer, sneaking around.

I paced along the perimeter of the woodland, staying almost parallel to the guy in the woods. His need to get away was growing more urgent as the copse began to thin towards the side of the house.

'You'd best get the hell out of here,' I said loud enough for my voice to carry. 'The police are on their way and will be here in no time.'

The sounds of crashing footsteps and splintering branches faded abruptly, but not because the prowler had stopped running, only that they'd broken from the cover of the trees onto a short strip of lawn at the far side of the copse. I jogged around the trees, and made it to the fringe of longer grass that formed the demarcation zone in time to see the back end of someone clambering over the top of the boundary wall into the adjacent property. He paused briefly, clinging to the wall for stability before leaping to the ground.

'Yeah, you'd better keep running, you arsehole!' My holler was for effect, because I'd no intention of pursuing. 'And don't show your damn face around here again.'

I'd only got a fleeting look him as he scrambled to freedom. But it was enough to spot unruly brown hair poking from beneath a wool cap. A dark jacket and trousers. Sneakers on his feet. But the odd thing was I saw both hands as he'd clung to the top of the wall, and only one of them was gloved. I turned and scanned the woods and saw a few freshly broken twigs, the paler interiors bright against the deep grey bark. I moved closer, but it was too dark within the woods to see anything. I took out my cell phone, and brought up a torch app. I swept the beam away from the broken twigs, calculating his path through the woods and spotted more signs of passage. I entered the woods, feeling the tug of spreading vines around my ankles. Spanish moss netted my path, and I used my free hand to sweep it aside. Insects dropped on me, but I ignored the wriggling and scratching as they got under my collar. Maybe twenty feet in I saw the dropped glove. Actually, that wasn't correct. The glove wasn't dropped but snagged on the tip of a sturdy branch. It had caught, been pulled off the prowler's hand as he yanked away to free himself, and had partly turned inside out.

I thought for only the briefest of moments, then immediately switched my phone to the camera application and snapped a few shots of the glove *in situ*. Then I found a couple of pencil-length twigs on the ground and used them as chopsticks to pick the glove from the branch, and finally made my way out of the woods. As I walked back towards the house, I spotted a figure standing on the lawn, but from his build immediately recognised him as Andrew Clayton.

'What's going on, Hunter?' he asked, as I approached juggling the glove between the two twigs. 'I could hear you hollering from inside.'

'Just chased off a prowler,' I explained, and held up the glove. 'He dropped this.'

'You get a look at him?' he asked hopefully.

'Not a good look. Too dark.'

'But you saw him drop that?'

I only lifted my eyebrows. 'I found this after he'd fled, but it could only have been his.'

'So what're you going to do with it?'

'Got a plastic bag I can use?'

'Got some sandwich bags in the kitchen.'

'Good. I'll call Detective VanMeter first thing and have her come pick this up.'

'You think they'll run it for forensic evidence?' Clayton sniffed. As if he thought it unlikely.

'If it were only a one-off prowler, I don't think they'd bother. But I think there's more to this guy coming round than satisfying a sense of curiosity. Whoever put that brick through your front door meant business. If this was the same guy, he came prepared again.' I held up the glove for emphasis. 'He wasn't some kid trying to get his kicks; he was up to more. He had on a hat and gloves, and it isn't exactly the weather for either.'

'The son of a bitch,' Clayton said. 'If I get my hands on him...'

'You'll do nothing,' I warned. 'Beating the crap out of some nut job isn't going to help your case.'

'My case? What do you mean by that?'

'You know what I mean, Clayton. Let's not try to kid each other.'

Clayton pushed out his chest. 'The police have already investigated me. I've been questioned, cleared *and* released without charge. So I'm not too sure *what* you mean.'

'Your alibi stood up,' I told him. 'But don't think the cops aren't looking for another way to get you.'

'You think I had something to do with my wife's murder?' His cheeks had grown tight, his mouth a slit.

'It has nothing to do with what I think. It's what the cops think. And giving them a reason to suspect you're a violent man won't help.' I glanced at the ground, then up again and met his stare. 'If there's any reason to get violent, leave it to me.'

He appraised me with keen interest. I wasn't as big or imposing as him. But that didn't mean a damn thing, and I knew he knew it. He'd fought in tough guy contests, and understood that some of the most dangerous adversaries weren't muscle-bound hulks, or overblown thugs; they were often the unremarkable guys you least expected. But that wasn't all he was thinking about. I'd given him the suggestion that I had his welfare in mind, that I was an ally. The best lie is one where you conceal it with part of the truth.

'I've nothing to hide from the cops, or from anyone else for that matter,' he said, and I watched him relax. He shoved his scarred hands into his jeans pockets.

'Want to get one of those sandwich bags for me?' I asked.

6

When Bryony arrived at the Clayton place the following morning she had a partner along with her I wasn't as happy to see. Detective Holker and I don't share the mutual respect I have with Bryony. In fact, if Holker had his way he'd see me behind bars, or at least he'd have my green card rescinded and have me kicked out of the country. He abides by the old fashioned notion that the law always wins out, whereas I have more faith in justice. Sometimes the two aren't the same, and he wasn't a fan of my methods. I'd no rancour for him, not that I particularly liked him either, but he had only sarcasm and disdain for me.

'Putting your nose where it isn't needed again, Hunter,' was his opening remark as I handed over the glove I'd found. 'You should've left it where it was til we got here. Now you've broken the chain of evidence it'll be inadmissible in court.'

'I've no interest in taking it to court,' I answered.

'I'm surprised you didn't just gun the guy down and have done.'

Holker's salt and pepper hair looked much darker than usual, and glistened like oil under the sun, and there were a couple of stray hairs he'd missed with his razor on his left cheek. There was a small weeping nick on his narrow jaw. He hadn't showered this morning, and his shaving had been rushed. His clothing looked rumpled too; a cream linen jacket, open-necked white shirt and black slacks, all piled loosely on his spare frame atop his obligatory Cuban-heeled shoes. Tampa CID was under a lot of pressure to get results, so I forgave him the snarky remark.

Bryony pursed her lips, shooting us both withering glances. 'You two should go out and have a beer together. Get over yourselves, why don't you?'

'Maybe we'd be better putting boxing gloves on and duking it out,' Holker suggested.

'Who needs boxing gloves?' I asked.

Holker flicked back the bottom of his jacket, hooked a thumb on his belt. It served the dual purpose of displaying his detective's shield, and the Glock holstered on his hip. I smiled at him.

'What's this?' I asked. 'You show me yours, I show you mine?'

'Jesus,' said Bryony. 'Once you two are finished comparing the length of your dicks can we get back to what's really important?'

'Fine by me,' I said. Holker only exhaled through his flaring nostrils.

I'd told Bryony about finding the glove when first I contacted her that morning, and I'd also forwarded her the photos of it when it was still hanging on the broken branch. Nevertheless I still led them around the house and across the lawn towards the copse of tress. As we walked I mentioned the thrill-seeking kids at the front gate and how I first thought the prowler could have arrived with them, but had changed my mind when spotting his attire. 'He was older, too,' I added.

'You could tell that in the dark?' Holker said, unconvinced.

'Yes. When he was climbing the wall, the moonlight was on him. It was how I spotted he'd lost a glove.'

'But you didn't see his face?' Holker asked.

'Didn't need to. I could tell from his movements he wasn't a teenager. He wasn't the most agile. Kind of struggled to pull himself over that wall.' The perimeter wall was about six-feet tall, hardly an insurmountable barrier. 'His hair was brown, maybe light brown seeing as I could tell colour, and looked as if it needed a cut. White guy,' I added, before either detective could prompt me. 'I got a look at part of his face and an ear, his hand too.'

'But you couldn't pick him out of a line up?' Bryony wondered.

'Maybe if you had him dressed the same and climbing over that wall I'd identify him, but that wouldn't stand in court.' My words were a barb aimed at Holker, but I was also confident that if the circumstances were repeated then I could positively ID the prowler. I held a hand level with my eyebrows. 'He was about five feet nine tall, I'd say, slim build.'

The problem was that the description could fit countless thousands of guys, probably dozens in the local vicinity. It didn't help much. The glove wasn't latex that'd hold a fingerprint inside, but there was always the possibility that there were viable prints on the cheap leather exterior. If they were interested in discovering the prowler's identity then they could run the glove for forensics, but my guess was they had more important things on their minds.

'Where was Clayton when all of this was happening?' Holker asked.

'Inside the house. When I chased off those kids and came back down the drive I saw him in the living room. After I saw off the prowler he came out and met me on the lawn back there. He said he heard me shouting and came out to investigate.'

'What was his demeanour?' Bryony asked.

'Angry.' I didn't elucidate. 'But that's understandable.'

'Anything?' Bryony asked hopefully. She meant had he incriminated himself in any way.

'Not yet,' I said.

'What happened then?' Holker asked.

'We went to the kitchen, and I bagged the glove, kept it safe. Clayton checked on Cole and then went to his own room. I made another patrol and was satisfied all was quiet so went back inside and locked up. Called you guys at first light.'

'Didn't you sleep?' Bryony asked. I wasn't showing signs of fatigue.

'No. Stayed awake all night. Rink's coming over to spell me in an hour or so,' I said with a cursory glance at my watch. 'I'll sleep then.'

'Is Clayton home now?' Holker wondered and turned to look back at the house.

'No.'

'You allowed him to leave?'

'He isn't under house arrest,' I reminded him. 'And I'm not here to hold his hand. It's the boy I'm here to protect, and he's safely at school.'

'That's not the only thing,' Holker said. 'You're here to help us determine if he had anything to do with his wife's murder. How do you suppose you're going to do that if you let him out of your sight?'

'Softly softly catchy monkey,' I said, and received an incredulous squint from Holker. Perhaps he was unfamiliar with the saying. 'If I'm constantly in his pocket, Clayton will be more guarded. He's more likely to trip himself up if I keep some distance between us.'

'That isn't the way I'd do things,' Holker grumbled.

'Good job it's not you staying here then, Detective,' I remarked. 'What would you do: shoot him and have done?'

Holker gave me the stink eye. I turned my back on him, joining Bryony as we began walking towards the house. I didn't need a heightened sixth sense to tell Holker's gaze was boring between my shoulder blades. I nudged Bryony's elbow, saying *sotto voce*, 'You told him why I'm here?'

'He's my partner, Joe. What did you expect?'

'Fair enough.' I expected a worse reaction from Holker than I'd received. Not only did he despise my tactics, he wasn't hugely impressed that Bryony had been intimate with me. I believed he held a candle for his beautiful partner, but had never had the nerve to show her his true feelings. Perhaps he was frightened that she'd turn him down flat, or worse, his wife would find out and trim his wick. I glanced back at him, and he was tight-lipped as he followed us.

'So you shared with Holker, how about you share a little more with me?' I asked.

'What do you mean?' Bryony asked innocently.

'I need to know if there's any progression in the case. If I'm going to wrangle some kind of confession from Clayton, I need to know the pertinent facts, otherwise how will I know if he's tripped himself up?'

'We're still concentrating on identifying the home invasion crew. We've some leads we're following up on before we can start affecting arrests.'

'I'm not talking about the robbers, and you know it, Bryony. You know there's something wrong here; details that just don't fit with their M.O. and probably never will. You don't think the ones who killed Ella are the same people, do you?'

'I don't,' Bryony said, 'but you already knew that. But we've also investigated Clayton thoroughly, and we can't find any evidence to say he organised the hit. We've checked his phone records, his email accounts, all the usual routes, but haven't found anything suspicious. No big payments going out of his bank accounts, nothing to indicate he paid anyone for their services.'

'Maybe payment was made in what they were allowed to carry away with them,' I said, though it was a poor theory. I recalled what Clayton had said about Ella's ring being stolen from her finger, and I doubted he'd have agreed to that. 'Or maybe he's totally innocent.'

'That's what we have to find out,' she said.

'What about other suspects?'

'Other suspects?'

I nodded at the bagged glove. 'The guy who left that has something to do with Ella's murder.'

'Or he's just a crazy guy who gets a kick out of being so close to a murder scene. There are plenty nut jobs like him.'

Holker had caught up as we slowed to speak. He surprised me by saying, 'You tell him about the emails, Bryony?'

'Not yet,' she said, and shrugged as if the messages were unimportant. 'We've been receiving anonymous messages criticizing us for our failure to catch the killer. The killer accused us of clearing Andrew Clayton, and concentrating on the unconnected home invasions, more or less stating that we were being racist, because Clayton is a successful white guy while the crew's obviously a bunch of underprivileged blacks. His words not mine. You ask me, he's the racist when jumping to conclusions like that.'

'Sounds as if he might have some insider knowledge,' I said.

'We've wondered the same,' Holker said, again surprising me by electing to share with me. 'The emails could even come from one of the home invasion gang, who are pissed that they're being blamed for Ella's murder. But that theory doesn't hold much weight with me. I'm thinking it's someone else who has a grudge against Clayton. There's one person of interest we're looking at.'

I waited. Both detectives glanced at each other, wondering how much they should divulge. Perhaps Holker believed that by telling me about a possible culprit he'd be sealing the man's doom. Finally he nodded, giving Bryony the go-ahead.

She waved her arm, taking in the house and grounds in one gesture. 'Did Clayton tell you how he could afford all this?'

'His boat supply company,' I said.

'Did he mention his business partner?'

'Yeah, but I haven't learned his name.'

Bryony sucked in her bottom lip, then released it with a tiny smack. 'Parker Quinn,' she announced. 'The two of them go back a-ways. They started off as a two-boat outfit, taking tourists out on the Gulf, built up their business from there.' I'd heard the story from Clayton already, but suspected there were parts of it he'd left out. Bryony confirmed my suspicion. 'Theirs is a shaky business relationship, has been for a number of years now. Clayton has tried buying out Quinn, but Quinn's not for moving. The way I've read things between them, Quinn also wants what Clayton has.'

'He hasn't done as well out of the partnership?' I asked.

'He's done OK with the cash, it's other things Clayton has that Quinn supposedly covets.'

'Hmmm,' I said, understanding what she was hinting at. 'Quinn had his eye on Ella? Any suggestion that she reciprocated?'

'Not that anyone is admitting to it, but I have a sense that Quinn and Ella enjoyed some sort of relationship. If Clayton suspected, he isn't saying a thing. You know to admit as much would give him a motive for having his wife murdered.' Bryony shrugged, and again looked at Holker, seeking his in-put.

'I know what you're thinking, Hunter,' said Holker. 'Why would he have Ella murdered, and still engage in business with the man who was jumping his wife's bones? Why not have Quinn murdered, and have done? That way he'd not only inherit everything he did from Ella, but also the entire business. That's what I've been thinking, too.'

'You suspect Quinn's behind the anonymous emails?'

'Yeah, But we've been unable to trace them back to him. Whoever's behind them is covering their tracks, sending them through anonymous Hotmail accounts. We've been able to identify the IP address of the computer used to send them, but not its location. Once we find the computer, we find the sender, but we haven't any reason to go hunting for it yet. These emails are only a few compared to the dozens of others we've received from all the haters. The only reason they're of interest to us is because they firmly accuse Clayton, seem to have some insider knowledge about the man, and have purposefully been kept anonymous.'

'Could be the killer,' I said. 'Throwing you off track by having you concentrate on Clayton.'

'Could be,' Holker admitted, and actually offered me a nod of mutual respect. But that was all I could expect from him. He walked away, his built-up heels leaving small crescent indentations in the lawn.

7

Once Rink arrived and took over guard duty, I collapsed on the bed in the guest room, and slept like the dead for six hours. When I woke, and had showered and shaved, and taken a bathroom break, I let my big buddy get off again. Before he got in his car, he raised his eyebrows at me in question, but I'd not a lot to tell him yet. I'd mentioned the prowler that dropped the glove when he arrived earlier, and guessed he'd spoken with Clayton about the incident while I slept. Because Andrew and Cole were home, I told him I'd give him a call later and bring him up to speed on my suspicions.

'I've nothing much on tonight,' he said. 'Want me to come on by later as a second set of eyes?'

'There's no need, yet, Rink.'

'What if the creepy dude comes back for another look?'

'I want him to,' I said. 'But he might be put off if security's too tight.'

'He'd never know I was here,' Rink said, and he wasn't boasting, though he'd earned the right. For all he was the size of a pro-wrestler, and almost as flamboyant in dress at times, Rink could be an invisible man when he wished. There'd been times when he'd infiltrated the strongholds of terrorists and enemy fighters under their very noses, and completed his mission without anyone suspecting he'd ever been there – until they found the evidence of his work; usually it had been bloody.

'I'm just on the other end of the phone if you want me,' he said.

'I know.'

He flicked a salute and took off, the thick tyres of his Porsche kicking up a mini-tsunami of crushed shells in his wake. There was an electronic sensor on the gate that allowed him easy exit, and I waited until the gate had fully locked again before going indoors. Clayton was in the kitchen. He heard me enter, and walked out from behind the central counter to meet me.

'What did the cops have to say about the prowler?' he asked without preamble.

'They're following up on it. I gave the glove to Detective VanMeter and she promised to get back to me once it's been examined.'

'I guess these things can take time,' he said.

'It's not like you see in the movies,' I told him. In fact, from what I'd learned, a lot of forensic investigation was determined by budgetary constraints and how important any single piece of evidence was to a case. On the face of it, the glove I'd seized had nothing to do with the murder inquiry Bryony was investigating, so it might be put aside altogether. Then again, she'd be a fool to discount the presence of the prowler because I for one hadn't changed my opinion: he was involved somehow, I just hadn't figured out how yet.

'Think he'll come back?' Clayton asked, and I noticed him again rubbing at his forearm. I wondered if it was a nervous tic.

'He might...then again he might not. He must realise he dropped his glove and that he might've made himself a suspect.'

'What are you planning on doing if he does show up?'

'Grab him, hand him over to VanMeter and have him answer some difficult questions.'

Clayton adjusted his spectacles, his mouth puckering slightly as he turned. My answer hadn't been what he wanted to hear. Perhaps, like Holker did, Clayton expected me to gun the guy down. As tempting as the notion was, we'd no evidence yet that he'd done anything to harm Ella, or even if he was the person responsible for hurling the brick through the door. Until I knew otherwise I wasn't going to jump to conclusions.

'As long as my boy's safe,' Clayton said, 'I don't care what happens to the bastard.'

As if mention of his name had summoned him, Cole appeared in the doorway. He was looking at his feet, shuffling his sneakers on the tiled floor.

'Everything OK, son?' Clayton asked.

'I'm thirsty,' said Cole without raising his head.

'I filled your bottle for you.' Clayton gestured towards a sports bottle on the counter, containing some kind of purple juice.

'I want chocolate milk,' Cole said.

'We don't have any,' Clayton said. 'You finished it yesterday, and I didn't get a chance to go grocery shopping today.'

Cole hung his head even lower.

'How about I go out and get some? I can be back in no time,' said Clayton.

'Can I come with you?' asked the boy hopefully.

Clayton glanced at me. I was about to suggest accompanying them to the nearest convenience store, but Clayton pre-empted me. 'No, you have to wait here with Mr Hunter. I won't be long; promise I'll be back before you know it.'

I could tell Cole was displeased, and was about to argue, but it was as if he knew his appeal would be pointless. 'Can I have Yoo-hoo?' he said instead.

'Yoo-hoo it is,' said Clayton. As an afterthought he looked at me. 'You're OK with keeping an eye on Cole, right?'

'It's why I'm here,' I said, more for the boy's sake than anything.

Clayton nodded. 'You want me to grab something for you?'

'Maybe I'll try some chocolate milk too,' I said, and caught a flick of Cole's attention directed my way. For the first time I noticed his mouth curl up at one side. There were better ways of bonding with a child than over a glass of flavoured milk, but I couldn't think of one right then. Somehow our shared taste for Yoo-hoo made us allies.

'…and some Goobers, Dad,' Cole added, now that he was on a roll.

'Goobers? They're chocolate-coated peanut's, right? I think I'd like some of those too, Mr Clayton.' I winked at the father, who appreciated what I was doing. He made a pistol of his fingers and pointed them at me.

'You got it,' he said, and pulled an imaginary trigger.

Cole barely moved, as Clayton swept past, rubbing his fingers through the boy's mass of hair before heading for the front door. Cole still toyed at the floor with his sneakers.

I wondered why he looked so different from his father. The boy was tow-headed with expansive curls hanging over his eyes, jutting over his ears and extending over the collar of his T-shirt. He was small for his age, slim to a point of fragility, and had vivid green eyes, though they appeared a little muddied by fatigue as he glimpsed up at me from under his wavy bangs. I knew that some small kids could fill out in puberty, but Cole would have to grow a lot before he matched his dad for brawn. I'd seen photographs of Ella, his mother, and assumed that he'd inherited more genes from her. Ella too had those same green eyes, and wavy hair, and had been tall and willowy. For all I knew Andrew Clayton could have celebrated a full head of curls once, but that was years ago and before his scalp became acquainted with a razor. There was no doubt in my mind whose sweet nature the boy inherited though; he had nothing of Clayton's pent up aggression, even though he was hurting badly from his loss and could have easily raged at his grief. Right now he only appeared shy, unsure of himself, and more so of me.

'So you like chocolate milk, huh?' I said, and immediately felt stupid. I was pushing the flimsy connection too much.

Cole shrugged his narrow shoulders.

He just stood there in the doorway, waiting.

'You want to ask me something?' I said. 'Go ahead. I'll answer anything you want to know about me.'

'Are you a police officer?' he asked timidly.

'No. Not a policeman.'

'I thought you were Detective Bryony's friend.'

'I am her friend, but I'm not a cop. I'm more like a private cop, if you like?'

'Oh, a private investigator you mean?' said the boy.

I laughed in good humour. 'Yeah, but I'm probably the world's worst private eye. I'm pretty useless at Cluedo.'

Cole squinted up at me, so maybe he hadn't heard of the board game.

'I thought you were here to protect us, not investigate,' he said.

'I am. I should have said that I work for a private eye – you met Rink earlier, right?'

Cole nodded. 'Rink's funny.'

'Yep. He is that,' I said and grinned. I earned a conspiratorial smile from the boy. 'And incredibly ugly,' I added with a wink, and this time he laughed. 'Well, Rink has a private investigations company and I work with him. Usually though, I do -' I opened my hands, taking in Cole and the house with the gesture '- this kind of stuff. I look after people, keep them safe.'

'So you're more like a bodyguard then?'

I nodded.

'Do you have a gun?'

At first I didn't know how best to answer, except honesty was the best policy in this instant. 'I do.'

'The bad men had guns too, when they…came here.' His voice had faltered towards the end, and I knew he was about to say "when they killed my mom" but couldn't bring himself to give the words sound.

'That's the only reason I'm carrying one now,' I reassured him.

'Will they come back?'

'I won't lie to you, Cole. The truth is I don't know, but if they do I won't let them hurt you.'

He thought about what I'd said. 'I don't like guns.'

'Good boy,' I told him. 'Guns are horrible things.'

He looked up at me again, and I'd swear that the mind behind his gaze was much older and wiser than nine years old. 'But you still carry one.'

'Do you know what a deterrent is?' I asked him, and realised I was probably insulting his intelligence. 'Course you do. Well, my gun's just a deterrent. I won't use it unless I absolutely have to.'

'I don't mind,' said Cole.

I waited, unsure what he actually meant.

'If the bad men come back, I don't mind if you shoot them. They shot my mom. They should be shot too. I don't like guns, Mr Hunter, but I positively hate what they did to my mom, so they'd deserve it.'

To say I was uncomfortable was an understatement. I quickly changed the subject. 'Call me Joe, why don't you? When you call me Mr Hunter it makes me feel old.'

'You are old,' said Cole. Then smiled again at the poke he'd delivered. 'Not as old as Mr and Mrs Huckabee who live up the block, but you're as old as my dad…and he's ancient compared to my friends' dads.'

Guys in their forties probably looked like withered mummies to most nine-year-olds, I decided. 'I'm not as old as I look,' I reassured him, and poked a finger into my own cheek, 'I'm in disguise. This is a mask like they wore on Mission Impossible. I'm only eighteen really.' Being eighteen years of age was a mark of adulthood to kids back home in England, and I hoped it was the same here in the US.

'If that's a mask, you didn't pick a very good one,' he said, then grinned at my look of mock affront. His chuckle as he walked from the room was musical. I liked the kid, he shared a sense of humour common to me, and I momentarily wondered how much of it he'd picked up from Rink while my buddy was here earlier. Nah, I decided, if Cole were following Rink's cue he'd have been much cheekier.

Clayton had only been gone minutes, but I heard a vehicle approaching the house, the tyres crunching on the shells. I moved from the kitchen into the vestibule and saw Cole had only got as far as the stairs. He'd screwed up his nose, as he looked at the door, probably thinking the same as I. This wasn't his dad returning with the promised treats.

'You want to go on upstairs?' I said, and it wasn't really a question. I placed a hand on his shoulder, gently steering him for the stairs. 'I just want to see who this is, OK? I'll call you down again when I know everything's alright.'

Cole glanced at me, and I knew he was checking to see if I'd drawn my gun. I hadn't, it was firmly wedged in the carry-holster in my lower back, hidden beneath my shirt. I showed him my empty hands. Cole appeared unsure at me being unarmed.

'Go on up,' I said, 'and don't you worry, everything will be fine.'

Cole paused only a few seconds longer, but it was as if I'd won his trust for now and he went up with no argument. I should have ordered him into his room, but that would have been over-reacting. Visitors weren't banned from the house, so there was probably nothing sinister about the arrival of this unexpected caller. When I checked, I saw Cole watching from around the bannister rail. His face was motionless as he gazed at me with serious intensity. I winked at him, as though we were partners in this now, and his smile flickered into place once more.

From beyond the plywood barrier on the shattered window I heard the clunk of a car door shutting. I waited, heard the measured padding of feet up the steps and onto the porch, waited a few seconds more then yanked open the door.

The guy standing before me was in his late forties or early fifties, about five-feet nine-inches tall, and with unruly greying brown hair. His eyes were bloodshot and almost forcing their way out the sockets. Earlier I'd told the detectives I'd be able to identify the prowler if I again saw him scrabbling over the wall out back. Now I wasn't as certain of a positive ID, because from the icy chill that went through my guts, I would also swear this was the same man. But unless he was insane, he wouldn't present himself at Clayton's door to ask if he could please have back his misplaced glove. Not that that was what he did. No. On seeing me, he took a jerk backwards, landed solidly on his heel, and shoved a hand quickly inside his jacket front.

Maybe I should have drawn my gun before opening the door.

8

Drawing my gun would have proved a matter of a second, and firing two bullets into the man's chest a half second more. It would probably take longer for him to fall backwards on the porch, wheezing out his last breath. In the same short space of time, he too could draw his gun from inside his coat, and similarly put a round in me. Sometimes mortality is measured in instants, and there are no guarantees who would be the one left standing afterwards.

Instead of reaching for my SIG, I lunged forward, my left hand snapping out and grasping his hand as it dipped in his jacket. I yanked his hand out, my fingers curled around the base of his thumb, and my own thumb-tip digging between the metacarpal bones. I rotated his hand outwards, locking it painfully at the wrist and elbow, even as my right hand shot in and grasped his trachea with crushing force. The guy gasped, and his spittle covered my face in a fine spray.

A quick anticlockwise rotation of his trapped hand would ruin his day; a concerted squeeze to his throat would finish it totally. But there were factors piling in on me that halted further injury. First, I could see no gun in his hand, just a folded piece of paper. Second, the man was already swooning out of shock. Third, and probably most importantly, I heard Cole's yelp and the rat-a-tat padding of his small feet down the stairs.

'Don't hurt him!' the boy squealed. 'Please don't hurt him, Joe, it's only my Uncle Parker!'

I glanced at Cole. He was a few feet behind me, bent at the waist, head rammed forward on his straining neck like a hirsute tortoise. His green eyes were huge, and strings of saliva meshed his open lips.

'It's OK, Cole. I'm not going to hurt him,' I reassured the boy. Whether my captive heard, or understood, I couldn't tell, because he was almost sinking to his butt. I relaxed my grip on his throat, grabbed his collar instead and hauled him to standing. Now my hold on his wrist helped steady him. I steadied him until some cognizance came back in his eyes. Cole had moved closer, was almost pressing up against my thigh, but it was so he could check his uncle was unhurt. 'He'll be fine in a second or two,' I added.

'G...get off me...' said the man.

'If I let go you'll fall on your arse,' I told him.

'I'm...' He probed at his reddened throat with his free hand and found everything was still in the correct place, though not necessarily in full working order. 'I'm...OK. Let go of me.'

I propped him against the doorframe, releasing my hold, while scooting Cole clear of us, should his uncle turn obstreperous and require controlling again.

'Jesus, man, who the hell are you anyway?' the man said.

'I'm looking after Cole,' I said. 'Who are you?'

He didn't answer my question. 'Where's Andrew?'

'Out,' I said. 'What do you want with him?'

He worked his aching wrist, while shaking his head at me. 'You must be the damn bodyguard he told me about.'

I didn't bother agreeing.

'And you're Parker Quinn,' I said, recalling now the full name of Clayton's business partner. Quinn wasn't actually a blood uncle to Cole, but I guessed he'd be the next best thing. I was in an awkward position, because according to the investigating detectives, this could be the man behind the anonymous email campaign pointing the accusatory finger at Clayton. But he might not be. I studied him, trying to imagine him clambering over the wall in the dark, moonlit, but not presenting his face to my scrutiny. He was alike the man I'd chased, but how could I be positive?

'How'd you get in past the gate?' I asked.

Quinn scowled at me, took a quick glance at Cole for support, then regained his scowl for me. 'I have the code for the gate. Jesus, man, how'd you think I got in, rammed my way through?'

I made a mental note to have the security code changed once Clayton returned home. I should have thought about it sooner, considering I'd been with Bryony when she had punched in the four-digit code to allow us access on my first arrival. All other visitors, Rink among them, had to press a buzzer and announce himself over an intercom, and Clayton had allowed entry, remotely opening the gate from a control panel in the house. Access to the property was an issue for security, but it also begged questions about the home invasion. The robbers had carted away some large electronic devices, and I doubted they'd carried them all the way up the drive to where they'd left their vehicles. They must have brought them nearer to the house. Had one of the robbers known the access code, or was there something I was missing? I supposed that they could have opened the gate from the control panel once inside the house, and accomplices had then driven closer, but it was a push. If Clayton were behind his wife's murder, he'd have told the crew the code to get in, but then if he were that organised he'd have made sure they damaged the gate to cover the trail back to him. As far as I knew there'd been no damage reported to the gate. As with the taking of Ella's wedding ring, the manner of the opening of the gate was an anomaly to be considered further, points to be talked over with Bryony next time I saw her.

'So why are you here?' I prompted Quinn.

'I told you already,' he snapped.

'No you didn't, you asked where Andrew was.'

'Well isn't it obvious? I want to see him.'

'About what?'

'It's…private.' Quinn stared past me and I knew he was eyeing the boy. I watched him smile sheepishly at Cole, reassuring him he was OK. I also caught the subtle undertone of his words. He didn't want Cole to hear. I turned to Cole, and saw that he'd retreated to the bottom of the stairs. He held the upright of the bannister as if in need of a crutch.

'Cole. It was just a bit of a misunderstanding between your Uncle Parker and me. Everything's fine now, so will you be a good boy and go upstairs a few minutes?'

Our shared connection had been tenuous to begin with, and now severely tested, but Quinn also nodded and pointed his chin upwards, silently asking the boy to do as he was asked. Cole pouted slightly, but he turned and went up the stairs, his treads heavier than when he'd pelted down. I closed the door, and pressed Quinn to go to the kitchen, where there was less likelihood we'd be overheard.

When he'd settled his lower back against the kitchen counter, I said, 'We got off on the wrong foot back there.'

It wasn't much of an apology, but I didn't think he deserved one. What the hell had he been thinking reaching into his jacket like that when confronted by a stranger?

He shrugged. 'Maybe I should've announced myself, but I've never had to before, normally I just come on up to the house…'

'Things aren't normal just now,' I reminded him.

'No. No they're not.' I watched sadness follow his words, and he looked down at his feet, started toeing the tiles underfoot.

'I guess Ella's murder hurt more people than her immediate family,' I said.

He placed a shaking hand over his eyes and I expected tears to follow, but then his shoulders straightened and he looked directly at me and his eyes, though still bloodshot, were dry. Anger sparked in them. 'It's the real reason I'm here. I do want to speak with Andrew, but it's to ask why the hell I've spent all afternoon at the goddamn police station answering hurtful accusations.'

I experienced a twinge of guilt, because Clayton had nothing to do with Quinn being dragged in for questioning. I wondered if, after we'd spoken about Quinn as a suspect behind the hate campaign, Bryony or Holker made the executive decision to bring him in, put some pressure on him and hope he'd fold - before they had any tangible evidence on him.

'What have you got to complain about?' I said. 'Evidently you answered to their satisfaction or you wouldn't be at your liberty now.'

Quinn went for his pocket again, but jerked to a halt, anticipating another throttling and painful wristlock.

'Go ahead.' I said, confident he wasn't carrying a weapon having discretely checked while propping him up minutes ago. All that was in his inside pocket was the folded paper he'd originally gone for, dropped from his spasming fingers as I'd wrenched everything out of place.

'I had to stand my own bail, goddamnit!' He rattled the paperwork under my nose, before throwing it on the counter. 'I've to report to Franklin Street to answer more of those goddamn questions in two days time. Those goddamn jackbooted Nazis are currently at my house executing a search warrant. God knows what I'm going to find when I get back home.'

I thought that at the very least he'd find his computer missing. I assumed his cell phone had already been seized when he was at the police station.

'It was a stupid move coming here, Quinn,' I told him. 'What if there's a tail on you? Fronting Clayton in his own home won't help your case if the cops think you're the one harassing him.'

'I'm the one harassing *him*?'

'You tell me,' I said.

'I just got my ass hauled to jail, had my hair yanked out and got grilled by some prissy A-hole in stacked heels, and now my house is being ransacked, and Andrew's the one being harassed?' Quinn rubbed his mouth with both hands. Then used his saliva-damp fingers to push back his hair. When he realised what he'd done, he looked in disgust at his palms, and then scrubbed them down the thighs of his jeans.

'You saw the front door, right?' I said.

'I had nothing to do with that!' Quinn's sclera began turning red again.

'I believe you,' I said, and wasn't lying. I really didn't think he was involved in Ella's death, in the vandalism of Clayton's home, or in sending the emails. But he could have a stake in the outcome if Clayton was charged. He stood to inherit control of their boating and supplies business, and that could be seen as a motive to want Clayton out of the way. Also, there was something else that might fall in his favour if my suspicions were correct. What that inkling was, I chose to keep it to myself for now. 'Look, Quinn. It's like I said, you're doing yourself no favour coming here like this. Maybe you should leave, and wait until you've thought things through before you see Andrew. How is throwing any of this at him going to help? Trust me, it isn't.'

He threw up his palms. 'You might be right. I was just so mad…'

'And getting into an argument with Andrew was your first idea?'

'I didn't come here to argue, only to speak. He's my friend, my business partner, who else would I go to?'

'You don't have a wife or girlfriend whose ear you could bend?' I asked.

Quinn's face almost folded in on itself.

'It's only me, man,' he said, 'only me.'

'Then don't go doing something stupid like spoiling a friendship,' I counselled him, even as I surreptitiously began leading him to the door. 'Go on, Quinn. Get yourself out of here before Andrew gets back. If I were you I'd be home, ensuring none of those jackbooted Nazis are tracking dirt all over your house.'

'I, uh, yeah,' he said, at a loss now I'd taken the wind out of him. 'Look, man, I'm sorry about the way I showed up at the door. It wasn't the best idea I've ever had.'

I shrugged, unconcerned. After all, I wasn't the one who'd ended up semiconscious, and with an aching wrist. I kept him moving past the stairs, and to the door. He opened it himself, probably having done so a hundred times in the past. But then he paused and glanced up. 'I hope I didn't frighten Cole. The boy's got enough on his plate without seeing me like that.'

'I'm sure he'll be fine. To be honest, Quinn, I'm the one who might have frightened Cole. I think I've some making up to do with him.'

'Aw hell, I didn't mean to cause any trouble for you,' he said.

'Forget about it,' I said.

'Man, I don't even know your name,' said Quinn, and tentatively offered me his hand.

'Hunter,' I said, and accepted his grip.

'Hunter,' he repeated by rote. He shook my hand, but was too embarrassed to meet my gaze. He stepped outside. As he walked to his car he slouched with each step, his hair hanging over his face, and I genuinely felt sorry for him. The guy, I'd already decided, was a threat to nobody, except perhaps himself.

9

Bryony VanMeter put away her cell phone and thought about what Joe Hunter had just told her.

She was standing in the service yard at the rear of Tampa PD HQ on Franklin Street. Jurisdiction for the murder of Ella Clayton came under the Hillsborough County Sheriff's Office, but being part of a larger picture where the home invasion crew had struck throughout the various districts of Tampa Bay, all investigations were being conducted under the direction of the Major Crimes and Strategic Investigations Bureaus based at One Police Center, of which she was a single spoke in a much larger task force wheel. She was waiting for Dennis Holker to join her, but he was taking longer than he'd promised. She didn't hold his tardiness against him; Holker had no control over when their captain got through tearing strips off him. She was thankful that he'd attended the summons to Captain Newburger's office alone, and for once saw a benefit in being junior in rank to her partner. Before joining CID she'd attained Master Police Officer rank, whereas Holker had been a uniformed sergeant before making the switch. If there was a ranking system in CID, Bryony could probably claim she was equivalent to a sergeant now, but Holker had stepped up to lieutenant. Lieutenant or not, it didn't stop a captain mauling you half to death when things weren't going to their satisfaction. She was fortunate not to be on the end of a stripping down too, so waited patiently for Holker to join her without complaint, though she was antsy and raring to go.

There was a storm brewing. The evening sky was deep orange and purple; the heavy clouds fit to burst at any second. The light pollution from the city added to the ominous cast of the bruised heavens. It felt as if the humidity had gone up by about forty per cent in the last few hours, and most of it was gathering in her clothes and hair. To avoid the promised downpour she stood beneath an overhanging concrete ledge that was one of the integral supports of the tower block behind her. She was at the bottom of a slope, up which trash was ordinarily wheeled to a series of trashcans and Dumpsters arranged out of public view in the service yard. Her lower angle gave her a skewed view of the yard where she could see only the tyres of the squad cars that came and went. She was standing in what was affectionately known as "the lepers pit" by the other officers and clerical staff that enjoyed sneaking a cigarette when opportunity arose. It didn't happen very often, smoking on duty being frowned upon by the politically correct brigade upstairs, but it was tolerated – as long as members of the public didn't see, when disciplinary procedures usually followed.

Bryony smoked. Not very often. Days, and sometimes weeks, went by before she relented to her habit, when she was careful only to have one cigarette. More than that and she suspected she'd be back up to twenty-a-day in no time. Under so much pressure from above, she could forgive herself the cigarette she sucked on now, and relished the cold buzz of nicotine through her system. It wasn't cold enough to balance the sticky heat, but it was better than nothing. She stepped from under shelter, walked up the ramp to squint around the corner at the CID squad room door, but there was still no sign of Holker. She trembled from the hit of nicotine, and her thoughts were a bit woozy. But she didn't douse her cigarette, returning to her hiding place she made certain she smoked it down to the stub.

She heard the squeaking of the door, followed by the clip of heels on asphalt. Time to go. She emerged from the ramp, popping a Breath Savers peppermint in her mouth as she searched for Holker. He knew where she'd be waiting, but walked away, across the yard towards their pool car, and she followed. His back was rigid, his steps more mincing than usual, as if he'd been reamed a new butthole. She guessed the shit storm he'd weathered had been epic.

Thinking of storms, the first fat droplets splattered her as the heavens geared up to end Holker's day on a similar note. She jogged for the car, aiming for the passenger side as Holker was already settling into the driver's position. As she slid inside, the rain intensified, drumming on the windshield like the claws of a horde of starving scavengers. She pulled the door shut, and sat steaming in the cooler air within the car. She glanced over at Holker.

'Don't ask,' he said.

So she didn't. Instead she said, 'Hunter called me while you were upstairs.'

Holker hit the ignition, and pulled away. 'What did Rambo have to say for himself?'

Bryony settled her mint in the corner of her mouth. 'He said there was an interesting visitor to the Clayton house earlier. Apparently Parker Quinn showed up full of piss and vinegar.'

'Don't tell me, we've another shooting to investigate?'

Bryony snorted in forced humour. Holker's disliking of Joe was growing tiresome on her, and he damn well knew it but still persisted.

'Hunter managed to calm the situation down before it could develop. He's beginning to doubt that Quinn's our man.'

'Shows you how much *he* knows then,' Holker said, as he drove through the deluge. 'I rushed that glove through forensics and they got a match on a hair they found caught in the inner lining, and the sample we took from Quinn today. I'm not talking a DNA match, that'll take longer as you know, but the hair samples are a colour match. It's enough to pull Quinn in again, even if it's only to ask what the hell he was doing lurking in the woods last night.'

'He's due to report back in two days,' Bryony said, 'and we haven't had the results back from the computers we seized from his home yet. Don't you think we might jeopardise things by jumping the gun and grabbing him now?'

'If Quinn's just been acting up at Clayton's place as you say, it tells me he's struggling to contain himself. If we pull him in, throw the evidence from the glove at him, it might be enough to make him fold, and tell us everything. I don't know about you Bryony, but even catching whoever's harassing Clayton is a win for us. It'll show that we're taking this case seriously, and a result is a result.'

'But it puts us no closer to catching Ella's murderer, and that's the only result I'm interested in right now. I know it's the same for you, Dennis.'

Holker aimed a thumb over his shoulder, before quickly returning his hands to the steering wheel. 'Captain Newburger wants Quinn interviewed, and preferably charged before the evening's out. For once I tend to agree with him.'

'Fair enough,' Bryony agreed, 'but I think we're making a mistake.'

'You know I don't like Hunter, right?'

'I think you've made your feelings known,' Bryony said, and couldn't help a rueful smile.

'It's not so much the guy; it's his goddamn blasé attitude to law enforcement. I don't know why he feels he's got a God-given right to dispense his own brand of justice. You ask me it's criminal, and he's a borderline psychopath who should've been locked up years ago.'

'Hunter works from a different rule book than us,' Bryony reasoned. 'You can't judge him because his rules of contact don't fit neatly into our police guidelines. He comes from a totally different world, don't forget, but intrinsically he was doing the same thing as us: taking out the human garbage. If I'd to be honest, there are times when I wish we weren't as restrained by rules and regulations…'

The tumult suddenly intensified. Bryony could barely hear herself think. The view through the windshield was obliterated, but for ribbons of leaping foam as the wipers fought the downpour. Holker slowed marginally, aware of brake lights flaring up ahead as other drivers responded to the washout. He said something but his words were lost under the drumming rain. Holker shook his head, and steered the car to the kerb. It didn't help alleviate the noise, but at least they wouldn't rear-end another vehicle.

Bryony stared at him, as much to read his lips as to hear.

'I said I don't like Hunter,' he said loudly, ' except there was a "but" I was going to add. It doesn't mean I don't trust the guy's instincts. He said he doesn't think Quinn has anything to do with harassing Clayton, and he's possibly right. But we have to follow the leads we're given, Bryony. Quinn might not be our man, but someone is going to great lengths to make him look guilty. We need to get Quinn in and see where it leads us next. If someone's trying their hardest to make Quinn look responsible, it's to divert attention away from them. For all we know he's not behind the harassment, but he has his suspicions who is. We have to investigate *every* angle if we're going to get to the bottom of this.'

Bryony couldn't argue. Holker was a good detective, with good instincts of his own. But solving any case took more than instinct. It was about following every lead, investigating them to a point they could be discarded as unimportant. Solving the case of the harassment of Andrew Clayton was a minor consideration against the much bigger problem of finding who'd murdered his wife, but the two cases were linked, and it only got in the way of the other. Some major cases could be broken through identifying the culprit in a minor related incident; once one thread was severed all the others could suddenly begin unraveling.

'Joe said he advised Quinn to return home; that where we're going now?'

'We are once it's safe to drive. Can you believe this?' Outside, the storm met Holker's disbelief with a crackle of lightning that sundered the heavens. The thunder that followed was like a barrage of cannon-fire that Bryony felt as vibrations in her chest.

'Hellish,' she muttered in agreement, as more lighting ripped a jagged course overhead. Thunder boomed almost instantly. This time she'd swear the actual car shook, and she was glad they had rubber firmly planted on the road beneath them. The rain clattered on the roof with renewed ferocity. 'But it'll pass in no time.'

Sustained rainfall could prove a law enforcement officer's ally. As a rule, criminals didn't like to operate in the rain, and when there was a continuous downpour criminality was drastically cut for the period. It didn't mean that a cop's workload got any easier though, because the rain brought its own problems. Traffic tended to back up, clogging or stalling the roads, and when that happened it was inevitable that the number of traffic collisions multiplied. Basically cops swapped one priority for another, but at least with the criminals laying low it allowed them the time to deal with the traffic chaos. Thankfully, detectives didn't answer road traffic calls, so for the duration of the storm they'd get some thinking time. That at least was the norm.

Holker had turned on the in-car radio, and the chatter between dispatch and patrol officers was a background buzz of accompaniment to the drumming on the windshield. It was too early for the reports of car crashes to begin, though it was inevitable, and the chatter was primarily people commenting on the unexpected deluge. Bryony had switched off from it all, but apparently Holker still had one ear tuned to the radio. He leaned down, hit a button and turned up the volume.

'Man, we could be on,' he announced, as the dispatcher announced a burglary in progress. A silent alarm had been tripped, but there were also separate 911 calls coming in from concerned neighbours who'd witnessed a group of people making forcible entrance to a family home in the upmarket Sunset Park neighbourhood. Patrol officers were already responding in force, and Tampa PD's Tactical Response Team was being mobilised.

As Bryony snapped to attention, reaching to switch on their siren and the blue lights in the front grill of their unmarked car, Holker announced they were en route. The rain hadn't lessened, the conditions on the road still atrocious, but it didn't mean a thing now. He peeled out, sending the car hurtling towards West Kennedy Boulevard, to pick up Henderson Boulevard and an arrow straight shot into Sunset Park. The rolling thunder followed them as the tyres sent up sheets of water in their wake.

10

It looked and sounded as if the gods were engaged in celestial warfare. I'd witnessed plenty of electrical storms since basing myself in Florida, most of them benign, but the occasional one being frightening in its intensity. I was hard put to recall one as violent as the storm that had hit with little warning only minutes ago. The rain came down in torrents, battering flat the Star and Stripes banner on Clayton's front lawn, throwing small fragments of crushed shell in the air as the raindrops impacted the drive. It was as if a thousand Irish dancers were doing a jig on the roof. So what the bloody hell was Andrew doing outside?

Cole was in bed, but he had been allowed to watch a Disney movie before lights out, so I was confident he was safe enough to leave alone while I went out on the porch for a minute or two. I'd been in the kitchen eating supper, and downing my second coffee from the jug I'd brewed, when I heard the thunder and watched the rear lawn, the pond and the surrounding tress flicker beneath the neon glare of lightning. The storm had arrived without warning, and it had held me mesmerised for a moment, and I'd barely registered the clicking open of the front door, and had only turned away from the lightshow in the heavens when hearing the thud of the door closing again. I padded through to the hall, couldn't see Andrew for the plyboard covering on the door, so went into the living room and looked out the huge plate glass window there. I couldn't immediately see Andrew, the deluge was solid, but a sudden squall of wind parted the sheeting rain and I caught a glimpse of him jogging up the drive, bent over in his pointless fight against getting a soaking, pulling the collar of his jacket as far up the back of his shaved head as he could. Moving away, I checked the control panel on the wall and saw that Clayton had disarmed the locking mechanism on the gate. I'd had him reset the code earlier, after telling him about Parker Quinn's unannounced arrival at the front door. I wondered if Quinn had returned against my advice, and Clayton had slipped out to meet him before he'd come all the way up to the house. Shaking my head in frustration, I grabbed my own jacket and shrugged into it, made sure my SIG was secure in its carry position, and opened the door. I stood on the porch searching for Clayton, but could see nothing of him now.

'Son of a bitch,' I muttered under my breath and went down the steps. The storm gods punished me mercilessly for my bad language the instant I stepped out from under cover. But I didn't learn my manners. Cursing again at Clayton's stupidity, I jogged after him, but avoided the waterlogged drive, sticking instead to the equally soggy but firmer lawn. My boots were awash in seconds, my trousers soaked through, and my jacket did little to hold off the rain either. But I pushed on with dogged resolve: I wanted to know what the hell Clayton was up to.

Lightning flashed but it did little to aid visibility, it simply washed everything over with stark blinding white. As I approached the perimeter wall though, I could begin making out identifiable form and shape amid the torrent. The gate was open, though the vehicle beyond hadn't entered from the outer track. Two figures stood close to each other, one of them recognisable as Clayton's thick-necked form. The other I couldn't make out beyond dark clothing and some kind of peaked cap. Neither man was aware of my approach. I began treading forward slowly, settling my feet on the spongy grass, while trying to hear anything above the constant pummeling rain and grumbling thunder. I couldn't hear a damn thing of their words, but Clayton's hands were held up in a placating gesture.

I'm unsure how Clayton sensed my approach, but he turned abruptly, his head cocked to one side. His spectacles were beaded with rain, as was the rest of him. I couldn't tell an expression from his gaze, but I watched his mouth slip open, then snap shut in the next instant. When he spun back to his visitor, his entire demeanour had changed, and it heralded a response from the man facing him. The guy cold-cocked him with a punch that flew from beside his hip and impacted Clayton's chin with a noise I heard even over the storm. Clayton was a tough guy, but it didn't help: anyone could be caught cold, and knocked out. Clayton went down on his butt, flopped over backwards, and lay with his arms spread and his mouth hanging open.

'Hey!' I shouted, and lurched forward, even as I reached tentatively for my gun. 'Hold it right there!'

The guy ignored my shout, rushing instead to open his car door. He glanced back at me from under his cap even as he yanked the door wide.

I got a glimpse of Clayton's assailant, and it was as brief as I'd seen of the man clambering over the wall last night. Then the guy was climbing back in his car, and hitting reverse. He must have kept the engine running while talking to Clayton because there was little pause between him piling inside then the car hurtling backwards up the track. I ran to Clayton, saw him begin to come round from the sneaky punch, and decided he'd survive, but not if he lay there in the pouring rain with his mouth open. I grabbed him by one wrist and tugged him over on to his side, and then immediately left him lying in the dirt as I chased the car up the drive. I'd no hope of catching it, but all I wanted was for a look at the licence plate. The driver hit a skid, yanked round the vehicle, engine roaring and tyres digging for traction, and then took off for the highway at speed. It had Florida plates but I couldn't make out the numbers, though I did make a note of the colour and positioning of the bumper stickers riding its rear fender. I regretted not taking out my gun and putting a round through the vehicle's body, that would have made it identifiable again. But doing so would have definitely ensured trouble from the police, and Holker in particular. It'd only prove his point that I not only lacked restraint but I was too hotheaded for my own good. I'd be kicked off the job, and to be honest, I was too involved in finding out the truth now to step aside.

Returning to Clayton's side, I found him stirring. One elbow was propped under him as he raised his head from the ground. His other hand probed at his jaw, checking for serious injury, even before he was fully aware of what he was doing. I crouched alongside him, helping to support him as he sat. 'You OK, Clayton?' I asked.

His spectacles were awry. He adjusted them, felt at his jaw again. He worked his lips, writhing them over his teeth, and tilted his face to one side to spit. If there was any blood in his mouth he'd swallowed it. 'I, uhm, I'm OK...I think. What the hell happened to me?'

'Sucker punch,' I told him, as I checked him over. There was reddening to his jaw, but his injury was superficial. I guessed he'd suffered worse during his career in the ring.

'That sneaky son of a...' Clayton attempted to stand, but his legs betrayed him and he sat down heavily in the sopping grass. I offered him a hand and hauled him up: the guy weighed a ton. I kept hold of his elbow as I steered him within the gates. He waved me aside, propping himself against the wall. He again probed his jaw, checking for injury, inserting fingers in his mouth to check for loosened teeth. He spat a string of saliva between his teeth. When he looked at me again his vision was a little clearer.

'Some bodyguard you turned out to be,' he muttered. 'If that asshole had a weapon I'd be dead now.'

The ferocity of the storm had abated in the last minute or so, but I still stood with rain pattering on my face, plastering my hair to my forehead. I expelled air in disgust. 'I thought we understood something: I'm not here for you. I'm here for Cole's sake. And besides, if I were looking after you, you aren't making my bloody job easy. What were you thinking sneaking out the house like that?'

'Who was sneaking?' he said gruffly.

'You didn't tell me you were leaving,' I pointed out.

'Am I obliged to? I can't come and go from my own home without your permission?' He snorted. 'I don't need your fucking permission and I certainly don't need you to babysit me.'

I looked at him.

He touched his mouth again.

'I was caught napping,' he said. 'When you came up behind me you distracted me. That punk wouldn't have had the guts to hit me if my back wasn't turned.'

He was massaging his ego, trying to redirect his downfall onto me. If I hadn't turned up when I did his injuries could have been much worse. But was he purely being ungrateful or trying to further throw our conversation off track? I wasn't going to allow it. 'So, are you going to tell me who that was?'

'How the hell would I know?'

'Don't come it, Clayton. You left the house in a fucking storm to speak to the man, so don't tell me you don't know him.'

'You're the one who told me I had to control access to the house, and check out those I let through the gate,' he said angrily.

'I didn't necessarily mean you had to do that in person,' I said. 'You could have checked over the intercom…'

'I did. Guy said he was delivering a package. How was I to know otherwise, when I receive deliveries for my company all the time?'

I bit my lip. He had a fair point; trouble was I wasn't buying his explanation. He'd opened the gate from the control panel in the house before checking whom the visitor was, not after he arrived at the gate. So he could have made an error in doing so, but I thought he was lying. 'So there was no package,' I said, 'so what did he say?'

'Told me I was a murdering asshole and I'd get what was coming to me. I felt like slapping him upside the head, and putting the record straight, but that was hardly going to convince him otherwise.'

'And you didn't know the guy?'

'Never seen him before. But he sounds like the same guy you chased over the wall last night.'

'I only got the briefest look at him,' I said, but didn't acknowledge if it was the same man or not. I couldn't be certain.

'We should call the cops,' Clayton said, 'and let them know what's happened.'

I looked sharply back at the house. The rain was diminishing, and I could see the hazy lights from the upper floors above the treetops. 'We should get back to Cole,' I corrected him. 'I'll phone Detective VanMeter as soon as I've checked on him.'

Clayton nodded at my wisdom, pushed away from the wall, and set off down the drive. 'Wait up,' I said, 'there's something you have to do first. Lock that goddamn gate.'

He turned and peered at me, angrily working his jaw. 'Who pays your wage?' With that he didn't wait for an answer but turned and marched off, the shells crunching under his deliberate footsteps.

11

'Joe, things are kind of hectic for me right now,' said Bryony VanMeter as she stood in the back yard of a house a few miles to the south of Andrew Clayton's place. The storm had passed but water still cascaded from the eaves of the house and the nearby live oak trees. The waves out on Old Tampa Bay were rougher than she had seen them in years, but the storm had passed. Wisps of steam rose from the boardwalk at the edge of the sea, and from Bryony's damp clothing. There were cops in numbers all over the place, and flashlight beams danced each direction she looked, reflecting off the wet walls and rooftops, as if their wielders expected to find a robber clinging to one of those surfaces in a desperate bid to escape discovery. They were wasting their time, because the home invasion crew had been and gone before the first patrol car arrived. Thankfully the homeowners were unhurt, and because the crew knew the game was up they'd fled the scene without any ill-gotten gains.

A cordon had been thrown in place, but neither Bryony nor any of the other cops on the scene believed the robbers were still inside it. The elderly homeowners had been disturbed from sleep by a ringing phone when the company responsible for monitoring their alarms called to check their authenticity via a code word. This was prior to alerting the police to the break-in to avoid a false call out. Only then did anyone know the house was actually under attack. When the husband hit the audible alarm and he and his wife barricaded themselves inside their panic room, and half their neighbourhood was roused by the wailing klaxon and flashing beacons the gang had fled, but not before a number of witnesses had stumbled from their front doors. There were thirteen eye witnesses at last count, but sadly not one of who could give a good description of the robbers or the vehicles they'd made off in. Perhaps the police would glean more facts with pointed questioning later, but right now Bryony felt everything about the situation was in chaos. She could do without Hunter complicating matters.

'I won't keep you,' Joe said, in that matter-of-fact way of his, but he didn't mean he was going to hang up, quite the opposite. He intended carrying on, but would be concise and to the point. That was one blessing.

'Tell me,' she sighed.

'Clayton was just assaulted at his front gate. Could have been by the same man I chased last night.'

'Parker Quinn,' she said, recalling the identifying hair found on the dropped glove.

'No, not Quinn, this was a totally different person. I met Quinn earlier, don't forget.'

He had indeed. And Bryony trusted that he wasn't mistaken this time. But if Hunter had seen the same man he chased yesterday evening, how could the glove he'd dropped contain hair matching the sample taken from Parker Quinn? She had an idea, and immediately looked for Detective Holker. She couldn't see him, so began walking around the side of the house, towards the front drive where they'd left their car. Cops milled around, some working search grids in hope of finding evidence, but there was little hope. Bryony felt they were all wasting their time here, when the gang was already long gone.

'Interesting,' she told Hunter as she walked.

'There was something weird about the incident,' Hunter went on.

'I hear you, Joe. It just doesn't add up.' She still couldn't see Holker. 'Give me what you have and I'll issue a BOLO.'

Hunter described Clayton's attacker, the same height and build as he had the person he'd seen scaling the wall. 'He was wearing a dark coverall and wool hat with a peak. Couldn't see his hair this time, but I got more of a look at his face. Definitely a white guy in his late thirties or early forties. Nothing distinctive about him though, except Clayton tells me he noticed a tattoo on the guy's right hand. Spider web on the flesh between his thumb and index finger.'

'Clayton didn't recognise him, then?'

'Claims not to, but I don't buy it.'

'And he didn't say why the guy assaulted him?'

'Another lie,' Hunter said. 'Supposedly the guy presented himself as a delivery driver, then when Clayton went out to meet him at the gate the guy accused him of murder, then punched him in the jaw.'

'You witnessed the assault?'

'I did, from a distance and through pouring rain, but to be honest I'd say my mother hits harder than that guy does. He dropped Clayton on his arse in the mud, but caught on the right spot it doesn't take much doing, I suppose.'

Bryony rubbed a hand over her face. She had to ask the inevitable question. 'Did this guy give any hint he's the one that murdered Ella?'

'Couldn't say,' said Hunter, 'and now Clayton isn't speaking to me. Maybe if you come over he'll speak to you...'

'Can't, Joe. Like I said it's kind of hectic right now. We've had another home invasion.' She scanned the nearby faces for Holker, and though she recognised a few of her fellow officers, her partner wasn't among them. 'Before you ask, they got away. But at least this time nobody was hurt.'

'That's one good thing at least,' Hunter agreed, though his tone implied differently. 'Something I have to throw by you about that,' he went on.

'Not now, Joe. I've enough on my plate as it is.'

'I hear you. That BOLO you mentioned putting out? The guy was driving a dark blue Toyota, a Corolla maybe, with Florida plates. It was a little beaten up and had bumper stickers: one of them said WPB, another said "Southern Fried Florida Native", and was set against a confederate flag.'

'WPB,' Bryony ruminated. 'West Palm Beach, you reckon? So the guy's an out-of-towner?'

'Or his car is,' Hunter said. 'Doesn't prove who he is, but it's something that might help identify the car.'

Bryony heard her name called. She turned and saw Holker walking out the front door of the house, accompanied by another man, this one tall, and square shouldered, with a mop of dark curls crowning his long face.

She recognised Kyle Mercer, a District 3 detective who'd also been seconded to the task force. It appeared from Holker's grateful handshake that Mercer had accepted the lead investigator role on this aborted home invasion. As Holker clipped down the steps towards Bryony, Mercer offered her a "*WTF?*" expression. She'd seen similar on the faces of many of her colleagues since arriving late to Sunset Park: raised eyebrows and a tight-lipped grimace.

'Joe, I gotta go,' she said into the phone. Without waiting for his answer she ended the call. Holker was almost upon her.

'We're wasting time here,' he said, echoing her feelings. 'Let's go.'

Their car was at the end of the drive; thankfully it wasn't penned in considering the fleet that had converged on the residential street. Holker strode for it.

'You still intend going for Quinn?' Bryony asked.

'We need at least one positive result tonight,' Holker said without turning or breaking stride.

'Lets go get him then.'

'You've changed your tune,' he said, 'earlier you thought we'd be wasting our time with Quinn.'

'I just learned something that changed my mind. I'll tell you about it on the way there.'

Holker turned so abruptly she halted in her tracks or else she'd bump into him. 'Tell me now,' Holker said.

'Quinn isn't the one personally harassing Clayton, but I think he might be behind the one who is.' Bryony decided she'd tell Holker about the guy who'd just assaulted Clayton once they were moving, but right now he needed something. 'And if he's put someone up to harassing Clayton, who's to say he didn't originally send someone to hurt him through his wife?'

12

I kicked out of the easy chair in the sitting room, reaching for my SIG out of reaction to the soft clunk that had roused me. I dropped my hand, changing the move to a scratch at my waistline; I didn't want Cole to know I'd almost drawn on him. But there was little chance of that. He stood fidgeting in the doorway from the hall, dressed in wrinkled Spiderman pyjamas, and his empty juice bottle lying between his bare feet. His wavy hair was mussed, standing up on one side where his head had met the pillow, and his green eyes were wide, though cloudy with sleep. I'd turned out most of the lights on the ground floor while I sat guard, but had left on one in the kitchen and it cast a faint ambience along the hall and up Cole's right hand side, his left was in silhouette. He would only see me as a dim figure illuminated by the meagre starlight coming through the large windows, and only when the ragged clouds allowed. I reached for the switch on a table lamp, and flicked it on. Cole blinked, then rubbed the balls of his thumbs into each eye socket.

'Cole, you OK, buddy?' I asked softly.

He smacked his lips, rubbed them with the back of a fist, then his gaze fixed on me. He took a half step backwards, as if unsure of my presence. I wondered if he'd staggered down here in a daze, and had only fully wakened when the lamp came on. 'I…I'm thirsty,' he croaked.

His juice bottle oozed a few dregs on the floor. It was the sound of the plastic sports bottle dropping from his lax fingers that had startled me out of the chair. I silently admonished myself for snoozing on the job, but not too hard because no harm was done. I'd missed a barefooted child coming downstairs, but things would have been different if someone had tried forcing a way inside. I moved towards him, and he looked from me to the bottle. He sighed heavily, but didn't reach for it.

'Let me get that for you,' I offered and scooped the bottle up. 'You want me to refill this for you?'

He nodded, then scrunched up his nose. I laid a hand on his head as I passed him in the doorway, gave his hair a quick tousle, and he turned to follow me to the kitchen. His bare soles sucked at the tiles as he trod behind me. 'What'd you like, Cole? Juice again?'

Clayton had prepared a jug of Cole's favourite fruit drink, and left it chilling in the refrigerator. I pulled open the door, and the contents inside tinkled, as the vacuum seal was broken. I reached for the large plastic juice container. The boy shook his head. 'Just water please.'

'You sure?' I said, and showed him the jug.

He wiped his nose with the back of his hand.

'You're the boss,' I said, and winked at him, as I set the container back in the fridge. I looked for bottled mineral water instead, but there was none. 'Tap water OK for you?'

Cole looked at me as if I was speaking an alien tongue.

But on reflection I was. He didn't understand the nuances between the English language spoken either side of the Atlantic. 'I'll run the faucet, get it nice and cold,' I said, and he got me.

'You speak funny,' he said.

'Do I? What, you mean like Donald Duck?'

He snorted out a laugh, but wasn't exactly impressed with my comedic skills.

I set the tap running at the kitchen sink, felt the water with my fingertips and found it tepid. While it chilled, I picked up his bottle off the counter where I'd set it down, and gave it a shake. Some purple gloop was gathered in the bottom, full of sediment. I twisted off the cap and upended the bottle and the mush slid out, though there were still a few crystallised lumps sticking to the bottle. I held the bottle under the tap, got it about half full, then put my thumb over the bottle's neck and shook. I splashed the gunk into the sink, and watched it sluice away under the running water. Being so full of impurities, I wondered if the water was safe to drink. The sediment was probably mineral, I decided, and filled the bottle anyway. On inspection it looked pure enough, so I twisted on the ergonomic cap and handed it back to Cole. He took an immediate glug, and smacked his lips with an audible sigh.

'Sounds as if you were *really* thirsty,' I said. My conversational skills with nine-year-olds were limited. But then his were too. He only grunted in answer. We simply stood there while he took another drink. 'Maybe you should take it easy, or you'll be in the bathroom all night.'

'Do I have to go back to bed?' Cole asked, and I thought I saw a faint tremor pass through him.

'You've school tomorrow,' I said, 'can't have you falling asleep in class.'

'I'm scared,' he said, 'I don't want to go back to sleep. In case it comes back…' his words petered out. I wondered if the storm had troubled him, but as far as I knew he'd slept through the thunder and lightning. It wasn't the storm though. How much had he heard when I'd come back to the house with his dad? Had he learned Clayton had been attacked, and feared it would be his turn next? But he'd said "it", not "he".

'In case what comes back?' I asked.

'The dream.'

'You had a nightmare?'

He scuffed his bare toes together.

'I hate scary nightmares too, but they can't hurt us,' I said.

He wasn't convinced.

'It can see me when I sleep with its big eyes,' he said, and it made me ponder what kind of boogieman he'd conjured. Since his mother had been murdered I made myself a bet he'd suffered a few tortured nights.

'It's not real, Cole. It's just a bad dream, and can't hurt you in real life.'

'Detective Bryony said the bad men hurt my mom, but she's wrong. I think it was the monster with the big eyes that hurt her.'

'Detective Bryony wasn't wrong,' I assured him. 'And she's going to catch the bad men responsible and put them in jail for a long, long time.'

'It got my mom,' he stated as if he hadn't heard me, and his lip trembled. 'I was asleep when it got her, and it might get me the same way. I don't want to ever sleep again.'

How the bloody hell did I answer? The only way I could. 'I won't let anything happen to you,' I promised. 'Now come on, let's get you to your room. And don't worry; I'll be right outside your door all night, OK? Nothing will touch you. I won't let it.'

Although I tried to steer him for the stairs he dug in, and it was surprising how much traction he generated with those tiny bare feet. I was nervous about being tactile with the kid, but maybe all he needed was a reassuring hug. I laid a hand on his shoulder, gave it a gentle squeeze. 'Don't you believe me, Cole?'

He again ignored my question and instead posed one of his own. 'Do you dream, Joe? Like nightmares?'

I dreamt all right, and they were probably worse than the ones the boy suffered. His nightmares were populated by imaginary bug-eyed monsters while mine were more depraved, replays of incidents from my past. Dead people came to me in my sleep, and it was as if they wanted to claw me down to the same hellish place they resided now.

'I do,' I said, 'but do you know what I do when I'm scared? I laugh.'

'Eh?'

'You heard me. I laugh, because I know something the scary things don't. I know I'm dreaming and that I control their actions, not them. I laugh at them and chase them away with good thoughts.' I knelt down in front of Cole, meeting him eye-to-eye. 'That's what you should do. Laugh at the bad thing.'

'I would,' he said, then paused, a little unsure of his next words. 'But in my dreams my mouth doesn't work.'

'Well that is odd,' I agreed, and I touched a finger to his forehead. 'But it doesn't stop you thinking, which is all a dream is don't forget. So next time you're afraid, just think how funny it is and send the bad thing packing. And if that doesn't work and you wake up, just give me a holler and I'll send it packing for you. Deal?' I held out a bent pinkie, and Cole squinted at it in confusion. 'What? Kids don't do pinkie deals these days?'

Cole shrugged, but offered me his own pinkie, and I wrapped mine round it. 'That's like a solemn bind between brothers,' I told him. 'And brothers always look out for each other, right?'

'Right,' he said, and we shook. His enthusiasm wasn't great, though. 'I haven't got any *real* brothers. Have you?'

'I did,' I said, thinking of my half-brother John. 'And you've met Rink. He's like my brother now. We look out for each other like real brothers; it's what we do, and now you're one of us.'

'Did you make a pinkie deal with Rink as well?'

'Yep,' I said. 'And you can too when he comes by tomorrow. But you'd best get some sleep first, or you'll be napping while he's here.' I stood, and used the moment to turn him and walk him for the stairs. This time he padded alongside me, but I rested my steepled fingers between his shoulders to keep the momentum going.

Clayton was waiting for us at the head of the stairs, dressed in boxers and a t-shirt. He'd lost the spectacles.

'Something wrong?' he asked, and they were the first words we'd shared since he'd sulked off earlier.

'Not now,' I said, speaking for us both. 'Cole had a bad dream, but he's a brave lad and isn't afraid anymore.'

'You OK, son?' Clayton asked.

'I'm fine,' Cole said, and went directly past his dad, holding himself rigid. I wondered what was worse; that Clayton didn't offer his son a hug or that Cole didn't welcome one. Clayton simply watched the boy return to his room and close the door. He looked back at me, rubbed a hand over his shaved head.

'Kids, huh?' he said, and moved his hand to his jaw.

'Don't you want to tuck him in?'

'It's like you said; he's a tough kid. Doesn't do all that touchy-feely stuff with me.'

'He's missing his mom,' I said, trying to give him a hint.

'Yeah, well he's not the only one.' Clayton touched his mouth, then inspected his fingertips, as if there'd be something to be discovered.

'Mouth still sore?' I asked.

'Nah, not too bad.'

I aimed a nod at his forearm. 'You get that when you fell down?'

Clayton rolled over his arm to look, and it was as if he'd noticed the purple bruise for the first time. He frowned, then rubbed his hand over it as if it were dirt to be brushed away. 'Must have done. Didn't feel it,' he said.

I didn't reply.

Clayton dropped his hands by his sides. Watched me.

'I told Cole I'd be outside his bedroom if he got scared again.'

Clayton shrugged. 'Don't let me stop you.'

With his announcement he turned on his heel and returned to his own room. As he walked he cupped his bruised arm with his other palm, massaging it as I'd noticed him doing in the past.

13

'Bryony and Holker struck out with Parker Quinn,' I told Rink the following morning as we ate breakfast in Clayton's kitchen. Clayton had seen Cole on to the school bus, before heading off to his office, giving us the opportunity to speak in private. 'But between me and you, I warned Bryony that they were concentrating on the wrong man.'

Rink had arrived at the Clayton house about ten minutes earlier, ready to spell me while I got some rest, but that wasn't why I'd asked him over. I'd told him about last night's antics, the mystery man turning up at the gate and how Clayton had been sucker punched to the ground. Rink's mouth had turned down at the corners, and then he'd said something about nobody being infallible, to which there was no argument. I described the assailant, including what little detail Clayton had added concerning the spider web tattoo, and the Toyota with its distinctive bumper stickers. I also mentioned that Bryony had initiated a "Be On the Look Out" with law enforcement agencies, but that I didn't expect the car to be found considering half of Tampa PD had been engaged in hunting the home invasion crew at the time. She hadn't mentioned last night that she and Holker were on their way to lift Parker Quinn when they'd detoured to the scene of the attempted robbery, but she'd rung me first thing to tell me that Quinn was again in the wind.

'I thought they had some decent circumstantial evidence with the hair pulled from the glove,' Rink said.

'So did Holker. But he jumped in with both feet and questioned Quinn before they got the results of the DNA work up. Quinn's legal brief tore holes in Holker, and - even if there was a match – Quinn had a plausible answer. He said he'd regularly visited Clayton's home, so the hair could easily have been transferred to the glove from Clayton or me after I found it. You can bet your ass Holker's thinking the same thing; he already had a go at me about seizing the glove instead of leaving it to the pros. Quinn's lawyer has already demanded that the glove and hair are both deemed inadmissible in evidence. Bryony expects he'll get his way.'

'You don't think Quinn has anything to do with Ella's murder or the harassment either.' Rink was no fool, and he'd come to the same conclusion as me, and based on far less facts than I'd already learned. 'So what? You think the real murderer is setting Quinn up as a patsy.'

'Yeah. I thought Bryony was thinking along those lines too, but now she's got it in her head Quinn has probably put this other guy up to harassing Clayton, to divert attention off him: but only as the stalker, not the murderer. The thing is, there was no evidence found on his phone or computer to suggest it. They got the results from the examination of all the equipment seized from Quinn's place last night, and there was no unusual correspondence found. None of the kit had the same IP number as the computer used to send the emails to the police either. Like I said, they struck out.'

'Bryony's a good detective; she'll come to the right conclusion once she's followed the clues. She'll get her man in the end.' Rink popped a chunk of bagel slathered in cream cheese in his mouth and chewed slowly, while eyeing me steadily. He was still playing at matchmaker.

'Hopefully I'll be able to help her,' I said, not taking the bait. 'But things are moving too slowly for me. You warned me this was an easy job, but I'm finding it difficult sitting on my thumbs like this.'

'You wish I'd never gotten you involved, brother?'

'It's not the work. The money's good and we can't turn it down, Rink. Plus Cole deserves to be protected, but I can't help feel he isn't the one in danger. I guess my problem is with his dad. He's paying top dollar for protection that he blatantly disregards, and makes no pretense that he appreciates me being here.'

'Maybe you challenge his machismo. Some guys are like that. They don't want to be seen as weak, or to admit they need help, and they respond negatively to it.' Rink toyed with the remainder of his bagel, his large hands ripping small morsels from it, but dropping them uneaten on the plate.

'That's why he makes all this about looking out for the boy, not him. I bet you feel like a glorified babysitter right now.'

I raised my eyebrows briefly. 'Like I said, I don't mind watching the boy, but I need to be doing more, Rink.'

Rink smiled slowly. 'I wondered how long it would take. You never were very good at sitting around waiting for something to happen.'

He had that right. Whereas Rink had the patience of a boulder, I always was too impulsive for my own good. Before we'd been enrolled into Arrowsake, I'd been with 1 Para, the airborne infantry regiment whose motto was "Ready for anything". The motto suited me, because I always felt like my fuse was lit and I was apt to explode at any second. While recuperating from the recent events up in Washington State, the most frustrating thing about working my way back to fitness was the temptation to leap back into the fray, knowing full well that I couldn't. Rink had eased me back into work with this job, thinking it was untaxing, but it wasn't having the desired effect.

'I'm itching to get moving, to do *something* worthwhile,' I admitted.

'You need to get some sleep,' Rink told me.

'I'm fine. Maybe I shouldn't admit it, but I napped on and off last night in a chair. I couldn't sleep now if I tried.'

Pushing aside his plate, Rink said, 'Well there doesn't appear to be much happening here just now. But I'll hang on, keep an eye on the property: won't look good if another brick gets chucked through a window. So you can go do whatever you gotta do.' He held up a finger. 'Can I ask what you have in mind, brother?'

'I'm planning on knocking on a few doors, maybe twisting a few arms while I'm at it. As you know there are people who'll talk to us who'd never crack their lips for a cop…with the correct motivation.'

'You planning on walking?'

My car was still parked on Rink's drive at Temple Terrace.

He fished in his jeans pocket, rattled the keys to the company Ford on the table. 'I'm only glad I didn't come in my Porsche,' he said.

'I'll bring it back in one piece,' I promised, and cupped the keys in my hand before he changed his mind. I stood.

'Before you go…'

'Don't tell me you want me to wash the dishes first,' I joked.

'No, just wondered what it is you aren't telling me.'

'What do you mean?'

'Joe, brother, I know you too well. You've something spinning around in your fat head, and I know it's bothering you. You've a theory on what happened here, right?'

'It's too soon to say, Rink.' I offered him a sad smile. 'Let's just say it's more a hypothesis than it is a theory just now. Soon as I'm more certain about the way my thoughts are heading I'll tell you everything, OK?'

'And there was I thought we shared all our secrets,' he said.

'Only the sordid ones,' I said, and he grinned. 'No, I don't want to put anything in your mind that turns out wrong. But as soon as I know I'm on the right track, you'll be first to know.'

Rink stood from the counter. 'When'd Clayton say he'd be back?'

'He didn't. Just that he'd stuff to do at his office. The impression I get is he doesn't like to spend too much time in my company.'

'Good,' Rink said, and nodded to himself as he mulled things over. 'While he's out I'm going to do a little digging round of my own.'

I'd been tempted to make a search of the house myself. After Ella's murder, the house and grounds had been subject to an extensive search by the police and crime scene investigators, but once it was completed there'd been nobody back to conduct any kind of follow up investigation. I didn't doubt the investigators had done an exemplary job, but they were searching for clues in respect of the original crime only, but of nothing that had happened since.

'If you find anything interesting, give me a shout, will you?'

'You too, buddy,' said Rink.

I left him to it, got in the Ford and went up the drive. The motion sensors on the gate opened it for me and I went up the track and onto the highway, and following an internal instinct turned right. I'd no exact destination in mind, but I did have a few ideas. When anyone wanted to off-load stolen property in Tampa there were any amount of customers in some of the seedier neighbourhoods. The cops would already have pulled on their snitches, trying to identify who the home invasion crew were shifting their ill-gotten wares through, and had probably come to the same conclusion as me: their stolen product was being shipped out of state. A missing gold wedding band wouldn't require transportation in a container truck. There were plenty of "We'll Buy Your Scrap Gold" outfits in the Tampa Bay area, but I didn't think Ella's jewellery would have passed through them – there was usually CCTV surveillance in most of those stores, a paper or digital trail too – and I guessed the murderer would have chosen a different type of purveyor of used gold. Coming to a decision, I went in search of the nearest friendly neighbourhood fence.

14

There's plenty said about the long arm of the law, but it's not often that the weary feet get a mention. Private Investigators used to be called gumshoes, and that's for good reason. Brass tacks investigating means getting your feet on the ground, and knocking on doors where you're not exactly a welcome visitor. I'm uncertain how many miles I'd put in, or how many flights of stairs I'd climbed, but I wouldn't need my customary run along Mexico Beach to match the steps I'd taken. In the five hours since I'd left Rink, I'd met with four backstreet fences who I knew of, and two that had come up through questioning. None of them gave me any leads to follow on the gold ring, but the last fence I spoke with was known as "Emilio the Blimp" and he said something that sent me on a different path.

Emilio looked younger than he was. He was fat. I'm not being unkind for the sake of it; he was seriously overweight, to a point that the skin on his face ballooned so that it stretched out his wrinkles making him more youthful-looking. He had a neck beard, and a spray of acne on his forehead, and where his voluminous shirt gaped at his waistline the flesh was as pallid as a dead squid. He didn't carry his weight well and relied on a stick to get around. Despite his unhealthy carriage he seemed gloriously unaware he was killing himself one double cheeseburger at a time, and acted with the confidence of someone certain they were immortal. He had a large personality to match his girth, and sometimes that was all it took to attract others into his circle, like a planet's gravity draws moons and satellites into its orbit. When I met with Emilio four other guys circled him, and not one of them understood what the ultimate fate was of orbiting dirtballs. Usually they got burned up as they continued to fall or they were engulfed in searing flame when their host exploded. Crappy metaphor or not, it was poor judgement when they'd allowed themselves to fall under Emilio the Blimp's influence.

My sleuthing had brought me to what might once have been referred to as a breaker's yard, and it still resembled one, with stacks of rusting cars piled high on all sides, awaiting the crusher. The ground underfoot was pure poison, black with perished oil, shredded rubber, and God knew what else. It was gated and fenced in with chain link, and once inside the gate there was a wooden shack, adjacent to an industrial-sized weighbridge. At the back of the junk-strewn compound were another set of sheds, and a red brick-built house that would've been at home on a British train station platform. For all intents and purposes it appeared that Emilio dealt in scrap iron, but his sideline was in precious metals, and he did his business with the expensive stuff back there in the most secure building. Not that I made it as far as the house before I was met by one of Emilio's lickspittles. It wasn't the man who stopped me in my tracks but the pit bull terrier he held, that strained at its leash to get at my throat. Two more of his guys stood outside the house, one of them clutching the handle of a baseball bat. The other was subtler about where he kept his weapon, but I noticed the handle of some kind of knife in his belt as he turned to call inside the open door. The fourth of Emilio's lackeys stepped outside, and he was nodding into a cell phone as he confirmed I'd arrived.

Apparently the last fence I'd spoken to had phoned ahead to warn Emilio I was coming. Honour among thieves wasn't an admirable trait, I decided, when it brought complications like the presence of a welcoming committee with an attack dog.

'I come in peace,' I said, holding aloft both empty hands, and grinning to add emphasis to my witty announcement. 'Take me to your leader.'

'Don't move another step, pal,' warned the dog-handler, and he gave the dog an inch or two of leash. The mutt jumped, dancing on its back legs to get a few more inches closer to my neck. Its front paws scrabbled at dead air, its teeth gnashing ineffectively, probably while it wondered what my blood tasted like.

'Trust me,' I told the lanky, greasy-haired punk, 'if I didn't have to I'd be happy. I already trod in two mounds of crap on my way through the yard. Get that dog trained not to shit in its own bed, why don't you?'

The dog looked as insulted as its handler did. It dropped to all four paws, its broad head low to the ground as it growled deep in its throat. Its handler made a similar sound and I stared him in the eye, dropping all pretenses at joviality.

I always was a dog person. If my work didn't often take me all over the country and beyond, I'd like a dog as a companion, and my greatest dream was to send for Hector and Paris, who I'd left back in England with my ex-wife. They'd adore the beach, love running the sands with me, but I knew it would never happen. Diane would no sooner allow it than she would giving up our real children - if we'd ever been blessed with them. Under different circumstances I'd like to have patted the dog, maybe have it lie down and give it a belly rub; I really didn't want to hurt the mutt. But I didn't love dogs enough to let them rip out my throat on command.

'I'm not leaving until I speak with Emilio,' I said, 'so he might as well dispense with the theatrics and come on out. Either that or you-' I took in all four dopes with one sweeping glance '-get the hell out of my way and let me go inside.'

'Are you deaf, buddy?' It was the guy with the baseball bat who took the lead. 'You don't take another step.'

To show his warning didn't faze me, I stepped forward, and I kept on going.

'Hey!' The dog handler actually pulled back, keeping the dog between him and me, and the dog reared on its back legs again. I was no dog behaviourist, but even I could tell it wasn't an immediate attack mode, though it would take only a split-second for the bull terrier's jaws to snap onto me if it was loosed.

'How does Emilio ever conduct business with you bozos around?' I challenged.

'You aren't here on business,' the man with the cell phone said, as he trod deliberately down the steps. 'You're here poking your nose in ours.'

'I don't give a shit about you,' I told him. 'My business is with Emilio.'

'You're a fucking detective,' said the guy with the knife in his belt. 'You're that fucker that offed Mick O'Neill and got away with it.'

'Buddy,' I told him, 'you only got one of those things right. Anyone who knows me would tell you I'm a pretty crappy detective.'

I waited for them to process my words, to figure out what exactly I was admitting to, and what the consequences might mean to them. Mick O'Neill was a dangerous gangster; they were just pathetic street punks. To add weight to my warning, I nodded at the nearest door. 'Do I go in that way, or does one of you want to pick a window and I'll follow you in?'

I hoped that they'd see sense and back down from a confrontation. They were four, and not forgetting the dog. I was one man. They knew of me by reputation, but the stories they'd heard were probably delivered with a great amount of doubt and disparaging comments. They were unconsciously doing the math, and coming to the wrong conclusion. I was woefully outnumbered, and despite my confidence, I couldn't possibly do a thing against them before I was overwhelmed. They shared glances and nods, formulating their plan of attack, and the guy with the knife even adjusted it in his belt.

'What?' I demanded. 'If I don't leave you're going to beat the crap out of me? That the idea, boys?'

'You're asking for it, buddy,' said the one with the cell phone, and the others agreed with grunts and curses.

'No. I'm asking to speak to Emilio. Do any of you really want to get into this because of a stolen wedding ring?' As I spoke steadily, I again looked each of them in the face. They'd spread out in a loose crescent before me. The dog handler was to the extreme left, baseball bat guy to the far right. Cell phone and the knife guy stood almost shoulder-to-shoulder in front of me, blocking access to the redbrick house. They didn't realise it, but they'd stood exactly where I wanted them. I stepped directly up to the two in the middle and it forced them apart, and to turn side-on to keep an eye on me while I still faced the door. One of them blocked the dog, the other the baseball bat. Cell phone guy was obviously marginally higher in the pecking order, because the knife man glanced at him for instruction. I purposefully directed my question at Knife. 'You did hear that the ring was stolen during a robbery, right? That an innocent woman was murdered for it?'

'Like I give a shit about some rich bitch out in the burbs?' he snorted, but I noted the discomfort worming its way behind his features.

'You'll give a shit when you're all pulled in on a homicide charge,' I told him. 'You maybe didn't do the robbing, but the cops might think otherwise. Emilio, for all they know, ordered the robbery, and you were the guys who kicked your way inside and shot that defenceless woman so you could take the ring from her finger like a bunch of ghouls.'

'We had nothing to do with...' Knife man shut up at a warning hiss from Cell man.

I glanced down at the guy's belt. 'I know that. I can see you don't use a gun. You prefer to stick people with a blade?' I sneered at him. 'Nah, I think that's only for show. You ever stuck a guy for real? Looked him in the eye, watched the life ebb from him even as the blood pools around his feet? You haven't, have you? I have. It's not a nice way to die. See, when you gut them the stink is almost enough to make you puke, and that's before you see their intestines sliding out.'

The colour washed from Knife's features. He made the mistake of lifting his left hand to wipe at his face. His hand obscured his vision, while his bent elbow was in the way of his right hand if he reached across for the hilt. In that instant I plucked the knife from his belt. He didn't know I'd liberated his weapon until he felt it prick under his left earlobe.

'Quick jab here,' I went on, 'and your brain is cabbage.'

I put a bit more pressure on the knife. But stabbing him was never my plan. It was making him shit his pants, and I'd take literally if it came to it. He jumped as if I'd stuck the knife through his neck, and the only way to escape the blade was to go sideways, into Cell phone man. Now I had two of them positioned between the dog's jaws and me, but that advantage was only for the briefest window of time. In my periphery I caught movement. The baseball bat was being wound up for a crack at my skull. But I'd manoeuvred its wielder so that to take an effective swing he had to first turn to his right, pull back the bat and then sweep it round again as he launched himself across the intervening space. I only needed to take a step sideways and he'd miss, but that would only encourage him to take a second swing. I had to stop him before he got up a good rhythm, so I didn't step aside. I went towards him, chambering my right knee, and stamped into his gut. My heel dug in just above his pubis, sank deep. The guy's legs straightened as his butt was punched backwards, and his torso jutted forward as his breath exploded out of him. The bat was still somewhere behind him but had lost all momentum. I elbowed him in the chin, to avoid him skewering on the knife I still held.

Tougher than he looked, the guy didn't immediately fall. But that suited me. I dropped the knife even as I swerved round him, grasped the bat out of his hand with my left hand, and then I was behind him. I could have easily crushed his skull with the bat, but didn't. I gripped it two-handed, one at the handle, one nearer the tip, and thrust it flat against his back. He staggered forward, just as Cell and Knife were trying to untangle themselves, and all three ended up stumbling and falling on the filthy ground. They formed a mound of struggling humanity that the bull terrier pounced on, and then launched off like a frothy-mouthed missile. I'd swear I could see all the way down its throat as it came directly for mine.

Its teeth were huge, gleaming against the wet darkness of its cavernous mouth. The bite pressure of a pit bull is incredible. Gladly for me it didn't crunch down on my flesh but on the baseball bat I'd jammed crosswise between us. I actually felt the teeth go into the wood as a tremor that shook my entire frame, then the dog yanked its head savagely from side-to-side far too fast for my senses to follow. Its claws scrabbled at my chest and upper thighs; the violent worrying of its jaws shook me. But I'd been turning as it hit and the frantic, and admittedly terrifying, moment was over with as the dog was cast aside, still clenching the bat between its teeth as it sailed away and then landed on its side on the junk strewn earth. My hand immediately went for my gun, and it was up and ready even as the dog found its feet in a scramble. The dog wasn't the least bit interested in me. It had the baseball bat, and it wasn't going to let go of its prize. It shot away with the bat clenched in its teeth, and disappeared behind one of the stacks of junked cars.

Fuck me, I thought, when I tell that story nobody will believe me. But there wasn't time for thanking my mad luck, or the odd whim of an animal's nature. I swung my SIG on the dog handler whose face was a picture of disbelief.

'What now?' I demanded.

The greasy-haired guy didn't have a clue. He was looking for an escape route, and I expected him to try to scurry for the cover of the nearest stack. His three pals had disentangled themselves, but hadn't yet risen. They all stared at my gun, and their pale faces made a triptych of ovals framing their incredulity.

'Now you put away the gun,' said a voice from the doorway.

I glanced over my shoulder and saw Emilio's huge bulk filling the aperture. His right hand rested on a stick that strained to hold him up. His left held a .38 revolver but it was down by his side. If I wished I could've spun and emptied half a clip into his ponderous body before he got a bead on me. But that wouldn't get me the answers I desired. I faced him while slipping my gun back in its carry position, and offered him a convivial smile. 'It's good to see you at last, Emilio. Did we really need the dramatics first?'

'You put on quite a performance,' Emilio replied, his small mouth puckering and drawing up the folds of hairy skin from beneath his chin. The effort must have been tremendous because the smile lasted a heartbeat then dissolved.

He checked out his followers. They'd clawed themselves back to their feet. Of the three I'd tussled with only the owner of the bat had been injured, but it was pain that'd pass, nothing permanent. He rubbed at his sore chin and aching gut, undecided on which required most nursing. The others only suffered bruised egos. The dog-handler looked most disturbed by the abandonment of his dog, which was currently hiding somewhere chomping merrily on the bat.

'There was no need for any of them to get hurt,' I pointed out. 'I only wanted to talk, to ask you a few questions.'

Emilio slipped away the revolver so he could brace both hands atop his walking stick. The stick was bent into a crescent. He looked over his buddies the way he would a piece of base metal, then shook his head in regret. 'Maybe I shouldn't have had them bait you like that,' he admitted.

'No, you shouldn't have,' I said, and thought about what he'd said; one word in particular was pinging like a warning beacon. I made myself a mental note to check it out later. First I wanted answers about Ella's ring. I hoped because of his reticence to speak with me that Emilio was holding some good information. 'I take it you already heard I was coming, and what I want to know about, so I'm going to get straight to the point. Ella Clayton was murdered during an alleged home invasion a couple of weeks ago. You heard about it, right?'

'I heard. What's it got to do with me? I'm an honest businessman, I don't consort with thieves and murderers.'

I gave his gang a scornful glance, and couldn't help sneering.

'Those boys are loyal to their employer, faithful as hounds you might say. They want to protect me. Pity the same can't be said for Caesar,' Emilio said. He caught them looking at him for instruction and he jerked his head. They slinked off, looking for their own hiding places.

'I take it that Caesar was the mutt? The only one out of the bunch with any brains,' I said.

'It's a dumb piece of shit, too. You should have shot it and saved me the bullet,' Emilio grunted.

'I'd rather shoot you,' I told him. 'Don't touch the dog or I'll be back.'

Emilio chuckled to himself. 'You'll happily throw a man off of a tower block, but won't see any harm coming to a dumb beast. Maybe you're not the hard ass I've heard about.'

'It's not a good idea to test me,' I warned.

He flapped one hand in the air. 'This ring you're looking for? Why come to me?'

'Trust me, you're not alone in this. I've been around a bunch of other guys before you. If you'd given me the opportunity to explain, we could've had this over with by now and I'd be out of your hair. What can you tell me about the ring?'

'Nothing. And that's the damn truth. I won't lie to you and say I don't handle some questionable merchandise, but that ring you're looking for…I'd be stupid to get within a mile of it. I just bet those others guys you spoke to said the same damn thing: it's not worth it.'

'You're saying you've never bought jewellery from a thief before?' I said.

'Nope. I've done it a hundred times. But I've never bought gold from a murderer before.'

'Not that you know of.'

Emilio shrugged his expansive shoulders. 'That's all I'm saying on the subject. Now if you want to beat anything more from me, I'd best call back those boys. They won't be caught cold like last time. They might get hurt, but so might you. Too much trouble, right? Same as it's too much trouble for me to handle the goods from a murder scene. You get me?'

'I get you. So,' I said, 'who else can I ask about them?'

'You'd be wasting your time, buddy. This ring, it's either hidden somewhere or been melted down for scrap. You'd be better following other leads, believe me.'

The thing was, I did believe him.

I pointed at a nearby stack of junk cars. 'That car up there, third from the top?'

Emilio followed my gaze. Nodded. 'Want to buy it?'

I ignored his stupid question. 'You see the bumper sticker, the one that says WPB? What do those initials stand for?'

'West Palm Beach,' Emilio said.

I nodded in agreement. 'You see many of those stickers round here?'

'Plenty,' Emilio said. 'Why?'

'No reason,' I said, but I was lying. 'Just wondering if it were a generic thing.'

'You get other designs, but the black oval and lettering on a white background is the most popular I've seen.'

I smiled at him. 'Thank you, Emilio. After our false start, you've actually proved helpful.'

My next bout of sleuthing wasn't as tough on my feet, or on the chins or egos of criminals on the lower rungs of the Tampa underworld. After driving away from Emilio's junkyard, I parked outside a Walgreens and took out my phone. Though I rarely used it to surf the web, it came with a browser app and I tapped in the initials WPB, but added "Tampa" after it, to differentiate my search from West Palm Beach. As an afterthought, and recalling the mental note I'd made earlier, I included the word "bait" in the search criteria and set it to work. The signal was decent, so I didn't have long to wait until a list of hyperlinks built in my browser, and I saw a likely candidate for what I'd been searching for. I followed the link.

'Wild Point Bait,' I read aloud. 'We specialize in live bait and fishing tackle.' I sank a little in my seat as I saw the banner at the head of the website. I recognised the same font and colours from the bumper sticker on the car I was seeking. Now that I had a closer look, the lettering sat atop a diagram of a fishing rod from which hung a leaping fish: through the teeming rain last night the picture of the rod and catch hadn't been visible to me, but I was certain the sticker on the Toyota Clayton's assailant took off in was the same. On the Wild Point Bait webpage was a side banner, and in it was a "Southern Fried Florida Native" announcement. It was advertising Saturday evening cookouts - or more likely fish fries – held at the bait and tackle shop's location off Shore Drive near Oldsmar. I knew the area, and it was only a few miles north along the Old Tampa Bay shoreline from Andrew Clayton's house. That both graphics I'd seen on the car were also present on the website was too much of a coincidence to ignore. When I thought about it, Clayton was in the boat and fishing business, so who might have a grudge against him more than a rival outfitter? I closed down my phone, started the Ford and headed west on Hillsborough Avenue.

I passed Clayton's house and felt a trickle of guilt for not pulling in and appraising Rink of what I'd discovered. But as I'd said to my friend, I didn't want to put any ideas in his head that might prove untrue. I wanted to follow the lead I'd found, see if it went anywhere of value, then I'd bring Rink up to speed. It'd be best to update Bryony and Holker, too, but only when and if I was on the right track. Holker especially wouldn't appreciate it if I complicated matters, further muddying the murky waters they were already wading through.

Then there was that selfish part of me that wanted more "me time". The brief scuffle I'd enjoyed with Emilio's punks had whetted my appetite. It was the kind of action I'd missed for months. And now I was hungry for more.

15

It was nearing four p.m. by the time I turned off Shore Drive. At this end of Oldsmar there were a number of residential properties, but there were also an equal amount of commercial premises, some of them arranged as short strip malls, others seated in their own private lots. Wild Point Bait enjoyed a position near the water, which was fitting, but to reach it I had to follow a beaten dirt track that zigzagged through a small industrial complex. Chain-link fences at the trackside seemed pointless considering they were rusted, bent out of shape and even collapsed in most places. The verges hadn't been attended to in years and were weed-strewn and collecting places for wind-blown trash. I wasn't sure it was somewhere I'd come to enjoy a cookout, but that was before I drove round the last building and onto the eastern shore of Safety Harbor. The bait and tackle shop wasn't much to look at, but its grounds were admittedly impressive and evocative of a certain way of life. I suppose it depends on your personal eye for beauty, but the rustic sheds strewn with old fishing nets, the sloping grassy embankment on which stood an upturned weathered old rowing boat, the sun-faded wooden jetties and small boats bobbing on the lazy tide all appealed to me. After last night's storm the sea was cerulean, and the water reflected the sky in a similar hue, twinkling in a million highlights where the sunlight caressed the gentle waves. Out on the bay was a small fleet of boats, some under sail, and a flotilla of kayaks originating from a rowing club over towards the Bridgeport side of the harbour. How the owner of the bait and tackle shop had come up with the name "Wild Point" was beyond me, because I thought the place serene. Perhaps the name meant something to fishermen, perhaps not.

I could feel the warmth through my clothing the second I stepped out of my car onto the pale dirt that served as a parking lot. I'd parked alongside a GMC Suburban, and there was some ancient truck that was so faded under the sun I couldn't determine its original colour. It couldn't be road worthy but fitted nicely into the rustic setting and it'd be a shame if it were removed. Sadly there was no sign of the Toyota I sought. I wondered if I'd jumped to a conclusion – a trait I was guilty of at times – and the car didn't belong here: for all I knew the Toyota belonged to a customer who'd slapped on the bumper stickers after a single day out on a hired boat.

I didn't immediately approach the shop, but took a look around.

A couple of workers were down by the water, tending to the small boats tied off to the jetty. A man was washing the boats with warm soapy water from a bucket, while a woman sat cross-legged on the jetty fiddling with some equipment I couldn't identify. I ignored the blond woman, checked out the man, but he was old, with a shaved head and thick white moustache, not the man I was looking for, so I ignored him too. Pushing my hands in my pockets, I strolled towards the upturned rowboat, and made out I was admiring the lines of its hull the way an artist might before settling down to forming a composition. I ran a hand over the wood and it was smooth and warm. While I did so, I glanced at the shop. The sign above the window gave the shop its full title. On the door itself I spotted smaller signs, and one of them was identical to the bumper sticker I'd followed here. Because of the glare of sunlight off the window there was no way to tell who was inside. There wasn't a hint of movement within. Checking on the couple down at the jetty, they were blissfully unaware of my presence. I walked nonchalantly, still admiring the view, towards the shop. My gun was in its usual position, nestled in my lower back, but I fully intended it stayed there this time.

A doorbell tinkled as I pushed inside. It was my first time in a bait and tackle shop, but it looked exactly as I'd imagined. Maybe there were more modern shops in the area, that had brighter lines and décor, but WPB had a retro feel to it, with an old wooden counter running the length of the shop, under which were dozens of individual storage boxes, over which were hinged clear plastic lids. More shelves behind the counter held hundreds of packaged items, and also myriad types of lures, floats, hooks, weights and God knew what else. There were fishing rods by the dozen arranged in racks. Reels. Landing nets. Gaffs. Spear guns. Kit bags. Folding chairs. You name it, whatever you required for a fishing trip, it could be had there. There were a few refrigeration units and a couple of chest-style freezers where they kept the bait; I wasn't sure where the live bait was stored. Another fridge looked anomalous in one corner, this one stacked with soft drinks and beer, but I supposed fishermen needed to rehydrate regularly when out under the Floridian sun.

The squeaking of hinges announced the arrival of a man who pushed his way through from a storeroom. He had his back to me, struggling to haul an oversized cardboard box through the gap. He cursed softly under his breath, juggled the box about, angrily kicked open the door with one foot, then turned abruptly and placed the heavy cargo down on the counter. Aloud, he suggested the box was of unknown parental lineage. Only then did he look up at me, his expression briefly startled. I nodded in greeting, and he flushed slightly, realising I'd seen and heard his unprofessional antics.

'Uh, help you?' he asked, and came out from behind the counter.

He was tall and sinewy, with a tan like polished chestnut. Blond hair, thinning on top, cut short around his ears. He was wearing canvas shorts, sandals, and a baggy T-shirt with the WPB logo on a breast pocket. He was younger than me, maybe in his early thirties. He wasn't the guy I was looking for.

'To be honest,' I said, 'I don't really know where to start. I've never been fishing before...' I scanned the shop as if it was a museum of curiosities.

'Well, wherever you want to start, I can hook you up.' He smiled. 'No pun intended.'

I grinned back at him. 'I've been thinking about getting some tackle and stuff, maybe doing some fishing off the beach first.'

He made a motion with one hand to a rack of long poles. 'I'll show you a selection of rods if you like? You got a budget in mind?'

I shrugged. 'Don't want to waste your time or anything. Not sure if I want to buy today, just wanted to get an idea about what I'd need to get started.'

There was a moment's disappointment he couldn't hide, but then the businessman took over again and he began his spiel, hoping that I'd be leaving with a trunk full of tackle by the time he was done. I allowed him his lead, nodding and agreeing with him as he showed me various rods, then led me over to the counter, and began taking down smaller boxes from the shelves and showing me different types of reels. I played at being interested, but was thinking how to broach the actual subject for being there without it sounding obvious.

'Not sure I want to lay out as much to begin with, I'm only in town for a few days before going home.' I allowed him to make his own decision about where home might be, based on my English accent. 'I was talking to one of your staff who said you might be prepared to hire me some gear...'

There was a visible slump in the man's shoulders, and I watched the dollar signs fade from his eyes. Before I'd lost an advantage, I carried on: 'At least I took him to be one of your staff. We got talking in a bar yesterday, and the subject turned to fishing. He gave me directions to get out here, otherwise, well, I wouldn't have known where to come.'

The man only nodded; giving me no clues to the mystery man I'd alluded to.

'I didn't catch his name,' I went on, and held my hand level with my eyebrows. 'He was about yay high. Brown wavy hair, medium build. Maybe forty years old.'

I elicited another nod. But then the man exhaled noisily, and said, 'Yeah, that'll be Benson.'

'I expected him to be around today...'

The guy shook his head. 'Not today. Not ever again if I have my way.'

'Jeez, I hope I haven't got him in trouble over this,' I said.

'Benson doesn't need any help getting himself in trouble, Mister.' He folded down the lid on the box of the latest reel he'd been about to show me. 'Look, buddy, no offence, but you've got no interest in fishing, have you? You're here about Benson. Why not just come out with whatever it is you want to ask? I'll decide if I want to answer or not.'

I'd been caught in my lie, but it didn't matter. The man wasn't being belligerent; he only seemed resigned.

'A full name would help,' I admitted.

'Tommy. Thomas Benson. You're right. He *was* an employee, but I had to let him go. Conflict of interests, is all I'll say on the matter.'

'Do you know where I can find him?'

The guy looked me over. Came to a conclusion. 'You aren't going to hurt him in any way? I don't have much nice to say about him, but I wouldn't wish harm on him.'

'I only need to speak with him about something.'

The man grabbed a pen and tore off a strip of receipt roll from his till. He jotted down an address. 'You didn't get that from me, right?'

'I wasn't even here,' I reassured him.

He thought about my answer, then handed over the note. I didn't look at what he'd written, just slipped the paper in my pocket. 'Can I ask you one last thing?'

'Why not?'

'Does Benson have a tattoo right here?' I touched a finger to the webbing between the thumb and index finger of my right hand.

'Not that I ever noticed,' he said. 'But I haven't seen him in about ten days, so who knows what the fool's been up to in the meantime?'

I nodded, shelved away another mental note. I went to the fridge and pulled out a six-pack of Budweiser, and counted fifty dollars on to the counter.

'That's too much,' said the man.

'It's for the beer and your time. Thanks. I appreciate it.'

'No worries,' he said as I turned for the door, carrying the beer under one arm. 'And, hey, buddy, if you ever do get serious about fishing come back, why don't you?'

'Will do.' My promise was empty, but then again so had been his offer. He meant unless it was to buy tackle, don't bother returning.

Back in my car, I put the beers aside. I'd no intention of drinking them yet. I'd discovered the name of Clayton's assailant, but it was too soon for celebration.

'Tommy Benson,' I said aloud, 'what exactly is your part in all this?'

Delving in my pocket, I found the slip of till roll and read the address. The street name was unfamiliar, but I knew the neighbourhood. I thought again that I should call Bryony and Holker, or Rink at the very least. But I didn't. All I used my phone for was to bring up the location of Benson's house on a sat-nav app. Time to go, I hit the ignition.

16

Tommy Benson wasn't home when I arrived at his small, dilapidated house a couple blocks west of Nebraska Avenue. But I wasn't at a loss, because I chanced upon him as he drove his Toyota off the short strip of pavement that served as his parking spot. He was fiddling with his CD player, thumbing up the volume on some country rock track, so didn't meet my gaze as he drove by. I watched my mirrors and saw him head towards Waters Avenue. As soon as he'd made a right, I pulled my Ford into a quick Y-turn and went after him. He was gloriously unaware of a tail as I followed him under the I-275 towards a small commercial strip adjacent to the Hillsborough River. He'd the choice of various stores including a Kmart, an outlet store selling last season's men's wear, and a dollar store among others. He pulled his Toyota into a parking space outside a laundromat. He was still unaware of me as he got out the car and lugged a bag of laundry to the shop. He was wearing a red T-shirt, jeans and high-top sneakers, and had a baseball cap pulled low, his hair jutting out from under it. I drove past his car, and got a good look this time at the bumper stickers. Now I could read it clearly, I committed the licence number to memory, though doing so was academic now.

Should I need to leave in a hurry, I reversed my car into a space outside a nearby Chinese restaurant, from where I had a view of his car and the laundromat. The windows of the shop reflected the late afternoon glare, so I'd no view of the interior, but I guessed Benson was currently stuffing his dirty laundry in one of the machines. For a brief moment I considered going inside and stopping him, in case he was washing clothing that might hold some trace evidence from when he was at Clayton's house. Why bother? All he was guilty of was planting a sucker punch on Clayton's chin, and nothing else that I knew of. Barring a couple of aches and pains, Clayton was unharmed, and he had given the impression he wasn't interested in pressing charges against his attacker. I decided to wait instead, but didn't know how long I was committing to: how long were the wash and dry cycles in a laundromat?

As it happened I didn't have to sit for more than a few minutes before Tommy Benson pushed out the front door. His hands were empty of laundry, but he soon filled them with a pack of cigarettes and a Zippo-style lighter. He sparked up and took a grateful pull on his cigarette. As he stood filling his nicotine quota, I got my first sharp look at him. Even without the evidence presented by his car I would have recognised him as the man who'd struck Clayton, knocking him on his arse during the thunderstorm. And, now that I had a good look at him, I was sure he was the also same man I'd startled from the copse of trees the night before the storm, the same one who'd dropped the glove during his escape. Recalling the glove, and the hair found inside it, it made me reconsider Benson's involvement in everything, including Ella's murder. The guy was tangled deeper in everything than I'd first thought, though I couldn't yet imagine how. So that left me single recourse. I got out my car, and walked towards him, my footsteps hushed by the traffic whistling by on the nearby elevated interstate. He was blissfully unaware of my approach, busy squinting up at the early evening sky as he smoked, and possibly plotting a return trip to the Clayton house as soon as it turned dark.

Less than ten feet separated us when he heard my footfalls and glanced my way. He was unconcerned by my presence, and turned away again. But a sudden tenseness went through him and he rounded on me, staring directly in my face. Had he too recognised me from our two brief interactions? I'd no real plan of approach, because I'd no idea of his level of involvement, but that was good because he'd have blown it. He acted exactly as a guilty person might in such circumstances: he let out a croak of alarm and began backpedalling away, his head snapping this way and that as he sought an escape route.

'Hey! Just hold it, Benson,' I said, lifting an empty palm towards him. 'I only want to speak to you.'

'Fuck that, man!' he replied.

I should have foreseen his next move, but I was preparing for a run. As he'd exhibited at Clayton's he was prone to violence, and apparently Benson's favourite method was delivering it without warning. He suddenly skipped towards me, and jabbed a kick at my balls.

As Rink mentioned earlier: nobody is infallible. His words almost rang true in my case; I came so near to having my testicles driven up inside me. But at the last instant I sucked in my gut, jerked back my pelvis and Benson's foot barely scuffed the front of my jeans. I thrust my palm into his chest, but it wasn't enough to halt his forward momentum, and he swung a couple of wild punches at my head before I'd had enough. I nutted him, catching him with the top of my forehead on his left cheek bone. I'd delivered the headbutt to stun, not to drop him cold, and almost succeeded. He let out a shout of pain, but then grabbed at me, and I returned the favour. However he wasn't up for a full on tussle and only used his grip on my clothing to pull around me, and get a clear run at the parking lot. I grasped at him but he yanked loose, ducked past me, and was running like a lunatic for his car before I could spin in pursuit.

We'd attracted the attention of an older couple returning from the pharmacy to their car: they made exclamations of dismay and backed away. Further along near the Kmart a trio of boys riding bicycles whooped and hollered as I gave chase. They began pedalling furiously, keen to follow the action. The last I needed was an audience, but first and foremost in my mind was catching Benson. He charged for his car, but he watched me over one shoulder, and figured that he couldn't make it inside the relative safety of the Toyota before I caught up. He forwent the car, rushing instead for the low wall that surrounded this part of the lot. He hurdled it, skipped across the sidewalk and onto the asphalt road. He swerved around a slow moving van. I pelted after him.

'Just bloody stop!' I yelled at his back, but he had no intention of obeying.

He lunged over the opposite sidewalk, and on to an adjacent strip of spongy grass. A low fence separated the verge from an expanse of green through which wended a cinder path, possibly a route for dog walkers or joggers. On the far side of the recreation field was a small neighbourhood, and I thought that was where Benson was heading, maybe seeking the bolthole of a friend's house. If he made it inside I'd have to call Bryony, but really I wanted to speak to Benson before the cops got to him. I put my head down and pushed harder after him.

He jerked to the right, and I turned with him, but then he went left again but he'd failed to wrong foot me. I was still on his heels, but he maintained a lead I was finding it difficult to shorten. I shouted again, but my words sounded more like a clipped curse. He paid no attention and kept running.

I could hear the kids on the bikes attempting to keep pace with us, but they'd taken the route on to the field via a gate, and were pedalling like crazy down the cinder path. I threw a warning gesture and a shout in their direction, trying to chase them off but they disobeyed me with as much willfulness as Benson. I ignored them after that, concentrating on the chase. My feet slapped through the grass, kicking up clouds of insects. Benson was proving fleet-footed. But then, so was I, and finally gaining step by step.

Benson must have sensed how close I was. He again tried a zigzag manoeuvre, but it helped him none, and only allowed me to close the gap by another few feet. He knew he wasn't going to make it all the way across the field before I had him, and had two options. Turn and fight or try something new. He preferred a surprise attack, and that wasn't available to him now, so he took option two. He went sharply to the left, just as the kids streaked down the path between us. As the first kid coasted by, Benson slapped an arm across the kid's chest and took him out of his saddle. For the tiniest moment I thought he was going to try to highjack the pedal cycle and make off on it. But no. As the kid clattered to the floor with a cry of dismay, the other kids swerved wildly to avoid hitting him and one of them streaked towards me. I'd to slam on the brakes to avoid colliding with him. The kid wobbled as he also tried to avoid a collision, braked too hard and went headlong over the handlebars. He rolled across the grass, arms and legs akimbo, before coming to rest in the dirt. Thankfully he looked unhurt, but I was filled with ignominy at Benson's actions. It made me switch up a gear, and I no longer simply wanted to talk. If ever I was tempted to shoot it was now, though I'd only have to wing the punk if I did.

Benson didn't give a shit for the kids' welfare. While I made a brief check on the two spilled boys, he went for the third. This kid jumped off his bike and ran back a few feet from Benson. Ignoring the boy's four-letter exclamation, Benson grabbed his bicycle, lifted it in the air and slung it at me. I dodged, but the back wheel clipped my left thigh, and dull pain went through the muscle that left it leaden. I tripped over the frame before regaining my balance.

Benson was off again.

I checked all the kids were unharmed, hissing warnings at them to stay back. This time they'd learned their lesson, and I took off at a limp after Benson who now headed directly for a narrow strip of undergrowth that separated the field from an embankment up to the highway. As I ran the deadening pain in my thigh was replaced by a tingling itch, but that was good: it meant the effects of the charley horse were wearing off.

Benson's hat had fallen off. I stamped on it as I ran. Not deliberately, but I didn't make much effort to miss it either. He forced through the tangle of undergrowth with all the grace of a charging warthog, then scurried up the embankment on all fours. I kicked through the tangles of creepers and long grass and almost got a grip round one of his ankles. He kicked loose, clawed his way upward and I was forced to scramble in pursuit again.

'Just stop, for fuck's sake!' I snarled. My tone didn't promise good things if he obeyed. Unsurprisingly he kept going. I made it on to the verge as Benson fled alongside the highway. Cars and trucks zipped past, heading the same direction. As I pursued, I could feel tiny bits of grit striking my flesh, kicked up from the road by the speeding vehicles.

Benson glanced frantically over his shoulder. I was thirty feet back, but again closing on him as his wind began to leave him. Each step he took was growing more ungainly as if he was rapidly approaching fatigue, while each of mine grew a little longer and steadier. He wasn't only checking how close I was though. He glanced, glanced again and then swerved left. He was through a gap between the hurtling traffic in about three bounds. He stood there on the narrow median. Fuck that, I decided, and was about to give up the chase. While I had him in my sights I'd have been happy to continue the chase, but not when things had grown so desperate. I'd need only go back and fetch my car and I'd catch him when he inevitably returned home. I began to slow.

Benson saw I'd lost any enthusiasm for the hunt, and took a gloating grin across the lanes at me. He raised his right fist, and slowly extended his middle finger, even as he stepped back. "Fuck you," he mouthed in victory.

Jesus! Even I didn't see the camper van's approach, so Benson had no hope. He reversed directly in front of it, and the impact was so sudden I'd no idea where Benson was for a few seconds. Partly it was because I'd scrunched tight my eyes at the sickening impact, and partly because the VW ploughed him up and over its windshield, flinging him skyward. By the time I opened my eyes, letting out a groan of regret, the van was already a hundred yards further down the highway, swerving wildly as the driver fought to control his own shock. Benson had landed on the median once more. From the way his body was contorted I didn't give him much odds at life. 'Holy shit,' I wheezed. On both sides of the highway cars and trucks were coming to a halt. Further back, those who hadn't witnessed the accident had no clue why the traffic had ground to a halt, and I heard the angry blaring of horns. I also caught the soft crunch of a rear-end collision.

I checked that I wasn't going to be similarly mown down before jogging across the road between stalled vehicles. As I made it to the median, I'd a short run to where Benson lay. I could hear him moaning, and the sound was so full of torment that it pained my ears. Steam rose from him, and it wasn't through overheating through exertion. It wasn't a good sign.

I'd witnessed many horrendous sights in my lifetime. I'd seen people shot, burned, decapitated, blown apart by explosives, but they had been under warfare conditions, or during life and death moments of shocking violence, and I'd been able to compartmentalise the horror so it didn't affect me. There's always something you don't grow inured to. One of them is when the horrendous injuries come so suddenly in a mundane situation as they had now, and in a totally avoidable manner. Less than five minutes ago Benson had been laundering his clothes. Now he looked like a bundle of filthy rags. Benson's body had practically burst…

I almost lost my lunch on the grass alongside him. But I pushed aside any revulsion, and dropped to my knees, ignoring the gore that immediately seeped through my jeans. Moments ago I'd considered shooting Benson for his ill treatment of the kids, but now my emphasis was on trying to save his life. I knew it was a futile attempt, but still had to do something. Hell, if I stood and watched him perish, I would never feel human again. There was nothing I could do for his traumatic injuries, no way of halting the blood pulsing from his torn and exposed arteries, and I could do nothing about rearranging his spilled intestines. But maybe I could offer some comfort in his last few seconds on earth, and – guiltily – coax an answer to a question or two. I held his right hand as I looked down at him. Miraculously his eyes were still open, but he was staring at a point a thousand miles beyond my face. 'Why did you have to run like that?' I asked him. 'I only wanted to speak to you.'

He heard. Maybe he understood my words, but I didn't think so. He squeezed my hand, but his grip had less strength than a newborn. His hold on existence was as tenuous. His lips moved. I had to lean in to hear, but all I made out was the slight smacking of his lips.

'What are you trying to say, Tommy?' I coaxed gently.

Others were closing in on us. Some of the bystanders were suffering the immediate revulsion and shock as I had. But a young black woman steeled herself and came to help as the others reached for phones to summon expert assistance. She cupped Benson's head in her palms, as he again made those smacking noises with his lips. I leaned closer to hear, but couldn't make out what he said.

'Paid,' said the woman to my quizzical frown. 'He said "paid".' She also leaned closer, while muttering soft encouragement to him and Benson mumbled his last words. I felt the life go out him, and air leaked from him like a punctured tyre. His body deflated visibly, and to be honest it was for the best. The woman shook her head, and I met her gaze. She looked back at Benson's lax features, then back at me. 'He said he was "paid to run". What did he mean, sir? That's just nuts, isn't it? He was paid to run into the traffic like that?'

No. That wasn't what Benson meant at all. I had a good idea what he was referring to, but I wasn't in a position to admit as much to this Good Samaritan.

17

'Remember: don't touch anything. You're not supposed to be here, Joe.'

Bryony VanMeter stood to one side, allowing Hunter to enter the vestibule of Thomas Benson's house. He stepped in alongside her, his hands fisted at his sides. 'I understand the rules, Bryony,' he reassured her.

'Pity you don't stick to them,' Detective Holker growled as he pushed inside past them.

They'd already had this discussion earlier at One Police Centre at Franklin Street and Bryony didn't feel they needed to go over it again. Deputies from Hillsborough Sheriff's department were first on the scene at the fatal accident on the I-275, closely followed by highway patrol officers, and because Hunter had stuck around he was first questioned as a witness, then arrested because it grew apparent that Thomas Benson had been struck by the VW van while fleeing from him. Hunter didn't resist, but asked that Detective VanMeter be informed of his arrest. Hunter was subsequently released once he'd related the circumstances, how he'd repeatedly warned Benson against running, and three youths and an elderly couple who'd witnessed the chase corroborated his story. Benson had been proven to be the aggressor, while Hunter only beseeched him to stop and talk. Holker still felt Hunter was complicit in Benson's death and wanted to throw the book at him, but Bryony had told him – off the record - not to be an ass. For a change he'd listened to her, but the uneasy truce with Hunter wouldn't last long. She was certain Holker purposefully goaded Hunter, hoping to get some kind of rise out him, one he'd push and shove at until Hunter broke and crossed a line. Holker would love to have Hunter in cuffs having assaulted a law enforcement officer. Be careful what you wish for, she wanted to warn him.

Hunter had explained to them how he'd found Benson, following the tip from the owner of WPB, the bait and tackle shop, but didn't say how he'd got to that point. It was maybe best they didn't ask. He narrated the actions by rote, explaining how on approaching this very house he'd spotted Benson driving away and identified the vehicle and the man from their previous confrontations, and had followed him to the strip mall. He explained he approached Benson with a view to questioning him about his grievance towards Andrew Clayton, but how he never got the chance.

'I heard you head-butted him,' Holker had sneered.

'Only after he tried to kick me in the balls,' Hunter had responded. 'But the eye witnesses already told you that too.'

'Why didn't you draw your sidearm?' Holker asked snippily.

'I only do that when I mean to use it,' said Hunter, deadpan.

'I meant to make him stand still, to hold him until the real professionals could speak with him.'

'Legally I couldn't do that, Detective Holker. Are you suggesting I should have broken the law? That's quite a turn of events.'

Holker had cursed him, and Bryony averted her face to hide her chuckle at her partner's expense.

She'd had Benson's Toyota impounded, and currently a CSI team was going over it, checking for trace evidence to Ella Clayton's murder, but none of them believed any would be found. Hunter had told them Benson's last words, also corroborated by Shaneesha Dewitt, the off-duty nurse who'd assisted Hunter with Benson during the man's final seconds. *Paid to run.* None of them were sure what he'd meant, but they were all certain he wasn't referring to his final minutes on Earth. He was confessing to his previous actions, and they had nothing to do with murder. When Bryony thought about it, twice Benson had run from Hunter on earlier occasions: had he been paid to run both times, and if so, by whom? They'd come to his house hoping to discover a clue. Holker had been reluctant about bringing Hunter, but there was value in having him along. Hunter had learned more about Benson's involvement than any of them, so perhaps he could add insight to something the detectives might otherwise miss. But he was under strict instructions to touch nothing and do exactly as instructed without argument. Bryony's friendly reminder was so Holker wasn't fed the ammunition to provoke him again.

Holker flicked on lights as he progressed through the dwelling. The house wasn't a crime scene, so there was no need to take precautions against transferring trace evidence, but Bryony still treated it as such. She checked on Hunter, and saw that he kept his hands by his sides. He caught her looking and offered the ghost of a smile. He was going to behave, his smile promised. Shame, because she preferred him as a bad boy. OK, not that she'd ever describe him as bad, in the sense of the word, but she enjoyed the buzz of excitement he invoked in her when he was around. He always reminded her of some caged beast, raw and dangerous, his true nature confined by the veneer of civilisation but apt to be loosed at any instant. As a child she once saw a Bengal tiger in a zoo, separated from her only by a short stretch of beaten earth and some narrow bars. It had stared at her with implacable intensity, and she knew it wished to eat her, and yet her impulse was to reach out to it, tempting its ravenous appetite while ruffling her fingertips through its short fur. She'd evoked a shriek of alarm from her mother, who'd snatched her out of harm's way, then scolded her madly for her recklessness – while all the time her mother had also peered over her at the tiger, wishing she'd had the opportunity to stroke the savage beast herself. Being around Hunter was akin to petting a tiger: she couldn't help herself, even if it meant losing a hand or worse. Feeling warm, she returned his smile, then winked and nodded for him to follow.

She moved away from Holker, heading for the sitting room while her partner moved deeper into the house. It was a small dwelling, suitable only for one person: in fact it was barely fit for habitation, but that was primarily down to Benson's aversion to housekeeping. The sitting room was a tip. It was strewn with the detritus of bachelorhood, and stank like an ashtray and was coloured fifty shades of tar. In the living space, there was a recliner chair, bearing the indentations where Benson regularly slouched before the TV. There was an archaic sideboard unit, with drawers missing their handles. On top of it was a music centre, the old kind that took cassette tapes and CDs. An unruly stack of CDs showed Benson had a preference for Country Rock and Rockabilly music. There was a confederate states flag nailed to the wall, on it printed the epitaph "The South's Gonna Rise Again", but Bryony guessed it had more significance concerning the birthplace of his musical tastes than it had to do with any inherent racism or even homeland pride. His taste in music was probably also why he had fixed a Southern Fried bumper sticker on his car. On one wall was a framed print of Eddie Cochran slinging a Gretsch guitar, and another wall upheld a poster of Hank Williams, so faded it was almost translucent.

'Looks as if Tommy Benson was living in the past,' Bryony commented.

'For such a slob, he had good taste,' Hunter replied as he studied the CD cases. As Bryony recalled from her dates with him, Hunter too had a liking for oldie music.

'If you see anything you like, try not to touch it,' she said, and winked again.

He eyed her, his eyes smoky. Bryony tried not to sashay as she walked across the room and leaned over the TV to check the space behind it. 'When I said he lived in the past, I was thinking he wasn't the type to be up to date on computers and such like. By the look of things I might be right.'

'He'd no phone on him when he died; none in his car?'

'Nope.'

There were footsteps from upstairs, Holker making his way through the bedrooms. 'Maybe Holker will have more luck up there,' Hunter said.

Bryony held up a hand. 'You see that, Joe?'

He walked over and studied the floor next to the TV. It was strewn with dust balls, lint, grit and a torn strip of notepaper. Bryony crouched, and used the side of her left pinkie finger to adjust the paper so the writing on it was easier to read. Beside her Hunter grew still as he studied what she'd spotted. The words were written in pencil, and because of the way the paper had been ripped they were incomplete, but what were the chances "la Clayto" weren't part of a very pertinent name?

While she pulled a plastic evidence bag from her jacket pocket, Bryony said, 'Joe, do me a favour, will you? Take a look around and see if you can spot a waste basket under any of that crap.'

Hunter did as asked. He moved around the room, using the toe of his boot to shift aside some dirty laundry left behind by Benson when he made his fatal trip to the laundromat. Finding nothing, he checked the other obvious places where Benson tossed his trash, but there was no sign of a litter basket. 'I'll check the kitchen,' he offered, and left the room without waiting. Bryony studied the words on the torn paper while it was still in situ, then used the half opened bag to pick it up. She shook it inside the bag, before smoothing the paper so it could be clearly read.

She thought about checking the drawers on the sideboard, and moved for them. She employed the tail of her shirt over her fingers to avoid leaving her fingerprints on the broken handles and tugged open the drawers in turn. She was looking for the notepad from which the paper was ripped, but came up blank. From the kitchen she could hear Hunter rummaging, and also the soft thud of Holker returning downstairs. She met her partner in the vestibule. 'Lookit what I found,' she said, and flashed her eyes at him as she shook the evidence bag.

'I'll raise you a tablet,' Holker said, with a gloating grin, and held up an iPad, over which he'd folded an empty evidence bag. 'What are the bets this matches the IP address of those emails we received?'

'I can do one better,' Hunter called from the kitchen. 'One of you might want to seize this so the chain of evidence isn't broken.'

'What's he up to?' Holker demanded as he stamped down the last few stairs. 'I thought I warned him…'

'I asked him to look,' Bryony told him gruffly, and received a snort of derision, but Holker let it go. They both entered the kitchen, Bryony slightly ahead. Hunter was hunkered over a pile of trash he'd upended from a plastic sack – he'd barely added to the mess that already littered the floor.

'Lemme see that,' Holker demanded, snapping the tips of two fingers against Hunter's left shoulder.

Hunter rose, standing a few inches taller than Holker even in his stacked heels. Hunter wasn't huge, maybe just a shade beneath six feet, and his build was lithe as opposed to muscular, but alongside Holker he made her partner seem diminutive by comparison. Maybe Holker felt his overwhelming presence and was prickled by small man syndrome: he pressed Hunter aside with the back of his wrist, almost dismissing him. Bryony watched Hunter's eyes tighten a fraction, and a similar tightening of his lips implied he didn't appreciate Holker's treatment. Another man – one not wearing a badge of officialdom – might possibly have ended up nursing a bruised chin. She caught Hunter's attention with a flick of her head, and when he transferred his gaze to her, she offered a thumb's up at his discovery. He shrugged imperceptibly, then nodded down at Holker, who was now bent over the find: it's all his now, Hunter's expression said.

As he inspected the items on the floor Holker's slicked hair had parted slightly, flopping aside and disclosing a bald spot he'd worked diligently to conceal. Some of the hairs at the roots were white. Bryony blinked slowly at it, then lifted her gaze to Hunter's. He too had spotted Holker's vain attempt at covering up what the detective felt was a personal failing, but the shiny skin on his crown didn't hold Hunter's attention. He wasn't as judgmental as the man crouching in front of him.

'I already put them in some sort of order,' Hunter announced. 'Don't worry, I used the handle of that plastic spoon to move them, not my fingers.'

Holker squinted up at Bryony, ignoring Hunter completely. 'You see what we've got here?'

She did indeed. There were approximately two dozen pieces of torn paper, on which was a penciled message. She didn't require an expert analyst to tell her the notepaper matched the slip she'd found in the sitting room. Hunter had already begun arranging the message as if completing a homemade jigsaw puzzle. The scrap of paper she'd previously seized would sit near the top of the page.

'Looks as if Benson practiced what he wanted to write before transferring it to an email,' Holker said.

Who did that these days? Bryony had already concurred that Benson probably wasn't the type to embrace modern technology, but surely jotting a note on paper prior to transposing it into an email was a supreme waste of time and effort: judging by the state of the house Benson wasn't one for performing mundane tasks. 'Or someone else did,' she added, and caught a nod of approval from Holker.

'Check this out.' Hunter walked over to the fridge. There were a few post-it notes adhered to the front. Reminders of appointments, and some kind of list. On closer inspection Bryony saw Benson had jotted down a shopping list, but it was for sundry items, not groceries. Instantly she noted how spidery, and poorly formed Benson's letters were. His spelling was atrocious too. She snapped the list off the fridge and took it over to Holker, and he laid it alongside the partially reconstructed message on the floor. The writing on the shredded message was neat, spelled correctly and even used the correct grammar.

'I think we can safely assume Benson sent the emails from the iPad,' Holker said, 'but he did so on somebody else's behalf. You thinking what I'm thinking, Bryony?'

'It's time to go see Parker Quinn again. And this time we have to squeeze him a little tighter.'

18

At much the same time as Tommy Benson fled from outside the laundromat, doggedly pursued by Joe Hunter across the recreation field and to his inevitable doom, another chase was underway, though this one wasn't in the open and didn't offer the slightest glimmer of an escape route.

Having endured two unexpected visits to the police station in the previous days, Parker Quinn had just about had his fill of detectives and their persistent questioning methods. He'd spent yesterday evening tidying up his home after a search team had gone through it like a bunch of invading Vikings, pillaging his computer equipment, tablet and cell phones, as well as his notes, records and even bank statements – both personal and business accounts - under the authorisation of a warrant. They hadn't exactly wrecked his home, and had been respectful of his belongings in their own manner, but nothing was where he'd previously left it. All felt wrong in his home, every piece of furniture out by a fraction of an inch, the angles all skewed. When you were as familiar with your own space as Quinn was with his, it felt oddly alien when strangers disturbed the equilibrium.

He expected his equipment would be returned to him soon. Once the forensic investigation was completed, and it was determined that there was in fact no incriminating evidence on any of his electronic devices, or in his paper records, then everything would be given back, though he doubted he'd receive an apology. Even if somebody did say sorry, he couldn't give a damn. The cops could keep their apologies; he only wished they'd leave him the hell alone. They should concentrate on the ones truly responsible for Ella's murder, instead of trying to tie him to this nonsense about a harassment campaign against Andrew.

He believed that pinning a charge on him would somehow appease those criticizing Tampa PD for their lack of tangible results in the ongoing home invasion cases, that had culminated in Ella's brutal slaying. It was a diversionary tactic, but it would check a box in the correct column for Detective's Holker and VanMeter, and for their commanders by proxy, earning them some breathing space. Well, fuck them all; there was no way he was taking the heat off them, by sacrificing his own liberty. He knew he wasn't helping himself by acting aversive to their questions, and by telling only half-truths about certain aspects of his business and personal relationship with the Clayton family, but it wasn't yet time for the truth to come out. Perhaps he should tell the truth: while he continued being selective with the facts, he'd only fuel the detectives' suspicions, thus returning their attention to him.

He wondered when he could expect another visit from Tampa's finest.

He'd lost count of the times he'd snuck to the blinds, teasing them open a slit, to check each time a vehicle approached. He assumed he was under surveillance, and for all he knew there was a bunch of cops staked out in one of the apartments across the street, noting and cataloguing his every move. It was only late afternoon, still bright out, but he'd chosen to close all his blinds, and to lock every door and window. If there was a surveillance team observing his house, he'd give them nothing, and there was no way they could possible sneak inside for a closer look without him hearing. Earlier, he'd considered the probability that during the execution of the search warrant another team were also busy at work, installing listening and recording devices throughout his home. He should have been here when the cops were on site – as that Hunter fella had suggested – so he could watch exactly what they'd been up to. But, after his stupidity led him to go to see Andrew instead of returning immediately home from the station, he'd missed the opportunity to supervise what was going on. While he'd gone through his house, room to room, resettling his furniture and belongings in their correct places, he'd surreptitiously kept an eye open for anything unusual or demanding of a closer inspection. He hadn't discovered any hidden microphones or pinhole cameras, but he couldn't be certain there were none, so he'd made a deeper search again today before realisation struck him.

Jesus, he was losing it! Paranoia had overtaken good sense. He was jumping at shadows, forming conclusions based on wild fantasies, looking for things that weren't there. He had to chill out, relax, get his head in order, or it wouldn't be the cops coming for him next time but the men in white coats.

But paranoia was what came of hiding a secret.

It made you jumpy. Being in constant fear of everything coming to light wasn't good for the health, neither mental nor physical. His brain felt as if it was on fire, a swirling kaleidoscope of conflicting thoughts and emotions making it difficult for him to settle, while his body was almost numb with fatigue. One or the other would give out on him soon, and he hoped it was his body. He'd rather collapse from lack of sleep than suffer a complete mental breakdown.

He needed to shower.

In fact, he'd prefer to bathe in the large tub, but he was too nervous to commit to the time a soak would take. Then again, if he were in the shower, he might not hear if anyone crept close to his house with the water battering him. If he ran a bath, left the tub filling, he could stand guard until the tub was full. Once sunk to his nose in the bubbles, he would be able to hear the softest footfall.

"Jesus Christ, Parker, listen to yourself!"

If he'd done something wrong – and morally he had – it wasn't anything the cops would be interested in. Sure it might hint that he had a motive for harassing Andrew, but with no proof of any involvement what could they do?

'Have your goddamn bath. You stink like a polecat!' he scolded himself.

He knew his actions were illogical, yet he couldn't deny the impulse to go and check all was clear. He teased open the blinds in his living room. A cyclist rode past without giving his house the briefest of glances. There was no one else out and about. The apartments opposite could conceal observers, but he could spot no sign of anything untoward. But he wasn't done. He made his way to his kitchen and repeated the process of teasing open the blinds. Once he was satisfied nobody was skulking in his backyard, he went through to the small room adjacent to the sitting room that he used as a home office. He spied out of the blinds there too. Nobody around. Only then did he go upstairs to the en suite bathroom and turn on the faucets. While his tub filled, he sat on his bed, near enough to the window so he could see through a slim gap between the drawn curtains.

He must have zoned out for a few minutes. He heard the patter of water on the floor. Jumping up, he rushed for the bathroom. The bath was full to the rim, slopping over at the foot. A washcloth had dropped over the overflow, partly damming it. He tugged the sopping cloth aside, and heard a satisfying gurgle as the overflow took water down the drain, even as he shut off the faucets. Thankfully he'd got to it before the flood could spread beyond a small puddle. He rung out the washcloth and used it to dab up the spillage as he muttered at his carelessness.

Distracted he didn't hear the soft click from downstairs.

He continued mopping, then draped the freshly wrung cloth over the faucets. Poured in some muscle soak that he got up to a good froth after swishing his hands through the deep water. He was beginning to look forward to his dip.

But first he had to check.

Back at the window he snooped between the curtains even as he began stripping out of his clothing.

His back was to the bedroom door, so he'd no idea a figure stole up on him along the hall…

…The man who crept towards Quinn had already slipped away the key he'd used to let himself in, placing it deep in a pocket of his coveralls. Before proceeding through the house, listening to Quinn's soft self-derision, and the splashing of water, he'd pulled on his ski-mask and goggles, though he suspected Quinn would still recognise him the second he laid eyes on him. He paused at the threshold as Quinn stepped out of his jeans, then bent to take another peak between the curtains, dressed only in his jockey shorts.

Quinn was pathetic, half the build of the man who stalked him. But he could prove noisy, and an encumbrance if allowed to voice his screams while trying to kick free. The man stepped aside, concealing himself behind the jamb as Quinn turned for the bathroom, again muttering under his breath. For reasons known only to him, Quinn didn't close the bathroom door: maybe he was used to bachelorhood and didn't feel the need or the privacy of closed doors in his own home. That only made things simpler for the disguised man.

He stepped into the bedroom, feeling his boots sink into the carpet's deep pile. He would unavoidably leave tread marks, so must ensure he brushed them out before leaving the house. Covered as he was head to foot, his sleeves and trouser cuffs sealed to his gloves and boots with duct tape, hair and mouth covered by the ski mask, there'd be slim chance of leaving any trace evidence behind, best he remember to ensure he left nothing as obvious as a footprint.

He'd brought a gun with him, but that was only as a safeguard. He left it holstered on his thigh, choosing to go with the knife he'd already chosen for the task. It was a blade taken from Quinn's fishing tackle box, when the killer had earlier visited the office shared with his business partner. The knife was sturdy, and locked in place once opened. It was an ideal fisherman's tool, good for stabbing, gutting, or for snicking through snagged lines. It was scalpel sharp. Plus it wouldn't be an untoward discovery after Quinn's body was found.

The man took a quick peak around the door. Quinn stood with his back to him, his bony ass paler than the rest of his sun-touched body. He had his face in his hands, using the balls of his thumbs to compress the fatigue out of his eyes. He visibly trembled. The man shook his head in disgust. Pitiful as Quinn might be, the man had no pity for him. In fact he had only a deep-seated hatred of the skinny wretch, and it would please him no end when the little bastard was dead and gone.

'Knock-knock!' the man said, and Quinn jumped so high his outstretched arms almost scuffed the ceiling.

Whoever Quinn had been watching out for, it wasn't the man in full disguise. As Quinn had spun around, one arm out to the side, grabbing at the sink for balance, the man stepped deeper into the bathroom firmly blocking the only escape route. Quinn wore a dazed expression, as he looked the man up and down: he didn't appear conscious of his nakedness or vulnerability. But that didn't last. His gaze settled on the soulless goggles, and his mouth opened and a spark of comprehension lit his dull gaze.

'Wh-what are *you* doing here?' he finally croaked.

'Do I need give you three guesses?' said the man and held up the lock knife.

'No.' Quinn shook his head in disbelief, not in response to the man's snarky question.

'Yes.' The man caught the edge of the door and pushed it shut behind him.

'Please. Please don't do this,' Quinn moaned.

'I have to,' said the man, 'and to be honest I *want* to. In fact, I'm going to enjoy doing what should've been done a long time ago.'

'Please...I had nothing to do with...'

'There you go again, wasting your breath.' The man moved forward.

The bathroom was about twelve feet by fifteen: a fair size, but woefully compact when trying to avoid a remorseless killer armed with a sharp blade. It didn't stop Quinn trying to run. He threw his meagre weight past the man, but a slap of a forearm knocked him back into the narrow gap he'd previously occupied between the bath and the sink. Quinn kept moving though, ducking low this time and trying to dodge under the upraised knife. If the man wished he could easily jam the blade between his shoulder blades and that would have been it for Parker Quinn. But he'd brought the blade for a different reason. He merely lifted one leg, bracing it against Quinn's chest, then booted him back into the cramped space again.

Quinn was bleating, pleading, but the man was confident the sounds wouldn't carry. Quinn scurried by the sink, one hand braced on it, using it as a prop to help hurdle past the man. He was knocked backwards again.

'You can stop trying to run. It's not happening,' said Quinn's tormentor.

Quinn was still desperate enough to try to get by again. He almost succeeded, and got a hand on the door handle, slapping it down before the larger man grabbed the nape of his neck and dragged him around. The backs of Quinn's thighs butted up against the rim of the bath.

'Don't. Please! I beg you! Don't do this!' Quinn must have known his pleas were as pointless as his desperate attempts at flight, though it didn't stop him trying. 'We can sort this,' he cried, 'I'll give you anything you want. Money, I can get you money-'

'Shut up. Don't even go there.' The man clamped his left hand firmly over Quinn's mouth as he forced him backwards over the tub. To ensure compliance he held the tip of the blade under Quinn's chin. 'There's not enough money on earth,' he assured his captive, 'to buy back what you took from me.'

Quinn screamed in desperation, hollering the man's name for all who might hear. Muffled by the leather glove, Quinn's voice was nonetheless still recognisable to the man. He couldn't chance anyone overhearing. He immediately thrust Quinn down and the smaller man went butt first into the bath. He was forced around, his head jammed under water.

'Don't dare mention my name again, or I'll make you sorry,' the man growled. His words were wasted, because beneath the surface frothing bubbles surrounded Quinn, jetting from beneath his attacker's gloved fingers. There was no possible way he could hear the warning, not while his mind rebelled against drowning. His arms flailed at the edges of the tub, water splashing everywhere. His feet kicked and pounded on the foot of the tub. One of Quinn's knees thudded solidly in the man's gut as he leaned down, exerting pressure, forcing Quinn deeper. He held him submerged until the fight went out of him. For a moment he feared he'd held Quinn down too long, because when he released the pressure from Quinn's face, he stayed as he was submerged in the steaming water.

A second passed, and another.

It had never been his plan to drown Quinn. No, he had to make things look as if Quinn was behind his own departure. He was reaching to tug Quinn out the water, when the smaller man's eyes suddenly snapped wide, and he erupted upwards, gurgling out a stream of water that had invaded his throat. Relieved, but undeterred from his mission, the man grasped Quinn's hair and pushed him under once more. He held him for a count of ten, before again tugging him to the surface. Quinn's eyes rolled in their sockets; he coughed and spluttered but was still alive, though now sufficiently weakened.

The man grabbed Quinn's right wrist first, dug the tip of the blade into the radial artery and sliced lightly upwards towards the elbow. Blood jetted for the ceiling. Unavoidably it spattered the man's coveralls, but it didn't matter. He must avoid getting blood on his boots though. He pushed Quinn's arm under water, and immediately grabbed at Quinn's right wrist. He repeated the cutting, making tentative slashes, but then a final time with more effort and determination, as if Quinn had dithered at first before making the decision to end it all and had started with that wrist. Gore again squirted, but already there was a lessening in the blood pressure, so it didn't jump as high. It still got on the wall and over the faucets before the man shoved the bleeding arm under water. Lastly he dropped the knife between Quinn's legs. Quinn made a futile attempt at grabbing the knife, but as well as the arteries the tendons had been damaged, and his fingers wouldn't work to close on the hilt. The man stood over him, pressing him gently at the centre of his chest to keep him submerged in the bath. The blood pulsed from Quinn, steadily turning the water scarlet. As Quinn should have regained cognizance from his near drowning, equally his mind closed down through lack of oxygenated blood reaching his brain. He made the occasional feeble attempt at rising, and one time his left arm slapped out of the bath, spilling droplets on the floor, making the man step away. But he was going, and his dying was in near silence.

Things had gone to plan, his killer thought, and once he'd placed the other items he'd brought, and ensured there was no incriminating trail back to him as he left, then he could be home in time for dinner. He was glad, because murder proved hungry work.

19

'So? The wanderer returns, does he?'

Rink was ready to leave by the time I got back to the Clayton house. He didn't say as such, but I knew he was mildly pissed that the few hours he was happy to spell for me had turned into a long day. What could I say? It wasn't as if I'd taken a liberty with his generosity, things had simply overtaken me since the moment I approached Tommy Benson and he'd took to his heels. It was unavoidable that I ended up in an interview suite before being sprung by Bryony and Holker. After that, the time we'd spent at Benson's house had grown much longer after the discovery of the shredded note, which Holker subsequently discovered reflected the exact wording in an email sent via the iPad he'd seized from Benson's bedroom. Once that was done, and Holker called in the result, a warrant was obtained to conduct a full search of the property. Holker wanted to supervise the search; I wanted to get out of there. In the end a compromise was struck, and Bryony drove me back to where I'd abandoned my – or rather Rink's – ride outside the laundromat earlier, before she returned to the house off Nebraska Avenue.

While driving me to the Ford, Bryony had shared a hypothesis.

'Whoever is behind the emails is being clever or extremely stupid. From the look of things, they've been paying Benson to be a middleman for them. But choosing a semi-illiterate punk to pen the messages for them is nuts, particularly if they had to supply the wording like that. If it was unavoidable that he do it for them, you'd think they'd ensure that Benson fully destroyed the handwritten note afterwards.' She looked across at me, inviting my opinion.

'Maybe he was given clear instructions to destroy it, but Benson didn't follow them. You saw the state of his house; he's not one for menial tasks like cleaning up. Maybe he thought that ripping the letter was enough, and it was too much effort to do anything else.' I shrugged. 'He probably never expected to be found out. He'd trashed the letter, and if he hadn't been flattened by a van, there was no way anybody would have gone to his house and found it. The iPad is something else. He went to the trouble of setting up an anonymous Hotmail account, and I'm guessing that the SIM card is stolen or untraceable, so that tells me there was some effort made at keeping his involvement secret. I'm betting the iPad didn't belong to him; the same person who put him up to sending the emails, and to going to Clayton's house those times, supplied it.'

'That's what I think,' said Bryony. 'But I've no idea why.'

I told her about my visit to Wild Point Bait, and how the owner had told me he'd let Benson go. 'He mentioned there being a conflict of interests. I didn't push him at the time, and maybe we should confirm it with him, but I'm betting Benson was doing work for someone else in the bait and tackle trade. Someone who has also got a personal beef with Andrew Clayton.'

'The prime suspect being Parker Quinn. I told you Clayton tried to buy him out, right? Quinn resisted though, but theirs has been a shaky business relationship since. Is it too far-fetched to believe Quinn is trying to have Clayton implicated in Ella's murder? If his wife's murder was pinned on him, and Clayton imprisoned, Quinn would have the business all to himself again.'

'There was the presence of Quinn's hair in the glove Benson dropped that time,' I admitted.

'Transference could have taken place if Quinn also supplied Benson with the gloves. If Quinn had him throw that brick through the door, he'd have made sure the guy didn't do anything stupid like leaving fingerprints for us to find. Ironic that by doing so he'd give us evidence more damning.'

I exhaled. I still didn't buy it. I knew that Bryony didn't either, but what tenuous evidence she had was certainly pointing towards Quinn.

'Once we're done at Benson's place,' Bryony said, 'next stop will be a visit with Parker Quinn. The previous search didn't turn up anything that implicated him in sending the messages, but that was then. Before we had anything to compare against. For one thing, I'd like to seize a sample of his handwriting to compare against the letter we found.'

As she pulled the car on to the lot outside the now locked and shuttered laundromat, her cell phone rang. She pulled up shy of Rink's Ford and took out her phone. Her eyebrows went up. 'Holker,' she told me, and hit the answer button. I could have got out and walked the few short yards to the Ford, but I hung on.

'You're kidding me?' she said after making brief greetings with her partner. I looked at her for clarification, but she held up a finger, asking me to wait. 'Well,' she went on, 'that certainly changes things doesn't it? Look, I'm dropping Hunter now. I'll be back with you in no time.'

She ended the call, and looked over at me. Her eyes were dizzy by whatever Holker had told her. With the freckles, the pixie haircut, and the way her nicked bottom lip pouted slightly, she looked about twelve years old.

'What?' I prompted.

She blinked slowly, and emotions played across her features, and I couldn't tell if she was relived or bemused.

'Holker found a gun. It was wrapped in cellophane and hidden in the crawlspace under Benson's house. It's too soon to say, and we'll need ballistic reports back, but the model matches one of the two guns used in the shooting of Ella Clayton. It looks as if Benson was there when she was murdered, Joe.'

'Or he was given the gun to hide,' I cautioned.

'Yeah, there is that. But if his benefactor is the same person who gave him the iPad and has been paying him to cause trouble, we might be close to identifying what really went on that night. Evidence always pointed at more than one man, hence the home invasion crew theory, so maybe Benson went along with the killer that night. Rounds from two different guns were dug from the walls don't forget, and there were faint footprints from more than one pair of boots. It looks as if we might have gotten a break here.'

I opened the door, and was about to get out. Bryony reached across and laid her fingers on my forearm, halting me.

'Joe, despite how Holker comes across at times, he said to tell you thanks. If you hadn't followed this lead we wouldn't be anywhere with the case just now.'

I didn't know how to answer. Accepting thanks from Holker was akin to accepting an offer of cash from a loan shark – I dreaded to think what the return payment terms were.

Bryony smiled. 'I should say thanks too.'

'You should get back to Benson's place,' I told her.

'Yeah,' she said, but it didn't stop her leaning across and pulling my face to hers. She kissed me on the lips. Chastely. 'That's just for starters,' she promised.

I drove back to the Clayton house in a mixed mood. I don't know how I felt about what had gone on that day: I was saddened that a man had died, but any guilt I felt towards Benson's needless death was tempered somewhat by the knowledge he could have been personally involved in Ella's murder. I was happy that the detectives had got a break in their case, and that I'd helped get them there. But I was also slightly concerned that all emphasis would now be placed on Parker Quinn. I'd met the man only once, but he hadn't struck me as a violent man, or even anyone who could contemplate murder, let alone organise one. There was something decidedly wrong with the scenario, and there were clues in the case that just didn't sit in the correct row for me. The damned missing ring still bugged me. If it was found at either Benson's house or Quinn's then I'd be happier to go with the consensus that the two men had been working together to discredit Andrew Clayton. But somehow I didn't think it would be. The only thing that left me feeling mildly happy was the lingering feeling of Bryony's kiss on my lips, and the promise of more to come.

My happy mood was leavened as I pulled up at the house and saw the steepling of Rink's brows as he strode towards me, making the quip about the wanderer returning.

'You wouldn't believe the day I've had,' I said as I walked to meet him.

'Bet it was more eventful than mine,' he griped. 'Things have been so quiet, it was actually a highlight of the day when the kid got home and I got some conversation.'

'He ask you about pinkie deals?' I asked.

'Yup. Then he asked if it made us blood brothers. When I told him it was similar he went and got a pin and wanted to prick our thumbs.'

'You didn't go that far?'

'I told him that drawing blood wasn't necessary...unless you're a vampire.' Rink grinned. 'He told me I was funny. Not sure he was paying me a compliment.'

'Is Andrew home yet?' I passed over the car keys.

'Got back a few hours ago. Didn't have much to say to me. But that was OK.' Rink took a surreptitious glance over his shoulder to check he wasn't overheard. Not that he was fearful of Andrew's wrath, but the guy was paying our wages. 'The guy's a prick. He brought take-out Chinese food for him and the boy. Didn't offer to share.'

'He's a prick because he didn't give you any of his noodles?'

'No. He's a prick in general.'

Rink headed for the car, and I felt it was a good time to walk with him. With Tommy Benson out of the picture, my guard duties needn't be as vigilant as before.

'Find anything interesting?' I prompted.

Rink stood beside the car, looking back at the big house. 'Diddlysquat, brother. But that isn't to say there's nothing there. I managed to snoop around but didn't want to disturb anything in Clayton's private rooms. Maybe you'll get a chance next time he goes gallivanting.'

Gallivanting was a word Rink had learned from me. He thought it highly funny, and often poked fun at me for what he termed my strange Olde English vocabulary. This was the same guy who called people he didn't like *frog-giggers* and enjoyed knocking them *catawampus*. And who'd found *diddlysquat* during his snooping around the house.

'Who knows how that will pan out?' I offered a regretful shrug. 'Not sure how long we're going to keep this as a paying gig. See, the thing is, it looks as if the guy who was hassling Clayton won't be a problem anymore.'

A line appeared between Rink's brows, making the epicanthic folds in his eyelids deepen. 'You did have a more eventful day than me, then?'

I told him about Tommy Benson getting himself splattered on the highway, and what was subsequently found in his house and how the cops were now heading over to grab Parker Quinn.

Rink looked down and to one side. He wasn't seeing the crushed shells on the drive. 'I get where you're coming from. Cole won't require protection if the bad guys are out of the picture.' He shrugged. 'I guess Clayton will be glad to see the back of us: he was only going along with us being here for appearances sake.'

'I might be able to get one more night out of him,' I said.

'Maybe I shouldn't leave yet, in case you need a lift back home.'

'No. Get yourself off, Rink. You've been here longer than you should've been already. I'm going to go in and tell Clayton what happened with Benson; then I'm going to tell him to expect a visit from Bryony and Holker. They'll probably come by once Quinn's in custody, to update him.'

'OK. You've got my number. If you do get kicked out on your butt, gimme a call. I'll come fetch you.'

I smiled. 'When you do, I've a great shaggy dog story for you.'

He raised his thick eyebrows.

'Bet you don't believe me when I tell it,' I said.

'Hunter, when it comes to you, nothing surprises me.'

He drove away, and I stood outside until he was out of sight.

Then I went to tell Andrew Clayton the news, and try to gauge his reaction to it.

Once inside, I went directly into the sitting room. Clayton wasn't there, but Cole was. He was up late, but tomorrow wasn't a school day, so maybe his dad allowed him more leeway with his bedtime. He was sitting on the floor, his crossed legs under the coffee table, one elbow braced on its top while leaning over some open jotters. The boy glanced up at me from under his mop of wavy hair, and his mouth quirked into a smile. But that was all the attention I received. He immediately went back to his drawing. I watched as he poked out his tongue, deep in concentration as he tried his hardest to get things right. I moved towards him, glanced over his previous works of art depicting costumed superheroes battling monsters. They were damn impressive for a kid of his tender age. 'That's a fine talent you've got there, Cole,' I said.

'My mom showed me how,' Cole said.

'Then she had a great student. They're cool drawings.'

'Not really.' He shrugged off the compliment, bent back to the task. I understood why he wasn't too enthusiastic about accepting praise, because he was in fact tracing images from a comic book, and transferring the drawings to the jotter pad. I recalled completing similar art projects when I was a kid, overlaying tracing paper on somebody else's picture and making a line drawing of it. Flipping over the tracing paper, I would then follow the lines, pressing just hard enough to transfer the faint mirror image to a fresh piece of paper, that I'd then fill in with my own flourishes with felt-tipped pens and coloured pencils. It was good to see in this age of electronic devices that some kids still enjoyed good old-fashioned arts and crafts.

'Is your dad around?' I asked.

Without looking up from his latest masterpiece, Cole aimed his pencil over his head. 'He's in his den,' he said, and the impression I got from his tone, he felt his dad spent too much time in there, or maybe that it was because Cole didn't get to spend it with him.

It was good that Clayton was elsewhere in the house. I preferred to be alone with him when I told him his tormentor was dead, and his business partner – Cole's beloved Uncle Parker – was the prime suspect in Ella's murder.

20

'Thomas Benson?' Andrew Clayton echoed my announcement. 'Nope, the name means nothing to me.' Behind the lenses of his spectacles, there wasn't even a flicker of his eyes. Some people claim you can tell when a person is lying through observation of 'tells' in their features, the random flick of a muscle, the dilation response of the pupils. There is much talked about how liars' eyes flick up and to one side as they access the side of the brain most prone to fantasy, but in my experience it's bullshit. So much for the eyes supposedly being the windows to the soul. Some liars can look you square on and deliver even the wildest of mistruths without a ghost of movement in their features – anywhere. But to me, Clayton's lack of response told me more than any facial quirks or tics ever could. He was lying though his teeth.

I'd found Clayton in his den-cum-home office where Cole had directed me. I knocked and he bade me enter like he was the lord of the manor. He was sitting behind a large wooden desk, on which was a new computer, with a wireless keyboard and mouse. I couldn't see what he was working on, but assumed it had something to do with boats or fishing paraphernalia. After returning from work and greedily chowing down on take-out food without offering my starving friend a morsel, Clayton must have showered. He more or less glowed, his freshly shaved pate shiny under the lights, and was dressed only in a cotton shirt and leisure shorts. I could smell the fragrant aroma of soap that had pervaded the atmosphere, mingling with the ozone from his desktop computer. I fought the urge to sneeze.

There was nowhere to sit, but that suited me fine. I closed the door so that Cole wouldn't overhear us, and propped my hips against it, folding my arms over my chest. I told him about my eventful day: at least some of it, culminating in Benson stepping into the path of a speeding van on the highway.

'He was better known as Tommy Benson,' I clarified. 'Worked for Wild Point Bait until recently. Ever had any business dealings with them?'

'Wild Point…that's that chicken shack up near Oldsmar isn't it? Yeah, I've had dealings with them in the past. Not for a year or two though. I tend to leave the smaller stuff to Parker: he handles the wholesale end of our business while I go after the bigger fry. I deal mostly in boats, engines and outboard motors, jet skis, where the big bucks are.'

'Benson left his previous job under a cloud,' I said. 'From what I can tell his boss was pleased to see the back of him.'

'Can't say I'm sad to hear of his passing either,' Clayton said. It took him a moment to realise how harsh he sounded. 'Course, I wouldn't wish what happened to him on anyone. But the guy was causing me trouble, so I'm happy there'll be an end to it now.'

'You say you didn't know him, had no dealings with him, but this is the same guy who knocked you on your arse at the gate. He seemed to have some sort of personal beef with you.'

'Are you the cops now, Hunter? What's with all these questions? How do I know what goes on in the mind of a fuck-up like this Benson guy? You said yourself he attacked you, tried to kick you in the nards when you approached him. Well, he might just have done the same to me, without any reason.'

I hadn't told Clayton about finding the shredded letter, or that the detectives suspected it had been supplied to Benson by a third party. I hadn't told him about the iPad, or the gun, either, and wasn't about to. That was for Holker or Bryony to do. A small part of me wanted to secure my employment for another night at least. Rington Investigations could do with the incoming cash, but payment was only a tiny part of my motivation. I was intrigued by what was really going on and didn't want to leave before discovering the full story. 'The cops think Benson was working on somebody else's behalf, someone with a reason to discredit you. The fact Benson worked in the same industry as you is quite telling, wouldn't you agree?'

'Half the guys on Tampa Bay work in the same industry as I do.' Clayton made a dismissive noise in the back of his throat. 'Yeah, I've pissed a few of them off in my time. Look around you, Hunter. I'm a successful businessman who's made my millions while they're still doing fifteen-dollar trips with tourists. My success breeds resentment from others in my line of work. Any number of the jealous sons of bitches could've been behind Benson...' He grunted in thought. 'Some more than others.'

'Names?'

'Look in the yellow pages under "boat hire". Then take your fucking pick.'

I let it go. Changed the subject with a nod towards the computer. 'Is this also a replacement from what the home invasion crew stole?'

Clayton stared back at me. His spectacle lenses reflected the bluish light from the screen saver, and his mouth was down turned.

'I asked around about some of your things that aren't easily replaced,' I went on. 'The stuff taken that had sentimental value. Ella's ring.' I studied his response, but still there were no tells in his features or posture. 'I tried the usual suspects, even had to shake one bunch down, but...well, I'm sorry, I didn't find the ring.'

He exhaled slowly through his nose. Then he sat back, and laced his fingers over the dome of his stomach. 'I doubt it'll ever be found,' he said. 'But thanks for trying. I owe you one.'

'Forget about it.' I nodded backwards. 'Priority is that Cole is safe, right?'

'Right.'

'So until we know otherwise, we assume there's still a third party who intends causing you trouble. You want me to stay on until the cops give the all clear?'

Finally a reaction flickered through him, as if he knew something I didn't, instead of to the contrary. He checked himself saying something untoward. Yet in the next instant he'd recovered, and he opened his hands palms up. 'As long as it takes,' he said. As an afterthought he leaned forward and manipulated the computer keyboard. 'Now, if you're done questioning me, I've clients to get back to. Mind closing the door on your way out?'

I left without comment, or fuss. Closed the door respectfully. Walked away down the hall frowning. Whatever reaction I'd expected, Clayton's wasn't it. When I'd chased Benson from the trees down by the pond that time, Clayton had acted the tough guy, bragging about what he'd do if he got his hands on the prowler. This time he'd met the news of Benson's death coolly. Yeah, he'd made that remark about being happy there'd be an end to his harassment, but I'd expected more. Where were the questions: who, what, when, why and how? Clayton had been uninterested, no dispassionate. However, I had to remind myself that people reacted differently during phases of the grieving process. There were times when they'd rage and scream, others when they fell into a funk of despondency. Perhaps Clayton had hit a point where he'd thought so long about death that he'd resigned himself to its inevitability. I'd been in the same place in the past. Sometimes it took a catalyst to stir the emotions again, and I wondered how Clayton would react when another inevitability occurred. A visit from Detectives VanMeter and Holker wouldn't be long coming. When they informed him they'd arrested Parker Quinn, Clayton might go volcanic, but who knew? Whatever the outcome, I'd a feeling tonight was going to be my last in Clayton's house as an employee.

While I was in Clayton's office, Cole had taken to his own room. The soft strains of conversation came from beyond his closed door, and the flickering blue light around its frame told me he was watching TV at low volume. I thought about knocking, checking on the boy, but decided against it. Last night's nightmares might trouble him again, but for now it were probably best that I allowed the boy to settle. It'd be best if he were asleep by the time the cops arrived.

There was no imminent danger I could imagine. I hadn't slept but for some short spells in the chair last night, and was beginning to tire, and had to stifle a yawn as I trudged down the stairs. I hadn't eaten since breakfast, those bagels and cream cheese now a distant memory in my gut. I headed for the kitchen. It still held the odour of Chinese food. I began rustling up something less exotic, finding eggs, cheese, milk and a green pepper in the fridge that I began forming into an omelet. I layered butter onto some thick wedges of bread cut from the loaf. Not exactly a feast, but enough to put me on for the time being. While waiting for the omelet to cook, I stood in the kitchen, feeling out of sorts.

The day had been a busy one. Forward momentum always suited me best. But since Bryony dropped me back at the laundromat, it was as if a parachute had opened behind me, dragging me to a halt. Eating and sleeping were necessities, but they only added to the creeping torpor draping over me. I ate in a hurry, as much to be doing something as refueling, and washed it down with coffee from a pot Clayton had left on the hotplate. There was a dishwasher, but I elected to wash the dishes and pans in the sink. I dried them and put them away. Cleaned down the worktops. Menial stuff, but it kept me moving. Stopped me from concentrating on the odd feeling of being in somebody else's place. Back home at Mexico Beach I'd felt as if my beach house suffered the lingering effects from the violence that recently visited it, and the same could be said of now. In this kitchen, those violating her home had disturbed Ella Clayton. She hadn't died here, but through in the sitting room after being chased there, but this was where her terror had begun, and I felt the memory of that terrible incident lingering in the atmosphere, pervading it the way the smell of soy sauce, and now fried eggs did.

If I paused to give the notion of ghosts any credibility it might be enough to throw me over the edge. I'd killed many people during my time as a counter-terrorism operative with Arrowsake, and also a good few since: if there were such things as vengeful sprits stalking the earth then I would attract quite a crowd. It was enough that my dreams were often troubled by the accusing faces of the dead, without suffering their relentlessly pursuit through the waking hours. Yet there, in her kitchen, I could swear I could sense Ella's presence. It was probably my conscience on overdrive, and the sense that I should do something more, but I made a silent promise to her that I wouldn't let this go. I'd pledged to protect her son, and it went without saying that I'd adhere to it, but I added the extra assurance that I'd do all I could to bring her resolution too.

It prompted me to an act I'd have never contemplated otherwise.

Forcing entry to the house, Ella's attackers had kicked through the doors that led from the garage to the adjoined utility space, and hence through the kitchen door. Following the police investigation, the doors had been replaced, and new locks installed. Clayton kept a set of keys on his person, and the doors had spares inserted in the locks within the house that I'd used when locking the house down at night. They'd be missed, but I'd also spotted an extra batch of keys in one of the kitchen drawers. They were still attached to a plastic fob bearing the name of the locksmith. I withdrew them and secreted them in my trouser pocket. I might be leaving in the morning, but I'd be back.

21

Detective Holker shared a look with Bryony that expressed exactly how she also felt. Evidence that might break their case was right there in front of them, but it wasn't a sense of relief she experienced. It was frustration. No, it was a stronger emotion...*aggravation*. Was there anything worse for a cop than finding the murderer they'd been chasing, only to find they'd defied the proper course of justice by taking their own life?

Arriving at Parker Quinn's home a few minutes earlier, they'd found the house lit in a number of rooms, and his car parked on the drive, but repeated knocking on his door had failed to rouse him. His cell phone was still with Tampa PD, undergoing forensic analysis, so Bryony had called the dispatcher back at One Police Centre, and asked that she ring Quinn's landline. Standing on his threshold they heard the phone ringing inside the house. It rang out. Holker made an executive decision: they were here to arrest Quinn and it was highly likely he was hiding from them. He forced entry, first breaking the door pane, then reaching in and uncoupling the locks. Weapons drawn they entered, clearing each room before proceeding. Holker was first to reach the master bedroom, the first to see the handwritten note placed at the centre of the bed. Bryony followed him into the room, and turned towards the bathroom, her gun ready should Quinn make a break for it from within the en suite bathroom.

'Tampa PD,' she'd announced. Trusting Holker would cover, she reached for the door handle with her left hand.

'I think it's safe to go in, Bryony,' said Holker. He shook his head, and she followed his gaze to the bed. 'Suicide note.'

Taking no chances, Bryony still prepared for trouble, but the door swung inward on a scene that only forced a sour taste to her mouth.

Parker Quinn lay nude in his tub. Only his head was above the waterline, bent back over the rim, wedged slightly between the faucets. His mouth was wide, but his tongue had retreated back into the recess of his open mouth. He'd upper dentures and they were askew. In direct contrast to the vivid scarlet of the water, his features were bleached of colour. His bathing water was mingled with so much of Quinn's lifeblood that it served to protect his modesty, and concealed his hands that had slipped down either side of his hips, but there was no doubt what he'd done. Blood had sprayed up the walls, even touching the ceiling, and there was one diluted patch of blood down the side of the bath, various spatters on the floor.

Bryony's instinct was to check for life.

Holker caught her elbow, stalling her.

She didn't argue. Quinn was beyond assistance. But that wasn't it. Holker had halted her because they'd just come from another potential crime scene and were in danger of causing cross contamination.

Holker called in their discovery, requested that another detective picked up the reins, then secured the scene, from their place at the foot of Quinn's bed. From there Quinn's sightless eyes still bore into Bryony, but she didn't look away.

'This is bullshit,' she said.

'Couldn't agree more,' said Holker. 'The son of a bitch got off too lightly.'

They shared the glance, and Bryony exhaled in anger at how close they'd come to catching Quinn alive. There was no steam rising off the bath water, but she made herself a bet it still wasn't icy cold. She turned her attention to the note. Read it in monotone. Quinn bleating on about how he couldn't live with the guilt any longer. How he'd shot Ella, because he was too scared to confront her husband. How he'd tried to make the murder look like a bungled robbery, then thought how he could ruin Clayton after the event by making it look as if he had organised his wife's murder.

'*This* is bullshit,' she said a second time, placing emphasis on the first word this time, and indicating the note. She wished she'd brought the evidence seized from Benson's house with her for confirmation, but she was certain the handwriting was the same. But therein lay the problem for her. It was too alike. It was too neat, too precise to have been the final words of a man planning to slit his wrists, then sit calmly in his bath while he bled out. 'I'd stake my ass that it's a forgery,' she said.

'Must admit the thought has gone through my mind,' Holker said, and he walked to the bathroom door. 'You see that?' He indicated a bath mat alongside the bath. It was clean, as if recently laundered. 'And that?' This time he indicated the spillage down the side of the bath, the blood that had jetted on the walls and ceiling. 'There's not a trace of blood on it. You ask me, I'd say the mat was placed there after the real killer wiped away any footprints he made when he was holding Quinn down.'

Bryony had also spotted the obvious. The surface of the bath water was scummy with blood, but nearer Quinn's feet there were still frothy bubbles. A branded bottle of muscle soak sat on a tiled shelf behind the faucets. 'Who planning on bleeding to death would bother adding bubble bath?'

Holker was impressed, but being the guy he was, he didn't offer praise lightly. He pointed out the pile of Quinn's clothing, discarded on the bed. Top of the bunch were his jockey shorts. 'Something else obvious you might've missed. From experience, I can't recall a suicide stripping naked before they got in the bath and opened their veins. Most of them usually leave on their clothing, or only strip down to their underwear. Some have experienced enough shame before they do the deed, so when they are eventually found they want to retain some vestige of dignity.'

'So we're in agreement this is a set-up?'

'We'll have to wait for the full forensic report, but I think it's safe to say we won't be far wrong. This is first degree murder, Bryony.'

'It seems like a lot of trouble for the killer to have gone to; setting up the scene like this,' said Bryony, second thoughts assailing her.

'Unless Quinn already prepared his bath before the killer arrived. He filled the bath, undressed out here, and was truly caught with his pants down. I think the plan was always to pose the suicide – the murderer didn't write that note after killing Quinn – but made use of the tub when it was presented to him.'

Mulling over Holker's theory, she concurred with a nod. Though something was still troubling about the scenario. 'We had to break in. You've noticed that every window and door was locked, all the drapes and blinds shut tight? It's unlikely Quinn left an exterior door open. Now unless the killer went round and secured the house after he was done, which I doubt, he managed to get inside without causing any damage or noise that would've alerted Quinn.'

'That suggests he had a key, right? Which would also suggest he was known to Quinn.'

'Or working with him.' Bryony placed a hand over her face. 'Oh, crap.'

'Tommy Benson,' Holker said.

'Benson,' she echoed. 'It didn't occur to me before but when Joe first approached him, he'd taken a bag of washing to the laundromat. I mean, did his house look as if it belonged to a man who made regular trips to a laundromat? What are the odds he was trying to get rid of Quinn's blood off his clothing? It would explain why he was so desperate to get away that he ran into traffic: he thought Hunter was a cop about to grab him.'

'We're making an assumption here,' Holker warned.

'Based on what we've seen and found, it's a fair one,' Bryony countered. 'Whether we're proved wrong in the long run, does it matter? I think it's something we need to follow up on.'

'Call it in,' said Holker. 'I want someone at the laundromat a.s.a.p. and that clothing seized.'

'The shop will be closed by now.'

'I don't care how late it is. Whoever gets dispatched I want them to make the manager unlock the shop. After Quinn didn't return for his load, I bet a member of staff put it to one side for safekeeping. I want that clothing. Even if it has been laundered there might still be some incriminating evidence on it.' As Bryony pulled out her cell, Holker raised a hand. He'd more to add. 'And I want Benson's house searched top to bottom again. We weren't looking for evidence of this murder earlier. I want CSI to go over everything with a fine-toothed comb.'

'I'll get on it,' Bryony promised, but she didn't yet call in. She looked around the room again. 'To think we had nothing on Ella Clayton's murder a few hours ago. Now both of the suspected perps are dead. It's an unsatisfactory ending, Dennis, but at least it will quieten down a few of our critics. It doesn't escape me that we wouldn't have been here without Hunter's help.'

'We might still have a live suspect, though,' said Holker. 'What is it with your friend that people near him always end up dead?'

'That's a little unfair, Dennis…' Bryony halted. She stared at her partner, her mouth caught in a tight grimace. She'd often suspected that Holker wished their relationship were more intimate. From what she'd experienced he was a married man who actually loved his wife, so his feelings had always been at odds to her. But now she understood that the affection he had for her had nothing to do with getting in her pants: quite the opposite. He was disapproving of her relationship with Hunter because he feared for her. He acted more like a big brother looking out for a little sister. The realisation was endearing, and she reached out and placed her fingertips on his chest. 'You don't have to worry about me, you know.'

Holker looked faintly embarrassed. 'Just looking out for you, kid,' he said. 'At first I was only worried that your connection to him might harm your career, now I'm more concerned you'll end up as another fatality left in his wake.'

'Wow,' she said, allowing her fingers to drift away. 'I appreciate your concern, Dennis, but I think it's unfounded.' Hunter had a history of violence, there was no denying it, and even to date his line of work regularly placed him in the line of danger. Inevitably some people close to Hunter had died, but typically it was the criminals he fought who ended up on a slab. She knew Hunter was a good man at heart and despite what Holker thought, wasn't the demented vigilante he'd been labeled. He wasn't on a single-minded crusade to clean up the criminal element of the world; his motivation went deeper than that. And it was simpler. He was a protector. His methods might not sit well with some cops, but what Hunter did was defend the helpless. When she'd asked for his help on this case, she knew he'd be hooked as soon as he learned there was a vulnerable child involved. That told her everything she needed about him, and she wished Holker could see the same admirable trait in him. Holker however would always see Hunter as reckless, and those around him prone to the fall-out from his actions.

Holker snorted but it was in good humour. 'Quinn only met Hunter, what…two days ago? Benson, once they came face to face, only lasted minutes after his first encounter. You telling me that guy isn't cursed with the mark of Cain?'

'Now you're just being nuts,' she said, but she also chuckled.

This was no place for humour, though, and both detectives realised it. They squeezed away their smiles, and when Bryony made the call and relayed Holker's instructions she was clipped and professional about it, pacing back and forth. All the while, Parker Quinn's half-closed eyes seemed to follow her every move. Ending her call, Bryony turned her back on him and looked instead at Holker. Her partner was staring at the suicide note on the bed.

'Something stills bothers me,' Holker said.

'About Benson being the murderer?'

'The torn letter Hunter found at Benson's place: we thought someone had written it for him.'

Bryony immediately understood where his mind was leading. 'That's right, because the samples we compared it to of Benson's writing were barely literate. So we have to ask ourselves, if it wasn't Parker Quinn behind it, who wrote the bogus suicide note for him?'

'Fuck,' Holker snapped. 'There's a third perp still out standing.'

'Yeah,' Bryony said, and her aggravation at being denied the proper course of justice by both Quinn and Benson's deaths evaporated. 'And do you know what that means, Dennis? You might even get yourself a living suspect.' As an afterthought she pipped him to the post with a snarky remark. 'Don't worry, I'll make sure Hunter doesn't get to him first.'

22

Footsteps padding downstairs roused me from an easy chair in the sitting room. I'd rested there for hours, while still being on guard. There was no imminent danger I could think of so could have retired to bed, but I wasn't asleep, not fully, just drifting. All the lights were off on the ground floor, and my view through the large window allowed me to see across the grounds, past the American flag that the breeze fought to stir, towards where the driveway swept towards the electronic gate. I'd been watching for headlights, expecting Bryony and Holker to turn up, but then the hour had grown late, and segued into the wee small hours, and now into pre-dawn. Throughout the hours I'd mulled over what I'd learned and what still puzzled me about the mess I'd become embroiled in. Nobody has ever accused me of being a good detective: usually I'm forced to react and to think on my feet, where I don't have much time for navel-gazing while ordering and reordering clues in my mind. This job had been different, there'd been lots of time spent ruminating, and in some way it proved more tiring than fighting my way out of an ambush. There were things that bothered me still, and the more I gave them thought the troublesome clues were leading me in only one direction, and to one person in particular.

And then, there he was entering the sitting room as I stood up in the pre-dawn gloom before him.

Andrew Clayton regarded me from the doorway, his bulk almost filling it. His posture was wary, head hunched down on his wide shoulders. For an instant I felt the spurt of adrenalin shoot through me, and I tensed to meet an attack.

'It's only me, Hunter,' Clayton announced, his voice a low rasp. There was emotion in it that gave me pause, and forced me to relax.

'I know,' I told him. 'What is it?'

We were both standing in the dark, a bit ridiculously, but neither of us reached for a light switch.

'Could we step outside?' Clayton asked.

I would have asked why we couldn't speak right there, but was intrigued by his question, and where it might lead. Clayton immediately doused any suspicions I had about his motive to get me out the house.

'I don't want Cole over-hearing,' he said.

Instinctively my head rose, as if by looking through the ceiling I could check the whereabouts of the boy, and if he was sleeping soundly. There was no hint of noise to suggest the boy was out of bed and creeping along the landing to eavesdrop. But Clayton had a point: there was something he didn't want Cole to hear, and a walk outside together would negate any chance of it happening. 'You're the boss,' I said.

Clayton turned away, heading for the front door. When I stepped into the vestibule, he was eyeing the joinery work shoring up the smashed door pane. The ply-board was a reminder of his harassment. He glanced back at me, then at the door again. 'Think that will be safe to get fixed now that another brick isn't going to damage it?'

I didn't answer. He already knew Benson was out of the picture, so I took it he'd heard that Parker Quinn had been taken in by the police, the reason he didn't want Cole to hear about his Uncle Parker being a bad guy. He'd put off making repairs, expecting a repeat attack on his property; perhaps he'd been right to wait, because if I hadn't disturbed Benson that time down by the pond, who knew what the guy had been planning? Maybe he'd targeted another window for a lobbed stone. Anyway, now both conspirators were no longer an issue, there wasn't any likelihood of repeat vandalism. Then again, if my suspicions were to be credited, Clayton would know it was safe to make repairs.

He opened the door and went out onto the porch. He walked stealthily, conscious of his weight on the boards. He needn't have bothered tiptoeing because I'd already determined that none of the boards sung out. I followed, pulling the door shut as he went down the steps. Without waiting, Clayton walked along the front of the impressive dwelling, forcing me to follow. I did so with a sense of wariness that I might be being led into a trap. My SIG was snug in its carry position. I didn't bother reaching towards it. Only followed where Clayton was taking me. He went around the side of the garage, on to the lawn that sloped gently towards the pond. The same breeze that struggled to shift the heavy flag out front was having an easier time with the long reeds along the pond's bank, and with the treetops that surrounded it. The storm clouds had well and truly passed, and the sky was a deep indigo spangled with stars, even as the sun made its first stab at climbing over the eastern horizon. The tidal breeze was warm, and I suspected that by mid-morning it would be furnace hot.

Clayton had dressed for the day. He wore an open-necked white shirt, grey trousers and black loafers. On his left wrist was an expensive Breitling watch. The round lenses of his glasses reflected the still pond, making them equally fathomless. But that was only until he turned fully towards me and I got a clear look at his sclera, which were bloodshot. And the lids were puffy: I'd swear Clayton had been crying. He could be a good actor, he'd proven that already if my suspicions were to be trusted, but I doubted it when it came to the gentler emotions. Suddenly doubt wedged into my mind, like a rigid hand forcing back the accusations I was prepared to call Clayton on.

I waited for him to speak.

It took him another moment to gather himself. He looked out across the pond again; unable to meet my gaze for fear his tears would deem him weak.

'It's Parker,' he said.

'Yeah,' I replied.

'Did the police call you already?'

I shook my head, even though he couldn't possibly see me as he stared over the water. 'After Bryony dropped me, I knew she was going back to arrest him.'

'You didn't say,' he said, and his voice had taken on an accusatory tone.

'At the time there was nothing to tell,' I replied. 'The cops were following up on something they'd found at Benson's place. I wasn't party to the details, so didn't think I should be talking to you about it. Quinn's your business partner; it wasn't my place to tell you he might be the one behind Benson. I expected the detectives to come by last night. I guess events overtook them and they didn't get the chance.'

'Huh! Things certainly overtook them,' Clayton said, gesturing hard at the ground with one clenched fist. 'Detective Holker rang me on my cell; they're coming over in an hour, him and VanMeter. But he wanted to make sure I heard from him first, before I caught anything in the news.'

'They've charged him?' I asked, but felt that wasn't it. He snapped a look at me, sneering at my stupidity. Worse news was coming.

'Parker's dead!' His voice was raised, and it had been a good idea to walk some distance from Cole, because I felt the force of his words like a slap to the cheek.

What the hell happened? My first thought was that Parker Quinn had resisted arrest and been shot in the attempt. Holker and - more importantly to me – Bryony – were safe, because Clayton had just told me they were going to drop by, but had either of them shot Quinn?

'Not only is he dead, Parker was murdered!'

I was too stunned to reply.

'Didn't you hear me? I said he was murdered! Fucking killed.'

'I heard,' I said, 'I'm just trying to make sense of it.'

'Fucking Tommy Benson...' Clayton had restrained his anger for long enough. He suddenly kicked at the lawn, sending a divot of grass sailing towards the pond. It landed in the reeds. He rounded on me, and the ligaments in his neck were rigid, tight enough to strum a tune on. 'Holker says the sick fuck stole into Parker's house and killed him. Caught the poor schmuck in his bath and slit his wrists. Watched him bleed to death, then set up the scene to look like a suicide. He went to some detail, Holker said, even leaving a forged suicide note. They say that's why he ran from you when you caught him trying to wash the evidence from his clothes: he thought the game was up and was desperate to escape. No wonder the bastard jumped in front of a van. Can you fucking believe it?'

No I didn't. Sure I believed Quinn was dead, murdered even and posed to make it appear he'd killed himself, but I didn't imagine for a second that Benson was his slayer. The reason being, I believed the same man who'd killed Quinn was also the same as killed Ella. Tommy Benson just didn't fit the bill of someone capable of planning, let alone carrying out two murders, then elaborately dressing the scenes.

'I'm sorry to hear about your friend,' I said.

'Why? By all accounts he was the one sending Benson round, and the one sending those emails blaming *me* for Ella's murder. Why should you be sorry for the son of a bitch? I'm not.'

He was mixed up, or he was playing a role. His tears, and the tremble in his voice, told me that the news of his partner's death was as troubling as the thought Quinn had been plotting to ruin him.

'It'll be difficult for you when it comes to telling Cole. I think the boy was fond of his Uncle Parker.'

Clayton steepled both hands over his face. His fingertips dug into his forehead. 'Oh, God…'

I hadn't been around them when the boy had learned of his mother's murder, and for all I knew he'd bawled and screamed for a week, but from what I'd witnessed in the past few days Cole had been internalising his grief. It's often said that kids are resilient, and are able to bounce back from loss easier than most adults, but I knew from experience what it was like losing a parent at a young age. It can mess you up. Perhaps the news that his uncle had also been murdered would open the floodgates – the best of a bad situation – or it would send him deeper into his self-imposed hole. I didn't envy Clayton the task of telling the boy, but it was something that couldn't be put off. It was best that he broach it before Cole found out Parker was suspected of being responsible for Ella's killing.

'Do you want me to speak to Cole first?' I offered, though it was about the last thing I wished to do.

'No.' He lowered his hands, made an adjustment of his spectacles, and looked at me again. His anger of moments ago had dissolved fully, and now he only looked deeply sad. Was I totally on the wrong track?

At a loss at what to say next, I sighed at the floor between my feet.

I was prepared to ask some pointed questions, there were still anomalies that troubled me, but the sudden doubt held my tongue.

'Thanks for the offer, Hunter, but there are some things a son deserves to hear from his dad.'

'You're probably right,' I said.

'But I would like to ask you one thing?'

'Go on.'

'I'd rather Cole didn't hear anything until after the police have left. You were planning on leaving this morning. Do you mind sticking around for a few extra hours and keeping an eye on him?'

I hadn't planned on leaving, but I'd expected to. Clayton had obviously made a decision on ending my employment, and if not for the phone call from Holker I'd have been sent packing at first light.

'I don't mind one bit,' I reassured him.

He nodded, and turned towards the house.

'I'd like to ask *you* one thing, too,' I said to his back.

'What is it?' He stopped in his tracks, listening with his ear cocked over one shoulder.

'That time at the gate, when Benson hit you,' I said, 'you described him as having a tattoo on his hand.'

Clayton turned, peering at me quizzically. 'That's right,' he said, and tapped his left fingers on the skin between the index finger and thumb of his right. 'A spider's web. Why?'

'No reason,' I said, but he knew I was lying.

'Do you think it's important?'

'I was thinking about the home invasion crew. Some gang members tag themselves with tattoos. Just wondered if Benson might be part of the crew after all.'

My explanation sounded feasible. While asking him about the tattoo I'd been watching him for 'tells' again, and this time, judging by his forthright description of what and where it was coming without pause, I believed he was being truthful. But that only complicated matters.

23

The following evening found me in a bar off Nebraska Boulevard, not far from College Hill. It wasn't an establishment I'd normally frequent. The neighbourhood had a crime rate twice the national average, and was a well-known hangout of gangbangers who weren't shy when it came to car-jackings, drive-by-shootings, muggings or assaults with a deadly weapon. This end of Nebraska Boulevard was also notorious for five-dollar hookers, streetwalkers, rent boys and others catering to wilder vices. Ergo it attracted some unsavoury clients. Whenever I'd been on Nebraska in the past it was while engaged in my job. This evening was in part a social occasion, seeing as Bryony VanMeter had joined me. She'd chosen the bar, being roughly mid-way from where she lived and where I'd travelled via taxi from Andrew Clayton's place. We'd found a quiet corner in what was largely a quiet bar, but I expected that once night began to fall things would heat up quite a lot.

'I asked to meet here because they stock a full bar of imported beers, even Brit ones,' Bryony said, as she eyed my bottle with a slice of lime wedged in its neck.

'I like Corona,' I replied. 'What can I say?'

'Nothing.' Bryony picked up her glass. The beer in it was so dark it had to be Irish. She held its bottom towards me, and I obliged, knocking my bottle to it. 'Cheers,' she said.

'Cheers,' I replied. I'd no idea what we had to celebrate, though I was content to go along with her, and was happy in her company.

Bryony had foregone the semi-businesslike clothing she wore on duty, electing for a coral-coloured satin blouse over blue jeans, and heels that added a few inches to her willowy frame. The left side of her auburn hair was clipped back over her ear, disrupting the pixie cut, and making her all the more lovely for it. Her smatterings of freckles were actually complimented by the colour of her blouse, as were her deep honey eyes.

Sitting opposite her, I must have looked like a slightly worse for wear older colleague, fresh from a hard day's work, but a long way from a shower and shave. Then again, the few patrons in the bar appeared further removed from a wash, so perhaps I didn't look too bad by comparison.

'This a usual watering hole for you?' I asked.

'I chose it for the beer, and the music. I thought both might be to your taste.'

The Rolling Stones were doing their stuff on the jukebox, Mick Jagger claiming that time was on his side, and proving that there was more to him than a strutting rooster. It was my kind of music, though sometimes my Rhythm and Blues was from an even older school. 'You did well,' I assured her. 'But let's not plan on eating here, eh?'

'I'm not suicidal,' she quipped, then realised she might have spoken in bad taste, considering the events of yesterday.

It was a good point to discuss what we were really there for, while we still had some relative privacy. 'So you're positive Quinn was murdered, then?'

'We can't say one hundred per cent, not until the pathology reports come back, but everyone who's been to the scene are in agreement. There are too many inconsistencies for it to have been done by Quinn. Holker has had the evidence we've collected fast-tracked, now that we're investigating another possible murder and not just a stupid harassment case. We hope to have something solid to tell the press by end of day.' She thought for a moment. 'Remember the letter you found at Benson's house? Well it doesn't need an expert to tell the same person who wrote it also left the suicide note on Quinn's bed. At first we thought Quinn supplied the one to Benson, so he could follow the wording when sending the email, but that doesn't make any sense now. On the surface it appears to be Quinn's handwriting, I was able to do a comparison against other samples we found at his house, and at his office. We've brought in a forensic handwriting analyst to see what they make of it.'

In the old days criminals used to mock-up letters using words snipped from newspapers and magazines. Things had moved on, I guessed, then changed my mind. The way these letters had been created could be by an even older method. 'Could somebody have traced samples of Quinn's writing? If they had enough samples they could pick and choose the letters and words they needed to fashion a bogus letter.'

'Good thinking,' she said, with another tip of her beer glass, 'but we have already considered that. The analyst will be able to confirm it.' She squinted slightly as she considered me. 'How did you come up with that theory, anyway? Is it you're not as dumb as you look?'

'It's just something I saw at Clayton's place. Cole was tracing comic book characters and making a collage out of them. I asked him about it and he said his mom showed him how to do it.'

'You're thinking Andrew Clayton got the same idea from Ella?' Bryony asked.

'I did, the second you mentioned it. But why send emails blaming him for Ella's murder, if he is guilty? Sounds a bit too "Murder She Wrote" to me.'

'It wouldn't be the first case where it's happened. I did a database search and there was a doctor who murdered his wife, who went on to taunt the FBI to try to catch him with letters claiming to be from the killer, who also happened to be harassing the good doctor. He was trying to waylay blame from himself by inventing this mysterious game-playing killer. He was caught in the end.'

'You'll catch this killer too,' I reassured her.

'You've changed your mind about Clayton?'

'You put me in that house to find evidence pointing at him being Ella's killer,' I said. 'I've been unable to do that; but there are things that I can't quite get my head around.'

'Like what?'

'Ella's wedding ring for starters.' The original idea that a home invasion crew were responsible for the robbery never quite sat with me: not when they'd shown how cautious they were, and with their reluctance to kill anyone. I didn't see the crew responsible for the other robberies gunning down a woman, then looting a ring from her finger, when there were easier targets to concentrate their greed on. 'OK. Maybe one of the crew couldn't pass up the opportunity to snatch her jewellery, when it was there for the taking, but I get the sense that we're on the wrong track. Taking her wedding ring feels more personal to me. That initially made me feel that Clayton had done in his wife, and kept her ring as a memento or even sick trophy. I can't quite shake that feeling, but am having doubts.'

'What else? You said there were *things* still bothering you. Plural.'

'Clayton lied to me.'

'Perhaps it's simply in his nature to lie.'

'He said he didn't know Thomas Benson.'

'Maybe he didn't,' Bryony said, and took a long gulp of her Guinness. I watched her tongue darting as she mopped the froth from her lips.

'But he didn't correct me when I told him it was the same guy who knocked him on his arse that night.'

'Sorry? You're saying it wasn't Tommy?'

'I asked Quinn this morning about the guy who struck him, and he again described a tattoo, right here.' I touched my right hand next to my thumb. 'A spider's web. Well, I've been thinking. After Benson got run over, I tried to ease him on when it was clear he was dying. I held his right hand. It didn't have any tattoo, Bryony.'

She was frowning long before I'd finished. She had seen Benson's corpse at the scene, and at the morgue afterwards if I understood police procedures, and had viewed photographs in the murder book she and Holker were compiling. She knew I was correct: Benson didn't have the tattoo. 'Originally I thought Clayton invented the tattoo, to further muddy the waters,' I said, 'but now I'm not sure. When I spoke with him about it this morning, he didn't falter when asked about it. Even the best liars have to have very good memories to answer as quickly and forthrightly as he did.'

'So why do you think he's lying?' Bryony said, but I watched the penny drop, her head rolling slightly on her shoulders. 'You're suggesting Clayton *did* know Tommy Benson, but he didn't know the guy who attacked him?'

'No, that's not what I'm suggesting. It's the opposite: I believe he didn't know Tommy, as he claimed, but he knows exactly who the tattooed guy is. He gave me this bullshit story of going out to meet him at the gate when the guy pretended he was delivering a package. We were in the middle of a bloody thunderstorm at the time. You ask me, Clayton used the thunderstorm as cover, not expecting me to notice he'd left the house. He was talking to the guy at the gate in the pouring rain. After I'd had a go at him about protecting the integrity of the grounds, demanding for starters that he change the code on the electronic gate, he went out and opened it up. The guy was driving a Toyota Corolla for Christ's sake, not a delivery truck. This was a man who was being harassed, who'd agreed to hiring protection for his son, and he opens the gate to a total stranger he must've known was lying about a delivery?'

Playing devil's advocate, Bryony shrugged. 'Maybe he receives smaller deliveries by private car. Maybe he was suckered into opening the gate.'

'There was no delivery I could see. Besides, we now know there was none, it was just a story. The thing was, when Clayton saw me approaching, he said something I didn't hear. Next thing the guy hit him and took off.'

'You think he told the guy to punch him?'

'That's what it looked like to me. The guy hit him with a little love tap and he went down like a bag of crap. Clayton's a man who used to fight in bare-knuckle boxing matches and cage fights, not the type to have a glass jaw.'

Bryony considered my words. It took another gulp of beer before she had a comeback ready. 'So you're saying that Clayton knew the guy, and from what you're suggesting they've been working together. They're the ones who used Tommy Benson and Parker Quinn, setting them up as patsys?'

'The tattooed guy is still out there.'

'But if they'd been working together, why would Clayton describe him to you when he knows it might lead us to his partner in crime.'

'Yeah,' I sighed, 'there is that. Something you might want to look into though, Bryony…I'm now certain it wasn't Tommy Benson at the gate that night, but it was Tommy Benson's car the guy drove off in. They knew each other.' I thought about the bumper stickers that had led me to Benson, and though I didn't yet mention to Bryony, I made myself a mental note to go check something with the owner of Wild Point Bait.

'We found footprints from at least two different robbers the night Ella was killed. There were also at least two firearms used, one of which we think we found at Benson's house, and will know for certain once the ballistics reports come back. So, Benson and this tattooed guy were working together, perhaps on Clayton's behalf, and Parker Quinn was totally innocent in all this? When we spoke with Clayton earlier, he struck me as being genuinely heartbroken about Quinn, but I suppose he could've been acting…' In the background Jagger had finished his moody rendition and someone else was now growling about smokestack lightning: Howling Wolf, I bet. Bryony had barely heard her cell's ringtone over the music. She cocked her head to one side, then lifted a palm to me, begging a moment. 'Jeez, Joe,' she muttered, as she fished her cell from her purse, 'you really know how to throw a wrench in the works.'

'You going to tell Holker the same thing?' I offered my most self-effacing smile.

'Dennis?' she greeted her partner, then offered me a scowl, working her mouth at me. *How'd you know it was Holker*, her unspoken question said.

'Who else knew you were meeting me who'd want to break up the party?' I whispered. Bryony shook her head in amusement, but was busy listening to Holker. I watched as her features pinched in question, then creased up around the temples as she was struck with understanding.

'I'll be right there,' she announced.

Holker tried to say something else, but Bryony was already standing up, gulping her final mouthful of beer. I could hear the distorted tones of his voice as he said something about not waiting. 'I'm nearby,' Bryony told him. 'Just give me five minutes, please.'

She didn't want the five minutes to say her pleasant goodbyes to me, though, but to drive wherever Holker was waiting. 'Come on, Joe.'

'What is it?'

'I haven't time to explain; if you want to hear, you'll have to do it while you walk me to my car.' She was already heading from the booth, and as she passed the bar, she threw down twenty dollars. I took it that it was enough for both our drinks, so only went after her, lugging the knapsack I'd fetched with me from Andrew Clayton's place.

Out on Nebraska Boulevard, Bryony picked up pace. The heels didn't slow her, but accentuated her legs magnificently. I paused very briefly to admire the view before hurrying after her. People got out of our way on the sidewalk, and I admit it did look as if we were engaged in a chase. More than one hooker turned to check out who might be their new rival on the strip, and they were green with envy: there wasn't a professional girl in sight who could hold a candle to Bryony. Oblivious to the looks she attracted, Bryony headed for where she'd left her car, down a side street.

'You going to tell me where we're going?' I asked.

Without turning, Bryony said, 'Where I'm going. Sorry, Joe, but I can't take you with me. Not this time.'

'You're going to abandon me in the middle of College Hill? You're signing my death warrant. Holker put you up to this?'

She snorted at my attempt at humour. 'We've got intel on the home invasion crew. The task force are about to mount a raid and I intend being there when it goes down.'

'I'll come with you.'

'Holker would shit a fur ball.'

'So?'

'So this is *our* gig, Joe. Mine and Holker's. I'm not about to mess it up for him; no way.'

'The guy dislikes me that much? Look, I promise to be a good boy…'

'I don't want a good boy,' she said, as she approached her car. Remarkably it hadn't been stolen, broken into, burned out or jacked up on bricks. 'I only want to get these bastards, and I can't afford any distractions. Sorry, Joe, but you can call a cab, right?'

'I understand,' I said. 'You can't turn up with me, but at least tell me where you're going.'

She was getting in the car. 'Why, so you can follow me?'

'You'd expect anything different?'

'Shit. Get in, buckle up and shut the hell up.'

<u>24</u>

'What the hell's Hunter doing here?' Detective Holker gritted his teeth to hold back any expletives. 'Goddamn it, Bryony! What were you thinking?'

'What did you expect me to do with him; drop him in the middle of nowhere?' Bryony glanced back at where she'd parked her car, out of sight and sound of the target building in Tampa Heights. Joe Hunter sat resolutely in the passenger seat, as he'd been instructed. But how long would that last?

'You could've dropped him in the Bay for all I care,' Holker growled. He was vested up, had his badge on a lanyard round his neck.

'So what are you bothered about? Don't worry, he's under strict instructions to sit there and not move.'

Holker shook his head and stormed away, heading towards a tactical response team leader, who was currently instructing his men on the plan of attack. 'I haven't time for this shit,' Holker said. 'Just keep him well away from me. I'd like to live to see the end of the day.'

Bryony shook her own head, but it was at her decision for allowing Hunter along for the ride. Holker was already suspicious enough, without allowing superstition to add to his dislike of Hunter. She'd already kicked off her heels and squirmed into a pair of sneakers she'd brought from her car's trunk. She also strapped into her own ballistic vest, cinching the Velcro tight, then checked over her department issue Glock. She gave Hunter one last stern look, and he waved, offering a supportive grin. Rakish son-of-a-bitch, she thought, but couldn't help smiling. She turned, all professional-like and headed to join Holker and the other Tampa PD officers preparing for the raid on the building out of view around the corner. Prep would have to be swift, because already members of the public had noticed the arrival of the police, some with no love of cops, and word would reach the ears of their targets imminently. There was a second team of officers, backed by another tac-team a few blocks to the north, ready to coordinate their movements with Holker's assigned team. Hillsborough County Sheriff's deputies had formed a cordon that encompassed the neighbourhood between Woodlawn Cemetery and the western boundary of Robles Park, as far north as Martin Luther King Jnr Boulevard, and south to Columbus Drive, ready to move in as manpower necessitated. The plan was for a pincer manoeuvre, go in loud and fast, and catch the home invasion crew with their pants down: but as the clock ticked onward, their window for monopolizing the element of surprise was narrowing. If they didn't move soon, the bad guys could be the ones coming with all guns blazing.

There was the genuine possibility of a counter attack, and Bryony was aware that there was an element of residents in the neighbourhood who packed enough weaponry to give them a real fight. If you believed the FBI-reported violent crime rates, and certain opinion polls, the Tampa Heights district was once in the top twenty most dangerous neighbourhoods in the nation, with residents having a one in nine chance of being a victim of crime. That was a few years ago now, and some refurbishment and business revitalization schemes had helped rejuvenate the neighbourhood, but those who had to patrol it still regarded it as a crime-ridden blemish on Tampa's good name. Early opinions said the crime rate was beginning to decrease, but ask any cop and they'd tell you it was bureaucratic bullshit, politicians playing fast and loose with the statistics to make them look good. There were many law-abiding, decent, hard-working people living there, but it only took a minority – responsible for the majority of criminal activity – to keep a neighbourhood down.

Bryony glanced at the armament wielded by her colleagues, regretful that the good folks of Tampa Heights should witness what amounted to an invading force, but she was also grateful that the team was fully equipped. Who knew what they faced once they stormed the seemingly derelict office complex the robbers had commandeered for their base of operations? Another thing she was thankful for was that it was a Sunday evening, and therefore there were no kids around, especially when the office complex was in earshot of a nearby academy, and a play park. There were a few small businesses in the vicinity too, auto-repair shops and junk yards primarily, but all were closed for the night, so there was lesser chance of collateral damage from members of the public strolling into the danger zone.

The tac-team leader was finishing up his instructions as Bryony arrived alongside Holker, swiping off-screen the blueprints of the office complex he'd brought up on a tablet. They all trusted the construction plans meant little to its current state, but the blueprints had given them an idea on the main ingress ports into the building. Undercover officers had added extra intelligence, and Bryony caught the leader instructing two of his guys to cover the second floor windows, in case they came under fire from above. Bryony didn't require a briefing as such, because her and Holker and the half-dozen other detectives on scene would be following direction after the hard entry of tactical support. Already one team of six heavily armed and armoured TRT officers was queuing up at the near corner, and Holker moved to join the rear of the queue, his sidearm drawn. Bryony moved in close on his heels. She could smell nervous anxiety, gun oil, and not a little testosterone, and fleetingly wondered if the scent was rising off her.

Another tac squad trotted away along the block from where they'd assembled, their plain-clothed counterparts joining the back of their line, while other specialist officers moved to vantage points where they could offer cover. The team leader coordinating the raid was talking through the secure radio channel, but Bryony had no idea what was being said. Instead she watched the point man on her team for instruction; waiting as he counted down with his fingers, then gestured them to move. In a huddle they went forward, Bryony feeling like the tail end of an armoured caterpillar bristling with guns. As they approached the last corner, the point man again gave silent instructions and the stack of bodies drew to a halt. He used a mirror to check around the corner, and was happy the approach was clear. He relayed as much into his helmet-mounted microphone, then waited as another countdown began.

Greenlight!

The tactical response team surged forward, slick and practiced, ready for any eventuality. Further up the street the second team moved parallel to them, aiming for rapid entry via a fire exit door at the far right corner of the office complex. Bryony's team angled for the original entrance foyer, where the glass doors had long since been vandalised, but were reinforced with graffiti-daubed steel shutters. In instances where doors required breaching, the usual order of the day was by the use of Hatton rounds, a charge of compressed zinc powder fired from a shotgun into the locking mechanism, but in this instance the dedicated breach officer lugged a set of industrial strength bolt-clippers. They made short work of the sturdy chain padlocking the shutters to the doorframe, an instant before a second tactical support officer prised the door open with a short crowbar. The screech of twisting metal was obliterated by the shouts of the remaining four armoured cops who swarmed inside, clearing the vestibule. The breaching couple went inside after them, after swapping out their tools for more deadly ones. Only then did the detectives follow on their heels.

No shots were fired during those first few seconds, by either cops or villains, and Bryony hoped the status quo would last. Best-case scenario was that the gang were overwhelmed and controlled before anybody got a shot off, but that was expecting a lot. As corners were cleared, the tac-team moved on, and a size eleven boot breached the next door via a swift kick to the handle. The tac-team went inside, shouting commands. Distantly Bryony could hear the other teams making equally noisy ingress, and now another sound. There were startled shouts, and the rumble of feet.

The first gunshot sounded like the clap of hands. It emanated from down a corridor and beyond walls. It was faint, but it sent an electrical charge through Bryony that left her scalp tingling. She knew it was the herald of more gunfire to come.

'Stay tight,' Holker said to her.

She was so close she was almost climbing his back as it was.

Helmeted heads bobbed before them as the tactical officers covered a narrow hallway, ready to rain down overlapping fields of fire but there was no sign of resistance. Vandalised offices stood vacant along the hall, but each had to be cleared before anyone moved on. But the team was slick, and well practiced, so each room took a case of seconds before the calls of "clear" rang out.

Another gun fired. It was on semi-automatic. Three snapping sounds followed by a second of dead silence. Then the trio of snaps repeated.

'Contact, contact,' one of the tac-team barked.

A figure had materialised from an open doorway ahead. Bryony could barely see the man, but one of the tac officers fired a second before she heard the thunderous bark of a shotgun. Scatter-shot drilled holes in the suspended ceiling above the leading officers, and shredded polystyrene tiles dropped like a blizzard of confetti at a wedding. Commands were barked in short order, but the gunman wasn't listening. A single shot rang out, and was rewarded by the clatter of a falling body.

Most of the team surged onward, with one cop crouching to clear the weapon from the fallen man. Another checked him for vitals, but Bryony knew from the seeping wound in his chest the man was no longer a threat. She briefly wondered if she knew the man's face, but it was slack in death and being malformed by the second bullet didn't even look natural let alone recognisable. She glanced at Holker, who also checked out the man with a frown. He raised his eyebrows at her in question. Before she could reply in the negative, they were moving once more.

There was a stairwell to the left, another door dead ahead. On their right they were blocked from the street by nailed shut windows, or ones replaced by sheets of warped plyboard. It was a shooting gallery, should anyone come up behind them. Bryony was mindful of an attack from the rear, but was as keen to get through the door as the others in the team. Gunfire crackled from beyond the door, and she could tell from the way the point man flinched that shouted updates were coming fast and furiously through his earpiece. One of the team paused to guard the stairs; the others went through the door. Holker had his gun up near his right shoulder. Bryony's was in a two-handed grip at waist height.

Bullets scorched the air around them.

By the time they turned, the tac guy was returning fire up the stairs. A black youth, no more than in his late teens, ducked back from the bannister rail as the cop's bullets punched holes in the ancient wood.

'Tampa Police! Drop your weapon!' the cop yelled.

The youth's response was to fire again, but they were pot shots, his arm over the rail, but his body hidden by the upper level floor. Bryony skipped aside as one of his poorly aimed bullets exploded through the window next to her. Beside her, Holker fired. The armoured cop was already advancing up the stairs. Bryony would prefer to follow the team into the next room where larger numbers of the home invasion crew were sequestered, and by the sound of things giving almost as good as they got in the gun battle, but the lone tac guy needed support. Holker and she were it. They went up fast, following the cop to the head of the stairs. Holker took a knee, covering as the cop went to his belly and swung around the bannister. 'He's running,' said the cop.

He must have been running backwards, because the youth was still shooting. Bullet holes pockmarked the wall adjacent to them. Challenges rang down the corridor from both ends. The cop levelled his gun, preparing to fire.

'He's just a kid,' Holker whispered harshly, and the cop's finger paused on the trigger.

A kid who'd shoot them all like mangy dogs given the chance, Bryony thought. But her partner was right. The youth was shooting out of desperation and fear, and it might not be seen as a justified shooting if he was killed. Besides, they needed a live arrestee, and by the way things were going there might not be a robber left standing judging by the fury of the gun battle raging below them.

The youth stopped shooting, but only because he'd made cover at the far end of the corridor and didn't have a target. In a bunch, they moved forward, the armoured cop again taking point. Here some of the windows were open to the elements. Bryony was conscious of the snipers outside, feeling a prickle of unease at being in their crosshairs. Last she wanted was for any of them to be caught in a blue-on-blue shooting. She listened as their colleague made a running commentary, up-dating their progress, she thought: she wasn't the only one wary of being taken out by an itchy-fingered sharp-shooter.

The youth peaked out from the far corner.

'Police! Put down your weapon. Now!' roared the tac guy, even as he brought up his M16.

The kid's response was to fire.

The bullet took the cop in the chest, and he went to one knee, huffing out in pain. Thankfully his Kevlar vest saved him, but he was momentarily winded. Bryony patted him on the shoulder, as she stood to protect him while he was vulnerable. Holker's gun was up and firing, and a split-second later Bryony's Glock joined in. It was one thing hoping for a live captive, but not at the expense of a dead cop. The youth fled.

'That little punk isn't getting away,' Holker swore.

They raced after him, the armoured cop now on his feet again, but a tad slow to follow.

Holker made the corner first, and dipped out.

'He's going down,' he announced, and Bryony swerved around him and took the stairs three at a time. The young man was fleet-footed, his Converse sneakers slapping the steps on his way down. Bryony heard him pause, rather than seen him, and she flattened her back to the wall as she hit the landing where the stairs turned back on themselves. Now she covered while Holker came down. He bobbed out.

A bullet ricocheted off the bannister next to him, buzzing away up the stairwell, and bouncing off walls like a drunken wasp. Bryony leaned out, shouting a warning, but it was rhetoric because she was already firing.

Below her the youth cursed in pain, then called her some unsavoury names she'd heard a hundred times before.

'Drop your weapon and show yourself,' Bryony barked. 'There's no way out. The building is surrounded. *Do you really want to die?*'

In reply the kid fired.

It was a single shot, and it hit nowhere near her.

The youth cursed under his breath, and she heard the metallic rattle of shells on the floor. Either he was armed with a revolver and he'd just dumped the empty cartridges, or he'd dropped those he was attempting to reload with. She shared a knowing look with Holker: was it a chance they should take? Hell yeah, she thought, and hurtled down the steps.

As she rounded the corner she immediately saw her mistake. The young man was still reloading, yes, but another of the home invasion crew had joined him, materializing from a passage in the rear of the building in a hail of gunfire. A bullet nicked the barrel of her Glock, wrenching it from her numb fingers. The man, a tall, spiky-haired black guy in a wife-beater vest and baggy jeans, cat-called at her, gripping his groin with his cupped left hand, then fired again. Bryony's only hope of survival was to go flat on her face. She dived at the floor, and her momentum took her in a slide that ended with her scrunched below the boarded-up windows adjacent to the foyer they'd first gained entrance by. Slivers of broken glass pierced her jeans and her left shoulder, but the wounds were superficial to the one the man planned for her. He took three exaggerated steps forward, his pistol held sideways in his fist as he hollered words she didn't catch.

Holker shot from where he kneeled on the stairs.

His bullet took the man in the side of his neck, and it was as if the strings tethering him upright in the world were cut. The guy collapsed in a boneless heap on top of Bryony. She could feel his blood on her face, but wasn't repulsed: better his than her's any time. She kicked free of him, even as Holker pounded to her side. The other cop was at the bottom of the stairs, his rifle sweeping the scene.

'Where's the kid?' Bryony asked, her voice inordinately angry.

Holker glanced around, spotting the door to the foyer moving slightly on its hinges. 'He's gone.'

'Like hell he is! He's not getting away,' Bryony said as she struggled to rise. Her left knee felt twice as large as it should. Stinging cuts decorated her, and she foolishly swiped her palms down the fronts of her jeans, both to clean her palms and to knock away the splinters digging into her. She grimaced at her stupidity. She reached for her Glock. Holker pressed a hand to her shoulder, supporting her while he bent and scooped it up.

'Check that still works before you shoot it again,' he instructed her. The bullet had struck the slide, and it was slightly deformed. Bryony attempted to manipulate the slide but it jammed. Her hands stung like crazy, her right partly because of the impact on her gun. 'Right,' Holker said, 'you're staying put. Officer, cover her, will you?' The tactical cop nodded, and moved to literally shield Bryony, as Holker made for the swinging door.

'Wait,' Bryony called, but Holker pushed through the door, his gun ready as he sought the young man's whereabouts. The youth hadn't gone out the main exit. Had he done so, the cops waiting outside would have him. He had to have gone deeper into the building, perhaps looking for another exit. Bryony nodded at the tac cop. 'You OK?'

'I'm good to go.' The cop distractedly touched the spot where the bullet hit his vest, before adjusting his rifle. 'You want to go after your partner, Detective?'

There was simply no debate in her mind. 'Yeah. Let's do it.'

The cop went first, and Bryony paused only a second to secure the gun dropped by the dead man. Not that she intended using it, but she didn't want it to fall into the hands of another of the gang before the complex was fully secured. It was a Taurus 100 model .40 S&W with gold accents and a mother of pearl grip: quite a beauty – a trophy gun, she thought, for any self-respecting gangster. It was a bit large framed for her, but if it came to it she was confident she could handle it, even with sore hands.

She followed the cop through the foyer, and there at the far left, earlier disregarded during the initial forced entry by the team was another door. It had been missed because a sheet of plyboard had concealed it, now on the floor and baring the dusty footprints of both the fleeing youth and Holker. The tac cop tapped his throat mike, giving a status report, and heard instructions in response. He glanced back at Bryony. 'Building's secure back where we came from. There's another team sweeping the rear corridors, moving to liaise on our position.'

Bryony nodded at him, but waved him on. Before anyone could reach him, gunfire could pin down Holker seeing as the kid had now reloaded. In the minute-or-so the back-up team required to join them, Holker could be killed. Not on her watch, she swore.

It was apparent where the kid had left the building. He'd kicked open a fire exit door, that led directly into a loading bay area. Even as Bryony and the cop stepped out the door, weapons sweeping for target acquisition, she heard her partner holler at the guy to stop. He received no response, and Holker set off at a gallop. His hard-heeled shoes slapped the asphalt, just out of sight around a corner from Bryony. Holker was so keen on catching the kid he'd forgotten what odds he had in a footrace with a youth wearing sneakers.

Bryony took a quick recce round the corner, and saw Holker dashing across the street, heading directly for one of the nearby autoshop yards. He was exposed as he went, and Bryony cringed as the kid who'd proven so ready to use a weapon, suddenly popped out from alongside a parked van, his revolver aimed directly at her partner.

She yelled a warning, snatching up the gun she'd seized in evidence. Alongside her the tac guy also leaned into his assault rifle, picking a shot that wasn't really there, because Holker skidded into his line of fire. Holker braced his legs, bringing up his gun in a two-handed grip.

'Drop it!' he shouted.

But his words were drowned out by the sharp crack of the kid's revolver.

The kid was a good shot. He'd already demonstrated that when shooting the tactical cop earlier, and this time was no different. Holker was hit.

Bryony saw blood puffing into the air, and her partner sat down on his ass in the street.

She raced forward, even as the tactical support officer grabbed at her, trying to clear her from his line of sight.

'Dennis!' she cried out, because she knew what was coming next. The kid was still partly concealed by the van, safe enough from the shot that she fired at a run, and which missed by a mile. Yet he had a clear line of sight on Holker, and he levelled his gun on the detective's face.

There was a sharp *crack*!

But Holker didn't die.

The young man was propelled from concealment by the fist that had struck him savagely in the back of his skull. The kid went down on his knees, arms outstretched, even as Joe Hunter followed his punch with a kick to the would-be cop-killer's liver that firmly sent him to the asphalt, the revolver spinning out of his grasp. Hunter pinned him there, a heel between his shoulder blades, as he waved at Bryony with a wink.

25

Expecting me to sit quietly in Bryony's car while a gun battle was raging just out of sight – but definitely within hearing distance - was never going to happen. My patience lasted a few minutes, until Bryony disappeared around the corner at the tail end of a heavily armed conga line. Once the raid was underway, I vacated the car, moving away from the few officers still in the near vicinity, and walked away across the road to a vantage point where I could keep a distant eye on the proceedings. By the time I positioned myself on the sidewalk outside a converted church, now used as a drop in day centre for the homeless if I read the notices correctly, the tactical support team had made entry to the target building. It was a matter of less than two minutes before the first pop of firearms went off, and I barely resisted the temptation to go after Bryony and Holker. They wouldn't have thanked me for my help, and Holker for one would probably have arrested me for obstructing officers in the line of duty. Maybe he'd have shot me, I thought, and claimed he honestly believed I was one of the bad guys: it was a joke, but perhaps not too far removed from the truth.

I'd no place going along on the raid, and no right, but what can I say? I didn't want to see Bryony hurt, and as the gunfight intensified I realised the police had met tougher resistance than anticipated. I was only one man, lightly armed with a 9mm pistol, so wasn't exactly the heavy cavalry they required as back up. I held my ground. But I was on pins. As the fight continued, police activity intensified too, with Sheriff's deputies moving in from a cordon they must have set up, to secure the perimeter. Uniformed Tampa PD officers, engaged minutes ago in securing the nearest streets, also converged on the city block, but didn't enter the fight. They set up a second battle line from behind their cruisers. Lightly protected by ballistic vests, they would still be vulnerable to the heavy firepower those inside the office complex had displayed, so it made sense they squatted in concealment behind their vehicles.

I caught myself chewing my bottom lip.

I wandered down the adjacent sidewalk, behind the cops that had set up a barrier of their cars across the road. Inside the office building the gunfire was lessening in frequency. Those cops I could see were still on high alert, but from their general demeanour they were receiving positive reports over their radios. By all appearances the raid was largely a success and the last of the opposition now seconds away from defeat. Some of the cops were stirring to move in on the building, to assist in the arrests and in securing the scene. There was a junkyard, but unlike the one where I'd met with Emilio and his boys, it had open access. I walked inside, then moved between rows of cars that looked like insurance write-offs and fender benders destined for scrapping once they'd been stripped of salvageable parts. The junkyard was next to an autoshop – the first probably supplying the latter with spare parts – and I'd only to step over a small collapsed brick wall to get on to the adjacent property. From the autoshop courtyard I had a better view of the office complex and more chance of spotting Bryony when she came out.

I didn't expect to see a young black guy come sprinting from the rear of the complex and skid to a halt in the courtyard, concealed from sight by a van displaying the autoshop's decal. Some of the cops to my right had witnessed the youth's dash across the road, and some of them stirred to grab him, but in the next instant another figure appeared from the office building: Detective Holker was in pursuit.

He had no idea where the guy was, or that he was bouncing nervously on his toes, waiting for Holker to get closer. Holker was fully exposed in the street, and was still moving directly into the guy's line of fire. I was in the process of yelling a warning when I recognised Bryony's voice doing the same, and I clamped down on mine, knowing we were both too late. Holker knew too, but he braced for impact, bringing up his gun and commanding the guy to drop his weapon.

His answer was the sharp crack of the guy's revolver, and I saw Holker fall on his arse, his face twisting up in agony. I couldn't tell where he had been hit, but saw blood on the asphalt alongside him.

I'm unsure at which point I'd begun running, but I was swiftly approaching where the young gangbanger had concealed himself alongside the van. Bryony cried out Holker's first name, even as the guy leaned out again to finish her partner. A gun cracked, and I heard the slap of Bryony's sneakers. The bullet hit something metallic beyond the gangbanger, and it didn't trouble him one bit. He prepared to shoot, and if I'd to be honest I couldn't say if his target was Holker or my friend, but it didn't matter.

He heard me at the last instant. Began to turn fractionally, but he didn't see what was coming. My right cross hit him while I was still at a run, catching him on the back of his head. My fist felt as if it had been compressed in a vice, every bone and ligament, and all the soft tissue compressed into a dense mass half its previous size. But the sensation only lasted for a split second before the impact forced the guy's head away, and the rest of his body followed it. I was still in motion, and used my forward trajectory to slam my right shin into a point just below his ribcage, and I instinctively knew that was it for the youth's resistance. He flattened on the ground, his gun spilled from his lax grip, and I ended up standing on top of him like Tarzan the ape-man trumpeting his latest victory. I glanced across at Bryony and saw her running to help her downed friend, and gave a brief wave to assure her my captive was under control so it was safe to assist Holker. Perhaps I winked too, but it was to clear my right eye of a piece of grit stirred up from the youth's collapse.

Bryony immediately went to one knee at Holker's side, and his first instinct was to brush her off as if she was fussing over nothing. But Bryony insisted, pressing her hand on Holker's wound. Thankfully it was to his outer thigh, so he'd probably live long enough for paramedics to reach him. Bryony's face was a mixture of concern, and brash anger. She glared over at me, but her ire wasn't for me but for the punk who lay sound asleep under my boot heel. A fully kitted tactical support officer was moving rapidly towards me, and I won't lie: having his assault rifle poised to shoot at me wasn't a nice feeling.

'Relax, buddy,' I told him, and showed him my empty hands, 'I'm one of the good guys.'

He probably already knew that, but Bryony told him I was with her. I hoped her words wouldn't come back to haunt her. The tac guy's emphasis went from me to my prisoner, and I willingly stepped off the punk so the cop could secure him with plastic zip-ties he pulled from his tactical vest. He also cinched the youth's ankles, then immediately secured the dropped gun. Other uniforms were arriving by then, some of them giving me funny looks. One young woman even placed a hand on my shoulder and tried to manoeuvre me away, but I shrugged her off and went to assist Bryony.

Holker saw me coming, and even though he was dazed with agony he scowled at me, then across at the youth I'd knocked cold.

'Please tell me you didn't kill my prisoner,' he growled.

'He'll have a sore head and will probably piss blood for a week, but he'll be OK,' I told him.

Holker swore at me.

'It's OK, no thanks are necessary.'

Holker swore again.

I put his bad mood down to the fact he was in such pain.

He looked up at Bryony who was still compressing his wound. 'Jesus, Bryony, what did I tell you about that guy?'

'I think Hunter just saved your life, Dennis. Maybe a little gratitude wouldn't go amiss this time,' she scolded.

'Saved my life? Yeah, maybe fucking so, but it probably wouldn't have needed saving if he wasn't within the fucking city limits! I wouldn't have been shot if that cursed son-of-a-bitch wasn't here in the first place!'

Blinking in confusion, I searched for an explanation from Bryony. Holker's words obviously had something to do with an earlier conversation they'd had, but for now I was left in the dark. Paramedics were on the scene, and I was pressed aside by yet another uniformed cop, to make room. I backed off willingly, watching from a distance as dressings were applied, and Holker bundled onto a gurney. Bryony marched with him as he was wheeled for an ambulance beyond the police cordon. I kept back, until she'd said her goodbyes at the door of the ambulance, then she turned, seeking me. I waved, and watched her shake her head. She jabbed her finger in the general direction where she'd left her car, and I complied with her instruction, walking the opposite direction to all the cops now swarming into the scene. I took it all of the suspects in the home invasion robberies were under arrest, or perhaps permanently retired from their occupation. But Bryony's work there was a long way from done.

Now that the fighting was over, dozens of local residents were out on the streets, all speculating about what had happened and forming their own opinions on the right and wrong of it. Some of them were angry at the police, but most wore relieved expressions, though the emotion wouldn't last either way: one gang out of the way only left a void for another to fill. None of the residents had a clue I'd been involved, so I was able to thread my way through them without being challenged, or pressed for answers. I returned to Bryony's car, but didn't get in, as it was locked and I didn't have the keys. Just stood with my butt parked on the hood, and waited, while I massaged my aching hand. It was a good forty-five minutes or more before Bryony showed. She'd unstrapped out of her Kevlar vest, and had it slung from her left forearm, the way you once saw cowboys lugging their saddles. There was no sign of her handgun, and I thought it might have been handed in as evidence. Her coral blouse was soaked with sweat, darkest where she'd worn the vest. It was only when I studied her that I saw her jeans and her blouse were splotched with blood.

'You OK?' I asked as she approached.

'I asked you to wait there and not move,' she replied.

I opened my palms as I stood from my perch.

She shook her head in exasperation, and went past me to the trunk. She deposited the vest in it, and I noticed the car rock slightly on its chassis under the weight. The trunk thudded shut. As she returned to the front, she picked at small slivers of glass in her clothing, flicking them aside. Her hands bore dozens of tiny nicks and scrapes.

'Want me to drive?' I offered.

'No. I'll do it. I'll drop you on the way.'

'Where are you going?'

'Where do you think? I want to check on Dennis.'

'Any update?'

'Get in,' she said, opening the locks with a key fob. I got in. She settled uncomfortably into the driving position, and again picked at various shards of glass she flicked out the open door. 'Holker's going to be fine. He's going to be hobbling for a few weeks, but he should fully recover.'

'He always did hobble on those heels he wears,' I said to lighten the mood. Bryony didn't laugh though. She was concerned for her partner, and I'd no right making fun at his expense. 'I'm glad he's going to be OK.'

'Could have been much worse,' she said as she closed the door and fired up the engine.

'I'm happy to have helped.'

'I'm happy you helped too,' she said as she drove away from the scene, heading for the nearby highway on the far side of Robles Park. 'God knows what the alternative would've been, but, Joe, please, in future just do as I damn well ask, OK?'

'I didn't deliberately disobey,' I said. 'I stayed outside the police cordon, the punk who shot Holker just happened to slip through. I wasn't going to stand idle while you, or even Holker were in danger.'

'Yeah, I know. And I'm grateful.' She didn't sound it.

'Did I get you in trouble?'

'Possibly. I'm unsure. I just know Captain Newburger wants to see me when I get back to Franklin Street. He didn't ask me nicely.'

'He doesn't need to know I was there with you.'

'Dennis knows. So does any number of cops who were there when you almost took that kid's head off.'

'Forget "kid". Let's call him what he really was: a punk with a gun, and he was intent on killing a cop. It could have been worse, Bryony,' I said. 'I could've shot him.'

'Thank the Lord for small mercies,' she intoned.

'Worse still I could've stood by like a law-abiding citizen and let him kill Holker. Tell your arsehole captain *that.*'

She didn't answer. Her face was thoughtful, her bottom lip protruding as she stared through the windscreen. In profile she was even cuter.

'You ask me, Captain Newburger should be congratulating you on a job well done,' I said. 'They were the home invasion crew everyone has been hunting, right?'

'Certainly looks like it. We've seven of them in custody, including the-' she was about to say kid but changed her mind '-asshole who tried to kill Dennis. Three dead. A preliminary search found goods matching those stolen during some of the home invasions. So, yeah, a celebration could be on the cards, but it will be kept low key for now.'

'They definitely acted guilty,' I said.

'I know where you're leading, Joe,' Bryony said, and looked over at me. She only held the squint for a second, because she was steering up the on-ramp to the highway and it demanded her attention. 'Except for during the Clayton robbery they haven't been overtly violent. But that fight back there was probably down to circumstance more than anything; they probably fought back because they knew the game was up. It doesn't categorically prove anything one way or another. Maybe under the circumstances they felt they had to kill Ella because she was about to raise the alarm.'

'You don't believe that any more than I do.'

'Nope. But it's something we'll have to look at.' She snorted. 'It's just one of about a hundred things I've still got on my plate.'

From what I understood, Bryony and Holker were still primaries on the investigation into Ella Clayton's murder, and now Parker Quinn's. By association they had to investigate Thomas Benson's involvement, and try to prove he was Quinn's and possibly even Ella's murderer. She also still had to determine what if any involvement Andrew Clayton had in it all. Finally catching the home invasion crew was another box ticked, but it didn't lend an answer to the other ongoing facets of their investigation. Especially when a gun possibly used in Ella's murder was discovered at Benson's house, and then there were those damn letters, and Quinn's staged suicide. With Holker injured, and possibly out of action for weeks, it now put extra pressure on Bryony. She could probably do without the inclusion of a new suspect, but there was still the tattooed guy to take into consideration.

Maybe I could lighten her load a bit, I decided. But no way was I about to tell her what I had in mind. If I did, she wouldn't drop me at Rink's place, she'd show me the red card with the instruction "Go directly to jail".

26

The following afternoon found me driving my Audi down a beaten dirt track between twisted down chain-link fences towards the shoreline of Safety Harbor. The car was moving slowly enough that its passage didn't stir the trash in the weed-strewn verges, but it kicked up clouds of pale yellow dust. I closed the windows so I didn't choke to death.

Once through the industrial estate, the potholed track didn't get much better, but once I pulled onto the grounds surrounding Wild Point Bait it wasn't as dusty. I could see across the sparkling bay to Bridgeport, though there was a heat haze that caused the horizon to dance and jiggle in my vision. The scene closer by was vivid, and pinpoints of light lanced off every piece of reflective material, causing me to avert my gaze so I wasn't temporarily blinded. As I got out my Audi, I turned my head towards the grassy embankment, then the jetties and boats, but there was no sign of the workers I'd spotted there on my previous visit. Intermittent knocking emanated from inside one of the net-strung wooden shacks, which I took to be a storage lock-up, or perhaps a workshop.

The GMC Suburban had been moved to a position nearer the WPB shop, but the faded old truck hadn't moved an inch: it would probably stay there until it was merely a few flakes of reddish rust and hunks of unrecognisable metal in the dirt, the fossilised remains of late twentieth century engineering. There was also a motorcycle balancing on its stands, and a green saloon car, both of which might have belonged to customers. I pondered waiting before I went inside the shop, to let the customers leave, but for all I knew the bike and car were staff vehicles. Walking to the shop, I thought about Bryony and to what extent her butt-reaming had been once she'd reported to Captain Newburger's office. I hadn't spoken with her since she'd dropped me at Temple Terrace, and she'd made no attempt to call me. I hoped that no news was good news, and that extended to Holker's recovery. I'd caught the news this morning, watching on Rink's

TV as I breakfasted on bacon, eggs and toast, and about a gallon of coffee. The media was trumpeting about the raid on the office complex at Tampa Heights. Although they reported a successful outcome for Tampa PD in their search for the home invasion gang, equally they criticised the police for taking so long to catch them, and bemoaned the fact three young men had lost their lives, due to what some deemed over-excessive use of force during the raid. What did they know about anything that they couldn't invent? They only mentioned in passing that three cops had been shot during the raid, but that told me that the cops – one of whom was Holker – had not sustained life-threatening injuries. Already some campaigning liberals were trying to turn the police raid into a racist statement, due to the targeting of a gang comprising mostly black men. I wondered if I'd be accused of being racist if they heard I'd knocked out one of the gangbangers, something I definitely was not. My closest circle of friends was an Asian American, an African American, a Mexican and an Irishman – when we walked together into a bar it sounded like the first line of a joke.

The doorbell tinkled as I entered Wild Point Bait, and I forgot all about the home invasion gang. I'd returned about another matter that I wanted to check with the owner. He wasn't behind the counter. This time it was a young blond woman, who I thought was the same person I'd seen working on the jetty that first time. She offered me a pleasant smile as I stepped into the cool interior of the shop. She was tanned, with little white lines around her mouth: she was a smiley person, and the perpetual expression extended to her twinkly blue eyes.

'Hi, there,' she said, and fist bumped the air. 'If you need anything, just let me know, OK.'

'Thanks,' I said, but continued towards her. 'Actually, I was hoping to speak with the manager. Is he around today?'

'I'm the manager. Can I help you?'

'Oh,' I said. 'I didn't mean any offense. I was hoping to speak with the same guy I spoke with the other day. He was a tall guy, tanned, with blond hair. I took it he was the manager…'

'Well, I suppose he is, sir. He's the owner, but he's kind of hands on when it comes to running the shop. That's my husband Harlan you're describing.' The woman didn't make a move to hail him.

'Any chance I can speak with him?'

'If it's about anything I can help with…' she nodded at the sundry equipment, and I didn't doubt she was an expert.

'I'm not here about fishing,' I explained, 'I only need to ask him about a mutual acquaintance.'

Her smile stayed in place, but it grew more fixed. Her mind was working overtime as she stared at me.

'Are you here about Tommy?' she asked, and her voice had lost its pleasant edge.

It was pointless lying. 'Yes, I am.'

'Are you a cop?'

'No.'

'You're the man who chased him into the highway,' she said, and it was with a note of accusation I hadn't expected. She'd placed her hands on the counter, and now I watched them draw up into semi-clenched fists.

'I didn't chase him, I was trying to get him to stop running.'

The woman ignored my lame excuse, her mind working furiously in a different direction. 'Harlan mentioned you'd been in here asking about Tommy, then in no time poor Tommy was dead. It didn't take too much figuring out who it was that chased him.' Her twinkly eyes had glassed over as she spoke, on the verge of tears. 'What had that poor boy done to deserve *that?*'

I was tempted to tell her that "poor Tommy" might very well be a murderer, but I didn't believe it myself. I chose my words carefully. 'That's what I hoped to speak with Harlan about.'

'He isn't here,' she said dismissively.

'When will he be back?'

'A few hours. He took out some tourists on the bay.' She nodded at the door. 'Best you aren't here when he gets back. Harlan said if you ever set foot through that door again he'd…' she stumbled to a halt, looking down at her clenched fist, realising she might be inviting trouble none of us wanted.

'Look,' I said, 'there's been a bit of a misunderstanding. I don't know what you've heard about Tommy, but you don't know the half of it. I'm only looking for answers, and they might help clear up a murder. They might even help prove that Tommy Benson was an innocent man.'

'Murder? Tommy had his faults but he was no murderer!'

'I tend to agree with you,' I reassured her.

'He had a drink problem, and wasn't the sharpest worker we ever had, but he was a good guy at heart. He was quick to anger, but easily as quick to laugh and joke and would do anything for you. Easily led, yeah, but…'

I'd nodded as she mentioned Tommy being easily manipulated, and again she stopped speaking. 'That's what I wanted to ask Harlan about. He said he had to let Tommy go recently, due to a conflict of interests. Was Tommy doing work for a competitor?' She didn't have to answer for me to tell I was on the right track. 'Was he doing work for Andrew Clayton and Parker Quinn?'

A tear dripped from one eye, as realisation struck her. 'We heard about Parker taking his own life. It's very sad, it's…' again she stumbled to a halt, and one hand went to her throat as she understood the implication of Quinn's death, alongside that of Tommy. 'Oh,' she said, and for a second looked as if her knees might give out. Her clenched hands unfolded, but only so she could grip the counter top. 'It's all connected, isn't it? Tommy, Parker-' her eyelids slid shut '- and Emma Clayton. Oh, dear Lord.'

I allowed my silence to answer for me.

Her head began to shake. When she opened her eyes, they were tinged red. 'No. No, Tommy wasn't working with Andrew or Parker. He was doing something with his cousin, but it wasn't *for* CQ Enterprises.'

'His cousin?' I prompted.

'Royce Benson,' she replied.

'Did Royce Benson have a beef with Clayton?'

'Royce Benson has a beef with the world in general,' she replied. I could tell there was more she wished to say, but didn't. Perhaps she wasn't one to pay attention to rumours. I was going to push her on it, but decided not to. Instead I touched the web of skin between my right thumb and index finger and allowed her to fill the gap.

'Yeah. Royce has a tattoo right there. Not the only one either, I've heard. He has them all over his body from when he was in prison.'

'What does he look like?'

'You saw Tommy, right? They both come from the same blood. With Royce think bigger, but much the same to look at. Except you'd know you weren't looking at Tommy if you met him. Unlike Tommy he wasn't quick to laugh or joke, in fact he's more likely to spit in your face…' she snorted in derision '…or punch it.'

'He doesn't sound like the nicest of guys,' I said.

'Harlan warned Tommy to steer clear of him when he got out. Told him he was bad news. But what could he do? They were cousins. Tommy being the guy he was couldn't turn his back on a family member in need.'

'He gave Royce someplace to stay,' I said, and didn't require confirmation. 'You said, "when he got out". Are you talking about prison? He got out recently, then?'

She shrugged. It was obvious.

'Any idea what he served time for? Violence?'

'He was violent, but that wasn't why he was put away. Fraud, I heard. Stolen credit cards, forging cheques, and a few other scams.'

'He scammed Clayton and Quinn's company?' I posed, hoping I'd finally found a motive that tied Royce to the Claytons.

She shrugged again, and said something that made my thoughts shoot off in a totally different direction.

'Royce's beef with Andrew goes way back before he was imprisoned. About ten years at least.'

I waited to see if she'd expound, but she didn't. The arms that had supported her now folded, crossed protectively beneath her breasts. I recognised the defensive stance. Further questions were unwelcome. As was my presence. I thanked her but she turned her back on me, and I left the store. The tinkling of the bell wasn't half as merry on my way out. In the sunshine again, I didn't feel warm. I felt clammy instead, and an oily sensation wormed a sinuous track down my spine. Even the sight of birds skimming the cerulean sea didn't make me feel any better. I turned my back on the scene, and returned to my Audi. When I got in the car it was stuffy and oven hot, but I'd no intention of buzzing down the windows until I was clear of the dust track and back on Shore Drive. My pocket chimed.

Actually, it wasn't my pocket making the noise, but my cell phone in it. I took out my phone and checked for the text message, hoping it was from Bryony. It wasn't. It was from Rink, and he was never second best. I read it, and it was short and sweet. "Ring me". I checked and saw that I'd missed two calls from him while I'd been inside Wild Point Bait, having forgotten to turn on my ringer again after silencing it during my date with Bryony at the bar the night before.

'Howdy, Rink,' I said when he answered my return call.

'Where have you snuck off to now?'

'Just following up on something,' I said.

'You near Clayton's place?'

'I'm only a couple of miles away at Oldsmar. Why? Has something happened?' I reached for the ignition.

'Relax, brother. Andrew rang the office, officially terminating your employment, and paying up on the fee. He's of the impression he's in the clear now, what with the home invasion gang's capture and Quinn and Benson permanently outta the picture.'

'Yeah,' I replied. 'I saw that coming.'

'But he said he wants a word with you about something before you're done,' Rink went on. 'Asked if you could give him a ring.'

Rink's words weren't loaded with double meaning, but to me they were. I didn't tell my friend so, because my mind could still be on the wrong track.

'I can do better than that,' I said, 'I'll call by the house.'

Rink paused. 'There something you ain't telling me?'

'You know there is,' I said.

He sighed. But then he knew any counseling would be pointless. 'Don't do anything that I wouldn't do,' he said, resolved to my hotheaded ways.

27

I had to press the intercom button to hail Andrew Clayton. Ironically he'd changed the code on the electronic gate since I'd left, which was a lot like closing the stable door after the horses had bolted. He buzzed me in, and I waited until the gate was fully open before driving onto his grounds. Proceeding along the crushed shell drive, my tyres depressed them deeper but still cast up fragments by the handful. As I neared the house the flag on the lawn was fluttering in a stiff but hot breeze from the nearby bay. In daylight the house was as impressive as it had been the first time I saw it, but like my own little beach house it no longer looked like a home. I wondered if Andrew, or especially Cole, would ever be happy there again after it had been visited by violence, and bore the indelible stain of Ella's slaying. Andrew had mentioned getting the door pane fixed, but a glazier had yet to arrive.

He must have spotted my arrival from the sitting room window, though I couldn't see him. The windows only reflected the blue of the sky. The door opened on cue as I turned off my engine and got out the Audi. Andrew stood on the raised porch, at the head of the steps, looking down at me. His spectacles also reflected the sky and I couldn't read his expression. His mouth was still, turned neither up nor down. I'd considered what he wanted to speak about on the way over, and now wondered if he'd discovered my pilfering act. The keys I'd lifted from the kitchen drawer burned a hole in my pocket. I'd formulated a white lie to cover the theft, whereby I could claim I'd used the keys during my security rounds, and had forgotten to replace them, and hand them over now: one reason I'd called by in person. If he didn't ask about them…well.

'Thanks for coming,' he said.

'I thought it best,' I replied, but remained noncommittal.

He held up a can of Budweiser. 'Get you a beer?'

'I'd better not,' I replied with a nod towards my car. 'Not when I'm driving.'

'Something else then?'

'I'll take a cold drink, if you've got one?'

'Chocolate milk?' he said with a smirk.

'Water's fine.' I moved for the steps. 'Or a coffee if you've got a pot on.'

Clayton didn't move from the porch. 'Go round back,' he said, 'I'll bring you something.'

We shared a lingering look, and now I was closer and at a better angle I could see his eyes. His lids pinched a couple of times. He was no longer my employer, but he still wished to be the boss. I mentally shrugged. No matter. I walked round the house while he went back inside.

He'd pulled some garden furniture from the garage. Now there was no apparent threat to him and his property he had probably deemed it safe to do so. There was a table with wooden benches and a parasol that cast a good blot of shade. I sat, and from there had a view of the house to one side and the pond to the other. Ordinarily the shimmering pond, over which skated fluttering insects, would have won my attention, but I canted my head to watch for my host. A dribble of sweat ran from my hairline and I knocked it away with a finger. After the thunder and lightning storms, the temperature had risen steadily and was now ten degrees beyond comfortable for me. I'd done some acclimatizing in the years since I'd made Florida my home, but some days were just so hot it reminded me I still had northern English blood.

Clayton sauntered across the lawn towards me, carrying a tray on which he'd placed a coffee pot and cup, and another couple of beers for himself. There was no milk or sugar for my coffee, but that was fine, and actually the way I preferred to drink it. He looked uncomfortable carrying the tray, as if perhaps he'd have preferred ordering me to play server instead. He plonked the tray down unceremoniously. I waited while he seated himself on the bench opposite before reaching for the pot and tipping out a good measure of coffee. I didn't drink though.

'What are you waiting for,' he asked, aiming his can at me, 'an invitation?'

I'd entertained some suspicions about the preparation of drinks in the Clayton household, not least recalling the gritty substance I'd noticed in the bottom of Cole's drinking bottle that time. When Ella was attacked, Andrew's alibi stood on the fact he'd gone up to Lake Tarpon with his son, but I'd wondered about its validity. A few tranquilizers dropped into his juice would have sent the boy into dreamland long enough for Andrew to leave him in the car while he returned to the house to murder Cole's mother. After the deed was done Clayton could have easily driven up to his fishing cabin, put the boy to bed, and on waking the kid would have been no wiser about the lapse in time, or where his father had been in the meantime. I thought about other times I'd noticed the boy looking groggy, and thought perhaps his dad had continued feeding him a knockout drug to keep him manageable at bedtime. That damn bottle had become a fixture in Cole's hand.

It was a wild theory, I admit, but it had been in the back of my mind long enough to ferment into a firm suspicion I wouldn't shake until I knew otherwise. I'd look a fool if I drank something that didn't agree with me.

Clayton snorted. 'Want me to taste it first?'

'Why would you need to do that?'

'Just wondered why you're turning your nose up at it like that. From what I've seen you're a bit of a caffeine freak.' He shrugged, as if my reticence to drink was below his contempt. 'Suit yourself. Drink, don't drink. Maybe I hawked a lugie in it before I brought the jug out here.'

And there it was: an admission that he was pissed with me about something, and I no longer thought it was because of the keys I'd filched.

'I've given you reason to spit in my coffee?' I asked.

'For the record, I haven't.' He aimed the can at me again, and it was beginning to annoy me. 'But I sure was tempted.'

'You weren't happy with my work? You paid up. If you expected more from me I'll give you a rebate.'

'I should get a full fucking refund,' he said.

I didn't answer.

He aimed the can at me a third time. 'You were supposed to be here to protect Cole. OK, so you did what was asked of you, but that wasn't the only reason you were here. You were here to snoop on me.'

Again I didn't offer a straight answer. 'Where is Cole?'

'He's at school. Where'd you think?'

I thought that after the death of Parker Quinn, Clayton might have kept him away from school for a few days, to allow the boy time to come to terms with his latest shock. But perhaps it was best that Cole was at school, surrounded by his friends, rather than brooding in his room where his grieving would be all the darker. And that he wasn't around to witness things now.

'I was only checking it was safe to speak bluntly.'

'Be as blunt as you want,' he said, and gave me a sneer. 'I fucking intend to be.'

'Good. I hate when people pussyfoot around.'

He placed his beer can on the table. He stood slowly, stepping out from behind the bench while I remained seated. 'You're a real piece of work, ain't ya?'

'So I've been told.'

He thumped his chest with a curled fist in what I guessed might have been one of his prefight rituals from back in the day. His posturing also had an effect on his vernacular, and again I supposed his behaviour harked back to when he faced off against equally vulgar young bravos. 'So? Come on, asshole. Out with it. You've something you wanna fucking say bluntly. Do it now. Man-to-fucking-man.' He punctuated the last with another gorilla-like thump to his chest.

Without rising to the challenge, I only looked at him steadily. 'You told Rink you wanted a word with me. I thought it'd be something more erudite than "fucking".' I sniffed at his attempt at intimidation.

'You're a sanctimonious asshole, aren't you?'

'I've been told that before too. You asked me if I'd been snooping on you. Well, the answer's yes and no.'

'I didn't ask, I knew. You think I'm fucking stupid?'

'Would a stupid man need snooping on?' I countered. 'That's why my answer is primarily "no".'

'So you think I'm only a bit stupid?' He rolled his tongue against his bottom lip.

'I was here to protect Cole. But I was here with an open mind on whether you might be the one dangerous to him.'

'Son of a bitch! You think I'd harm my own son?' He took one step around the table, and I pivoted so I could keep my gaze fixed on him, but also to discretely move my feet out past the table leg.

'Relax, Clayton. I already decided you're no threat to Cole.' I picked up my coffee and swigged it down in one. As I set down the cup, I again stared at him. 'I've got to ask you, though. Cole? When did you find out he really wasn't your boy?'

'What the fuck?' He curled his fists. I held up a hand to stall him.

I slid out my SIG and placed it flat on the table next to the coffee pot. He eyed it spuriously.

'Don't worry about the gun,' I said. 'It was getting uncomfortable prodding my back when I'm sweating like a pig.'

He took off his spectacles and placed them on the table too. He dashed perspiration from his eye-sockets with both hands, swiped his hands out so the droplets arched from his fingertips. He didn't lower his arms all the way, making him look like he'd an invisible rolled carpet beneath each armpit.

'Well?' I asked.

'Cole's my son.' His words were cold.

'There was a time when I thought that maybe Parker Quinn was more than an uncle to the boy, but that wasn't it. Want to tell me about Royce Benson?'

'The fuck with him.'

'So you do know him?'

He seethed with poorly restrained anger.

'So why lie about him when I asked? You described him down to the tattoo on his hand. You know, if you'd mentioned his name after he punched you, two guys might still be alive.'

'Don't fucking dare try to blame Parker's death on me.'

'I'm not. But if you'd come clean about Royce in the beginning, then maybe he could've been stopped before he got to Quinn. Hell, if I'd known I was after the wrong man I wouldn't have bothered Tommy Benson, and he wouldn't have run into the traffic.'

'To hell with Tommy-fucking-Benson. He was working for that other piece of shit, wasn't he? I've no fucking regrets about him!'

'He was being used,' I said, and couldn't keep the recrimination out of my tone. 'You knew all along Royce Benson was behind this. Why the hell didn't you tell the police?' I held up my hand to stall him, because I'd my own theory. 'You didn't want anyone to know he was Cole's real father.'

'Fuck you.'

'You know, the more times you use that word, the less effect it has on me. And you can stop the denial: you've more or less admitted he's the real dad.'

'No! He was just a fucking sperm donor. I'm Cole's dad!'

'I'm not denying you've been a father to him, and yeah, it does take more than fathering a child to be a real dad, and you beat Royce hands down there. But is this what it's all about? Royce murdered Ella because he was denied access to his own son?'

'What do you mean Royce killed Ella? Are you nuts? It was the home invasion gang-' He came to an abrupt stop, as if only then realising the truth. 'Hold on! Royce murdered her? He set it up to look like…son of a fucking bitch!'

'Quit the lies, Clayton. You suspected all along. What bothered me is why you didn't tell the police, and put a stop to things. What has Royce got over you that he's made you keep his involvement a secret?'

Clayton stared down at me, his mouth working. Finally he swept an arm to one side. 'I want you to leave.'

I didn't move.

'Now. Get up, and get the fuck off my property before I throw you off.'

'That day at the gate,' I went on, 'you knew it was Royce. You went out to speak with him in the middle of a storm. What did he want that was so important that you did that? Is he blackmailing you or something?'

'I'm not answering another of your damn questions,' he snapped. 'Who the fuck do you think you are anyway? You're not a cop.'

'I'm not. But I can have them over here like that.' I snapped my fingers to clarify. 'In fact, if you don't speak to me, I'm duty bound to call Detective VanMeter and tell her what I've learned.'

'You've learned fuck-all, man.'

'I've learned enough to know I'm right. Royce Benson is Cole's genetic father, he's probably the one who murdered Ella, and Quinn, and has been behind the harassment of you, and setting things up to make you look like a murderer – and yet here you are, protecting him, like you're too afraid to come clean about him.'

'You calling me a coward?'

'I'm calling you a misguided fool,' I clarified. 'I'm not calling you a coward, no, but I do believe you're afraid of him, or what it will mean to your son if he ever finds out the truth about his real father.'

'I've asked you to leave.'

'I'll come back with the cops.'

'The fuck has anything of this to do with you?'

'I signed on to protect Cole. I'm not finished doing that yet.'

'Fuck you. Cole doesn't need your protection. I'm his dad, I'll be all the protection he needs!'

'You can't protect Cole *and* Royce,' I said. 'What happens when Royce comes back to finish things good and proper?'

'Whaddaya mean "come back"? I thought from the way you were talking he'd already been arrested. How'd you know about him otherwise?'

'I might not be the world's best detective but I can still ask around,' I said. 'This thing with Royce, it's been going on for more than a decade. Sounds as if it might've come to a head a lot sooner if he hadn't got himself put away in prison for...' Now it was me doing the old "Oh, I just realised" look. 'That's it. It was you that had him put away for fraud, right? Or maybe you were involved in his crimes in another way.'

'You don't know what the fuck you're talking about,' he growled.

'Then enlighten me.'

'Nope. I've said all I'm gonna say. Now, get up, walk away, and don't show your face round here again. Otherwise, I promise you, I will rearrange it.'

'Quit with the bullshit, will you?' I demanded. 'You've more to worry about.'

'Royce Benson? I'm not afraid of him, but you should be.'

'How come?'

'You're the one chased his cousin into traffic. Think he'll let that go without some sort of payback? I thought he'd already proved what he was capable of...' Clayton stumbled to a halt, realising the admission he had just made: yes, he knew much more about Royce than he'd previously let on. 'Right. Enough. Now like I said, get the fuck out or I'm gonna make you.'

We were both simmering for different reasons, both of us prone to blow at any second. I should've got up and walked away. But my impetuous nature simply wouldn't allow it.

'I shouldn't let the rest of that coffee go to waste,' I said.

Clayton swung for me, and I welcomed the move.

28

Old fighters often seek that one final battle, where they can prove they aren't over the hill, that they're still a contender for the crown. From the first time Clayton bragged about his prowess in the bare-knuckle ring, I suspected he'd been sizing me up, wondering who was the better man, and concluding that – of course – it was he. If I'd to be totally honest, I'd entertained similar thoughts, and knew in my bones that somewhere down the line we'd come to blows. Employing a bodyguard for Cole hadn't sat well with him; it suggested that he was too weak for the job, and in need of protection too. Hiring another man to protect his child was a personal failure in his mind, and now that there was no longer a requirement to go along with the police's suggestion, he wanted to prove that I'd been a spare wheel all along. I was also of a similar mind-set, in that I too had something to prove. Not so much to Clayton, but to myself. In my mid-forties now, I wasn't the soldier I was even five years ago, and goading Clayton into a fistfight was as much a test of my self-worth as stuffing my rucksack with bricks and running until I dropped ever was. Nobody is perfect, and some of us are far from it. There's darkness in me, I don't deny it, and it's prone to express itself in violence. I'm not proud of the aggressive side to my nature, but it's there and sometimes requires feeding. Thankfully I'm able to control the hunger most of the time, and target my lust for combat on deserving targets, and Andrew Clayton didn't fit the usual bill. But there were things about the man that had pissed me off, no less his lies, and his reticence to tell the truth sooner when doing so would have saved lives. Then there was the aloofness he'd showed Cole, when all the kid really wanted was a hug. He'd argued that he was a dad, more than a mere genetic father could ever be, but he sure hadn't shown it. I'd egged him into a fight, because he needed some sense of priority knocked into his fat head.

When he swung for me, a clubbing right hand at the side of my head, I'd seen it coming a mile off. I ducked, and his arm swept by, even as I began to slip off the bench seat. I didn't expect his next move though, and it told me that Clayton was a more dangerous fighter than his overblown fight record attested to. He grasped the opposite side of the table and heaved up, throwing it against me, and had I not adjusted my feet earlier I'd have been trapped between table and bench and at his mercy. My SIG skidded away on to the lawn, but that was OK, because I'd no need of it. His spectacles went flying too, along with the beer can he'd dumped, but I deliberately knocked aside the coffee jug to avoid a scalding. Under other circumstances the jug would have made a great weapon, but for this fight I'd other ideas.

Clayton was a big man, much heavier than me, but he was anything but slowed by his bulk. He knew how to use it to his advantage. He kept heaving, getting both arms under the table and using it as a battering ram against me, forcing me to get the hell out of the way. The umbrella was an encumbrance, both to my mobility and my vision, and I yanked at it, pulling the pole from the centre of the table. In my hands was an unwieldy lance, but I used it to jab at Clayton's chest, and he reared back from the dirt-encrusted tip, and he lost his grip on the table. As I gained clearance, I overhanded the parasol end, and Clayton batted it aside with both forearms. When he turned towards me, I was ready for him; both of my hands now up in a recognisable boxer's guard.

There's an enigma attached to fighting, where even someone more comfortable with striking will revert to natural instinct when grabbed: they'll also grab their opponent and grapple when they should be punching. Pro-fighters train out the instinct to needlessly grapple, but it's still there, and in the throes of battle they can't resist the urge. The opposite is said for when you lift your fists, their instinct then is to trade blows, and usually on the same plane. I made it look as if I was concerned about a punch to the head, and that of course made Clayton more determined to hit it. He powered a left jab at me that I slipped, and as his right cross to my chin thudded in, I caught his wrist in my left palm and parried it aside. My right fist hooked into his floating rib. Clayton grunted, but my short hook was never going to stop him. He back elbowed at my chin, and though it wasn't a clean blow his forearm smacked up against my right ear. I was knocked aside, but went with the flow, and gaining room to move I changed my plane of attack, and it was nowhere he was ready for. My heel struck the outer edge of his knee.

A warning to the wise. Never admit to having a weakness to a potential adversary. Early on Clayton told me his fighting career ended when he blew out his anterior cruciate ligament. He'd even helped highlight his weakness with an unconscious tap at his leg. I targeted the same knee with my kick, but only with enough force to wobble him: I could have immediately ended his comeback if I'd powered in the kick. As it was, pain shot through him and he staggered, and when I hooked him this time, it was a full shot to his chest with my bodyweight behind it.

'Son of a bitch,' he wheezed.

'Had enough yet?'

'I haven't even gotten started.'

He came at me again, this time mixing up his own planes of attack. A straight left and right punch, turned into a rapid hook/uppercut combination that set me rocking to and fro, and then he swept a knee up at my groin. I sucked back my gut, and his knee only skimmed me – thankfully on my pubis bone and not my testicles – and I dropped the tip of my elbow into the meat of his thigh. His weight was enough to force me backwards. I felt my heels sinking into the soft lawn, and had to settle before swinging a counter flurry of punches. Now Clayton was the one ducking and weaving, but he was timing my punches and dug in with a snappy hook of his own to my ribs. The pain exhibited in the gritting of my teeth and squinting of my eyes, and he knew he'd landed a good dig. It spurred him to capitalise on his advantage, and he got me again, this time with an uppercut that rocked me on my feet.

It was more by accident than design that when he drove in with a solid jab to the chin, that I pivotted to present my back to him, parrying his punch with my shoulder even as I wrapped my bent arm around his forearm. I snapped down on his wrist, hyper-extending his elbow over my shoulder. I thrust my hips backwards, and hauled him over the fulcrum in a cumbersome offside throw. He didn't somersault onto his back, just kind of staggered forward on one leg, and fought for balance, while I kept hold of his trapped arm stopping him from doing so. In desperation he threw a punch across his body, but missed me by a long way. But then he changed his punch so that it targeted my own bent elbow, and the shot to the nerves sent white fire up my arm to the fingertips. I lost my grip, and he spun, settling himself for another punch at my head.

My right arm was numb, a poor defence, but it was all I had when his fist powered at my chin. I tucked my head low, lifted my shoulder and absorbed the punch that should have knocked my lights out. Clayton was happy that he'd got in another hurtful punch, and grinned at me to show his pleasure. I edged back a few feet, and nodded at him in acceptance.

'Had enough yet?' he asked, mimicking my taunt of moments ago. 'Need a rest, buddy?'

'Still plenty left in my tank,' I replied, trying not to wilt under the agony in my right shoulder. 'If you want a second or two to catch your breath, feel free. I'll wait. Don't want to take a liberty with a washed-out old man.'

'I'm good to go.'

'Then come on.' I wiggled the tingling fingers of my right hand at him in what looked like a show of bravado, but was really an attempt to get the blood flowing in my shocked extremity again.

He danced in like a boxer, throwing short jabs to get me moving, trying to force me left so that my weakened right side was open to attack. I denied him his plan, skipping sideways, and chopping out at his pistoning wrist with the edge of my left hand. If I'd punched his exposed ribs with my right, I'd have undone what little feeling I'd regained in my arm, so I chose instead to snap a palm into the side of his head. I felt the contact of skin on skin, heard the sharp slap of my hand on his bald scalp, but I'd hit high and with little effect on him.

'Shit! You hit like a little girl,' he taunted.

'I'll make you squeal like a girl,' I promised.

He laughed.

The fucker was enjoying himself.

But then again, in a similar weird throe of masochism, so was I.

Grinning, I beckoned him in again.

Our tussle had taken us down the slope towards the pond. The lawn was spongier than ever, the water table having risen from the recent storm. My boots were waterproofed but I could still feel the added weight of cloying mud on the soles. I snapped a kick towards Clayton and watched a divot of muddy grass strike his belly. He frowned, slapped at the mucky stain on his shirt.

'Was there any need?' he demanded.

I wiggled my eyebrows, and it spurred him to attack. He yelled as he came, and I waited, allowing him to go for the grapple round my waist. As he snugged in, began squeezing, and lifting, I clubbed both forearms down on the back of his neck at the same time as I drove one knee into his chest. The double battering loosened his grip, but I made the mistake of returning his grapple. I looped an arm round his head, grabbed at the waistband of his jeans with my other hand. As he lifted me with an enormous grunt of effort, we both skidded off our feet. Because he was upslope, my back was towards the pond, and I'd further to fall. However, I kept a good grip on the levers I'd snatched and as I hit dirt, I rolled him over the top of me, kicking out with my legs at the last moment. This time he did somersault, but he didn't relinquish his hard won hold, and we continued the tumble I'd initiated. The tall reeds at pondside thrashed us. About a billion insects filled the scene, and we were both dotted with writhing bugs. One or two of the little devils were in my ears, and more in my nostrils and mouth. Clayton was no better off. We both kicked and pushed, as much to get away from the wriggling swarm as each other. On the way we landed a couple of sly digs apiece. Clayton was filthy, and I guessed I was equally as mud smeared. He smacked at my head with an open hand. I backhanded him. Then we were both on our knees, and we went for a grip on each other's heads. I had hair that Clayton got a grab on but his dome was shiny so my hold was on an ear: mine was the better and more painful grip, and I won the head control battle. I twisted him sideways, forcing him down and I fell over him, chest to chest, and my bodyweight helped press him further into the soggy reeds. Water pumped up through the spongy lattice of roots and flooded over his face. He cried out in panic and thrashed a hand at the muddy water to clear it from his mouth, nostrils and eyes. It was a battle he'd no hope of winning, because he only forced up more pond water that now invaded every orifice.

I could tell there was something decidedly wrong, and I relaxed my hold on his ear. He craned up, gasping for life, spitting the filthy water from his mouth. I poised to get in a good crack to his face, but held back. Clayton bucked and kicked and made a wordless roar. His eyes were startled, and his mouth wide in abject horror.

I sat up, then backed off him.

He struggled, but he couldn't get a hand under him that didn't sink deeper into the mud. He again cried out, and I knew I had to do something before he disappeared fully into the pond. I grabbed the font of his shirt, hauled him up. He windmilled his arms. Dirt and broken reeds clung to him, and his emphasis again went to clearing his face. While he was wiping away mud, I wrenched backwards and pulled him clear of the sucking mud, and allowed him to drop on the lowest edge of the lawn. He lay there gasping.

'For fuck's sake,' I said in bemusement. 'You can't swim?'

He coughed and spluttered, and it was enough of an answer to assume I was correct. It also explained why there'd never been a swimming pool added to his expansive property.

'You sell boats for a living and you can't even swim?' I asked again.

'Don't…need to swim…' he gasped, 'when you've a…good boat beneath you…' He again went into a coughing fit. I was sitting alongside him, equally covered in filth. Something alive and furious squirmed under the collar of my shirt. I swiped it out, saw something black and sinuous and dashed it away in disgust. Next I dug mud from my ears.

Clearing my ear canals made my hearing that much sharper and I heard the slow clap of someone upslope from us.

Craning round I spotted a figure limned by the sun, and instantly recognised her lithe and curvy shape.

'Hey, Bryony!' I greeted her.

'Well done boys,' she answered. 'Finished with our little mud wrassle are we?'

'If you're going to wrestle a swine, you have to do it in mud,' I commented. My words actually gained me a grunt of mirth from Clayton, who was now free of the panic his near drowning had brought on.

'Talk about a dirty fighter,' he put in, wiping mud from his face, and now I grinned at the lame joke. He sideswiped me with the back of his arm, and we both struggled up. It was as slippery as hell. In the end we held on to each other and made it to our feet. We stood there like two naughty schoolboys caught in a prank, both of us flicking muck from our fingertips. We shared a conspiratorial smile.

'What is this anyway?' Bryony asked. 'Some kind of homo-erotic male bonding session?'

'Let's not go too far,' I told her.

'Boys. You never grow up.'

'Nothing wrong with staying young at heart,' Clayton pointed out. 'Eh, Hunter?'

'Amen to that,' I agreed.

'What the hell do you think you were doing?' Bryony demanded, still confused by the scene she'd stumbled on.

'Just clearing the air,' I said.

'Yup,' agreed Clayton. 'Just putting a few things to rights.'

'And are we all sorted now?' Bryony asked.

I looked at Clayton.

'A draw?' he asked.

'Dream on.'

He shook his head, but it was with a laugh. He slapped me on my shoulder – the one he'd earlier tried his hardest to injure – but this time it was simply a clap of camaraderie. 'OK,' I acquiesced, 'Let's call it a draw.'

'Thank the Lord for that,' said Bryony. Then she aimed a beady eye at me. 'What's up, Joe? With Holker incapacitated you had to find someone else to piss off?'

'We're good now. Just had to clear up a few misunderstandings on both our parts. Clayton isn't your man, Bryony.'

'I know.'

Clayton squinted between us. 'You guys actually believed I had something to do with my wife's murder?'

'We couldn't discount you,' Bryony explained.

'Wasn't him,' I repeated.

'And you know that how?'

I could have explained that if Clayton was a murderer, he would have fought like one, and not stuck to a moral code of conduct like the sportsman he was. But that would have meant little. Instead I stated a fact. 'Because I think I know who was, and Andrew also knows.'

I was putting him on the spot, but there you go. I'd agreed our fight had ended in a draw, and now he owed me something in return.

He looked at the ground. Then slowly raised his head, his mouth pulled into a tight grimace. 'The man you're looking for is-'

Before he could complete his sentence Bryony finished it. 'Royce Benson.'

I was secretly pleased she'd beaten me to the punch. She was the real detective after all, and it wouldn't have been good for her career prospects if an amateur like me had solved the murder before she did.

<u>29</u>

Rink was unimpressed by my account of taking on Andrew Clayton *mano a mano,* **suggesting** I'd have been better served convincing him that with Royce Benson still on the loose the necessity for a bodyguard still existed.

'That's exactly what our little scrap achieved,' I reassured him. 'It also won me some respect from the guy, and he's now more inclined to work with me instead of putting up barriers.'

'You did talk fees, right, brother? I know what you're like when it comes to offering *pro bono* work.'

'We agreed the same terms as before, Rink. I told him we'd send over an invoice at conclusion of the job.'

Rink nodded. Satisfied. He wasn't greedy, but a business only survived when it had a healthy incoming cash flow. We were sitting in his office building, and the footfall of clients through the front door was slower than a glacier's progress. McTeer's work for the soccer star down in Miami brought some kickbacks to Rington Investigations, but the work for Andrew Clayton was the only real money-spinner we'd had lately.

I dug the house keys I'd appropriated from my pocket. 'Won't need these now, I suppose.' I'd planned on sneaking in, and conducting a thorough search of the house at my leisure. But that was when I was still looking for the missing wedding ring, and whatever it was I thought Clayton had used to dope the kid with, among other things – none of which I now expected to find there. I hadn't shared my plan with Rink.

'Spill,' he said.

'I thought Clayton was hiding something. He was, but not what I thought. The kid…Cole…he isn't Andrew's.'

Rink didn't look too surprised. 'Thought he looked more like Parker Quinn myself,' he said.

'That's what I thought at first. But then I saw Tommy Benson and changed my opinion.'

'The kid was Tommy's?'

'No. That's where I was still wrong. Cole's father is Tommy's cousin, Royce Benson.'

'This the frog-gigger who's been causing all the bother?'

'That's the general consensus.'

After our mud fight, and righting the garden furniture, Clayton and me had sat down at the picnic table with Bryony. While wiping broken blades of grass from his spectacles, Clayton had come clean about the secret he'd been hiding from us. 'Royce used to be Andrew's best buddy,' I explained. 'Apparently they met on the underground fighting circuit. Andrew was already a name, and he took Royce under his wing, got him a few fights, helped with his training.'

'He was managing him?' Rink posed.

'Yeah. But not in an official capacity. He was doing it through friendship, trying to help the guy out. Well, that's the way Clayton makes it sound, but you ask me he was using the guy also. He would give Royce other jobs, the shitty stuff he didn't want to deal with himself, and for a while Royce hung out with him like an extra member of the family, and was even involved when Clayton and Quinn partnered up to start their business. But he integrated into the family a little too closely, getting as close to Ella as he was to Andrew, probably closer. This was before they were married. Then Ella got pregnant, and Andrew popped the question. He'd no idea Cole wasn't his and Ella wasn't about to make him any the wiser until she had his ring on her finger.'

'So what part of his millions attracted Ella to Clayton?' Rink quipped in a world-weary fashion.

'Once the boy was born the truth came out of course, but by then Ella was Clayton's wife, and had a stake in the company, and in the home he'd purchased for them. If he'd kicked her out, he'd have been ruined. Instead Clayton knuckled down, accepted Ella's infidelity and took the boy on as his own. Course, he wasn't as forgiving of Royce. They came to blows. But that didn't satisfy Clayton, he wanted to punish Royce for what he saw as a massive betrayal of his friendship, and his trust. He knew Royce was up to no good, cloning credit cards, forging cheques, pulling other scams, and he tipped off the police. To prove her fealty to her husband, Ella apparently helped him set Royce up. Royce became the subject of an investigation and because his crimes were judged as federal offenses he earned himself a ten-year stretch in Zephyrhills Correctional Institute for his trouble.'

'With that in mind, I'm surprised the cops didn't finger Royce for Ella's murder first thing,' said Rink.

'Royce was clever and made the murder look like a bungled robbery. The cops were chasing their tails trying to catch the home invasion crew, and Royce had set things up to look like another of their jobs. You remember there was more than one gun used, and various footprints found at the house: well, Bryony now believes Royce set the scene to look as if there were a number of robbers. The way he tried to set the scene at Quinn's place, making his murder look like a suicide.'

'What was Tommy Benson's part in it all?'

'He was being used, but I don't think Royce ever intended for him to be connected to the crime or especially killed. Tommy was helping Royce get his revenge on the Clayton's, but only through smashing a window and that time he dumped the glove to point the blame at Parker Quinn. We thought at first that Tommy had been given the notes to copy so he could send the anonymous emails to the police claiming Clayton murdered his wife; but we now think Royce – the forger – was behind it. His fingerprints were lifted off bullet casings in a gun found concealed at Tommy's place, showing Royce was the one who hid it in the crawl space, and I also heard from a mutual acquaintance that Royce has been staying with Tommy since he got out of prison. I only discovered Tommy through chance, and now that we've a better idea about when Quinn died, it was around the same time as Tommy ran to his death. So it had to be Royce.'

'Why murder Quinn?'

I shrugged. 'Royce wanted a fall guy, and Quinn being Clayton's business partner, one who was in a current dispute over ownership, made him an ideal candidate. We're guessing that Royce didn't believe his home invasion scenario would stand up to deeper scrutiny, so instead tried to make it look as if Quinn was behind the set up. Don't forget he knew Quinn from before his imprisonment and probably thought he was also involved in getting him arrested, seeing as Quinn had replaced him as Clayton's new bosom buddy. He probably decided he could get two lots of revenge for the price of one in killing Quinn, and hurting Clayton again.'

'What is it with these bozo criminals? They think they're cleverer than they are. Why not just go after Clayton in the first place; a drive-by shooting or something and have done?'

'That wouldn't have been satisfying enough. He felt wronged, I guess. Particularly by the woman he loved, who'd chosen Clayton's money over him, and even denied him his son by helping put him in prison. Bryony for one believes that Ella's murder was a crime of passion; the rest is all about cold retribution. It's why he stole Ella's wedding band: he thought the ring she was wearing should've been his from the beginning.'

Rink pulled at his bottom lip, deep in contemplation. Alongside his index finger, a scar on his chin he wore from an encounter with a crazy knifeman turned white against his tawny skin. Coming to a conclusion he finally looked across at me. 'Why'd Clayton cover for him though? He must've know Royce was behind everything, especially when he got a good look at him that time at the gate.'

'Royce has been blackmailing him.'

'Ah,' said Rink. 'Something to do with Cole?'

'Yeah. But that's only partly it. He warned that if Clayton breathed a word that he was around, then he'd snatch Cole and bury him out in a swamp. Clayton swore he didn't think Royce was serious, but couldn't take the chance: hence he agreed to hire me as a bodyguard for Cole. But that's not what he was most afraid of. See, it appears that back in the day, it was Clayton who taught Royce everything he knew about fraud and deception, and that Royce was prepared to spill all to the police. If he did, then Andrew would be looking at a similar prison sentence Royce had already endured.'

'Clayton's an asshole,' Rink said.

'Yeah, he is. The way he tells things there was no real love lost between him and Ella since they first got married. In some respects Royce has helped him out, getting rid of both an unfaithful and loveless wife, and a troublesome business partner. I could tell Bryony wanted to arrest him, thinking maybe Clayton actually did put Royce up to the murders but that wasn't it. He might be looking at a police obstruction or perverting the course of justice charge, or whatever it's called here in the States, but as it stands it's only hearsay at the moment. Everything was off the record, Bryony hadn't read him the Miranda warning, and nothing is in writing, so everything he admitted to is inadmissible in court. Even if she pushed it, Clayton could easily lawyer-up and retract everything he'd said. Even if he is caught, Royce Benson's testimony would be deemed unreliable.'

'So Bryony let it go?'

'She's more interested in catching a killer than she is chasing Clayton for crimes more than a decade old, especially when there's little hope of proving them.'

'How's your buddy?' Rink asked, changing the subject.

'Holker? He's recovering. He's tried to discharge himself from hospital, but even if he were to get out, he won't be allowed back to work yet. Not on active duty at any rate – poor bugger is still catheted up and pissing in a bag.' I tried not to smile.

'Is Bryony now lead on the investigation?'

'It's why her captain pulled her in. She thought she was in for a kicking, but it turned out to be the opposite. She was given primary detective duties on Ella and Quinn's murders, the home invasion crew are now off her books, being looked after by other detectives from the task force seeing as they've been proved to be unrelated cases now.'

'She deputise you, then?'

I snorted out a laugh. 'She told me to concentrate on my bodyguard duties and leave the detective work to her in future.'

Rink also laughed. 'What are the chances, eh?'

'Have you heard the expression "in for a penny in for a pound"?'

'It's one of the less confusing sayings I've heard you use, brother. So what you got in mind?'

'There's a suggestion that an extra person has been added to Royce Benson's hit list, namely yours truly. For all he was using Tommy, it doesn't change the fact they were cousins, and he might blame me for Tommy's death. I'm hoping to use his need for revenge to my – and Bryony's - benefit.'

'He'd be a fool to come within a mile of Clayton's place now that the police are hunting him.' Rink suddenly realised where he was being led. He shook his head at me. 'He doesn't know he's a suspect yet?'

'No. He can't know what Clayton has told us, and probably doesn't know the police got his prints from the gun – which by the way the ballistics reports prove was one used to shoot holes in the walls at the Claytons' house. That time at the gate, Clayton was still protecting him, and actually told Royce to hit him and run when I approached, so he's probably confident that Clayton's still fearful of what will happen if he talks. But I'm with you: he won't come to the house, but he will want to speak with Clayton again, and I think I know how that can be arranged.'

'You're planning on setting a trap?'

'Yeah, and guess who's going to be the bait?'

'You're nuts, brother. I ever tell you that?'

'About ten times a day.'

Rink stood, glowered down at me with a look of reproof. He usually did that ten times a day too.

'I'm going to need your help, of course,' I told him.

'Well, didn't I just see that coming,' he scolded, but he was secretly pleased. He was curling up inside at the lack of activity he'd been engaged in lately, despite his Zen-like cool about it all. 'What do you want from me, brother?'

I laid out my plan as briefly as I could.

'Shit, man,' he said once I was done. 'If this goes wrong you'll be royally fucked. Actually, strike that: *We'll* be royally fucked!'

<u>30</u>

Jedediah Boaz was a respected detective in his days with Tampa PD.
Bryony remembered his name being mentioned around the precinct when
first she'd started work as a patrol cop in District 2, and vaguely recalled
that he'd been pensioned out on medical grounds following a car crash that
almost took one of his legs. In the intervening years she'd occasionally
heard his name come up in conversation, but as time passed it was with
more derision, and then with a note of ridicule. It saddened her to hear that
former colleagues now used the man's name as a cautionary tale for where
a reliance on booze could send you, and she'd been disgusted to learn that
there was even an "unofficial" sweep stake going around the office on
when he'd stop sucking on a scotch bottle and place the barrel of a
revolver between his teeth. Bryony had one time made her feelings known,
only for her colleagues to laugh her down, and tell her she was a victim of
her feminine sensibilities. Boaz was a hopeless drunk, playing at gumshoe
out of the back of a car that was falling to pieces around him. These days
patrol cops watched out for him behind the wheel, because they could
guarantee themselves a DUI arrest. Bryony had checked: Boaz had never
been arrested – let alone charged – with driving under the influence, but he
had spent a few nights in the County lockup's drunk tank.

It didn't surprise her to find Boaz was the detective who'd pieced
together the case against Royce Benson that had put him behind bars in the
correctional institute at Zephyrhills; this was back when Boaz was a good
detective, before the accident and his spiral into self-destruction. She'd read
the case files, and from them had formed the opinion that Royce was
indeed a criminal, but there was nothing to suggest he was capable of
murder. Yes, he was known to be aggressive and violent, but how could
she judge him on that when she saw those very same traits in Joe Hunter, a
man she valued as a friend, and possibly more? Royce Benson was a
fighter, but from what she'd learned he usually restricted his battles to the

ring – sometimes in underground arenas granted – but there was nothing on his record that suggested he took his battles to the street itself. That was before he spent eight years behind bars. Penned up like an animal, who knew how his nature had altered? Perhaps his incarceration had allowed his anger and frustration to fester into something unrecognisable in the younger fighter. She'd checked his prison record, and found that he had been involved in a number of minor altercations, but nothing that had stained his record too indelibly, and he'd made parole two years earlier than his original ten years sentence had demanded. She knew that a prison record was never complete. On his record were only incidents the correctional staff had learned of, and taken note; there would be much more that they had missed. She decided that to get the measure of the man she was now hunting she should speak with someone who knew him for what he really was. His parole officer was unavailable, on vacation on a cruise ship down in the Caribbean, but he'd only know the man Royce pretended to be these days anyway, so she decided she should go to source.

She'd attended Boaz's condominium in River Oaks, and having only walked up the filthy stairs to his upper floor apartment, had come away from the experience feeling grimy, sullied by the atmosphere. How did a decorated cop end up in such desperation as Boaz now lived? Easily, she concurred, and fleetingly worried about Dennis Holker and how things might have ended for him if his injuries had proved more serious. Knocking on the door had failed to garner a response, and she'd called Boaz's telephone numbers on record, listening first to the landline phone ringing out, and then to silence when she tried his cell. She thumped determinedly on the door with the ball of her hand, but with no success. Boaz wasn't home; so next she drove to a strip mall on West Waters Avenue, and looked up at the dingy office windows above a tool hire shop. She scanned the parking lot, and spotted an older model Honda Civic, dotted with bird droppings and a with a handful of flyers for take out food and escort girls – the required nourishment that fed many men – jammed under the windshield wipers. The car didn't appear to have been moved in a number of days. She checked the Honda's tag number against the one she'd jotted in her notebook earlier, and confirmed the car belonged to Boaz. She glanced up at the blind windows of his office and wondered if he was inside. She rang his cell phone again, and this time heard the faint strains of an electronic ditty over the swishing of passing traffic. But the phone went unanswered. Perhaps Boaz was out of his office and a likely contender for where he might be found was any of the nearby bars. But she couldn't walk away without checking. Equally he could be upstairs, perhaps worse for wear from the bottle he took refuge in these days, maybe passed out in his desk chair or sleeping in any available spot. She headed for the tool hire shop, because she could see no other way up to the office.

A middle-aged Floridian man of Spanish descent greeted her. He was propped on his elbows behind a scarred counter, looking as weary as the décor in the front of the shop. He was protected behind a wire screen, with only a small open hatch through which he slouched. Behind him was a storeroom, cluttered with faded boxes and tool parts. He was round faced, carrying a scattering of old acne scars on his cheeks, and his hair receded from a sallow brow. He blinked in surprise at her, and she wondered if it was because he hadn't expected a customer, or if it was because she wasn't the type who generally hired from him, or if – and it were more likely – he'd immediately made her as a cop. For a second she wondered if it were only tools that were passed to customers from behind the counter, and if at any second he'd slam down the security hatch hovering over his head, and flee for a back way out. He didn't do any such thing; he smiled at her and held up a pudgy hand as he said hi.

Bryony flashed her shield, and introduced herself. 'I'm looking for Jedediah Boaz,' she explained, as she glanced about seeking a door to upstairs, 'and believe he rents the office space above you. How do I get up there?'

'Jed's not in,' replied the man amiably, and there was no suggestion he was trying to deter her from finding him. His accent held no trace of his Mediterranean heritage. He looked up at the ceiling. 'In fact, I haven't heard him up there in a few days. Usually I can hear him clumping around on that game leg of his.'

'Are you here all the time?' Bryony asked.

'One man operation, ma'am,' he said. 'If I don't open up, the shop stays closed.'

'And you haven't heard or seen Mr Boaz in days?'

'Four days I'd say. Coulda been Thursday last week, but I could be mistaken.'

'Does Mr Boaz usually come in over the weekend?'

'Spends more time here than he does at home,' he said, 'when he isn't working from his car.'

'You know his car, right?'

'The Honda outside. It has sat out there since Thursday,' said the man without prompting. 'But that isn't unusual. You do know Jed has a problem, right?' He mimed taking a slug from a bottle. 'There are times he goes missing for days on end. That ol' car of his has become quite a fixture out on the lot. Was thinking of using it to my benefit, having an advertisement banner stuck on its roof to draw in passing traffic.'

Bryony didn't answer.

'I'd still like to go up to his office.' She craned to see past him, again looking for a way up.

'Sometimes, when he's not too soused I let him go on up through here.' He thumbed over his shoulder at some indiscernible stairwell hidden from sight in the storeroom. 'But usually he uses the entrance around back. The stairs are a bit cramped for a drunk, but it gives access to the office when I'm closed or when I don't want him knocking everything off my shelves.'

'Around the back?'

'Yup, 'round back. The service alley.' He pointed out snaking directions she didn't really require. 'But you can come through if you prefer.'

She could have easily made the walk to the rear of the building, but she expected the door in the alley would be only one of two she'd have to access. If Boaz were passed out in a drunken stupor, he'd be unlikely to hear her knocking on the lowest door. 'That'd be helpful,' she said. 'Thank you.'

'*No es problema*,' he replied, almost in mockery of his heritage. 'But you'll have to give me a second or two…' He grunted, and wrestled with bolts, and Bryony saw that a portion of the counter was a hinged doorway under the opening. He heaved it open and Bryony had to duck to get through. 'Crazy, no?' said the shopkeeper. 'The lengths I've to go to these days. I used to have an open counter, made things much easier, but I got sick of kids jumping it when I was through back, and stealing the cash from the register. Hah, you can probably tell that when I installed the door, it was before I got so fat.'

Bryony smiled at his self-deprecating humour. But she had wondered: it must be a squeeze for the rotund guy to fit through the gap, and especially for a worse for wear Boaz with a bad leg. The shopkeeper went through the process in reverse, locking the hinged door behind her, then security conscious as ever, dropping the grilled flap over the opening in the screen and also bolting it shut. 'This way,' he finally said, and led her into the dusty confines of his storeroom. They'd to squeeze between rows of shelving, then he indicated a gap in the wall, and the first of a few stairs.

'You don't happen to keep a spare key to his office do you?' she asked.

'I keep one in the safe. What? You want to go inside when he isn't there?'

'I'll see if he's in first,' Bryony said, 'but it sure would be helpful if you fetched the key.'

The guy shrugged.

Bryony went up the stairs. She didn't think it necessary to draw her sidearm, but nevertheless, her hand hovered near her shoulder rig beneath her jacket. The stairs were few, and not too wide, and the bulb the shopkeeper flicked on did little to light her way, being almost opaque with spider webs. She guessed Boaz didn't invite too many prospective clients to his office. At the head of the stairs was a narrow landing, from where a second set of steps descended in the other direction, leading to the fire exit door in the service alley. A flimsy door was all that gave Boaz any privacy in his office, and she thought that the shopkeeper was probably right about it being vacant. When he was in his office he'd hear Boaz pass wind from downstairs, she thought.

She knocked on the door.

No answer.

She rang Boaz's cell, and again heard the strains of music, now much louder and recognisable as a factory set ringtone.

'Mr Boaz,' she called. 'Mr Boaz! Tampa PD. Can you please answer the door.'

From below her on the stairs she heard the shopkeeper coming up with the key. She held out a palm to stall him.

'Mr Boaz? My name's Bryony VanMeter, I'm a detective with Tampa PD and need to speak with you urgently.' She rapped on the door again.

'Like I said, I don't think Jed's in,' offered the shopkeeper, who hadn't proceeded up the stairs.

The trouble was Bryony believed that Jed Boaz was in his office, just not in a state to answer. Over the dusty atmosphere, and the oil and iron smells wafting up from the tool shop, she could detect another scent: one that made saliva flood the insides of her cheeks, and raise her gorge. She didn't want to, but she put her nose to the doorframe, pressing on the door to gain a fraction of clearance between door and frame and inhaled.

'You'd best bring up that key,' she told the shopkeeper, after wiping at her mouth with the back of her wrist.

When he was slow to mount the stairs, Bryony went down and took the key from his outstretched hand. 'You should stay down here, sir,' she advised.

'Oh no,' said the guy, 'is he…?'

Yes, Bryony wanted to say, Jed Boaz is dead, but first she must confirm her suspicions. She was infinitely familiar with the sickly sweet stench leaking from beyond the closed door. Boaz was dead or he'd left the carcass of an animal to rot in his place.

She trembled as she unlocked the door, then took out her sidearm. She pushed open the door, grimacing against the anticipated waft of foul air, and entered the tiny room in one sudden rush. She checked the corners, the space behind the door, then moved forward, when really she could have seen everything she needed to from the landing. Jedediah Boaz was seated in his desk chair, his head lowered on his chest. His left hand was open on the desktop, but his right hand was fisted around the handle of an extendable baton also stretched across the desk. Congealed blood, torn scalp and hanks of hair adhered to the baton. The top of Boaz's skull showed where the baton had stripped the flesh from him with the ferocity of its impacts. On previous occasions, the murder scenes had been staged to look like something they weren't, but this was an exception. People simply didn't beat themselves to death with a steel baton whilst seated at their workstation.

She had come seeking answers from Boaz: primarily if he believed that Royce Benson was capable of murder. Well, even after death, Boaz told her everything she needed to know about the man she was hunting.

31

Cole was sitting on a tall stool at the breakfast counter in the family kitchen. Spread out on the counter was his schoolbooks, but he had forgone his homework assignment for drawing more of his favourite superheroes. He was blissfully unaware of the reason for the gathering of adults in the sitting room, from which I'd taken a break to grab a coffee and to surreptitiously check on the boy. He looked up at me from under his shock of curls, and offered a meek smile. I winked at him, and headed for the coffee jug to pour a cup. Cole leaned over his drawing, and I wondered if it was to conceal the fact he was again tracing images from a comic book. Recalling that his mum showed him how to trace, it made me wonder if Ella had also been involved in the fraud and forgery crimes of her husband and illicit lover, Royce Benson. It didn't matter now, I decided, and didn't make me think worse of her – not for her criminality or her infidelity, neither of which had anything to do with me or my opinion. Standing in the kitchen on a previous occasion, I'd promised Ella I wouldn't quit until she found justice. But now I didn't feel I owed her my pledge as much as I did the boy.

How would he react when he learned that Andrew wasn't his real dad, and that the man who'd murdered his mother and adopted "Uncle Parker" was actually his father? I was only glad that the task of telling Cole wasn't down to me: I wouldn't have known where to begin. The kid had endured enough upset to last anyone a lifetime, and I couldn't help worry that when the truth finally came out it would send him over the edge. I remembered when I was a boy, waiting at the factory gates for my dad, who I'd walk home with and he'd give me the leftover sandwich saved for me in his bait box. Or, when his wage was particularly flush from overtime, we'd call at the chippie for a fish and chips treat, or maybe a bag of crisps and bottle of lemonade from his favourite watering hole. The time I'd waited for him and he never appeared had stuck with me throughout life, and the most vivid thing about the incident was when I was approached by his workmates, all of them wearing haunted looks, who told me my dad had collapsed and died. They had been well meaning, but in hindsight it hadn't been their job to inform me of my dad's passing, and it's perhaps because I hadn't been at home, maybe sitting on my mum's knee, when I learned the terrible news that it had hit me so brutally. I'm sure the emotional distance that crept between me and my mum afterwards was down to the fact she wasn't there to hold me when I learned the worst news of my young life. I was much the same age as Cole was when he heard of his mum's murder, and I knew the distress would take a long time to subside; he didn't need any more shocking revelations piled on him at this time, and certainly not from a relative stranger, but it was unavoidable. I pitied Andrew when the time came, but more so the boy.

Propping myself against the kitchen counter I looked over at him, while holding my coffee to my mouth. He glanced back at me.

'Do you want to be a comic book artist when you grow up?' I asked him.

He shrugged.

'It's a great talent you have,' I said, and realised I was rehashing words I'd already shared with him before. But I didn't know what else to say. Diane and me had never had kids. I'd never really been around children, and even as a young boy hadn't had much to do with my younger stepbrother once John came along. Later in life I'd my dogs, and even now Hector and Paris, my German shepherds, were about the closest thing I'd ever had to children, and I was estranged from them. I struggled to find anything to say that didn't sound false to my ear, and where Cole would note the insincerity too. 'You should keep it up,' I said.

'I've decided when I grow up I'm going to be a police officer,' he said.

'Really? That's admirable, Cole.'

'Yeah. Then I'll catch all the bad men.'

'So you wouldn't prefer to be a superhero?' I smiled.

'Superheroes aren't real,' he told me matter-of-fact.

'They aren't?' I struck a pose, chin up, one fist on my hip, which probably didn't work when I was holding up a mug of steaming coffee in the other. 'You haven't heard of Caffeine Man?'

Cole scowled at my attempt at humour. I'd probably tried too hard. But I gave it another go. 'You ought to see Rink in tights: it's not a pretty sight.'

This time he curled a lip at one corner, and I could tell his mind was working on possibilities.

'How about doing a drawing for me? You could design costumes for Rink and me, and I'll stick it on a wall in our office.'

He pondered the idea, and I could tell I'd piqued his interest.

'Maybe I should let you come up with our superhero names, eh? Caffeine Man isn't that good, is it?' I wrinkled my nose in distaste at my suggestion.

'Not really,' he said.

'What do you think of the Scarlet Hunter?' I suggested.

His snort told me everything.

'What's going on in here?'

I turned and met Bryony's gaze. She'd progressed no further than the doorway from the hall.

'Guys' stuff,' I explained, with a wink for Cole. 'No girls allowed.'

She clucked her tongue at me. 'So how about you come and join us through here, Joe?' She went *sotto voce*. 'This was your idea, so some input would be helpful...'

'Yes, Detective VanMeter,' I said, and mock saluted. I turned to Cole. 'Maybe when you're a cop you won't be as bossy as Bryony is, eh?'

Cole's cheeks coloured because I'd shared his aspirations to be a cop with a genuine detective. He ducked back to his drawing. 'Hey, Cole,' I added, 'you might need a bigger piece of paper to fit Rink's fat head on it.' I left him chuckling, and when I entered the sitting room I caught Rink scowling at me. 'Oh, you heard that, huh?'

'I heard,' he growled.

He was sitting on an easy chair opposite the one I'd earlier vacated. Andrew Clayton was on the settee and Bryony returned after closing the door and sat down alongside him. I reclaimed my chair, and placed my cup on the coffee table that served as our war table. Bryony had supplied recent mugshots of Royce Benson, from when he was still secured at Zephyrhills, so we all would recognise him. In the photos his hair was much shorter than it had been when I'd had a brief look at him during the storm, but his face was so similar to Tommy Benson's that I was positive I'd have spotted him in a crowd.

'There's no guarantee he'll show up,' Clayton reminded us. 'You ask me, he's run for the hills by now.'

'Anyone with sense would have,' Rink said. 'But he's already proven he isn't the wisest guy around. He strikes me as having an over-inflated ego. Did he really expect to get away with setting up those murder scenes like that? If he did, it tells us he isn't as clever as he thinks he is.'

'He's a fraudster,' Bryony reminded us. 'And a forger. He gets a kick out of making things look like somebody else's work.'

'He wasn't very good at it. He got caught.' I glanced at Clayton to gauge my words on him. Maybe Royce would never have been caught the first time if not for being set up. But Clayton didn't react. 'His problem here was always being too elaborate. If he'd stuck to the one killing, he might have slipped under the radar. But not two times.'

'Three times,' Bryony said to our surprise. 'I've just come from another murder scene. I think I can reasonably add Jedediah Boaz to Royce's tally.'

'Who? Jed Boaz?' Clayton said, his eyes wide in recognition of the name. 'He was the detective who put Royce away when…'

Bryony nodded at him, and briefly told us about finding the ex-cop, and now low rent gumshoe, savagely beaten to death in his office. The timing of Boaz's violent death was far too convenient to be coincidental, and it went without much argument that the detective who'd sent him to prison had also been on Royce Benson's hit list.

'It suggests Royce isn't finished yet,' Rink said.

'Boaz died about four days ago,' Bryony corrected. 'Before Quinn was murdered. Sadly he'd nobody to miss him, so it has taken us this long to discover his murder. Maybe if I knew then what I do now, I could've been on to Royce much sooner, and stopped him before he got to Boaz or Quinn.' She snapped a glance at Clayton, but he purposefully chose that moment to adjust his spectacles and lower his face. Bryony shook her head, still glowering. This wasn't a time for recrimination: who knew what fate had in store for any of us, and even if Clayton had come clean at the beginning there was no saying what route Royce would have subsequently followed. In my estimation Quinn and Boaz would still be dead, whereas Tommy Benson might not have ended up pancaked on the highway.

Receiving no comment, or apology, from Clayton, Bryony went on. 'We've currently got a full-scale manhunt on for Royce Benson, but he's managing to give us the slip. It's my opinion that he's lying low, but like the rest of you I don't think he's finished yet. I've managed to cobble together a press release that should convince him that with the successful arrest of the home invasion crew, he's in the clear for the meantime. Quinn's death has only been reported as a suicide to date, and I'm holding off on announcing Boaz's murder – I've some leeway, while we wait for a relative to come forward and identify his body. His ex-wife Barbara is flying in from Seattle, but it could give us a day or two's grace before his identity hits the headlines. As far as Royce is concerned, we're still on the back foot and know nothing about him.' She looked directly at Clayton now, and his features puckered in anticipation of what was coming. 'You're the only one who knows who he is, Andrew. That suggests to me that he'll change tactics now, and instead of trying to destroy you through these theatrical shenanigans, he'll go for broke.'

I raised my eyebrows at Rink. He remained deadpan.

'I still don't think he'll come near me,' Clayton said unconvincingly.

'He's exhibiting typical serial killer tendencies,' said Bryony. 'And let's not kid ourselves, it's what he's becoming. Once serial killers get a taste for killing, their need for further death grows stronger, and the timescale between their killings usually narrows. Something else that's typical in many historical cases is how the psychos begin to enjoy the cat and mouse game with law enforcement. They inject themselves into the case, more or less taunting the police to catch them. Royce has done this, sending the emails, setting up the crime scenes, trying to avert blame onto innocent people, but all the while understanding the clues will ultimately lead back to him. But if he's true to form, then he'll also have a burning ambition to be identified at the conclusion of the investigation, to earn his notoriety. Where's the satisfaction in gaining revenge on those he feels betrayed him if he can't claim the accolades for all his hard work?'

'I think what Bryony is trying to say is he won't stop until he kills you, Clayton.' I took a sip of my coffee to punctuate my point, watching Clayton over the rim of my cup.

'He's had his opportunities to get at me before,' Clayton argued. 'I know for a fact he's been in my office, and that's where he got the samples of Parker's writing from, for when he forged the suicide note. He also took the spare key to Parker's place, which allowed him to sneak inside without alerting Parker. If he burglarized my office, what was to stop him waiting there for me to show up, and killing me when I wasn't expecting it? Or that time at the gate: he could have shot me instead of just punching me.'

'It was different then,' I pointed out. 'You admitted that he was using you then, blackmailing you with your involvement in the frauds. Killing you then didn't serve a purpose.'

'And it does now?'

'Of course,' Bryony said. 'You're the only one left he has a grudge against. Who else is he going to target?'

Clayton pointed a finger at me.

'You killed his baby cousin,' he said.

'I didn't kill Tommy,' I said, but I was under no illusion. Tommy had been the architect of his own demise, but Royce Benson might not see things that way. 'But I'm happy to paint a bull's eye on my back if it helps.

I'd rather he comes after me than you, Clayton. At least that way Cole won't end up in the crosshairs.'

Mention of Cole was a dirty trick on my behalf, but if Clayton was the loving dad he'd so ignominiously claimed to be, then he'd no option than give us all the necessary assistance we required to catch Royce. It hadn't escaped my notice that Clayton was still to fully condemn his old friend – and the fact Royce had aided him in clearing out a couple of troublesome relationships had to be taken into consideration. I'd a horrible feeling that Clayton might still feel some lingering friendship with Royce, or worse still was suffering guilt for having sent the man to prison and creating the monster he'd subsequently become. I had to play on his feelings for his son, and how vulnerable the boy was, if there was any hope of gaining his cooperation.

'I've resources to hand now,' offered Bryony. 'I can have a patrol allocated to watch the house until we apprehend Royce. Mr Clayton, I can have you and your son placed into protective custody if you prefer?' She paused and looked each of us in the face, before settling on me. 'But that isn't the plan is it, Joe?'

'If you make things impossible for Royce, he might go to ground. If he completely jumps ship you might never catch him. If what you said about his actions coming to a head is true, we should use that to our advantage.' I could tell she was bristling, about to remind me that this was Tampa PD's responsibility, *her* case, and I should damn well remember that my place in it was tenuous. I forestalled her with a lifted hand, patting down her anger before it grew. 'Like Clayton suggested, I'm probably now a target. I'm happy to be dangled as bait if it helps you catch him.'

'You'd be prepared to be a Judas goat for me?' Bryony asked.

I shrugged. A Judas goat was trained to lure other livestock to the stockyard for slaughter, while its own life was spared the knife. 'I can't say I'm happy with the name, but it pretty much sums up what I'm prepared to do.' To catch the killer, I had to portray something he recognised as a kindred creature and would follow to his doom. 'Mind you, I like the idea of being spared the knife. I'd prefer to come out the other end with my arse intact. That's where it down to you, Bryony.'

'I'll take your idea back to…'

I shook my head before she even got going. 'If you bring in a full SWAT team, chances are Royce will spot them a mile off, and he'll disappear. We have to do this under the radar, Bryony. Keep it between us.'

'Can't do it, Joe. I'm a cop; there are strict rules and regulations I have to follow. This isn't about killing Royce Benson; it's about arresting him.' She laughed but it was a sound of derision. 'If I leave his capture to you, I know he'll end up dead.'

'Hey,' I said, glancing around, 'did I just hear Holker's voice?'

Rink grunted in mirth, or more likely in agreement with Bryony. Clayton only stared at me, not getting the joke. Bryony pursed her lips.

'Who have I killed lately?' I asked innocently. Since my engagement on this job people had died, but none of them because of me. When I thought back, I'd tussled with a bunch of thugs in a junkyard, entered a footrace with a guy who tried to take a shortcut across a busy highway, punched out a gunman who was shooting at the cops – possibly saving her partner's life in the process - and even scuffled with my employer, but nobody had died at my hands. If I could keep my record as clean when bringing down Royce Benson then great. If not…well, I was happy either way.

'I solemnly swear not to kill him,' I said, with my hand on heart, 'unless I have to.'

'Don't even joke, Joe,' she warned.

Who was joking?

32

The killer was more patient than any of us gave him credit for. Three days had passed since our little war council in Andrew Clayton's sitting room, and still Royce Benson hadn't shown. It didn't surprise us, because none of us believed he'd turn up at the house again. We couldn't lower our guard though, in case he was stupid and decided a full frontal attack, or even a sneaky ninja-style assault on the estate was on the cards. Between Rink and me we set up round the clock protection of both Andrew and Cole, and we even called in Raul Velasquez to spell me, so that I could go out on the town and try to rustle up some action by motivating Royce a little. I visited various hangouts supplied to me by Clayton and bad-mouthed Tommy Benson, to see if it would stir some family loyalty from his cousin, who would decide now was the time to gain his revenge. Trouble was, without exception those I spoke to tended to agree that Tommy was a feckless asshole who did the world a favour by playing chicken with a speeding campervan. On my second return to Wild Point Bait, Harlan, the owner-cum-manager-cum-husband of the blond, didn't follow up on his threat to punch me in the face, but he made it obvious I wasn't welcome in his shop by telling me to leave his premises *tout de suite*: actually his French was a tad more coarse and ended with "off". When I didn't immediately go, he took out some sort of Billy club – I guessed it was employed to bash out the brains of large fish – and measured it in his palm with some meaty slaps. His bravado didn't intimidate me one bit, but I held no rancour towards the man, and had no intention of coming to blows with him. Without telling him that Royce was the prime suspect in three murders, I asked him in a reasonable manner if he knew where to find him.

'Who says I even know Royce Benson?'

'Your good lady wife does. She told me it was the reason you sacked Tommy, because he was working for Royce when he was still on your books. From what she said, you knew Tommy was mixing with a wrong one. You know Royce, and what he is, no doubt about it. He's the reason Tommy ended up dead, so if you have to be pissed off at anyone, make it him.'

'I've a good idea where he might be,' he replied, but didn't elicit any further information. Momentarily I thought about encouraging him to tell me, so I in turn I could alert Bryony. But where was the satisfaction in that? I'd done my best to set a challenge to Royce, and I wasn't one for backing down now.

'Then do me a favour, buddy,' I said, 'tell him he'll be wasting his time going near Andrew Clayton's place for the next few days. Clayton has gone fishing.' I left things at that, because to say more would make it obvious I was extending Royce a direct invitation to try his hand up at Lake Tarpon. I preferred that Royce came to the decision himself. 'Do that for me, and I promise I'll never bother you again.'

I left the bait shop, strangling an old ditty popularized by Bing Crosby and Louis Armstrong, my voice as gravel-laden as Satchmo's. I sang about going fishing by a shady wady pool to the accompaniment of the doorbell, and thought that it was enough to get the hint across.

When I arrived back at the Clayton place, everything was ready for the trip up to Andrew's lakeside fishing cabin. Tomorrow was Friday, but Clayton had already called in a sick day for Cole at school, to ensure we had a long weekend to spring our trap. Cole – oblivious to our actual reason for heading to the lake – was excited by the prospect of catching an elusive tilapia, and I could only smile encouragement having no idea what species of fish he was referring to. Velasquez had enjoyed his day out, the change of scenery from Rink's office doing him good, and it was a shame he couldn't come up to the lake with us, but somebody had to hold the fort, and Rink had pulled rank.

Once we'd grabbed our overnight bags, Rink joined Clayton and Cole in the family SUV, offering protection while we travelled in convoy to the fishing grounds. Velasquez took the pool car back to the office, and I was going to drive up in my Audi, watching for a tail of any kind. Who knew? Royce might already be watching, and have sourced himself another set of wheels after he'd lost the use of Tommy's Toyota after Tampa PD impounded it for forensic analysis. There was always the possibility that Bryony had put us under surveillance. She only trusted me to behave so far, and despite everything between us, she was still a cop, and as she'd pointed out had strict rules and regulations to follow. Her inclusion at the meeting three days earlier had been off the record, and it was only the friend part of her that had agreed to me staking myself out like a goat, whereas her detective part screamed at her in warning: if her commanders ever discovered she'd advocated vigilantism she'd be out of a job, and would probably join me in a jail term. She was no fool. She'd have a team on stand-by, ready to move the second she got a hint about what I was up to, and I couldn't blame her. If the shoe was on the other foot...

The thing was, she did know what the general plan was, but I hadn't told her the genuine timescale. I'd hinted that a fishing trip was planned for the weekend, but had also made it sound as if we wouldn't be going up to Lake Tarpon until Friday evening. By setting off a full twenty-four hours ahead of schedule it gave us some wiggle space, before the might of Tampa PD fell on all our heads. I didn't plan on excluding her – that was never my intention – and in fact wanted her there to snap the handcuffs on Royce, but I planned alerting her, and the inevitable stormtroopers that'd come running with her, only once we knew that the end game was on.

'Stay close on my ass,' Rink said from the driving seat of the SUV. Clayton was sitting in the back with Cole, who clutched his ever-present drinking bottle. There was a time when I found the presence of the bottle suspicious, and it had forced my thoughts in the wrong direction. Now I recognised the bottle for what it was: a comforter for a boy now too old to openly carry a stuffed toy.

'Alright in the back?' I asked.

Clayton scruffed his son's hair, and Cole grinned bashfully. 'We're good,' Clayton said. 'Let's try to keep things that way, eh, guys?'

'Stick to the plan, and everything should be just fine,' I said.

Clayton peered at me and I knew what he was thinking: "just fine" wasn't good enough when it came to Cole's safety. I tapped the tinted window. 'Roll it up, Clayton. We don't need to present any other targets.'

Cole, I suspected, knew more about what was happening than he let on. But he didn't appear frightened at the prospect, his eyes sparkled with barely subdued excitement, and I made myself a bet it had nothing to do with catching a fish. He was approaching our trip as some sort of grand adventure, and maybe now that we were rolling, he had given some thought to those superhero characters I'd asked him to develop. I only hoped Rink and me could live up to expectation.

The house was locked tight. I still had those keys in my pocket. To finally put my mind at rest I considered holding off following Rink so closely as he drove up the crushed shell drive towards the distant gate, and searching the house for missed clues. Yet, I told myself all my suspicions concerning Clayton's involvement had been unfounded. So I stuck to the plan, hopped in my Audi and followed close behind the SUV. The motion sensor on the inside opened the gate for us, and after we'd driven through we waited only a moment for the gate to close behind us. I watched the gate through my rearview, and one piece of the puzzle still bothering me settled in place. I'd always wondered how vehicles had been brought up to the house during the staged robbery, and thought that somebody – namely Clayton – had supplied the code to the gate to the thieves. But I recalled earlier that Clayton had said Royce had been to his office, and had taken samples of Parker Quinn's writing, as well as spare keys to Quinn's house. I just bet that he'd obtained the security codes to Clayton's house during a similar foray. It still presented another mystery to consider: after setting up Ella's murder, the house had been cleaned out of some large items of property, and I still thought that it must have been a huge task for one man to accomplish. Royce would have needed assistance. In all likelihood, he'd enrolled his cousin Tommy to help in the transportation of the stolen goods. Tommy must have known what Royce was up to, and he had to have seen Ella's dead body when helping shift the stolen property from the house. With that in mind, I didn't feel so bad about Tommy's death any longer. And I looked forward to a reckoning with the architect of his downfall.

I hit the gas and took off after the SUV.

The trip up to Lake Tarpon was uneventful. We cut up through Oldsmar and picked up East Lake Road as far as Lansbrook, where we headed west towards Juniper Bay. I'd been up that way before, but was still surprised to find the area around the lake so heavily populated. I'd have preferred somewhere more remote for a showdown with a murderer, but supposed I had to work with what I was presented with. As we got on a few minor trails, we passed more houses, but as we approached the lakeshore, I noted that the distance between the houses and fishing lodges began to thin out. We finally pulled up alongside what Clayton had described as his shack, and I should have known it was a misnomer. It was a plush cabin, which put my small beach house to shame. It enjoyed a private plot a few acres in size, hidden from its nearest neighbours by groves of moss-strung cypress and other trees I didn't recognise. A lawn sloped gently to the lake, and down its centre was a boardwalk, that extended five or so yards over the water as a jetty. A flat-bottomed boat - I'd heard them called pirogues – was moored to the jetty. There was also a speedboat of some kind up on a metal plinth, currently swathed in a weatherproof tarpaulin. It was approaching evening, but still light. Around here the sunset came quite abruptly, and getting some lights on in the cabin was a priority. Still. There was another thing we must do first.

'OK, everyone out,' said Rink as he got out the SUV.

Clayton and Cole slipped out and stood alongside him. They were carrying bags stuffed with the necessities they wouldn't find to hand at the shack.

'Put those in here,' I said, opening the boot of my Audi, 'then make yourselves comfortable.'

Cole glanced at his dad.

'We aren't staying here, son,' Clayton explained, as he took the boy's bag from him and dumped it in the trunk.

'Why not? I like it here, Dad.'

'I know you do, son, but we're going on up to a different place tonight. Only Mr Hunter is staying here.'

'Can't I stay here with you, Joe?' Cole asked.

'You'll be back here in a day or two,' I promised, 'but first your dad wants to show you a new place he's found for you. Has even better fishing, and if you're real lucky you might spot an alligator or two. Do me a favour, OK? Watch none of those gators eat Rink, huh?' I winked. 'We don't want any of the poor things getting sick.'

'Where are we going?' Cole went on, as unamused by my joke as Rink was.

Clayton pointed across the lake. It was dim enough on the far side that lights stood out in a jumble of pinpoints through the trees. 'See those lights over there? Well one of them is in the new place I've rented. Just thought it might be nice to have a change of scenery. If you look hard enough, you might even be able to spot Mr Hunter from the other side.'

'I'll wave,' I said, but we were over-egging the pudding. Cole wasn't stupid. He knew something was up.

'Why are you staying here, Joe?'

'I've a little job to do,' I told him.

He looked at his dad, then back at me. He leaned in conspiratorially. 'Is it something to do with the bad men?'

'No. Of course not,' I lied.

He snorted, shook his head at me, then crooked his little finger. 'Pinkie swear on it.'

His dad took him by his elbow and led him to the car, saving me any embarrassment. 'Cole. That's enough now. Mr Hunter told you he's a job to be getting on with.'

'Dad! I just want to…'

'That's enough, Cole!' Clayton snapped gruffly. 'Now come on. We're holding up Mr Rington.'

Rink had already climbed into the driving position in the Audi, his arm propped out the window. He drummed his fingers on the door, feigning impatience. To me, he said, "I'll give you a call soon as we're settled in.'

Once his passengers were inside, he backed the Audi up the short drive, leaving me standing alongside the SUV, with my overnight bag in hand. It seemed more effort than it was worth to swap out the vehicles, but as and when – if ever – Royce turned up, I wanted him to spot Clayton's SUV and conclude the family was here, and not safely out of harm's way on the far side of the lake.

As soon as the soft purr of my car's engine had faded, I turned and surveyed the lake. There were still a few fishermen in boats out on the water, but I assumed they were already preparing to return to shore. The sun was a bloated orange disc hovering over the distant horizon, minutes away from making a plunge to lavender twilight. On both sides of me the trees swayed with the breeze, the smaller branches rattling, and Spanish moss wafted like bunting at a celebration.

The woods would make good concealment for someone prowling up to the cabin. I stood, waiting, but got no sense of being observed. I turned towards the shack, striding a little way up the boardwalk to the screened entrance door. Clayton had already supplied me with the keys to unlock the padlocks securing the screens. I opened them, and then used a second key to open the door, pushing it open where it swung directly into the living room.

I didn't check out the décor or furnishings, or anything else for that matter, but for the barrel of the gun aimed directly at my face.

33

'Come on, come on, somebody answer, goddamnit!'

Leaning out the car window, frustrated by the lack of response she was receiving from pressing on the buzzer, Bryony VanMeter pushed open the door and went directly to the control panel alongside the gate to Andrew Clayton's property. A red light blinked intermittently above the keypad. She keyed in a code she'd used to get through on previous occasions, but the gate remained resolutely shut. Realising the code had been changed, she stabbed at random numbers, but there was as much chance of winning the lottery as hitting the correct sequence. Stubbornly the light stayed red. There was a "call" button on the pad, under it a small microphone and speaker. She pressed, waited, but got no answer. Leaning into the mouthpiece, she again pressed the button, though she already felt it was a pointless exercise. "It's Detective VanMeter. Anyone there?'

She took out her cell. Hit the stored number for Clayton's phone. It rang out.

'Goddamnit!'

She was already returning to her car. She should call Joe. But again she knew she'd be wasting her time, and the last thing she wanted was for him to try and deter her from joining them. She wasn't stupid. She knew Joe's agenda matched her own, but he was playing loose and free with the timescale. He'd informed her that the family was going to travel up to a second rental home on Lake Tarpon for the weekend and had even given her the address, but she sensed he was bending the truth when he mentioned they wouldn't leave until after Cole returned from school on Friday afternoon. Wait until she saw him, she was going to bend his goddamn ear for telling her lies. He was trying to do his own bit to help, but it was actually causing inconvenience she could do without, having to chase him like this.

She spun the car in the drive and headed for the highway, where she took a left and hit the gas for all it was worth. She used the in-car radio to request back up, and was reassured that Hillsborough County Sheriff's deputies were en route. Officers from Tampa PD also responded but would take longer to make it to the lakeside scene.

She'd come from the hospital, having checked on Detective Holker. Dennis was the proverbial bear with a sore head. He was mending, but still unable to return to active duty, and wouldn't be fit for the rigours of the job for weeks yet. He was exasperated as all hell, and more so because he wanted to be up on his feet again and chasing the bad guys. But that didn't mean he hadn't been mentally giving their case the attention it deserved: he had a lot of spare thinking time while lying in his sick bed. As Bryony had also considered, there was something decidedly wrong with what had previously been pieced together concerning Ella's murder, and what had led them to concentrate solely on Royce Benson. They both believed that Royce was their man. But there was something they were missing.

Holker had called her from his bedside phone, and asked her to check out some of the evidence collected during the search of Tommy Benson's house. Bryony had dutifully attended the evidence depository at Franklin Street HQ, and checked against listed evidence seized in the course of the search. Due to Holker's request, they had hit on something important enough that it was a game changer, and she'd driven directly to the hospital to tell him the news in person.

The iPad from which the emails had been sent accusing Andrew Clayton of murder matched an item stolen during one of the home invasion robberies. During the course of their investigation, and through subsequent admissions during the interrogation of those arrested at Tampa Heights, the gang had been implicated in three of the six known robberies, as well as the one aborted at Sunset Park when their plan was scuppered by the triggering of a silent alarm, and they had to flee empty-handed. Property found at the office complex matched items taken during those same three robberies, but two, and especially the incident at the Clayton house, remained unproved in connection to the gang. The iPad was identified as property stolen during one of the unsolved cases. It didn't implicate the Tampa Heights crew; it told a different story all together.

One man could have accomplished the murders of Jed Boaz and Parker Quinn, and both detectives were positive Royce was responsible, but for the workload at the Clayton house he'd have needed help. What they'd all missed was the fact that there was not one but two gangs active in the Tampa Bay area, and one of them was still in operation, and Royce Benson was managing their activities to achieve his own goal.

Joe Hunter thought they were up against one man, and had prepared to help catch him.

Sadly he was in for a rude awakening.

Bryony hit her lights and siren, pushing the car to its limit up the highway towards Oldsmar.

34

'Drop the bag, and show me both ya hands, asshole,' said the gunman facing me from the dimness inside the cabin.

I was standing in the open threshold, a sitting duck, and there was no hope of making a leap out of his sights before he could pop a round or two in my body. I dropped the bag, kicked it to one side, and held up both hands.

'Good. Now git inside and close the door with your heel. Try anything else and I'll shoot ya.'

The gun was fitted with a suppressor. He wanted me inside, the door closed tight, so that when he shot me there'd be no hint of my dying that would carry to any neighbours. I doubted anyone would hear a damn thing anyway, even if the door was wide and I let out a strangled cry. Exhaling in regret, I did as commanded, and kicked the door shut behind me.

'Are you armed?'

'No,' I said.

'Don't fuckin' lie to me.'

I shrugged.

'Git your arms high, asshole. I wanna see under your jacket.' The gun jerked up an inch or two as the gunman emphasised his point. He lowered it again, aiming at the centre of my chest, regaining a more viable target than my skull. I lifted my arms, causing my jacket and T-shirt to ride up, displaying a lack of weaponry in my waistline. The gunman grunted. 'Now, turn around. Hands still high.'

'I've a gun in my belt,' I admitted. The alternative was he'd spot my SIG and, pissed at my lies, he might shoot me while my back was turned.

'Turn around,' he commanded again.

I turned. My hands still reached for the ceiling.

I hoped he'd do something rash like press the gun to my head while he removed my weapon from my belt, where there was a chance I could surprise him by spinning abruptly, where I might be able to take away his gun before he got me back in his sights. He was cautious though. He moved closer, but not within striking distance.

'Use the thumb and index finger of ya left hand. Take out the gun and throw it away. Nice an' easy now.'

I didn't move.

'You haffa problem with your hearin' buddy?'

'I heard you loud and clear,' I reassured him. 'Just not too keen on throwing away a good gun.'

'I'll shoot ya,' he warned.

'I believe you. But it doesn't change anything. You're going to shoot me, so I'd prefer to keep the gun incase I get a chance to shoot you back.'

'Who the fuck d'ya think you're messin' with, buddy?'

'Actually, I did wonder,' I confessed.

As Rink had previously mentioned, it's true that nobody is infallible. Certainly not me, it seemed, because I'd walked directly into the kind of trap I'd hoped to set to catch a killer. We'd all understood that much of our plan's success was based upon pushing Royce Benson into making an ill-timed assault on his final targets. But he'd beaten us all to the punch, and I admit to stinging with embarrassment in being caught so flatfooted. While we'd been wasting time plotting, he'd acted, and had set up his own little trap, that I'd now sprung. I'd have congratulated him on his foresight and for taking the initiative, if he was around to accept the accolade. Because the gunman before me wasn't the guy I knew as Royce. The hand holding the gun didn't have a spider web tattoo, and though he bore a passing resemblance to both Royce and Tommy, he was older than both. This, not Tommy, I realised, could have been the guy who I'd spooked out of the trees that time, the man responsible for dropping the glove seeded with forensic evidence framing Parker Quinn. Then again, possibly not, because Tommy's dying words were that he'd been "paid to run", and Tommy had done so on both occasions I'd come across him. Nevertheless I wondered how many relatives the Benson clan stretched to, and how many of them were helping Royce on his revenge trip.

All along, the mystery of the transportation of the stolen goods from the Clayton house had itched like a burr in my mind. Earlier I'd concluded that the ill-fated Tommy had helped his cousin empty the house to make the scene look like a bungled robbery. Maybe Tommy had, but in hindsight, I now understood that even two men weren't enough to complete the task – not if Royce's priority was setting up the murder scene. The truth was, the murder had been only one facet of the robbery, and Royce had the assistance of his own loyal crew of burglars to do the heavy lifting. He hadn't snuck into Clayton's office to steal the code for the gate. He didn't need to do that. After Clayton and Cole drove away, he'd entered the house alone, killed Ella, then while inside and at his leisure had disabled the gate's locking mechanism from the master switch inside the house, allowing his buddies to drive up to the house with the vans and manpower necessary to move the goods.

The cops had grabbed the home invasion crew based at Tampa Heights, and everyone with the exception of Bryony and Holker were trumpeting about their success in ending the crime wave. But I also recalled Bryony telling me that evidence sifted from the derelict office complex implicated the Tampa Heights Crew in only "some" of the robberies. Some but not all. The reason they hadn't found evidence relating to the other home invasion robberies during the raid, and in particular the one at the Clayton house, was because there was a second gang in operation. Not only had we underestimated Royce Benson, we'd also misjudged the resources he had at hand. This man was only one who was helping him, and it worried me how large the gang really was.

'Where's Royce?' I asked the gunman.

'Ya shouldn't concern yourself with Royce. The only person ya hafta worry about is me, asshole.'

'I'm not worried about you, you dick,' I said. 'If you were going to shoot me, you'd have done it by now.'

'Don't try me,' said the gunman, but there wasn't much conviction in his voice. He was a robber. And possibly a violent one at that, but he didn't strike me as a stone cold killer. Royce held the distinct family honours on that title.

Unnecessarily, he took a step closer towards me. 'Put both yer hands on yer head. Twine yer fingers together. Do it motherfucker, or I swear t' God I'll plug ya.'

I placed my palms on my head as instructed, but only loosely fed my fingers together. Hopefully he'd seen cops grabbing the entwined fingers of a felon, holding them steady while they patted them down. What he might not understand was when cops did so a second armed officer was usually on hand to cover them. To remove my gun, he'd first have to put his own aside if his other hand was tied up holding mine.

The son of a bitch didn't grab my hands.

He kept his distance.

Called out to another of the crew to come in.

The door swung open inches from my nose, and in stepped another man, this one bearing no family resemblance to the Bensons. This guy was younger, maybe in his early twenties, and he had the sour disposition of many immature reprobates who raged at the world in general.

'Is this dickweed giving you trouble, Lonnie?' the new arrival growled.

'Won't do as he's told, Mike,' said his pal.

'That so?' Mike was holding a sawed-off shotgun that he took pleasure in ramming into my guts.

The air left me in a rush, and I bent slightly, my abdominal muscles contracting in agony. In reflex my eyes began to squeeze shut, even as my mouth opened wide to suck in the air displaced from my lungs. I tensed against the instinct, and my gaze remained clear enough to spot a third man crouching by a front tyre of Clayton's SUV, in the act of extracting a knife he'd just jammed in the sidewall. There was only one good reason for disabling the vehicle: it was so I'd no way of following them, or of trying to get to the real targets of Royce's trap if I managed to escape. It told me that

I wasn't scheduled to die just yet. Maybe they had orders to hold me here until Royce was finished with Clayton, when he'd return and dispatch me at his leisure.

That was good.

It told me that there was an advantage hidden within the dire situation I'd blundered into.

To Bryony, I'd pledged I wouldn't kill Royce Benson unless I had to. Well, I'd made no such promise concerning these bastards.

I played up the agony in my guts, wheezing some more, and surreptitiously lowered my arms to massage my belly. Mike grinned at my apparent discomfort, pleased with the amount of pain he'd inflicted, and behind me Lonnie was slow to register I'd lowered my hands. Neither of their minds was on shooting me and that was the brief opening I'd been hoping for. As the third man stood from puncturing the remaining front tyre on the SUV, I straightened at the waist, twisting away even as I swept the shotgun aside with a cupped left palm.

Behind me Lonnie yelped in shock, and he did the unthinkable. He transposed his surprise onto the trigger of his gun. The silenced pistol made a dull clacking sound, and the corresponding thud of the bullet striking flesh was equally as dull, and almost simultaneous. Mike took the bullet an inch or so above his navel. His eyes widened in disbelief, and he had no concept of sitting down, or that I'd continued the scooping motion, liberating the shotgun from his relaxing grip.

Lonnie was terrified when I spun the shotgun on him. He'd just shot his friend, and his mind was in a state of chaos. He took a second or two to realise that he should point the gun at me. By then it was too late for him. His only saving grace was that I didn't instantly blast him to death, but used the gun barrel to club aside his gun. I heard the sickening crunch of breaking bones, and his wrist went floppy. The silenced gun fell from his outstretched fingers. I didn't halt my movement, I continued swinging in a circular loop, backhanding the barrel against his jaw. Lonnie's head jerked almost a full one-eighty degrees, and the centrifugal force worked on his neck, then his upper torso, and he pirouetted away from me, a spray of blood-flecked saliva painting the air before he collapsed on his front on the floor.

By then I was no longer looking at him, but turning again, preparing to meet the next assailant.

The third robber had charged up the stoop, and his only weapon to hand was the blade with which he'd punctured the SUV's tyres. It was sharp, serrated down one edge, a vicious close-quarters weapon that'd seriously ruin my day. But he'd made the old mistake of bringing a knife to a gunfight. I fired the liberated shotgun, the buckshot tearing out a chunk of his pelvis before he got within stabbing distance. He collapsed, and it was partly on top of his gut-shot pal, Mike. I slammed the smoking barrel on the top of his head, almost in an act of mercy.

Mike was still conscious. Even severely injured, he could prove dangerous if he had another gun, or even if he snatched up the dropped knife. I lunged in and snapped a kick under his chin, and he went out like a doused candle, splayed in the doorway.

I swung quickly to cover Lonnie. He had a broken wrist and most assuredly a broken jaw. Groaning, semi-conscious, he was no immediate threat. I made a rapid check of my surroundings, collecting the dropped weapons, and thought that all was clear. But before I'd fully relax, I bobbed a quick look outside. There was nobody apparent. If there had been others of the gang in hiding, I'm pretty sure they would have come out once they knew I'd been secured, and especially when things kicked off so violently. I took it that the trio had been left here to capture me, with Lonnie entering the cabin through a window at the back in order to spring the trap while Mike and the knife man waited in the trees, and Royce and whoever else was helping had took off after the Audi when Rink drove it away. I hurled the shotgun and the silenced handgun into the nearest copse of trees, but held on to the knife, slipping it into my boot.

I grabbed for my phone.

Rink didn't answer.

Bad.

I wanted to get after him; to help him fight off the assault I believed was already underway.

But first I rang Bryony.

'Joe! What's going on?'

'It's happening, Bryony, an attack on Clayton,' I said in a rush. 'How close are you?'

'Already on my way to Lake Tarpon. Why did you-'

I cut her short. 'There's no time for that. I'm at Clayton's fishing place, but the others have gone to the second cabin we spoke about. Things just turned nasty here, Bryony, but I think I got the best of it.'

'What the hell's happened? Did you catch Royce?'

'No. There are others. Royce has his own crew.'

'I know, Joe. I know.'

I was unsure how she'd come to the same conclusion as me, but then wasn't the time to debate our theories.

'What's your ETA?' I asked.

'Ten minutes.'

'Too long,' I said. 'I can't wait. Go directly to the other place, but have some of your pals come here. Three down. All in need of immediate medical assistance.'

'Oh, shit, Joe…?'

I hung up.

The SUV was out of commission. I'd no idea if the trio had transportation nearby, or whether the plan was for them to be picked up after I was dealt with, and I'd no time to check. I looked across the lake, to where the sun had sunk below the horizon. Pinpoints of light danced like lighting bugs in the purple haze. Clayton had told Cole that he could probably spot me from where the safe house was located. My mind made up, I charged down the boardwalk for the jetty, hoping the pirogue I'd spotted came equipped with an outboard motor.

35

The distant pop of a handgun was barely decipherable over the roaring of the labouring outboard motor, and the pirogue's noisy progress over the lake. I was pushing the boat too hard, but I could live with a burned out motor: I couldn't live with the knowledge I'd arrived too late to help Rink, Cole or even Andrew Clayton.

I was standing to the rear of the boat, forcing extra effort from the engine, my legs braced, trying to ride as best I could the bouncing and shuddering of the boat as it dipped and fell in the water. Scanning ahead, I'd no real idea which of the lights in view belonged to the safe house where we'd originally intended hiding Cole and his father. The gunshot should have given me a clue, but the acoustics played havoc with my hearing. I squeezed my eyelids tight, then blinked, shaking my head. Tried to pierce the dancing horizon with my gaze.

Another gunshot rang out.

This time I spotted a corresponding flash, and I yanked on the motor to send me in a tight curve to the left – I'd almost overshot the gunfight, streaking initially too far to the north. I swore under my breath as I almost pitched from the boat, fought for balance, then nudged some more power from the throttle. As it was, I still felt as if I was only crawling across the lake.

What the hell was going on? How many guns had Royce brought to the fight with him? Had they ambushed Rink and the others outside, or waited until they'd entered the cabin? What about my friend and charges: were any of them hurt? They were all questions for later. The important thing right then was getting to the opposite shore as rapidly as possible.

Bryony was on her way. And for the briefest of moments I thought I heard the distant squall of sirens, and hoped it was cops she'd called in as back up. The sirens could have been miles away, and before the cops could arrive anything might happen. Gunfights could be fatal in a matter of split seconds.

The western edge of Lake Tarpon was shallow, and as I pushed for the shore, it became choked with long reeds, floating twigs and thick with silt. A normal keeled boat would have struggled, becoming mired in the entangling reeds, but the flat-bottomed pirogue was designed by fisherman working on the bayous and easily contended with it. Nevertheless, I had to pull the motor out of the water as I drew nearer shore, as the reeds began to entangle the screws. I allowed the boat to coast in, and was still a dozen feet out from dry land when I scrambled forward and jumped overboard. Bad idea. My feet sank deep in the mud, and I almost went face down in the filth I'd stirred up. Fighting at the cloying muck, swiping aside reeds, I pushed for the shore, gasping in effort with every step won. Only once I was on dry land, my feet settled under me, did I draw my SIG out of my waistband. After the scuffle with Clayton, and its unceremonious dumping on the lawn when he overturned the picnic table, I'd stripped, cleaned and oiled my gun, before reassembling and reloading it: I knew it was good to go. But I still gave it a once over having floundered about in the water, even as I ran at a crouch through a snarl of low bushes towards a stand of hard-packed dirt masquerading as a parking lot.

There was nobody in sight, but I heard rushed voices debating something from a few hundred paces to my left. A stand of trees made it impossible to see the cabin I suspected nestled at the rear of the trees.

I began to move for the trees but pushing through them would prove too noisy. Changing trajectory, I headed instead for the parking area. As my feet found the hard-pack, I moved more stealthily, edging along the lot with the trees as cover, until I got a look down a narrow trail dug from the earth by the wheels of vehicles coming and going over the years. It was a secondary route to the cabin, one where boats could be brought down to the lakeside on trailers. I moved down it, listening keenly, still unsure of the scene I'd find, or the number of enemies.

What the hell had happened? And to what extent did Royce Benson want revenge where he'd bring an armed gang to a shootout where a little child was involved? His own boy, if he had any sense of responsibility. I took it he'd no intention of snatching Cole as his own, and was more interested in putting down the last of those he felt had wronged him all those years ago, even if Cole was in the firing line. Suddenly I hated the man with a passion.

The cops were still a good way off, the distant warble of sirens barely reaching my ears from somewhere across the lake. They'd headed directly for the cabin on the other side of the water, and would be even longer in arriving here. I had mixed feelings; at least with the late arrival of the cavalry it gave me an opportunity to get on with what was required.

As I reached the end of the trail, the woods to either side opened up, and in the dimness of the sunset I made out the peeked roof of a fishing lodge even larger than the one I'd come from. It sat in an open spread of ground, bordered again on the far side by trees. The lawn was patchy, and partly cluttered by boats in dry-dock, sheeted up against the elements. A separate building down at the lakeside appeared to be a boatshed. My Audi was drawn up alongside the house, but there was nobody in it, and nobody nearby. A van was parked so close it nudged the Audi's crumpled rear fender. The van's doors were wide open. Another vehicle, some kind of pickup truck, was further back and its doors were open too, showing the speed at which its occupants had decamped.

There'd been no gunfire since I was still out on the lake. But the lack of a fight was more worrying than if guns still crackled and popped. It could mean I was already too late to help.

The house was in darkness and wasn't under attack.

I sprinted across the patchwork lawn, and sequestered myself alongside the van. I dipped a look in an open door and found nobody inside. Next, I duck walked to my Audi. The rear bumper was badly crumpled, showing that the van had shunted it the last few feet to its final resting place. There was a gouge in the paintwork of the roof where a bullet had struck it a glancing blow. Briefly piecing together what had happened, I thought that our switcheroo with the cars had been spotted back at the other cabin, and the gang lying in wait to ambush us had followed Rink and our wards as he'd driven away, leaving behind the trio to deal with me. On approach to this place, Rink must have spotted the tail, but only once on the way down to the house. The van had rammed him, while those in the pickup had jumped out shooting. I was only glad there was no presence of blood to show they'd been hit before Rink and the others got out. They didn't have time to get inside the house, and with no safe place to hide had gone the only way available. I ran for the corner of the house, and looked across more parched grass to where the beached boats stood. Somebody crouched alongside them.

There was enough ambient light to make out the figure of a man, holding a pistol, and to tell it was nobody I recognised. I doubted it was a well-meaning neighbour who'd come to help, which left only one thing: he was an enemy. There wasn't another person to be seen from where I stood, so I walked out determinedly. I'd approached two thirds of the way before the gunman was aware of my presence, and he turned and looked back at me. He had no idea who I was, and had no hope of making out my features, or even the gun I held at my waistline.

'Where the fuck are they?' he whispered, mistaking me for one of his pals.

'You tell me,' I said, and fired.

My bullet took him in the thigh, and he squealed like a stuck pig, as he collapsed on the ground, drawing up his knee into his arms. He'd dropped his weapon. I kicked it aside, even as I reached down and snagged a fistful of his hair. I stuck the barrel of my SIG under his jaw.

'Didn't you fucking hear me?' I demanded.

He was a man in his thirties, skinny to a point of emaciation, with teardrop tattoos dripping from the corner of his right eye. Prison tats, I thought, from Zephyrhills Correctional Institute maybe, where he'd made

Royce Benson's acquaintance. It was all supposition, and didn't matter one bit.

'What the fuck, man?' he cried, and real tears joined the stylized ones on his cheeks. 'You shot me, man!'

'Want me to shoot you again, *man*? How many of you are there?' I gave his hair an extra twist, forcing his chin tighter against the barrel of my SIG.

'Two, man! There's only two more of us. Royce and Bean. Fuck, man, I thought you was Bean.' He continued to grapple with his tormented leg, and I allowed him to wallow in his pain a moment.

'Where are they?' I asked.

He was too busy crying to answer.

Releasing his hair, I slapped aside his hands, and forced my thumb on to the wound in his leg. 'You have to keep pressure on if you want the bleeding to stop,' I said, and nastily ground my thumb tip deep into the pulped flesh. The guy squealed again, and I almost felt sorry for him. Threatening him wouldn't give me answers quickly enough, so good old fashioned torture was on the cards. 'Where are your friends?' I demanded to know, and dug in harder.

Through his bleats of agony, he stabbed a finger towards lakeside. In hindsight, he didn't have to, because as he was gesticulating frantically another gun fired and through cracks between the planks I saw the flash light up the interior of the boathouse.

Who was inside, friend or foe?

I snatched up the crying man's gun, checked it out. It was a revolver, with all six rounds still in their chambers. He hadn't fired, or he'd reloaded it. Whatever, I couldn't allow him to rejoin the fight. I clubbed him on the skull with the gun. It didn't knock him out, but gave him another painful wound to keep his mind distracted. He lay there mewling in abstract dejection as I trotted away, keeping the boats between the action and me.

Another shot rang from the boathouse, and there was a thunder roll of feet on a boardwalk.

Rushing forward, I aimed for a gap between two upturned rowboats, looking for a way to the far side of the boathouse. I was galvanised by the yelp of terror from a small boy, and let caution slip as I bolted now for the gap.

In my haste I stumbled over the legs of a man propped in the deep well of shadows against the upturned keel of the first rowboat. I skidded, going down on one knee before I could right myself, and snapped my attention on him. For the second time in less than half an hour a gun was pointed directly at my face.

36

'Thank your stars I'm not top of my game, right now. I almost ventilated your skull, Hunter,' said Rink as he lowered his sidearm.

My friend tried to express humour in his words, but he was too pained for them to sound sincere. His face gleamed slick with sweat in the gloom. Fearing the worst I leaned towards him, trying to see where he was hit. He pawed my hand aside.

'I took one in the side. Hurts like a bastard when I try to stand, but I ain't dead yet.' He straightened where he sat, but hissed in pain.

'Take it easy, Rink,' I admonished him, 'you're not helping yourself by trying to get up.'

'Ain't gonna sit here on my ass when the fighting's not done,' he said. 'There's some punk-ass creeping round back there with a hawgleg.'

'I got him,' I said, taking it he was referring to the crying man. I was surprised he hadn't heard our interaction seeing as it had gone down only a handful of yards away. Then again, bullet wounds, and the ensuing shock could play havoc on the senses. I bet that Rink's internal voice had been yelling in anger and frustration and blocked out everything else. That or he'd sunk into momentary unconsciousness. I was only glad he'd enough of his wits about him not to pull the trigger when I blundered over him in the dark. 'There are two more of the arseholes out there. What happened, Rink?'

'Got the drop on us,' he explained breathlessly. 'Royce rammed the car; another coupla punks came out of a pickup shooting. I got Clayton and the boy to cover, but only at the expense of my own ass.'

He hadn't literally been shot in the backside. I could see now where he pressed his left hand over a wound in his side, an inch above his hip. His shirt and the top of his jeans were sodden with blood.

'Through and through?' I asked hopefully.

'Not my day, brother,' he said, meaning the bullet was lodged somewhere inside him.

'Shit.'

'Don't worry about me. You gotta go save the kid.'

'Did you get any of them?' I asked.

'Man, don't go rubbing salt in my wounds, Joe.' His face pulled up into a grimace. I preferred to see that than him sinking into the calm resolution of oncoming death. If he was bleeding inside, hopefully it wasn't from torn arteries or he was finished. I hoped the fact he was in pain meant he wasn't succumbing quickly to an internal bleed. He stared at me a second or two too long, and I feared he was losing it, but then he said, 'How'd you get here anyway?'

I was soaked, and muddy, and bits of broken reeds had adhered to my jacket. From the look of things it was fair to think I'd swam across the lake. 'Tell you later,' I promised.

A shout snapped out from down near the boathouse, initiating another volley of bullets.

'Help me up, brother,' said Rink, grabbing at my shoulder.

'Stay down,' I commanded. 'You're going to bleed out if you try to move.'

'I can still shoot. Give you cover. Help me over there.' He nodded to the keel of the next boat along. From there he would have a line on the back end of the boathouse. And covering fire would be helpful.

'OK, but that's as far as you go. Got it?'

'OK, Mom,' he said, and twisted his mouth in the parody of a grin. I grasped his bent arm, and used it to drag him the few feet to the other boat. He tried to help, but his legs disobeyed him, scraping feebly at the earth. I didn't want to imagine what damage had been done to his insides, and if his spine had been hit by the tumbling bullet…

No. I couldn't allow myself to think the worst. It was only shock, his nervous system rebelling against the trauma.

'Here.' I passed him the liberated revolver. He tucked the gun down by his right thigh as a back-up weapon, needing one hand to compress his wound. Then he wormed around to a better position: he bit down on the agony even the smallest of movements set off within him.

I forced him a smile of concern.

'Go on, git outta here,' he growled.

Giving him a quick squeeze of his shoulder, I told him I'd be back.

'Make sure you bring Cole with ya,' he said, and it was the motivation I required to leave my injured friend's side. I slipped around the keel of the rowboat, scanning both sides of the boathouse. From my position I couldn't tell where Royce or his buddy, Bean, were, but one of them must have been in the nearby woods because that's where Clayton was shooting. As far as I knew Clayton had little experience with firearms, and I could only assume Rink had passed him a gun, or he'd found one in the boathouse. Whatever, he had little hope of contending with two gunmen on opposite sides of the building, while trying to keep Cole out of harm's way.

Coming to a snap decision, I ran across the lawn to the stand of trees. My hope was that in the dark, and with no idea I'd escaped the trap set for me at the other cabin, Royce or his pal would think I was their tattooed buddy rushing to help. Thankfully I didn't get shot, so my ploy must have worked.

The woodland had been abandoned to nature. In the gloom the branches were a snarl of tugging and scraping barbs that pulled at my clothing and hair. I almost took out an eye on a broken twig that speared the bridge of my nose. Underfoot the coarse grass was matted, and the earth spongy. It made moving both difficult and noisy, but I persevered. I forged through the woods towards the lakeside.

'Hart!' came a harsh whisper from a few yards to my left. 'Get back to the goddamn house. You're supposed to be stopping them running back that way.'

I stood still, peering at the shape crouching a few feet into the trees. There was no way of knowing who had spoken, but my guess was that Royce would be closer to the action.

'Bean?' I whispered, to disarm him, as I began creeping forward. He'd no way of knowing I was there, and hearing his own name would only enforce the notion I was his tattooed pal, Hart.

'Royce will tear you a new one if those fuckers get away,' Bean warned, but I was glad to note his attention was back on the boathouse. He was kneeling, holding a pistol with both hands. It wasn't aimed at any target, just ready for if he spotted movement.

I could have executed him on the spot. Moved in on him, put my gun to his skull, and spread his brains like compost in the grass.

As much as I was tempted, I didn't blow out his brains. The cops were coming, and even though I was trying to save an endangered child, my every move would come under deep scrutiny.

But I had to put the gunman out of commission, and in a way he couldn't continue the fight, even if he was left alive after it.

I shoved away my gun as I crossed the last few feet.

He glanced back at me at the most opportune moment...but only for me. Even in the dark my build registered, and he knew I wasn't skinny Hart. He began to turn, to bring round his gun. But my fast jab connected solidly with the side of his jaw. He began to sag, but wasn't unconscious. He jerked spasmodically, and again tried to bring his gun to bear. When questioned later, I could therefore claim I was fighting for my life. Grabbing both his hands so I had control of the gun, I yanked him off balance and he fell on his side. I continued the twist on his gun, and it rotated out of his grasp, his index finger misaligned on his right hand when it was caught in the trigger guard and wrenched out of its socket. A mere dislocation would slow but not stop him. I threw his gun behind me into the woods, and then rained blows to his head and neck.

Bean was totally overwhelmed, but I wasn't finished. I grabbed his right arm, pulled it straight with my right arm, and dropped my elbow sharply down on his. His arm broke. In case he was ambidextrous, I flattened him face down on the trampled grass, reached across and hoisted his left arm in the air. I folded his hand over the wrist until the metacarpals could withstand the force no longer and began to crackle and pop. With both arms so severely damaged, Bean would have to be some kind of kickboxing expert to rejoin the battle, but even then he wouldn't be throwing kicks any time soon. I hoofed him between the legs, to ensure he stayed down, and gave him an extra stamp to the liver just for the hell of it. His punishment was deserving of a bastard threatening the life of a child.

Bean, Hart, Lonnie, Mike and the nameless knifeman, all of them were scumbags in my estimation, and had gotten off lightly. The worst of them was still out there, though, and he was the real target. The fact that I'd heard no gunfire lately wasn't lost on me. Leaving Bean moaning in agony, I drew my SIG and headed for the boathouse.

37

She overshot the entrance to the fishing lodge in her haste. Bryony trod on the brake pedal, and her tyres shuddered on the rough road surface, pluming stinking smoke before she brought the car to a halt. She hit reverse, using her mirrors to guide her into a swooping turn, and then stamped the gas pedal again. She clipped a gatepost, but scratches on her car were the least of her concerns. She pushed down the track, and came to a point where it branched. To the left the track wasn't maintained, just two ruts in the earth that skirted a copse of trees towards the lake. She continued to the right, slowing now that she was almost on the scene.

All the way there she'd driven on lights and sirens, forcing her way past slower moving traffic, but as she approached the cabin had turned everything off. Alerting Royce Benson to her presence when her back up was still minutes away wasn't a good idea. She even turned off her headlights, so they wouldn't betray her position. The sun had set, but it wasn't yet full night, so she didn't fear colliding with anything in the dark. In fact, she could already make out a pickup truck abandoned a short distance ahead, and beyond it another couple of vehicles less visibly defined. Coming to a halt, she pressed down her window, listening keenly, and feared the worst. The absence of gunfire wasn't reassuring.

Rapidly she updated her responding colleagues by her in-car radio, having already been appraised of what had been discovered across the lake. Three down, two of them critical but expected to survive. Bryony had made a silent thank-you that Hunter hadn't dealt with his ambushers as uncompromisingly as usual. She made a second thank-you to whichever god or patron saint watched over warriors these days, because the alternative was that Hunter could have also fallen during the fight. She pinched off her thanks though, because who knew what had gone down in the meantime. The quietude she'd come upon could mean she was about to enter a scene of slaughter.

Once out of the car, she drew her sidearm.

She proceeded on foot, edging around the pickup, checking it for bodies alive or dead, but it was apparent that its driver and passenger had decamped in a hurry. The van was equally deserted, and so too Hunter's Audi. There was no sign of Clayton's SUV. Had Joe been chased here in his car, arriving before Clayton's? The alignment of the short queue of vehicles was a mystery to be cleared up later: right then it didn't matter. She scanned the house for any sign of life, but it was locked up, and in darkness. She jogged past it, staring into the deepening gloom. She thought she heard weeping.

Cautiously she approached some upturned boats on trestles, and saw a man curled into a fetal ball. He was unsure whether to cradle his injured leg, or his head, and was unaware of her approach.

'Police,' she whispered harshly. 'Do not move.'

'Aw hell, man!' groaned the man, as he blinked up at her with feverish eyes. She thought he was wearing mascara that had run, until she made out the black marks on his cheek to be tattoos. His face was skeletal, warped by agony, but Bryony thought she recognised his distinguishing factors, and even put a name to the lowlife she'd once arrested as "Scott Hartman". His presence at the scene wasn't an unfortunate coincidence.

'Show me your hands, Hartman.'

'I'm hurt, goddamnit. You have to help me.'

'Your fucking hands,' she emphasised. 'Now, or I swear to God, I'll give you something to really cry about.'

Hartman held up his skinny wrists. His palms were sticky with blood, as was the side of his head, and now she could see more clearly his left thigh. Questions might later be asked about her treatment of a wounded prisoner, but he was still dangerous, so she'd no qualms about pulling out her handcuffs and snapping one bracelet round his right wrist. The other she clipped onto the trestle he lay alongside.

'Help's coming,' she told him as she quickly patted him down. 'If you know what's good for you, *don't* move.'

'You can't leave me! I'm bleeding to death,' Hartman keened plaintively.

'I've left you a hand free. Slap it over that wound in your leg. Then shut the hell up.' She stood from him, again scanning around. From a distance she heard the sirens of responding patrols. She looked down at Hartman. 'By the way, you're under arrest, asshole. We'll sort out the charges later. You understand your rights, yeah?'

Hartman nodded by rote.

'Well, forget about them,' Bryony snapped. 'If you give me a reason to come back I'm going to shoot you in your other leg.'

She stalked away, smiling grimly at her warning, feeling empowered. She could understand Hunter's attraction in taking off the kid gloves now and again.

'Bryony…over here.'

The whisper stopped her in her tracks.

She brought up her gun, but she'd already identified the slow drawl.

She paced quickly to Jared Rington's side.

'Rink? What's going on?'

Rink was seated with his legs outstretched, though he'd his back propped against the keel of a boat, and a gun in one hand. Another revolver lay on the ground next to him. Rink was a powerful man, but she knew from one single glance that right now a kitten would overwhelm him in a competition of strength. 'Hell, Rink, are you hit?'

His left hand was pressed to his side. His clothing and hand shone wetly.

'I'm good,' he said, though it was obvious he was spouting the kind of macho bullshit usually reserved for his banter with Joe.

'How bad?' she asked, and crouched to assist.

'Bad enough, but I'll live.' He pressed her away, leaving a bloody handprint on her wrist. 'Tell me that's an ambulance I can hear?'

'Help's coming,' she reassured him.

'Go help Hunter then.'

'I can't leave you here like this.'

'Sure you can. You just left that punk bleeding back there.'

Allowing a scum ball like Scott Hartman to bleed was one thing, quite another when it came to a man she considered a friend. She and Rink hadn't shared similar intimacy as she had with Joe, but she was still fond of the big lunk.

Rink held up his pistol. It was an effort that set his forearm trembling. But he seemed satisfied. 'I can still do my bit if needs be,' he said. 'You go do yours. Hunter's down there someplace, but so's Royce Benson and some other frog-gigger.'

'Where are Andrew and Cole?'

'Down there too,' he said, with a nod at the boathouse. 'We got ambushed, and I sent them down there to hide after I got shot. I don't know what's happened in the last few minutes, but I'm sure I heard Joe wailing on somebody in the woods.' He squeezed her a grim smile. 'Things have been awful quiet since.'

Exhaling, Bryony mentally prepared herself for what was to come. Her entire body was shivering with adrenalin, and – she had to admit – a touch of fear. It had been some time since she'd felt as edgy while performing her duty, and it was because nothing that had happened as yet could be described as police procedure. If she lost Royce Benson, her ass and career would be in a sling. God forbid if she were to lose Clayton or Cole.

'Right,' she said, in decision. 'Sit tight, Rink. I'm going down there.'

'Git. I'll cover ya.'

She raced directly for the back end of the boathouse. It was a large construction, built to house a powerboat or cabin cruiser. At the front would be a portal big enough to allow a boat to sail inside and berth inside the shed. At the rear there was a second large door – this one to allow loading and unloading of a boat onto a transport trailer or truck. The door was padlocked shut. There had to be a normal entrance door, but she didn't know if it were to the right or left. By chance she went right, listening to what she thought was the grumble of an idling engine.

From inside a gun cracked.

Yelping, Bryony dropped to her knees, slapping at the stinging splinters of wood that had struck her neck and chin. She hissed in pain, checking her fingertips, and found them smeared with blood. Her hiss became an exhalation of relief. The blood was mostly Rink's, from when he'd grasped her earlier: her wounds were minor. Though she dreaded to think how close the stray bullet had come to taking off her head.

From inside the shed she heard muffled grunts and thuds, feet pounding on a boardwalk, something heavy avalanching down.

A child screeched.

A huge splash followed, and a muffled curse.

Bryony fought back to her feet, and ran for the corner, her left hand grabbing at the boathouse wall for stability as she took the corner.

There was no damn door that she could see, but there was a way inside at the front of the boathouse. She ran for it even as guns cracked in competition, drilling holes in the shed wall mere feet behind her.

She hadn't made the front of the building when the engine roared, and the thud of a boat striking wood shook the boathouse to its foundations. Bryony dodged to the right, fully expecting the entire building to collapse down on her. Her angle allowed her an oblique view of the front of the shed, and from it a boat forced a passage out on to the lake. Bryony hollered an inane "stop", even as she equally ineffectively rushed towards the shore. What was she going to do? Scupper the boat with a few well-aimed pot shots?

Somebody had an equally insane idea to stop the boat.

She heard the staccato thud of running footsteps, then a figure hurtled along a short boardwalk jetty projecting from the inside of the boathouse. The runner didn't stop; he dove headlong off the jetty, arms stretching for the side of the cabin cruiser at least ten feet away.

38

There was a cabin cruiser inside the boathouse. When I stole a glance inside the building its engine was already running. I'd left the guy called Bean incapacitated in the woods, and his skinny pal, Hart, equally out of commission, so was happy Royce Benson was the only attacker left to contend with. But this, I knew was the difficult part. Because one glance was all it took to determine that my task wasn't going to be a walk in the park, considering he was holding Cole by the scruff of his shirt, and had the barrel of a gun wedged under the kid's ribs. Royce was on the rear walkway, his back to a wall, dressed in a dark blue coverall, and boots. The kid held in front of him was a small weeping captive but an effective shield against the gun Clayton held, as well as my SIG.

Andrew Clayton was on the boat, his back to me, and the gun held out at his side as he pleaded with his old friend to let the boy go. It took little guessing to figure out what had happened since the ambush. While Rink had tried to cover them, Clayton had brought the boy to the boat, and got it running in an attempt at escape. But while Clayton was busy at the controls, Royce must have rushed in and grabbed the boy off the boat, and now held him hostage.

'It's me you want, not Cole,' Clayton said, his voice plaintive and high-pitched. 'Let him go and you can do whatever you want to me. Don't hurt Cole. Please, Royce? See sense, for God's sake!'

'No,' Royce snapped, his mouth so close to Cole's head that his breath whipped the boy's hair. 'You took everything from me. I'll take everything from you, you bastard. Don't you get it? You have to *suffer...*'

I was hidden at the edge of the portal, listening, but also weighing my options. If I entered, Clayton and I would have two angles of fire on Royce, but I doubted Clayton's skill with a handgun. Not only that, but would he even shoot when his son's life was in peril? Even a marksman would be pressured by such a dilemma. And to be fair, I wasn't keen on taking a shot either. It would only take Royce to move a fraction of an inch, and he could tug Cole into my line of fire. Even if I got him, and didn't kill Royce with my first shot, he might pull the trigger, and Cole would die. It wasn't a chance I could take.

From nearby the sirens of rapidly approaching police cars warbled. Royce might not hear them being so intent on arguing with Clayton. His focus was so pinpointed he probably wouldn't hear the cops until they came charging inside the boathouse. A full-scale assault was only minutes away, but I was under no illusion: there weren't minutes to spare. I took another peak inside, staying close to the edge of the wall.

'I have suffered,' Clayton cried, as he moved a step towards the aft of the boat. 'You killed Ella. You killed Parker. Royce! For God's sake, man, how many more have to die?'

'Don't pretend you miss either of them, you lying piece of shit! When I think about it, taking those cheating bastards out did you a goddamn favour. Where's the suffering; where's the fucking payback?' Royce shook Cole savagely. 'This brat is the only thing important to you. I should shoot him right now, and see some real pain in your face before I take your fucking head off.'

Cole yelped in terror, and I almost stepped inside the boathouse.

'How can you threaten him like that, Royce? You know he's…' Clayton bit down on his words, understanding their repercussions if Cole managed to get out of there alive.

Royce shook his head, and looked down at the boy with what could only be described as abhorrence. 'You think I feel anything for this little *bastard*? Who's to say who the real father is, eh? Ella was free and easy with me; she was free and easy with any fucker with a dick. You know what she was, Clayton. A fucking whore when you met her, and a fucking whore to the very end!'

'Shut your filthy mouth!' Clayton hollered, enraged now.

Royce laughed bitterly. 'What? You don't want the boy to know his mom was a dirty stinking whore? You do know Parker was sneaking behind your back, right? Fucking her because you couldn't?'

'I told you to shut your filthy mouth!' Clayton jerked up his gun again, and I steeled for the worst.

'Go on,' Royce taunted. 'Shoot if you want. It'll be the first time you shot something that wasn't a blank.' He shook Cole again. 'But I bet it's him you hit. Go on, Clayton! Fucking shoot.'

Clayton dropped his arm, the gun again out to his side, and I sighed, while Royce only laughed at him, calling him a coward.

'Let Cole go,' Clayton said, and his rage had diminished to some form of resignation. 'Do what you want to me, but the boy's innocent. He has nothing to do with this.'

'Hasn't he?' Royce turned his attention to the boy. 'What do you say, Cole? Do you want to tell your daddy about Uncle Parker visiting when he was out of town.' Royce laughed nastily. 'Do you want to tell daddy about the other man who used to visit too. Do you remember you called me a *monster*? That time I was humping your mom and you walked into the bedroom.'

Clayton's spine went rigid. Cole had suffered nightmares inhabited with what he'd called "the monster" and we both knew now who had fixed that image in the boy's psyche.

'What? You didn't realise I'd been with her since I got back?' Royce asked. 'Jesus, Clayton, how gullible are you? If it's any consolation, it was only revenge fucking on my part. Didn't enjoy it, not one bit. Ella, though, she loved every goddamn second; said she hadn't been satisfied by you in years. You know...' Royce shook his head at the absurdity of where he was leading. He walked the boy along a boardwalk towards the far side of the shed, forcing Clayton to follow him every step, taunting him to take a shot. He again planted himself, with Cole as a human shield. Grinned at his old friend. 'Ella asked me to get rid of you. So we could be together. Can you believe it? I was tempted, but that was never my plan. Oh, yeah. I was

265

always going to get rid of you, that never changed, but it wasn't to play fucking happy families with Ella and this little brat.' He paused to think, then juggled the gun under Cole's armpit so he could momentarily release his hold on the boy's shirt. He plucked something from around his neck, and hung it up in the air. It was a gold wedding ring knotted on a string. Ella's wedding ring. 'Don't know why the fuck I held onto this piece of junk,' he said and tossed it away. It plonked into the water between the jetty and the boat. 'I don't give a damn about Ella, *him-*' he shook Cole, having regained his hold at the scruff of his neck '-or you, Clayton. Every last fucker that ruined my life is going to pay.'

Clayton shook with rage. The discarding of Ella's wedding band, plus Royce's latest admission — be it truth or simply another attempt at hurting Clayton - had just tipped the situation into an inevitable decline. It was time to act, and my gaze fell on something I'd previously missed that gave me hope. I immediately crept away, then once out of earshot, made my way around the boathouse to the far side. Immediately I reached my objective I secured my gun in my waistband, took a few steps back, then charged forward.

There was a Perspex window in the wall, designed to be semi-opaque for privacy or security purposes but also to allow natural light inside. It was set into an aluminium frame, held with simple pop rivets. It was no barrier to my weight as I crashed through it, and immediately on to Royce Benson's back. I hit him kind of side-on, with a large chunk of Perspex between us so I'd no easy way of grappling his gun away. But that hadn't been my intention. As I collided with him, he was thrown sideways, and his reaction was to throw out both arms for stability. He dropped Cole, but maintained a grip on his gun. One out of two good results weren't bad. But my small-odds win was only fleeting, because my kamikaze dive took me to my knees, and I felt the brunt of the collision go through my entire body in a raw wave of agony. Royce was startled by my sudden appearance though, and didn't immediately shoot me dead. He staggered against the wall, slid along it, while his head swept back and forth between me, Cole and Clayton.

Clayton fired.

His bullet missed Royce by a mile. But it kept the killer's attention off immediately ending my days. Cole was on the boardwalk decking a few feet from me. I scrambled for him on hands and screamingly painful knees, grasped him by his waistband and immediately slung him off the boardwalk into the lake. I caught a fleeting image of his face before he plunged into what looked like a bottomless abyss of black water below. It was a pale oval of shock. It was only once I threw him to safety that it even occurred he might be – like his dad had proven - unable to swim.

The water was deep enough for a boat to float inside the shed, deeper than a small boy's height, but not for an adult to stand safely in it I hoped. I looked for Clayton, about to tell him to jump overboard, but in the few seconds my attention was off him, Royce had moved

He was now on the boat, and he clubbed at Clayton with a balled hand. Clayton took the blow on the side of his head, and I watched his spectacles fly away over the side of the cabin cruiser. The only reason Royce didn't shoot was because Clayton had hold of his gun hand, wrestling it in the air. Clayton had dropped his gun after his first poor shot, and he drove a punch of his own at Royce. Now I was in no fear of losing my sidearm, I pulled it out again. Seeking a shot.

Royce's gun went off.

The bullet snapped the air alongside my head, and I jerked away as it punched a hole through the wall. I was sure I heard a woman's yelp of surprise, but had no time to consider it further. I sought a target, but Clayton's back was to me now, and Royce out of my line of fire. I glanced down, looking for Cole. He was nowhere to be seen. Panic threatened to swell my heart, but I fought it down, moving rapidly along the walkway, trying to get a clear shot at Royce. I crashed up against a stack of plastic iceboxes, or bait chests, or whatever the hell they were, and they avalanched around my feet. I kicked clear passage through, again distractedly searching the water for a sign of Cole, while Clayton and Royce grappled furiously for control of the gun.

I searched for my shot, but suddenly the surface of the water broke, and Cole clawed at the air, screeching in animal-like terror. As he sank again into the depths, it caught us in tableau, as all eyes turned his way. The temptation to leap to his rescue pulled at me, but to do that would mean the death of another, and quite likely mine and Cole's deaths too when finally we resurfaced into the gunman's sights.

Suddenly Clayton let out a shout, and it was in fear. Overbalanced, he fell sideways over the side of the boat. The smack his body made as it hit the water was thunderous compared to the dull *plunk* Cole made when he went under moments ago.

'Ha! Drown you bastards!' Royce Benson crowed, but then his view snapped around. He swung his liberated gun at me.

Dodging, I again went down on one knee on the boardwalk. But Benson didn't shoot; he took his time, holding me under guard while he walked backwards to the cabin. It didn't take much figuring out what he had in mind.

I bobbed up and fired.

Missed him.

He fired back, but missed me too.

He hit the throttle and the cabin cruiser's engine roared, and the boathouse was filled with smoke and diesel fumes. The boat began to surge ahead, pushing frothy water before it.

'You're not getting away, you bastard,' I said, and shot at him. Royce grunted in pain, but returned fire. His bullets punched the wall, even as I began a run down the side walkway. Intent on killing me, Royce lost his hold on the steering and the boat veered into the dock, the full thing shaking under my feet, and items of equipment stored in the rafters rained down. An ancient wooden oar came close to smashing my skull, but I jerked my head away and took the knock on my shoulder. It was the same arm that Clayton had targeted during our scuffle, and though the aches in my muscles were memories now, they were brought back to life in glorious Technicolor flashes of pain down my chest. My gun slipped from numb fingers. I groped for it, but couldn't immediately see where it fell for the clutter on the boardwalk.

Up from the depths Cole again broke the surface. He clawed ineffectively at the water as if it would hold him up. Ten feet away, his father had finally found his feet and erupted out, shedding water in a shout of panic. He swept his hands over his features, clearing his eyes and nostrils, spitting and coughing.

'Clayton! Get Cole!' I hollered at him, jabbing a hand at the floundering boy. Cognizance entered Clayton's expression, and he called out for his son as he lurched forward.

Royce aimed his gun at me.

I ducked and weaved, but he didn't fire. Or if he pulled the trigger, the hammer had fallen on an empty chamber. Royce swore at me, then hit the throttle again, the boat banging and nudging at a jetty that extended out over the lake, before he found a straight line to freedom.

One last glance showed me Clayton wading chest deep for Cole, his hands reaching to pluck the boy to safety, and it was good enough for me. Being a man who laid much emphasis on a promise, I ran after the boat: Royce wasn't getting away. I hurtled along the jetty, and threw myself after it; sailing through the air with less grace than would any superhero I'd joked with Cole about.

My headlong dive proved almost too impressive, because I landed half on and half off the boat, my gut slamming down on the side rail inches from impalement on a brass lug. The wind blasted from me, and my kneecaps slammed the hull with another twin explosion of pain shooting through them. In such discomfort, I almost slipped overboard. But I was incensed enough that I fought the urge to flop backwards, and instead grabbed at the rail, and heaved myself over it on to the deck. I lay on my back for a moment, stunned, gathering my wits and my strength, sucking in the oxygen my winding had displaced, before recalling exactly what had motivated me into my punishing dive. I began to pull my legs under me to help me stand, and all I managed was a graceless slide across the deck. With nothing for it, I rolled on to my front, grabbing at the rail to starboard for assistance. My grip slipped and I went again to all fours. Royce's boot found my guts while I was still doing a poor impression of a wobbly coffee table.

The muscles in my stomach contracted in waves. I felt nauseous, on the verge of vomiting. But I'd been in worse shape before and fought back. I did then. I backhanded Royce between the legs, forcing him away, and scrambled to my feet, holding the rail tighter this time. It was fortunate I found my feet because suddenly the boat lurched into a turn, then immediately shuddered, and the prow forced a line through the water in a different direction. The boat pitched wildly, and I almost went overboard and had to fight the motion just to retain my wits. It was hardly surprising that the boat rolled and danced as it surged across the lake, with nobody at the helm.

'You've a lot to answer for, you bastard,' Royce spat at me as he aimed a punch at my head. I dodged and he withdrew his jab.

His accusation was rich, considering everything he'd done. But I guessed he was referring to his cousin Tommy's death, or maybe he was concerned for the welfare of Lonnie and the others, because my presence didn't bode well for them. Perhaps that wasn't what he meant, and it was the fact I'd spoiled his chances of killing Andrew and Cole back in the boathouse, and forcing him to make a break for it. Frankly, I didn't give a damn about his disappointment. I punched at him.

Royce palmed my fist aside, and struck me with a hammering blow of his tattooed right hand. The swine still had hold of his revolver, but I'd no way of knowing if it was armed. He battered my shoulder with the butt of the handle, causing the numbness already in it to buzz with an electric charge: he'd got me sweet on a bundle of nerves. I couldn't forget that he was once a pro-fighter, and knew exactly where to hit so it hurt. Fair enough, I decided, because I intended hurting him equally.

The cabin cruiser rocked to and fro. We went from one side of the deck to the other, then back again, in what to an observer might have resembled a drunken waltz. All the while we punched, and grabbed at each other. The deck was too unstable to throw a kick, or even a knee to the balls. Royce again used his revolver to hammer me, this time with the barrel that abraded skin down my left pectoral muscle alongside my recently healed bullet wound. Our fight took us into the open cabin. Royce's back bent over the steering wheel; aided by the fact my left hand was gripping his windpipe. He swayed to the right, forcing my reach to over–extend, and he pulled loose, and again struck at me with the gun butt. It got me down the side of my face, feeling as if it almost ripped off my earlobe. The boat dipped to the right also, and we fell in a tangle of limbs against the cabin wall. There were storage compartments and equipment, electronic components and other stuff I was unfamiliar with. Nothing I could use as a blunt weapon, though.

I chopped at his wrist, and he relinquished his grip on the gun. It fell between our feet. As we struggled I stood on the damn thing, and my right leg skidded out from under me. Royce powered me backwards further off balance, and I spilled onto the deck once more. I half expected Royce to take a second to adjust the steering, giving me an opportunity to rise, but he was too engaged in the fight to bother where the boat was heading. He came after me, and sacrificed his own stability by kicking at my side.

Balling up around his foot, I wrapped my arms and knees around his shin. Royce swore, realising his mistake and tried to wrench free, but I hung on with the tenacity of a tic dug into a bull's hide. He hopped, trying to dislodge my clinging weight, and it was obvious to me where we'd end up. He toppled, smacking face down on the deck near the aft of the boat. I wrenched him over, climbing his body like a demented ape. Royce punched up at me, and I batted aside his arms. Got a hand round his windpipe and squeezed.

Royce's hands pushed at my jaw, and he worked his fingertips into my eyes, forcing me to twist away to save my vision. His fingers scrabbled down my face and found purchase on my bottom lip. He was seconds from ripping it off, when I thrust down again and got his fingers between my teeth. I crunched as hard as I could, and he hollered in ignominy more than in pain. What? He expected a fight constrained by rules? He bucked wildly, and I fell sideways, aided into my roll by a wild dip of the boat to starboard. The damn cabin cruiser was still racing forward at top speed, with no hand at the helm. Hitting the hull, I rebounded slightly, and got my feet between us, kicking at Royce with both heels. He scrambled for the port rail, grabbing it, and hauling himself to standing. He took a moment to crane around, and his eyes went wide, and a curse broke from his lips. He began to pull along the rail for the cabin. I launched up, and dove at him. He rammed an elbow between us, but I swept it down, and head-butted him cleanly in the jaw.

He was stunned, and I swung a clubbing right at his face. It might have been the sweet punch, except the boat's keel suddenly hit something, and it rose a foot or so in the water, and with it me. I was weightless for a second or two, before crashing down on the deck. My punch had barely clipped Royce, but he was also down. The engine roared still, and we were still moving, but more sluggishly than before. The boat was towing something, and whatever it was it acted like an anchor, but not enough to halt all forward volition. Clambering up, I looked, and saw that we were barely fifty yards from shore, on a straight line for impact. Perhaps I shouldn't have stopped Royce gaining control of the steering. I lurched for the cabin.

'Hold it, mother fucker!" Royce snapped.

A quick glance showed me a sight I'd grown used to lately. A gun was aimed at my face. Royce was bluffing though, because we both knew it was empty. I lunged for the cabin, reaching for the wheel.

The gun cracked, and a bullet smashed a chunk of wood from the cabin a few inches from me.

It wasn't the empty gun he'd used to club me. Royce had found the gun dropped earlier by Clayton, and this one could have plenty bullets left in the chamber to finish me off. I'd no idea how many times Clayton fired during the standoff in the boathouse, but even a single remaining bullet was enough to drop me. It was a chance I'd take.

I didn't go for the wheel. I charged Royce, and he was surprised by my recklessness and it took him a second longer to react. I threw myself at him, but in a way he'd never expect, going sideways, as if rolling over a fence with little regard to where I landed. The gun barked, but by then I was past the barrel and caromed into him, knocking him backwards at the same instant the boat hit the sloping shore and tore a shuddering path through loamy earth.

Entangled we went overboard, striking the aft rail, and spilling away as the boat continued its forward plummet to land. The water was shallow, but deep enough to completely submerge me as I hit. Royce was on top, and his weight bore me down into the silty mud. My vision was filled with gritty darkness, and I'd no way of seeing the fist Royce drove into my face before it battered me further into the muck. My mouth opened in reflex and foul slime flooded in. The darkness in my vision grew deeper.

In desperation I groped for the knife I'd inserted in my boot.

My fingers only found soaked cloth, and in regret I realised the knife had been lost when we'd tumbled overboard. I had no weapon to fight back with, and was rapidly weakening.

Fuck, I thought, as my lungs pulsed agonizingly through lack of oxygen, this was what drowning felt like.

39

Stunned by his insane leap after the boat, Bryony could only gape at the antics of her friend. Joe impacted the boat solidly, and judging by the nasty thwack of his body against the keel he could be in trouble. But then he swarmed over the rail, on to the deck. Before he could right himself, a man in coveralls - who could only be Royce Benson - aimed a punishing kick at him. Then the boat was careening away, but it was at a wild curving tangent. She lifted her gun overhead, hollering a command, and let loose a single round. But she was wasting her time. In their fight, neither man aboard the roaring craft would hear let alone obey her command to halt.

From within the boathouse sounded splashing, highly-pitched voices, but no words she could decipher. Edging inside, with her gun extended, she searched for enemies, but the only people present were Andrew Clayton and his son. Clayton was shoulder deep in the water, hugging the boy to his chest, and an arm round Cole's head, as they slumped against the jetty. Bryony jogged along the boardwalk towards them, still checking for attackers. 'Everybody OK?' she demanded.

Cole wept inconsolably, drenched through, but otherwise he seemed fine. Clayton looked up at her, big-eyed. He coughed out words, then without asking handed Cole up to her. Bryony slipped away her gun to help, hauling the boy up on to the jetty. He sat between her knees, still weeping dejectedly, while Clayton hauled himself on to the boardwalk alongside her. He reached for the boy and pulled him into an embrace.

'Wait here,' Bryony told Clayton. 'Help will be here in no time.'

The sirens keened wildly now, and she was certain she could make out dim blue flashes dancing on the lake beyond the aperture.

'You have to stop that son of a bitch,' Clayton told her. 'He won't stop until we're all dead.'

'Don't worry, sir,' she said. 'Everything's in hand.'

She didn't believe her own proclamation, so wasn't surprised at the scowl Clayton shot her. She held out a calming palm, then nodded in some kind of silent promise, and turned to jog along the jetty again. Once outside, she searched the lake for the boat and saw that it wasn't as far off as she'd expected. It was zigzagging through the shallows near to shore. It was night now, but the hull was almost phosphorescent against the dark waters, and in its radiance she could see two small stick figures engaged in battle.

'Bryony!'

Hearing her name snapped her attention on the person leaning up against the wall of the boathouse. Rink offered her a grimace, and clutched at the bleeding wound in his side, but evidently his injury wasn't as debilitating as she'd earlier feared. He'd found the strength to get up and follow her, his need to assist his friends overcoming good sense perhaps.

'Is that Hunter out there?' He nodded at the swerving boat.

'Who else?' she asked, and raised her eyebrows. For a moment they shared a look, as if they were the long-suffering parents of a misbehaving child.

'Best you get after him then,' Rink said. 'You know he won't be happy til he hands you Royce's ass as a trophy.'

What could she do? There wasn't another boat she could use to give chase.

'Lookit,' Rink said, and she followed his gaze.

The cabin cruiser was heading in a curving line back towards land. Unless someone got a grip of the steering, it would make landfall a few hundred yards down shore.

'Go on, I'll watch Clayton and the kid til your buddies get here.'

Cops were already on scene up towards the house. The gumball strobe lights flashed intermittently on the boathouse and in the trees surrounding the property.

'Put away your gun, Rink. We don't want anyone making any stupid mistakes.'

'Good call,' he said, and dropped the gun at his feet. It had been a struggle to hold it, she bet. 'Being shot once in a day is enough for me.' Rink slid down the wall, on to his butt. He waved her away. 'Go on. I'm good. Help Hunter; he's the one needs you now.'

Bryony edged away, checking on the boat's trajectory. Then when she was fairly certain where it would beach, she set off at a gallop towards the trees. From behind her she heard the shouted commands of armed officers, and took it they'd discovered Scott Hartman chained to the trestle. She used the edge of the trees as a guide towards shore, and moments later came upon another man sitting on the grass. Both his arms were folded up towards his chin, and he was shivering, abjectly miserable, and in obvious pain if the cold sweat lathering him was any indicator. His arms looked oddly shaped, and it took a second or two before she understood what must have happened: Joe had left this would-be killer in no fit state to continue the fight. She turned and hollered for help, and a flashlight beam danced across the lawn towards her. She waved a cop towards her, identifying herself, holding up both her shield and her sidearm. 'This asshole needs a medic,' she told who she now saw was a Hillsborough County Sheriff's deputy. 'But first take him into custody.'

Before the deputy could question her further, she took off at a run for the shore. She trusted that by now the boat had run aground, or it had swerved wildly back to the middle of the lake. When she hit the waterline, she peered to her right. The boat was indeed beached on the shore a few hundred yards away, the engine continuing to roar in defiance as it fought to gain a few more inches up the slope. Behind it was a snarl of branches and reeds, driftwood left over from the recent storm dragged there by the boat as it pushed through the shallows, and outlined by the raggedy canopy a man punched down at another pushed beneath the surface. The edge of the lake was a boggy morass. But she slogged along it, fighting the clinging mud that attempted to stop her in her tracks. At a dash she could cover a hundred yards in no time, but here it felt as if time had slowed, as if it was an age before she took each hard won step.

Who was killing whom up ahead? She couldn't make out any features, just the movement of the man sitting on top of the other, now forcing down with both straight arms in an attempt at drowning their opponent. She'd prefer that it was Joe on top, but not that he was intent on killing Royce. She wanted the bastard alive. Justice must be served, the multiple murderer tried and convicted and sent to prison for the rest of his life.

She was within twenty feet before she got a look at the victor in profile, the longish hair, and knew she faced the worst scenario possible. Royce had bettered Hunter, and was even now only making random shoves at his opponent to ensure the weakened man stayed submerged. Hunter was dying.

She came to a halt, the mud instantly sucking her down to the ankles. Raised her gun in the air, and fired.

Royce Benson snapped a glance at her.

'Police!' she yelled. 'Get up off him now!'

Royce laughed, a sound so heartless it chilled her.

'Arrest me. Go ahead. You're too late to save him, anyway,' he said, his hands still submerged.

'Get off him now, or I will shoot.'

'So shoot me. You think that will save him? He's gone.'

Bryony took a lumbering step forward. Her gun now in both hands, aimed directly at Benson's chest. 'Last warning,' she said.

'You aren't going to shoot me. You're a cop.' Royce sneered at her.

He was right. She was a cop. But not of the stick-up-the-ass, rule following-type epitomised by Dennis Holker. First and foremost she was a human being, with the same fears and insecurities, or the same hopes and dreams as anyone else. Arresting a felon wasn't as important to her as saving the life of someone she cared deeply for.

She fired.

The bullet struck Benson high on his left shoulder, and its impact made him slump sideways. He groaned in pain, but began to turn towards her.

'Next bullet's in your heart, asshole,' she promised.

She was an instant too late in seeing his right hand break the surface. From beneath the water he barely raised the barrel of a gun a few inches, and only when it flashed brightly in the gloom, and she sat down heavily in the mud did she understand he'd returned fire. As she dropped, her own gun slipped sideways, and she almost lost a hold of it, and her mind was so bewildered by the turn of events, that she had to grab at it a few times before she had it gripped tightly enough to control. Benson hove up, and she knew she'd made a bad decision in going only for a debilitating shot, rather than a fatal one. He stood, bringing what she now saw was a revolver to bear, and in their hurry to find a target, he found his first.

He fired, and once again the night was split by a sharp crack of thunder and lightning. Bryony's eyelids flickered in time with the single shot, and she waited for the dull impact of metal tearing through her body. Yet it never came.

A leg had rammed up from under the surface, water surging up around it, so that she didn't see where it impacted a split-second before Royce fired. Wherever the heel struck him, it lifted Royce off his feet and propelled him backwards, so that the bullet flew high overhead. Before she could make clear sense of what had just happened, or before she could finally put a stop to Royce Benson's killing spree, Hunter erupted from the water with a furious roar, and she knew now that arrest was no longer an issue.

Then again, who was she to stand in the way of true justice? She lowered her firearm, and instead watched as Hunter plunged after Royce, shooting two pummelling palm heel thrusts into the killer's chin. Royce made a futile attempt at shooting, but the gun was empty now, and of no use to him. He struck at Hunter with it as a club, but Hunter was undeterred, taking the blow to his shoulder in order to deliver his own. He threw a straight right into the centre of Royce's face, and even over the distance, the grunting, the stamping, the slosh of mud and water, she heard the impact, and the resulting crack of breaking bones.

As Hunter slumped to one knee sluicing water, gasping to catch his breath, she couldn't credit her eyes. Royce was still standing. She brought up her weapon, a warning shout dancing on her lips, but it never found voice. She understood now.

She struggled to stand, but got her feet beneath her.

Where had she been shot?

She couldn't tell, because there was no indication, neither blood or pain, nor any other sign of trauma.

She'd sat down in surprise she realised, but wouldn't dwell on it. Her shock at being fired at so suddenly had saved her life, so where was the shame?

Forging through the muck, she didn't lower her gun from Royce. But he was no threat, and she took a few seconds to grip Hunter's shoulder and give him a squeeze of thanks. He winced at her touch, and hardly surprising after the pounding his body had taken. He glanced up at her, still expelling dirty lake water from his lips and nostrils, and nodded his own thanks. They'd both played a part in saving the others' ass.

And, the best part of all, Hunter had handed her Royce Benson as a trophy as he'd promised.

The killer was snagged among the branches of the tree towed up from the bottom of the lake by the cabin cruiser, his spine wedged in the V of two thicker limbs. He was barely clinging to consciousness, but while he fought the escape into oblivion, he was barely aware of his surroundings, and no threat. He bled profusely from where Bryony had shot him, and from his mashed nose and split lips. It was only a pity that he hadn't been impaled on one of the branches, to cause him further torment, Bryony thought in a spike of delicious sadism. It was what he deserved.

Instead she told him he was under arrest, and took delight in her proclamation instead.

40

There were five of us sitting on the balcony at the rear of Rink's condominium, and an observer would have been forgiven for thinking they were looking at a bunch of war-wounded veterans taking the air as part of their recovery. Of us all Rink was the most severely injured, and the little gathering was to toast his release from hospital after a ten-day stay following emergency surgery to fix his damaged insides. Thankfully the trauma team had saved his life, halting the internal bleeding and patching up the tears in his intestines, and the nick to his liver where the tumbling bullet had finished up. The wound was harsh enough that it would have killed a lesser man, or an unluckier one, and it still surprised me how he'd managed to survive, let alone hang on until Clayton and Cole were safely in the hands of the responding police officers. Then again, it was Rink, and he was one of the toughest most resilient son's of bitches I'd ever known, so I shouldn't have been surprised at all.

Bryony VanMeter carried healing scratches on her cheek, forehead and down her neck, courtesy I'd learned of splinters of wood when a stray round fired by Clayton almost ended her days. Dennis Holker, as sour-faced as ever but more affable towards our little company than I'd seen him, wasn't yet fit for an active role at work, but was planning a return to office duties soon. He walked with a stick, but hopefully it was something he'd be able to cast aside before long. His leg was already on the mend, and his doctor's anticipated a full recovery. My right arm was in a sling, and I'd stitches in my scalp, an ugly scab on the bridge of my nose, and about a million fading bruises under my clothing, but otherwise was fine.

The only one of us who didn't look like the walking wounded was Andrew Clayton, but his injuries were hidden deeper than my bruises, and would take longer to fade. He was under no illusion that the actions of his younger self had taken such a toll on the lives around him in later years, and that in part he was responsible for setting Royce Benson's actions in motion, when first he'd chosen to betray him to the authorities, while later keeping his lips zipped from dropping him in it when it was apparent who was behind the killings. He was a lucky guy, I guessed, not to have been arrested on a conspiracy charge by the detectives who now welcomed him into our gathering. His saving grace was that there was no way to prove he was guilty. After my previous disliking of the guy, I could only feel sorry for him now. Especially after he handed us a drawing done for us by Cole. It featured three muscle-bound supercrocs in gaudy costumes and masks, and our names written above each: Joe, Rink and Bryony, with the private message of "Thanks for catching the bad men for me" penned underneath. It must have stung Clayton not to be featured in the little group of crime fighters, considering it was Clayton who'd plucked Cole from the lake when I'd almost gotten him drowned.

There was a collection of beer bottles on the table between us, some empty, but other full ones in reserve. Out of the norm for me, I'd chosen a Budweiser from the pack I'd bought from Harlan that time over the Corona I usually imbibed. I finished it in a slug before hitting my companions with the ending of my shaggy dog tale, from when I'd been led to West Point Bait and Tommy Benson via the kick-off in the junkyard with Emilio's boys.

'The goddamn dog ran away with the bat?' Rink wheezed in incredulity, and slapped a palm down on the table, setting the beer bottles jiggling. 'You gotta be freakin' kidding us, brother?'

'It's true,' I said with a self-satisfied nod, which engendered a peel of scornful laughter from my disbelieving friends.

'Man, I used to try that excuse on the principal when I didn't deliver my homework assignments on time,' Holker said. 'He didn't buy that lousy defense any more than I do.'

'Suit yourselves,' I said, with no real animosity at being called a liar. 'Believe me. Don't believe me. It happened, and that's the story I'm sticking to.'

'So Emilio the Blimp set you on the right track, huh?' said Rink.

'Oh, you know him?'

'I know him, have come across him on some other cases. He's even proved helpful to me in the past,' Rink said with a mischievous nod. 'You only have to look at him to tell he's a talented guy.'

'He is?' I was doubtful.

'Sure he is. I heard he can fart the theme-tune from Hawaii Five-O on request.'

We all laughed too hard at the joke, until Holker waved a hand for calm. 'I've got a question for you, Hunter. Why didn't you just shoot the goddamn mutt?'

'I like dogs.' I shrugged. 'I was tempted to shoot its handlers, if it's any consolation?'

Holker grinned in good humour. He aimed a finger at me, and his pointy chin dimpled round a drunken smile. 'You know, Joe, I didn't give you much credit before. But I've been keeping a running tally on the bad guys you encountered and am happy to say you managed not to kill a single one of them this time. OK, there was the Tommy Benson thing, but I'm happy to discount him. Wasn't you that killed him, but his own stupidity.'

'Not to mention the fender of a VW van,' Rink added, with an equally drunken grin and Holker mimicked him.

Hell, I thought, neither of those guys should be drinking while on their meds, but when I figured things out they were only on their second beers. They were drunk on euphoria, rather than alcohol, and to be fair I was feeling a little tipsy in that department myself. Holker was right; I hadn't shot anyone dead, which to him was a small miracle but cause for approval.

Both Holker and Bryony were the toast of the Tampa PD Major Crimes Bureau, and up for official commendations for their part in catching not one but two home invasion gangs, and for clearing up a murder spree unprecedented in Florida in the past few years. There was even talk of Rink and me being rewarded for our public spirited actions with a civic reception and commendation from the mayor's office, of which neither of us wanted any part. But we had to admit; the certificates of merit and any accompanying news clippings would look good framed on the wall at Rington Investigations, alongside Cole's superhero drawing. Maybe there was benefit in not killing *everybody*, I laughed to myself.

'I still think you're bad luck to hang around with,' Holker went on, 'judging by the look of us.'

I took his comment in the good humour it was meant, though Bryony tutted at him.

'Hey, I'm right,' he said in a goofy voice, and earned himself another round of tipsy laughter.

'It wasn't Hunter who got you all injured though, was it?'

Hearing his sobering tone we all looked at Andrew Clayton, and he stood slowly from the table. 'I should make my apologies,' he continued somberly. 'For getting you all involved in this. But I'd rather make my thanks.' He'd replaced his spectacles after losing his usual ones in the lake, alongside Ella's ring. The ring had later been recovered by a police diver, but was currently being held in the evidence repository at Franklin Street for when Royce Benson and his gang came to trial. The broken glasses also dug from the lake bottom had been cast in the trash, so Clayton had fitted himself with some designer brand. They became his focus now, adjusting them so he could surreptitiously wipe at his glassy eyes. 'If not for you folks, I don't know what would've happened to me or my boy.'

'You played your part in protecting him,' I said, by way of commiseration.

'It was through me he was in danger in the first place,' Clayton sighed. 'I know it. So, I also know who to be truly grateful to.'

He was nearest Rink, and he held out a hand to my buddy.

Rink shook with him, then eased his hand away and pressed it gently against the dressing on his abdomen.

Clayton then made his way round the table, first thanking Holker, then Bryony, before ending up at my side.

'Joe?' he said, and offered his hand.

I paused, but only so I could shrug my arm from its sling, tentative because of the fractured clavicle I'd sustained. Ironically the break hadn't been caused by Clayton, the falling oar, or Royce Benson when he'd been pounding on me with his gun butt, but when I'd mashed Royce's face with such desperate power that some of the kinetic force had flashed back up my straightened arm and found release in the abused collarbone. It'd be a while before it was fully healed, but a handshake was manageable, I thought. Noticing my discomfort, Clayton was careful to only squeeze my hand briefly, and I returned the favour: the gesture was so unlike during our first meeting. 'Thank-you for everything,' he said equally as softly, 'and I mean that from the heart.'

He used the excuse of leaving to go collect Cole from a babysitter, and we allowed him to leave with no further fuss.

Once he was out of earshot, Holker snorted, and was in danger of slipping back into his usual sarcastic mode, but Bryony beat him to the punch. 'Andrew isn't responsible for any of this. Only Royce Benson is,' she announced. 'But we caught the murderous bastard, all of us, and he'll serve his dues. All's well that ends well, right? So let's not forget that.' She grabbed her beer bottle off the table. 'This *is* supposed to be a celebration.'

'You got that right,' Rink said, and raised his bottle.

Holker thought for a moment, and his gaze was fixed, but then his chin dimpled again, and he raised his bottle, and Bryony mirrored him. I also tipped my bottle, still using my right arm.

'To good friends,' Bryony toasted, and we replied in kind and clinked over the centre of the table. 'And a speedy return to health,' she added and smiled at each of us in turn.

'And here's to Joe keeping his weapon firmly tucked in his pants in future,' Holker blurted loudly.

I laughed at his double entendre, but only after I caught a sly smile and unflinching gaze from Bryony. I was happy when she didn't echo his toast.

Thanks

As ever my gratitude goes to my literary agent Luigi Bonomi, and all at LBA, and to all my family, friends and colleagues whose collective support is unflinching. In my humble opinion, a book is never a book until it is read, so my thanks also go to my readers, without whom I'd simply be making pointless scratchings on paper. Big thanks to Debbie at The Cover Collection for her excellent work on the cover. Also a special thank-you must go to fellow author, Graham Smith, whose wise words delivered at the most opportune time sent this tale down a different track than first I'd been following.

And now for a brief explanation…

Regarding Joe Hunter's shaggy dog tale: as unbelievable as it sounds, his encounter with the dog matches one I experienced as a police officer, where a bull terrier did indeed snatch a length of wood out of my hands just after I'd liberated it from a man trying to bash in my skull. I had the onerous task of explaining why I was unable to seize the weapon in evidence to an unbelieving desk sergeant on my return to the station with my prisoner. Luckily my previously obnoxious arrestee was as equally amused by the incident that he admitted that it was the truth. As Joe Hunter said: 'It happened, and that's the story I'm sticking to.'

About Matt Hilton

Matt Hilton quit his career as a police officer to pursue his love of writing tight, cinematic action thrillers. He is the author of the high-octane Joe Hunter thriller series, including his most recent novel **'No Safe Place'** – Joe Hunter 11. His first book, **'Dead Men's Dust'**, was shortlisted for the International Thriller Writers' Debut Book of 2009 Award, and was a Sunday Times bestseller, also being named as a 'thriller of the year 2009' by The Daily Telegraph. **Dead Men's Dust** was also a top ten Kindle bestseller in 2013. The Joe Hunter series has been widely published by Hodder and Stoughton in UK territories, and by William Morrow and Company and Down and Out Books in the USA, and have been translated into German, Italian, Romanian and Bulgarian. As well as the Joe Hunter series, Matt has been published in a number of anthologies and collections, and has published novels in the supernatural/horror genre, namely **'Preternatural'**, **'Dominion'**, **'Darkest Hour'** and **'The Shadows Call'**. Also, he has a brand new thriller series featuring Tess Grey and Nicolas "Po'boy" Villere that debuted in November 2015, with **'Blood Tracks'**, and the second book **'Painted Skins'** will be published in August 2016 by Severn House Publishers. He is currently working on the next Joe Hunter novel, as well as a stand-alone thriller novel.

www.matthiltonbooks.com
@MHiltonauthor
www.facebook/MattHiltonAuthor

Other Books by the Author

Joe Hunter thriller series:

Dead Men's Dust
Judgement and Wrath
Slash and Burn
Cut and Run
Blood and Ashes
Dead Men's Harvest
No Going Back
Rules of Honour
The Lawless Kind
The Devil's Anvil
No Safe Place

Joe Hunter e-book short stories:

Joe Hunter: Six of the Best
Dead Fall
Red Stripes
Joe Hunter: Instant Justice

Tess Grey and Nicolas 'Po' Villere

Blood Tracks
Painted Skins (August 2016)

Lightning Source UK Ltd.
Milton Keynes UK
UKOW01n2327100616

276060UK00001B/13/P